PENGUIN BOOKS

THE KNACK OF LIFE

Trisha Rainsford was born in Chicago, but grew up in Ireland. She is a writer and former teacher of Classical Studies. She lives in Limerick with her husband and three sons.

The Knack of Life

TRISHA RAINSFORD

PENGUIN BOOKS

PENGUIN BOOKS

Published by the Penguin Group
Penguin Books Ltd, 80 Strand, London WC2R ORL, England
Penguin Group (USA) Inc., 375 Hudson Street, New York, New York 10014, USA
Penguin Group (Canada), 90 Eglinton Avenue East, Suite 700, Toronto, Ontario, Canada M4P 2Y3
(a division of Pearson Penguin Canada Inc.)
Penguin Ireland, 25 St Stephen's Green, Dublin 2, Ireland
(a division of Penguin Books Ltd)
Penguin Group (Australia), 250 Camberwell Road,
Camberwell, Victoria 3124, Australia (a division of Pearson Australia Group Pty Ltd)
Penguin Books India Pvt Ltd, 11 Community Centre,
Panchsheel Park, New Delhi – 110 017, India
Penguin Group (NZ), cnr Airborne and Rosedale Roads, Albany,
Auckland 1310, New Zealand (a division of Pearson New Zealand Ltd)
Penguin Books (South Africa) (Pty) Ltd, 24 Sturdee Avenue,
Rosebank, Johannesburg 2196, South Africa

Penguin Books Ltd, Registered Offices: 80 Strand, London WC2R ORL, England

www.penguin.com

Published by Penguin Ireland 2005
Published in Penguin Books 2006
1

ISBN-13 978-1-844-88009-6
ISBN-10 1-844-88009-5

This book is dedicated to my family and friends.

Acknowledgements

I'd like to thank Patricia Deevy, my Irish editor, for her unending patience, humour and tact. The woman deserves a medal. Thanks also to Ann Cooke at Penguin UK, Fred the Band, Michael McLoughlin and all at Penguin Ireland.

I

'Wish You Were Here'
Pink Floyd, 1975

I could never really see why Mattie was killed. Well, that's not entirely true. Strictly speaking I now know why and, in a sense, I even understand what happened – the sequence of events and all that. But still. I mean, why kill him? Why not just drive away?

But they didn't drive away, they killed him, and as close as I can figure if Mattie had stayed home and pared his corns or read the newspaper he'd still be alive. But he didn't. He took his dog for a walk, and maybe planned on a little poaching and one way or another ended up in the wrong place at the wrong time.

Before Mattie was murdered I hadn't realized that life was so arbitrary. I thought the world was a reasonable and ordered place where we make our own fate. After Mattie was killed that world view shattered and I became obsessed with accidental happenings.

And that wasn't even the worst part. Much worse than that was finding a way to live with the fact that I wasn't even scratched that night, while Mattie was shot dead. That's probably why I thought about it so much.

Now it's not so bad. Now, when I look at what happened I can see that I couldn't have helped him. He was dead before he hit the tarmac. The blood that was pooled all around him on the road flooded out of the wound in his chest *after* he was already dead. Or so they told me when I asked.

I still dream about that night. In my dream I see Mattie's body falling for a long, long time through the frosty night air. His eyes are open and he's smiling and waving at me. Calling my name over and over in his raw smokers' voice.

Then he falls and his body breaks apart as it hits the ground. Smashes the way a jigsaw would if you dropped it on to the floor. Pieces of Mattie everywhere and I'm covered in his blood and I wake up and I'm crying. It never ends any other way.

Sometimes I visit Mattie's grave and once – when I was very upset and more than a little drunk – I walked through the night until I reached the graveyard. When I got there, I stumbled through the rows and rows of headstones until I finally found the rectangle of earth that was Mattie's grave.

The grave was still pretty fresh then, there was no head-stone. I was the one who eventually put up the headstone that recorded Mattie's details. I bought the headstone some-time later so that other people could find out who he was and when he lived and where he was buried and, more importantly, so that they could see that somebody cared about him enough to be bothered to make a record of his existence for posterity. But that was still in the future that night.

As I stood at his grave, everything that had happened ran over and over in my head like a looped video. What had happened and how and why I hadn't stopped it and if I could or should or might have saved him. Did he feel pain as his life seeped away? Was he afraid? Did he hear me there? See me?

Eventually I just crumpled on to the grave. And though it was true that I was drunk, it was more than drunkenness that made me fold in that way. The strength ebbed from my legs and I literally couldn't stand any more, and it was less because of alcohol and more because of despair and self-loathing.

I dropped on to the compacted soil that was still too freshly dug to be populated by grass and as I hit the ground I began to cry. A cold, hard crying that pushed itself throughout my body and made me want to die. But I didn't die. Instead I lay there on the ground, my body turning to ice and I spoke to Mattie.

'Sorry,' I whispered into the earth, 'I'm sorry.'

Tears filled my throat again and I hugged my stomach as if it was about to explode. And then, wiping sodden earth from my face with my hand, I rolled on to my back and fell asleep.

When I woke up I was stiff with the cold and completely sober and began to walk towards home. But even that couldn't go smoothly. Not for one night could I manage to get away without a shitload of crazy stuff happening.

And still. Still none of the mad things that happened mattered in a way. That night when I lay on Mattie's grave, talking my drunk talk to the worms, something changed.

Even all the things that happened afterwards never made me go back to the place I'd been before that night. That awful place, completely barren of forgiveness and hope about Mattie's death. Why? I don't know why, except maybe I was absolved, somehow. Made clean by some wisp of Mattie that hovered near his grave.

It took a while, but eventually I managed to stop feeling responsible for Mattie's death. I understand it all a bit better, of course, and see that there really wouldn't have been anything I could have done.

But I still dream about what happened, though it's less frequent now. I still dream that I'm covered in his blood. Maybe I'll always have that dream. I don't know.

*

Cassandra happened to be staying with me when Mattie was murdered. She often came to stay with me after Jessica left. Mattie was murdered on a Sunday night and the week before I'd had to drive to Limerick to collect a special order of books for school.

As far as I knew Cassandra was in Spain compiling photographs for an exhibition. Last I'd heard she'd just left Pamplona and the stampeding bulls to go on tour with a troupe of acrobats. Even so, I decided to call and see her mother, my aunt Lucy, while I was in town. Not that it was a hardship – I liked my aunt Lucy.

'Séamus,' Aunt Lucy said, smiling her huge smile and hugging me against her scratchy, plaid dressing gown.

'Come in, come in. Good to see you. Nothing wrong, is there? What brings you to town?'

'Books,' I said, picking up the heavy terracotta pot she was pushing along the hallway with her foot. 'Where do you want this?'

'Just outside the back door, the bloody thing needs re-potting,' she said, and I could hear the relief in her voice and I knew that it wasn't just that she was relieved to have me carry her heavy plant.

It was more than that. It was relief that my life wasn't falling apart again. Relief that I wasn't slithering into depression again. Relief for me. For her. For my parents.

Lucy led the way to the kitchen. I carried the chipped pot through the kitchen and placed it on the step outside the back door.

'Well, now,' she said, 'how is Séamus?'

'I'm grand. How's Uncle Leo, by the way? Mam said he sprained his ankle.'

Lucy rolled her eyes. 'Still complaining and limping, but well enough to go golfing.'

'It'll be good exercise,' I said, laughing.

'That's what he says.'

I looked out the open back door at Lucy's neat garden. 'How about yourself? How are you?'

Lucy smiled. 'There's fear of me,' she said, adjusting the rope belt of her dressing gown. 'In fact, I'm just about to have my breakfast. Would you eat a couple of sausages yourself?'

'Absolutely. I'm starving.'

'Run up so and call Cassandra and I'll get started here.'

'Cassandra?'

Lucy nodded.

'I didn't know she was home.'

Lucy looked at me over her shoulder as she lit the gas under the frying pan. 'Since last week.'

I ran up the stairs taking the broad steps two at a time and banged hard on the door at the top of the stairs.

'Drop dead, Rachel!' a voice snarled.

'Get up this minute!' I shouted, flinging open the door.

Cassandra sat up, knotted into a muddle of sheets and blankets.

I opened the curtains and wintry daylight streamed into the clothes-strewn bedroom. Cassandra covered her head with a sheet.

'Get out. Have you no respect for a woman's privacy?'

'No,' I said, leaning on the end of the old-fashioned wooden double bed, 'especially as you never even bothered your arse to ring me since you got back from Spain.'

'I was going to ring you today.' Cassandra pulled the sheet off her head so that it looped around her neck like a cowl. She squinted her brown eyes to look at me. 'I've been busy. I took some really, really good shots in Spain and I was hoping I might even have the bones of an exhibition but I need to develop everything first. And I *was* going to ring you today. Honestly, Séamus.'

'Liar. Get up. Your mother says you have to get up.'

'OK, OK,' she said, falling back on to the bed with a groan. 'I'm awake, I'll be down in a minute. Get out.'

'Fine. Just one thing.'

'What?'

'You really should take your mascara off at night, it makes you look like a battered panda.'

'Drop dead,' she said, head disappearing under the sheet again.

'Be down in five minutes or I'm coming back up to get you,' I said, and left the room.

'I'm really terrified!' she shouted.

'Yeah, yeah, yeah,' I shouted back as I went downstairs.

Aunt Lucy was slicing white pudding on a breadboard when I walked back into the food fragrant kitchen.

'Is Rachel around?' I asked, as I stood beside her and watched her chop.

'At Emily's,' she said, scooping a handful of pudding and transferring it to the sizzling pan. 'She's staying with her for the weekend. Emily lives in Cork now, she has a job in the bank there. Do you know Emily?'

I shook my head.

'Yes, you do,' Cassandra said behind me, as she padded past in stockinged feet and opened the fridge. 'You went out with her sister when you were at college.'

I shook my head again.

'Jesus, Séamus,' Cassandra tutted, as she poured herself a glass of orange juice, 'what kind of a man are you? Don Quixote?'

'Or maybe you mean Don Juan?'

'Whatever. You must remember. Her name was Aoife or Amanda – something like that.'

'Oh, Amelia.'

'Amelia,' Cassandra repeated, sitting on to a wooden chair and tucking her knees inside her long nightshirt. 'That's it. How quaint.'

'That's rich from a woman called Cassandra.'

'Blame my mother,' Cassandra said, shading her eyes from

the wintry, low-in-the-sky sun that was streaming through the kitchen window.

'Leave me out of this,' Aunt Lucy said, as she placed plates of food on the table. 'Stop talking and eat.'

We ate in silence for a few minutes.

'I think I might as well go back to Castleannery with you,' Cassandra said, breaking the silence.

I looked up.

'A couple of weeks in the country will do me good.'

'What about your photographs? I thought you had to develop a load of fabulous photographs?'

Cassandra sighed. 'It's too near Christmas. I can't really do much about it now, can I?'

'Mind you, you could get a job *easily* as it's so near Christmas,' her mother said. 'The weather has been terrible. I'd say half the art teachers in the country are out with the flu. They must be desperate for substitute teachers.'

'Nah. I'm finished with that. No more teaching – no offence, Séamus. I spoke to an agent in Spain.'

'An estate agent?'

'Haw-haw. She's English and has helped loads of artists. Anyway, I met her in Pamplona and she thinks she might be able to place my work.'

'That'd be great,' Aunt Lucy said. 'Séamus, have you finished eating? Will I get you an ashtray?'

'No thanks. I quit.'

'Good for you,' Aunt Lucy said. 'How long are you off them?'

'A month.'

'Well, done. How are you finding it?'

'Not too bad,' I said. 'I have my moments, but I think I'll succeed this time.'

'I'm sure you will – anyway, Cassandra – sorry, love – what were you saying about the agent and all of that?'

'Just that I'm going to go for it this time. Who knows I might get some good pictures in Castleannery.'

'You might,' I said. 'I'll line up the locals and ask them if you can take pictures. I'd say Pakie Hayes would look frighteningly gorgeous in a bikini.'

Cassandra pushed back her chair and stretched her arms high above her head, then she stood up and walked over to her mother and draped her arm around her shoulders.

'You can mock now, but you'll all be glad when I'm famous and they're writing articles about me in the Sunday papers.'

Aunt Lucy nodded her head. 'I'm sure we will, love.'

'And if I can't make some sort of a career for myself this year, I'll look for a permanent teaching job.'

Aunt Lucy looked at me and raised her eyebrows and then we both looked at Cassandra.

'Or maybe next year,' she said, holding her hands up in the air. 'These things sometimes take a bit of time. Anyway, back to Castleannery. The more I think about it the better it seems. I'll definitely go back to Castleannery with you. I could do with a break.'

I looked at her.

'Don't you want me to come?'

'Of course I want you to come. I just don't want you skiving off when you should be working.'

'Slave driver. Anyway, it'll be good for me. Help me to get my head together.'

'Always a blessing,' Aunt Lucy muttered as she left the kitchen to go upstairs. 'Ring me when you're coming home.'

It was raining hard by the time I pulled into the conifer-lined yard in front of the small farmhouse Jessica and I had bought after we were married. Prince came bounding up as Cassandra stepped out of the car.

'Hello, boy,' she said, bending down to rub his big, black, bony head. 'Did you miss me? Is he treating you properly?'

I lifted the box of school books from the boot of the car and started towards the house.

'Lock your car,' Cassandra said.

'Why?'

'The usual reasons,' she said, following me to the red front door.

'City girl,' I said, as she and Prince queued behind me in the rain, 'nobody is going to steal my car, for God's sake.'

'This could be a hotbed of crime for all you know. Castleannery – crime capital of the mid-west.'

'I doubt it.'

'Well, you never can tell, Séamus.'

'It's the middle of nowhere. Nothing ever happens here.'

'You've obviously never seen *Deliverance*,' she said. 'These backwaters can be the most dangerous of all.'

'Sure,' I said, closing the front door against the rain. 'Sure they can, Cass – whatever you say.'

The night of Mattie's murder Cassandra and I were invited to a dinner party.

'Pádraig Harrison never invited me to any of his soirées before,' I said to Cassandra, as we drove the half-mile to his house.

'Maybe he's inviting the neighbours in relays.' Cassandra flicked down the passenger visor to examine her face in the tiny mirror. 'This bloody mirror is useless, by the way.'

'Well, in my experience it's a perfectly good mirror, but to give it its due it's not going to be much good at eight o'clock at night in the pitch dark. Anyway, you look fine.'

Cassandra tutted and pulled her coat closer around her shoulders.

'We should have walked,' I said, as I peered into the night and up at the clear, starry frost-promising sky. 'The roads will be like glass by the time we're coming home.'

'I have no intention of arriving at Pádraig Harrison's with a red, frost-bitten nose,' Cassandra said, shuffling her short black hair as she pulled round the rear-view mirror to face her.

'Hey!' I shouted, as I fixed it back in position.

Cassandra tutted loudly.

'Get over yourself,' I said, peering in the mirror as if I was likely to see something charging behind me along the dark, country road. 'Anyway, I don't know why you're so nervous. I can't imagine that he'll be too critical of you. He already seems to like you.'

'Really?'

'Jesus, Cassandra, how stupid can you be? He's only inviting me to dinner because of you. That's as plain as the non frost-bitten nose on your face.'

'Really?' she squealed, turning to look at me. 'No way.'

'Yes, yes. Look at it like this – he's called to the house three times in the past two days. I've lived four fields away from him for months and I'd say he's probably only called twice before in all that time.'

'I thought teachers were very important people.'

I snorted and laughed at the same time. 'In the 1950s, maybe. Generally speaking I wouldn't think I'd be interesting enough for a computer whizz like Pádraig unless I had my lovely cousin in tow.'

'Aw, thanks, Séamus,' Cassandra said, reaching over to pinch my cheek.

'Get off.'

Cassandra laughed. 'Sometimes I remember why I put up with you.'

A tall house with pointed dormers and yellow light streaming from its many windows appeared, suddenly, as we drove around a hairpin bend on the road.

'Oh, look – is that the house?'

'Yes, indeed,' I said, pulling into the driveway and coming to a halt behind a black car. 'Let's go and impress the natives.'

*

It was only two weeks earlier that Mattie and I had found William Ormston at the side of the road just across from Pádraig Harrison's house. It was a Monday, about half four. Cold, rainy, grey – almost dark. I was on my way home after school.

As I drove I was trying to plan something for dinner that wouldn't take long to prepare so that I could start correcting the thirty-two essays that were slithering around on the back seat of my car. Pádraig Harrison's house came into view over the tops of the trees, and as I was rounding the bend I saw a dark green BMW jammed in the ditch. I slammed on my brakes, jumped out into the heavy drizzle and ran towards it. Just as I reached the car, Mattie appeared on the road.

'Mattie!' I shouted to him before I bent down to peer inside. A square-shouldered, heavyset man with silver hair was leaning across the steering wheel. I opened the car door and laid my hand, gently, on his shoulder.

'Sir?' I called, softly. 'Hello? Excuse me, sir. Can you hear me? Are you all right?'

Mattie arrived behind me as I grasped the man's shoulders and tried to sit him back into his seat. A low moan came from the slumped figure so I immediately let go. I turned to look at Mattie who was staring at the driver.

'What'll we do?' I whispered, standing up.

'Have you your phone?'

I patted the pockets of my jacket and ran back and frantically searched the car. No phone. Fuck it. Why did I never remember to bring the fucking thing with me? I ran back to Mattie.

'I can't find it. Must have left it at home. I'm so stupid, I'm always . . .'

Mattie held up a hand. 'No matter. Don't worry. Try the house there, see if anybody is home. They'll surely let you use the telephone.'

I ran across the road and hammered on Pádraig Harrison's

front door. When there was no reply I made my way to the back of his house. Maybe the back door was open? Or even a window. Surely nobody would mind if I went in to call an ambulance? But the whole house was locked up tight. I ran back to Mattie who looked up as he heard me approach.

'Nobody home,' I said, pausing to take a breath and rub the rain from my face. 'Locked up.'

'Look, the fastest thing is if you just hop into the car and go up home and phone the doctor, and maybe an ambulance as well while you're at it.'

I nodded and ran across the road to my car and drove home and made the phone calls. When I got back, Mattie was crouched beside the clenched body in the car, talking to the silver-haired man as if he was an old friend. He looked up at me.

'They shouldn't be long.'

Mattie grinned. 'Good man.'

Mattie rubbed a cracked, leathery hand across his face and readjusted the rain-soaked cloth cap on his head. The other hand was still resting on the stranger's arm. 'Good man, yourself,' he said, and I didn't know which of us he was addressing and I didn't care. It made me feel better. I strained my eyes and ears for evidence of an ambulance.

'You'll be grand,' Mattie said, to the man behind me. 'The doctor'll be here in a minute and he'll fix you up and you'll be right as rain. Right as rain. Won't he, Séamus?'

I started at the sound of my name.

'Yeah,' I said, tearing my eyes, momentarily, away from my vigil. 'That's right. You'll be fine.'

I looked at the hunched figure and I didn't think he'd ever be fine, but I knew Mattie wanted me to say it anyway. So I said it again, hoping that the repetition might be taken for conviction. 'Just fine. Just fine.'

A silver car appeared suddenly around the bend and stopped abruptly. The door opened and a tall, thin, nearly albino blond man jumped out. I almost shouted with relief.

'You'd think a doctor'd have enough money to buy himself a good warm coat,' I said, as he walked towards us.

Tim Winter grinned and pulled at the collar of his pale-green linen jacket in the vain hope of protecting himself from the elements. 'It's only a myth that doctors make loads of money. So? How are you doing? Saw you in the paper with the under-elevens – well done.'

'Thanks,' I said, as he came to a stop beside me. He shivered and buttoned his jacket, but the rain was already creating dark-green epaulettes where it was soaking his shoulders.

'Well?' he said. 'Who have we here?'

'I don't know who he is – never saw him before. I just found him here on my way home.'

'All right. Great,' Tim said, as if it was. 'Can I have a look?'

Mattie stepped back.

'How are you, Mattie?' Tim asked, patting Mattie on the arm as he moved in closer to the collapsed man.

'Grand, Doctor Winter. Just grand.'

Tim Winter forgot about us then as he leaned into the car. Right at that point an ambulance came screeching around the corner, its blue lights flashing in the dusk. The ambulance was followed closely by two police cars.

People poured from the vehicles and the whole stretch of road was transformed into a scene from a film. Police cars and an ambulance parked at angles. Uniformed men. A middle-aged woman in a beige raincoat and a young woman in a nurse's uniform. They talked and bustled and worked and the ambulance driver stood by the ditch smoking a cigarette as he waited.

Mattie and I watched as they carefully lifted the silver-haired man from the car on to a stretcher and into the ambulance. We stayed standing in the same spot until both the ambulance and doctor's car had disappeared from view.

'The Guards'll mind the man's car,' Mattie said, looking at me as the air became thick with silence after the ambulance left.

'They will,' I said, as we looked at two policemen who had taken our names and addresses in case they needed more information.

'I suppose I should really go home,' I said.

'You should,' Mattie agreed.

'I should,' I said.

Neither of us moved.

'Come on, so,' I said, after a few silent seconds. 'I'd say we could use a hot cup of tea.'

Mattie nodded and we both sat into my car. It wasn't until I sat down that I realized my clothes were soaking wet. Neither of us spoke until we were in my house.

'Grand and warm in here,' Mattie said, as soon as I turned on the light in the kitchen.

'God bless the inventor of central heating.' I began filling the kettle.

'It's marvellous, right enough,' Mattie said, gravitating immediately towards the navy range that was radiating its heat throughout the kitchen and the house.

'I'm just going to go upstairs and change out of these wet clothes,' I said. 'Make yourself at home.'

Mattie nodded.

When I came back downstairs with an armful of dry clothes to offer Mattie he was still standing in front of the range, rubbing his hands together.

'I wonder is that poor man dead, Séamus?'

I held the clothes out to him.

'Change into these. You must be soaking wet.'

Mattie shook his head. 'Ah, no, thanks all the same, I'm grand. Nearly dry now. But do you think he's dead?'

I dropped the clothes on to an empty chair and made a pot of tea.

'I don't know, Mattie,' I said, pouring the tea. 'He didn't look too good to me.'

'Nor me,' Mattie said, spooning sugar absentmindedly into the mug of tea I had handed him. Five or six spoonfuls tumbled into the mug before he started stirring.

'Still, God is good,' he said before taking a sip of tea.

'Yeah. So they say. Have a biscuit, Mattie, and change into these, why don't you? You'll get your death in those wet clothes.'

Mattie laughed and took a fig roll in his big, coarse hand. 'Indeed I won't. I'm grand as I am. Wet clothes won't do me one bit of harm. I tell you, if wet clothes were to kill me I'd be dead long ago.'

And he was absolutely correct of course. His wet clothes didn't do him any harm. Not like the bullet in the chest two weeks later.

I lifted the brass door knocker on Pádraig Harrison's front door and it banged against its matching plate. The door opened almost immediately. A tall, gangly shape was silhouetted in the doorway.

'Séamus. Nice to see you,' Tim Winter said, reaching for my hand and shaking it as he stepped back to let us into Pádraig Harrison's airy, cathedral-ceilinged hallway.

'Tim, how are you? Bitter cold out there.'

'Desperate. Absolutely freezing. Can I take your coats?'

I shrugged out of my heavy woollen coat and handed it to Tim. It was a nice coat, not my usual style at all. This was a long, grey cashmere coat that Jessica had bought me.

Not really a teacher's coat, I thought, as I looked at it draped over Tim's long arm. More the kind of coat an architect might wear, I realized with a shock. My heart ached in my chest. For all I knew maybe the architect had picked it out.

Maybe they'd talked about me when they were together?

Maybe she'd shared her disappointment in me and they'd decided to try to smarten me up? Renovate me like a derelict property. Tear away the dreadful décor and make a silk purse out of a sow's ear? I wanted to cry and I longed for a cigarette. Why was it that the idea of Jessica made me want to smoke? Jessica always hated that I smoked. All the time we were together she nagged me to stop and now that I had it was too late.

'Thanks,' I said loudly, to clear my head. 'Thanks a lot, Tim.'

But my head didn't clear. Instead it began to fill up with Jessica and slips of what had happened. Single words and half phrases and pictures – water speeding down a rusty spout into a dirty bucket. I hated when that happened. It was a waste of time. A stupid, bloody waste of time and it was ruining my life. Why the hell had I stopped smoking?

'I don't think we've met,' I heard Tim say, in the distance.

'No,' Cassandra said. 'I take it you're Tim. I'm Cassandra O'Brien and, as you can see, my cousin has no manners.'

'Cousin?' Tim echoed, taking Cassandra's coat from her outstretched hand.

'Yes, this is my cousin Cassandra.' I forced myself into the present and made my mouth take the shape of a smile. 'And, Cassandra, this gentleman here is Tim Winter, local GP and trainer of St Nessan's under-elevens hurling team for years – long before I ever came along.'

Tim grinned. 'But I never won the League with them Séamus, not like you.'

'Just reaping the benefits of your hard work. Have you any notion of coming back to us?'

Tim shook his head. 'I'd love to, but I can't seem to manage it any more. I'm over thirty now – don't have the same stamina, I suppose.'

'You're the same age as me.'

Tim winked. 'But I'm not as fit and healthy as you.'

'Well, if you change your mind . . .' I began.

'Séamus! Cassandra!' a voice called from the top of the stairs.

Pádraig. He appeared to pause as if to let us look at him. We duly did so. 'You've arrived.'

He suddenly broke into movement and cantered down the mauve carpeted steps. 'Great to see you! You know Tim, don't you?'

'Sure.'

'And I've met Cassandra,' Tim said.

Cassandra pulled a face at me.

'I have good manners relative to everybody else I meet during the day,' I muttered to her as we filed into the sitting room behind Pádraig and Tim.

'They're all nine year olds,' she muttered in reply.

I shrugged.

'Lovely house, Pádraig,' I said, loudly, like an over-enthusiastic salesman. 'You've done a great job.'

Pádraig displayed his white, even teeth in a smile that only included his mouth.

'Thanks, Séamus. I like it. I really, really do.'

'How long have you lived here, Pádraig?' Cassandra asked.

'Since I came to Castleannery – about eight months now.'

'And how do you find it? Castleannery I mean? You lived in London before that, didn't you?' Cassandra continued.

'Love it. Settled right in. I'm a rural boy at heart, I suppose. Beats the hell out of life in London, anyway, eh, Séamus?'

'Definitely,' I said, thinking the only time I'd ever lived in London I'd been nineteen and just finished my first year in college. I'd spent three months there, carrying cement up and down ladders and sleeping in a hostel bed that stank of urine. It was many a cigarette I smoked lying on the bed in that hostel. 'You just can't beat the fresh air and open spaces.'

'You'll all have a drink? Séamus? Cassandra? Tim?' Pádraig interrupted.

Rude, arrogant bollocks, I thought.

'Great,' I said.

'Wine OK?'

We all nodded and Pádraig filled four long-stemmed crystal glasses and handed three of them to us.

'So, Séamus,' he said as he moved to stand in front of the huge fire that climbed up the inglenook chimney, 'I believe you've had an exciting time during the past few weeks.'

I considered him for a minute and the angular planes of his face and his clearly expensive clothes and state of the art house and wondered if he was being sarcastic.

'No,' I sort of drawled, after a pause, 'nothing too exhilarating.'

Pádraig smiled his smile again.

'I heard otherwise,' he said, in a low, coaxing voice that made me want to ask him what the fuck exactly he wanted from me. But I didn't. Instead I tried a smile of my own.

'Well, if you consider the confiscation of fourteen water-pistols and the breaking up of a fight in the boys' toilets exciting, then I guess the answer is yes.'

I paused to sip my drink. Everybody laughed except Pádraig. A look of annoyance flitted across his smooth-skinned face and his lips twitched. He coughed and swallowed and then he began to laugh along with Tim and Cassandra.

'Very good, very good,' he said, his laugh sliding into a chuckle until he was creating a fair impersonation of a warm, friendly person, 'but I wasn't talking about that. I was thinking more along the lines of your episode with William Ormston.'

I looked at him and shook my head.

'*William Ormston?*' Pádraig repeated.

'Nope. Sorry about that. Can't place him. Not a pupil. I

don't think I ever taught a William Ormston and I'm pretty sure he isn't a parent.'

Tim laughed. 'The man you found?'

I shook my head again and shrugged.

'The man in the BMW?' Tim said.

'Oh, right. *That* William Ormston. Right. It was me, that's true. Me and Mattie Ahern, actually.'

'That's right, Mattie was there as well,' Tim said. 'Can you believe I'd forgotten that he was there.'

'Well, he was. Good job too, Tim. I was worse than useless.'

'Mattie?' Pádraig interrupted.

'Mattie Ahern,' I said. 'I don't know if you know him. A farmer. He lives about a half mile down the road from you here. On the road to the glen. A great man.'

'He is,' Tim confirmed. 'A great man.'

'He was more use to that poor man – William whatshisname – than I was.'

'Ormston. William Ormston,' Tim said.

'Right. Ormston.'

'Shock,' Tim said, 'you were in shock.'

'Maybe. Whatever the reason, Mattie had to take charge and sort it all out.'

Pádraig smiled, vaguely. 'Oh, right. Right. That's great. But what I find amazing is that you found William Ormston like that. Just there on the side of the road. It was quite near here, wasn't it?'

I remembered banging on his door in the rain 'Across the road. You weren't here.'

'Across the road from here?'

I nodded.

Pádraig put his hand to his face. 'I didn't realize it was as close as that, everything was pretty much cleared away by the time I got home.'

I shrugged.

Pádraig shook his head with regret as if he'd missed the main event. Pompous, materialistic bastard.

'I can't believe it. I'm never out any more – but I was in London all that week.'

'Oh, right,' I said.

'But he had you to help him, anyway,' Pádraig said, furrowing his brow as he fixed his eyes on my face. 'You and your friend Martin.'

'Mattie. Not that it did him much good. He died anyway.'

'Well,' Tim said, pausing to sip from his glass, 'you can never tell for sure, but I'd say he'd have died even if he'd been in a hospital.'

'But *William Ormston*,' Pádraig said.

'Just who the hell *is* William Ormston?' Cassandra interrupted, looking at me; everyone turned to look at her and she blushed slightly. 'It's just that you never told me about this Séamus.'

'I forgot.'

'So? Who is he? Or should I say, who *was* he?'

'No idea.'

'You never heard of William Ormston?' Pádraig said.

I shook my head. 'As far as I'm concerned he was just some unlucky old bastard who had a heart attack or a stroke or something and died on the road near Castleannery.'

Pádraig winced at the swear word and it made me want to swear again.

'Who was he?' Cassandra repeated.

'Just the owner of one of the most important computer software companies in Europe,' Pádraig said, looking at Cassandra and pronouncing each syllable slowly, as if she wouldn't understand his words if he spoke at a normal pace.

'Like Bill Gates?' Cassandra said.

Pádraig laughed. 'Maybe not as big as Bill Gates, but big enough. Important. Powerful.'

'Well, he's dead now anyway,' I said, as my irritation with

Pádraig threatened to move into my hands and make me punch him in his shiny-toothed mouth.

Pádraig looked at me. I stood up and walked to stand beside him at the fire.

'You know what they say, Pádraig,' I said, irrationally glad to see that I was at least a head taller than him, 'there are no pockets in a shroud.'

Pádraig continued to stare at me. 'Mmm,' he said, looking away abruptly and bringing his long-fingered hands together in a sudden clap before rubbing his moisturized palms, loudly, together. 'Anybody for a refill?'

Fuck you too, I thought.

'That'd be great,' Tim said, holding his glass out towards Pádraig and looking at me. 'You're right, there, Séamus.'

'Did he have a heart attack?' Cassandra said.

'Stroke,' Tim said, 'that was the final verdict. He had a pre-exisiting condition, anyway, and it appears that he had a stroke that day and it's what killed him. He never regained consciousness – died on the way to the hospital in the back of the ambulance.'

'And was there foul play suspected?' Cassandra said.

Tim and I looked at her. She blushed again. 'Sorry, I just wondered that's all. If he was rich and powerful then maybe somebody bumped him off.'

Pádraig had turned his back as he refilled glasses.

'Who was bumped off?' a woman's voice said.

We all turned towards the voice. A tall, fair-haired woman in a full-length, sleeveless black dress stood in the doorway.

'Chrissie,' Pádraig said, rushing forward to kiss her on the cheek. 'Everything work out?'

The woman held his hand and smiled. Wisps of blonde hair trailed down the back of her long neck from her loosely pinned-up hair.

'Not too bad,' she said, taking a seat in the centre of the cream couch. 'I finally managed to get somebody to answer the phone. They should have the stuff by morning. Thanks, Pádraig.'

Pádraig smiled and returned to pouring out drinks.

'You haven't met our guests, have you?' Pádraig said, handing Cassandra and I our refilled glasses of wine.

Chrissie shook her head and looked at us.

'OK – Chrissie – I'd like you to meet Séamus and Cassandra.'

I walked over to the couch and offered her my hand. Chrissie stood up and shook hands with me.

'Hello,' Cassandra said.

The two women smiled at each other as Chrissie sat back down on the couch.

'Nice to meet you both. So, tell me – who was bumped off?'

Tim laughed and took a swig from his drink. 'Nobody.'

'William Ormston,' I said.

Chrissie turned to look at me.

'But he wasn't,' I continued, 'murdered, I mean. He died in his car just across the road from here.'

'Séamus found him,' Tim interrupted.

'Really? I think I remember something about that, now that you mention it. And who thinks he was murdered?'

'Nobody,' Tim said. 'Well, Cassandra – but she was just speculating as he was so wealthy she thinks that maybe somebody may have wanted to kill him.'

'For his money?' Chrissie asked Cassandra.

'I wouldn't know William Ormston from a blade of grass,' Cassandra said, shrugging and waving her hands in surrender. 'Don't ask me.'

Chrissie laughed.

'Nobody really thinks he was murdered,' Tim said, quietly, 'not even the police. A couple of tall Guards with Kerry accents nosed around for a few days. Did that door-to-door thing.'

'Not that there are many doors around here,' I said.

Chrissie smiled. 'No. But they could ask in the village, I suppose. Did they, Tim? Ask in the village?'

'Yes,' Tim said, 'but there was nothing to find out so they went away.'

'And did they search for clues or whatever it is happens in these cases?' Cassandra said.

Tim shrugged and looked at me.

'Yes,' I said, 'they did. A swarm of them searched, but they mustn't have found anything because they left after a couple of hours. Asked their few questions, searched the ditches and left.'

'Unless they've just gone away to collate all their information and maybe they'll come back again and re-open the investigation?' Cassandra said, grinning.

'I doubt that,' Tim said, 'as I just said, the man definitely had a stroke. Simple as that. He was on medication to stop his blood clotting. It was a question of *when* rather than *if* he'd have a stroke.'

'Really?' I said.

'Seemingly,' Tim said, 'so, no foul play suspected.'

'But perhaps the police know something we don't know,' I said. 'Maybe a detective will have one of those hunches they always have on TV and come back and poke around and find something? You never know.'

Tim laughed and stretched his long legs. 'Unlikely,' he said, rubbing his hands over his face as if he was washing his face. 'Extremely unlikely.'

'Pity,' Cassandra said, 'it might liven up the long winter evenings to have a little bit of murder and mayhem going on in sleepy old Castleannery.'

Everybody laughed.

'OK,' Pádraig said, as the laughter subsided. I realized he hadn't spoken for a while. 'Time for dinner. If you're all ready?'

We all stood up, making various assenting noises.

'Great,' Pádraig said, putting his glass on to the beeswaxed pine mantlepiece, 'follow me into the dining room.'

Tim, Chrissie, Cassandra and I waited for Pádraig to lead the way out of the room towards the smell of food. As we crocodiled through the narrow but tastefully decorated hallway I wondered about William Ormston.

Where was he from? What had he been like? Did he have lots of friends? A big family? I realized that I had no idea. All I knew about him was that he owned a big, new, dark-green BMW, and that he'd had some kind of a bad turn and died in the ditch across the road from where we were about to eat our dinner. It wasn't a lot, really.

Pádraig's dinner was, naturally, delicious. Or 'delightful', as Cassandra said to him when we finished eating.

'Really, Pádraig, that was delightful.'

I looked at her and mouthed the word 'delightful' behind my serviette, but she slid her gaze away from me and back to our host. Pádraig smiled his wide smile. 'I'm glad you enjoyed it, Cassandra. Makes it all worthwhile. Coffee?'

Cassandra nodded her head and dropped her gaze on to the empty white porcelain plate in front of her. Pádraig stood up from the table. I looked at Cassandra again, but her eyes were firmly focused on her plate. Bored with trying to get her attention I looked around the table.

Tim was sitting with his eyes closed, humming gently to the ambient classical music that floated in the background air. Tim was a most unusual looking Irishman – blond as a Swede. So blond, in fact, that his eyelashes were almost white and his short hair a halo around his head.

I liked Tim. Straightforward, no shit. I'd known him for most of my time in Castleannery and while we weren't exactly bosom buddies, I really did like him. Jessica had been very fond of Tim as well, I remembered. She thought he was very clever, and I suppose she was right – he was a doctor after all.

Tim'd been great after Jessica left. We only spoke about it once – in the pub. I was pissed and crying. He was kind and bought me whiskey, and agreed that life was shit. But, better still, he never brought it up again. Just treated me as if I was normal – which meant a lot to me at the time.

Mostly though, when I thought of Tim, it was in the context of hurling. They still talked about Tim in St Nessan's Hurling Club and how he was well known for cursing at officious GAA officials and getting drunk each year at the annual fundraising dinner dance and singing 'The Copacabana'.

Entertaining as he was, Tim was easily replaced in the social structure of the club – not, however, as easily replaced as a coach. Without a doubt, he was handy to have around to tend to the myriad injuries caused by bad judgement, hurleys and quick tempers. But more than that was the way he could manage to shout exactly the correct words of encouragement at red-kneed, muddy-legged children wielding hurleys in frenzied contests. It was a great shame that he'd retired – the kids really missed him.

I moved my eyes off Tim and found that Chrissie was looking at me. Returning her gaze, I noticed that she had a tiny scar near her mouth. A crescent-shaped colourless scar at the very corner of her lipstick-free mouth. It made her look like she was smiling slightly even when her mouth was at rest.

'Did you enjoy your dinner, Séamus?' she said, her lips lifting into an actual smile.

'Delightful,' I said.

Chrissie's smile turned into a grin. Cassandra looked up from her plate and glared at me.

'Oh, look,' I said, as the door opened, 'coffee. That smells delicious, Pádraig.'

Pádraig swept into the room carrying a large silver tray, which he set in the centre of the white tablecloth.

'Delightful,' Cassandra said.

I winked at her as she pursed her mouth suppressing a smile.

'Absolutely delightful,' I said, as Pádraig began to pour the dark, aromatic liquid into fragile white cups. 'How do you manage it?'

'Practise,' Pádraig said, keeping his eyes on his task. 'I always think you can't beat a cup of real coffee, can you?'

'No,' Tim said, 'and you certainly can't beat a cup of coffee and a cigarette. Pádraig, is it OK if I take my coffee with me outside the back door to have a quick smoke?'

'That's fine,' Pádraig said, his mouth compressed into a disapproving line as he handed Tim a cup of coffee. 'Milk? Sugar?'

Tim shook his head as he stood up from the table. 'Black is great. Will you join me, Séamus?'

I sighed. 'I'd love that, but I've been off them now for almost a month so I'd better not.'

'Fair play to you,' Tim said. 'You must be delighted with yourself.'

'Well, not really, but I suppose I'll keep going as I've gone this far,' I said.

'It's the wise thing,' Tim said, giving us all a small wave as he disappeared into the kitchen clutching his cup.

Pádraig finished serving coffee and resumed his head of table position. 'Chrissie – while I think of it. I'll be gone at six – my plane to Frankfurt leaves at seven thirty and there are workmen coming first thing in the morning.'

Chrissie sipped coffee and nodded.

'Are you having more work done on the house?' I asked to distract myself from envying Tim the nicotine that was by then pumping up his heart and flooding his brain with illusions of relaxation and relief. How I wanted that – even if it was an illusion.

'Well, yes,' Pádraig answered, pausing to sip coffee.

'There can't be much left to do,' I said.

Pádraig shrugged and nodded, and swept his eyes around the room in an unfocused way. 'Just a few jobs.'

'Jobs?' I repeated.

'Anybody for more coffee?' Pádraig stood up and grabbed the coffee pot. He walked around the table and topped up each small coffee cup without waiting for an answer. When he reached me I put my hand over my cup and looked up at him.

'Is it a swimming pool?' I said.

Pádraig looked at me as if I'd lost my mind.

'Maybe it's a cinema or a shrine to Elvis?'

Pádraig tutted and everybody else laughed.

'I just can't imagine what *jobs* you'd need to have done,' I said.

'I suppose there's no harm in telling you,' he said, pausing as if to think something out. He nodded and took a deep breath. 'I'm having the garage converted into a secure unit.'

'Like a prison?' I said.

Pádraig gave his half smile. 'More like a vault.'

'Why?' Cassandra asked.

Pádraig turned his attention to her, and I could see her sit up straight in her seat. 'It's my line of business,' he said.

'Are you afraid somebody is going to steal your computers?' she said.

Pádraig smiled and I thought for a minute he was going to lean forward and actually pat Cassandra on the head. 'The stock I have to protect is a lot more valuable than any computer hardware.'

'Stock?' Chrissie asked.

'Software. It's what I do and nowadays, as you know, it's

the pivot of the whole IT industry,' Pádraig said. 'One can't be too careful.'

I wanted to puke. Or smoke. 'Industrial espionage?' I said instead. 'Don't you think it's all a bit James Bondish?'

Pádraig shrugged. 'You'd be surprised. Once the job is done I'll be able to relax.'

'Job? What job?' Tim said, walking back into the room accompanied by a delicious scent of cold air and cigarette smoke.

'Pádraig is having something built tomorrow,' Chrissie elaborated.

'Not built – modified. I'm having the garage converted into a sort of vault to store my computers and work para-phernalia.'

'Really?' Tim said. 'Your ordinary garage? Where you keep the deep freeze and stuff?'

Pádraig nodded.

'But why? What's the problem?' Tim said.

'Industrial espionage,' I said, nodding at Tim. 'Better to avoid that, don't you think?'

Tim grinned at me and sat down. 'Definitely. Why all the rush, though, Pádraig? Is somebody after you?'

'Yeah,' I said, 'how come there haven't been loads of gorgeous women with Eastern European accents in the pub trying to get us to give them information about you?'

'Or,' Tim said, 'maybe they'll just send guys in black leotards in the dead of night with those tiny cameras to snap pictures of your work?'

We all laughed again – this time Pádraig joined in, but I could see he didn't find our routine one bit funny. Dry balls.

'Very good, Tim,' he said as the laughter subsided, 'but what you don't realize is that it was hell to get these guys to agree to come all the way to Castleannery.'

'All the way?' I said. 'Where are they coming from? New York?'

'London. And the job itself will only take one day, but these are the top men in their field. There's nothing they don't know about security, so, when they said they could come tomorrow – I jumped at the chance. First thing tomorrow morning they'll be here, and I'll be damn glad.'

Pádraig paused and drained his cup. 'By this time to-morrow my humble garage will be as impregnable a fortress as any of your Fort Knoxes or National Banks.'

'That's great,' Chrissie said, nibbling on a thin biscuit, a smile curling the corners of her mouth.

'Makes me feel all safe and secure knowing that our neighbourhood is going to be protected from marauding hoardes of spies,' I said. Tim and Chrissie looked away, hands covering the grins that were spreading across their faces. Where did this Pádraig Harrison idiot get off? Delusions of grandeur *and* industrial espionage? It'd have been laughable if only it wasn't so teeth-grindingly annoying.

2

'(The Angels Wanna Wear My) Red Shoes'
Elvis Costello, 1977

Pádraig, Chrissie and Tim stood at the door breathing clouds of steam into the frosty November night as Cassandra and I sat into my freezing cold car. I waved through the foggy window and turned the key in the ignition. The car made a reluctant, choking noise. And then died. I tried it again.

The second time it was even more reluctant. Glancing quickly at the group huddled in the doorway I could imagine Pádraig assessing the age of my car and comparing it to whatever kind of big, shiny new car he owned and tucked up every night in his nice warm garage.

'What is wrong with this crock?' Cassandra said, teeth chattering like magpies.

'Nothing,' I said, 'it's just cold that's all.'

I turned the key again. It sputtered again and then silence.

'Shit,' I muttered, trying a fourth time to no avail.

'Everything all right?' Pádraig called, tapping on the window.

I rolled down my window.

'Oh, not a problem, thanks all the same, Pádraig, just a bit cold, that's all,' I called back in a high-pitched, happy voice. 'Just give her a minute to heat up.'

'I hate the way men always call cars, "her" and "she",' Cassandra complained as I rolled my window closed and placed my hand on the ignition key again.

'They don't always,' I said, to distract myself.

'Yeah, but they shouldn't do it at all. How would you like –'

'Shh. We'll argue later, OK?'

Slowly I turned the key and without warning the engine started. I smiled to myself in the dark.

'Good girl,' I whispered. 'I knew you could do it.'

'See! See! What did I just say?' Cassandra said.

Pádraig's face re-appeared outside my side window. I rolled down the window. 'Everything all right?'

'Great, great. No problem.'

'Yeah, the old jalopy started at last, thanks,' Cassandra said, smiling up at his shadowed face.

'It's not an old jalopy,' I said.

Cassandra laughed. 'Yes, it is. You're always complaining about it.'

'No, I'm not,' I said, glaring at her in the dark. 'I'm very fond of this car.'

'Yes, well, I suppose you would have to be fond of a car that tries so hard,' Pádraig said, burrowing his chin into the neck of his sweater and stamping his designer shoes against the ground to keep his feet warm. I hoped he got frostbite.

'They don't make cars like this any more,' I said, tapping the steering wheel with the tips of the fingers of my right hand. Even as I spoke I was wondering what the hell was wrong with me. Next I'd be saying 'Alrighty then' and 'Yessiree'. But I couldn't seem to stop myself.

'No,' I said, sagely nodding my head, 'we'll never see the like of this car again.'

For God's sake, what was I trying to do?

'I wonder why,' Cassandra said, looking at me as she huddled deeper into her coat.

'Well, thanks for a lovely evening,' I said, ignoring Cassandra completely and revving the engine. 'We'd better be off so.'

'Great to see you,' Pádraig said, stepping back a little from the car. 'Thanks for coming. See you soon.'

'Bye!' Cassandra called as I turned the car as quickly as I could and drove away from Pádraig Harrison's house.

I drove out the gateway pushing my foot to the floor until the car reached a pathetic thirty miles an hour, then I remembered that the roads were probably icy and slowed back down. Cassandra turned on the radio and fiddled with the heater.

'Thanks be to God,' she said, pulling her coat as high as it'd go around her ears and head and sitting back in her seat. 'It's heating up at last. I thought I was going to die of cold.'

I concentrated on the shadowy trees lining the road and thought how black they looked against the clear, starry sky. Cassandra hummed along with a Stevie Wonder song.

'So, Séamus, did you have a nice evening?'

I glanced quickly at her and then returned my gaze to the potentially icy road without answering.

'I did,' she said. 'Isn't it a great house?'

'Hmm.'

'And the food was delicious.'

'Delightful.'

'Pig. Still it was.'

I laughed. 'Delightful. Perfectly, perfectly, awfully, awfully delightful.'

'Oh, shut up. I'm going to sleep, so just shut up.'

'It's hardly worth your while. We'll be home in a minute.'

'Still, I want to, so shut up.'

We drove the rest of the short distance to my house in silence, relaxing into the low murmur of the radio.

When we arrived we both went straight upstairs without even bothering to take off our coats. Half blind with tiredness I undressed and climbed into my chilly bed, but as soon as I lay down I seemed to move into a different place. A sudden wide-awake nightmare place where I could hear the far-away sounds of cars and dogs and where I was exhausted to the point of nausea, but still couldn't manage to make that final leap into unconsciousness.

I thought about Pádraig Harrison and how much he annoyed me, and I tried to think of good reasons for it, but all I could come up with was that he had a nice house and a fancy car and he thought he was just fine in the world and I didn't like that one little bit. And of course he was rich – or at least much richer than I'd ever be – and he was also handsome and urbane.

I tried to think of ways these were faults, but failed except for the fact that every time I thought of one of them they made me dislike him more. And though the very idea of Pádraig Harrison annoyed me, I welcomed it and wanted to keep him centre-stage in my head because otherwise I knew I'd think about Jessica. And I didn't want to do that.

But, as usual, I had no choice. Gradually Pádraig Harrison and his annoying, superior ways receded and I slid into wondering about Jessica. Tumbled into the usual cascade of questions.

Where is she? Is she asleep? Is he there? What is it like in her new life? Does he rub her shoulders when her head hurts? Do they fuck all the time? Does she enjoy it more than she did with me? Does she ever kiss him while he sleeps so that he wakes to the smell of her face and the smile in her green eyes?

It was like probing an aching tooth, both irresistible and excruciating at the same time. I preferred it when I was thinking about Pádraig Harrison.

At two o'clock I surrendered and got up and went downstairs to the kitchen to search through the drawers for a cigarette. I was almost positive that Mattie had left a pack behind him one day recently, but I couldn't remember for sure.

In the kitchen I opened cupboard door after cupboard door and rummaged in the drawers behind bits of string and rolls of sellotape. Waves of fury rose inside me as I slammed doors and drawers and my toes went numb from the cold rising from the tiled kitchen floor.

I searched through old biscuit tins secreted at the back of cupboards. There might just be one cigarette. That wasn't a lot to ask for, was it? One measly cigarette. That would be plenty. But there weren't any.

Panting with withdrawal I stood in the middle of the kitchen and tried to think of a plan. There was no place to buy cigarettes, I knew that. Stupid bloody one-horse towns like Castleannery, where all the shops – such as they were – closed at nine o'clock.

And it was after two in the morning so the pubs were closed as well. I opened a drawer and slammed it shut in temper. Fuck it. What kind of a place has no shops that are open at night?

I could drive to town. That was a possibility. There'd surely be something open in Limerick. Some all-night shop or restaurant or at least a garage. But that would take nearly an hour and the roads were probably like glass with all that icy weather.

Why had I stopped smoking? It was a stupid thing to do. Totally fucking ridiculous. Especially with Jessica and everything. What was I thinking? It wasn't *that* bad for you. Better than a nervous breakdown, anyway. Better than tossing yourself under a train or into a river.

I banged a cupboard door with my fist and racked my brain for another place to search. Perhaps I still had that bottle of whiskey that Eamon brought back from America, I thought, vainly opening and closing the same cupboards I'd already searched, just in case I'd managed to miss a whole bottle of whiskey.

But I knew it wasn't there. I knew Eamon finished it off the last time he'd visited. Typical of that brother of mine, never thought about anybody but himself.

Anyway, it was probably just as well, considering that it was Sunday night – no, Monday morning and I had school in a few hours. Hard enough to teach thirty-two nine and ten year olds without having had much sleep. Absolutely impossible if I had a hangover as well.

I didn't want whiskey. I wanted a cigarette. I *needed* a cigarette. If only I could smoke a cigarette I just knew Jessica's face would dissolve from inside my eyelids and let me sleep.

I wondered why it was that I couldn't seem to stop thinking about Jessica. I didn't want to think about her. There was no point any more, and I knew full well there was no point.

It wasn't like it had been at the start when I'd thought if I stayed awake all night I'd think of a way to fix it all and make it all right. I didn't believe that now. But even though I knew that it was futile, it made no difference. I still couldn't get her out of my head or my gut.

The same had been true when I was happy and in love and overwhelmed with every part of Jessica and that was fine. That was nice, in fact. But not any more.

And maybe if the face inside my eyelids had been the sad or angry or sneaky and betraying Jessica I might have been able to get to sleep. But it wasn't. Even though I had seen all those faces of Jessica, it was never those that glowed in my brain like radioactive cells. Instead it was the fair-haired and bright, happy Jessica, appearing like a vicious reminder of everything I'd lost.

I gave up my search but I still needed to smoke. I knew I was so agitated that I'd never sleep. First thing in the morning I was going straight back on the cigarettes and that was all about it. First fucking light, I'd be a smoker again. Prince woke up and came to snuffle around my bare toes.

'Scoot!' I shouted at him, but he ignored me and licked my big toe. 'Stop it,' I said, shaking my foot free.

How would I last until morning? I'd go mad. Maybe if I took a walk down the road, I could just call and see if Mattie was still up? He often went hunting in the middle of the night so there was a good chance he'd still be up.

I'd get dressed and walk down and if there was a light on I'd knock, and if not, I'd come home and make a gallon of cocoa and try to fall asleep. OK, good idea. I felt the knot in my chest loosening a little. That seemed like a plan.

I ran upstairs and remembering the frosty night outside, dressed in layers and layers of woollen clothes. In the hallway I pulled on gloves and boots and a hat my mother had knitted that I'd never wear during daylight hours. I eased the creaky front door open. Prince galloped up to me.

'OK,' I said, letting us both out into the bright, frosty darkness, 'but don't try to eat sheep or anything Prince, I'm warning you, or you'll get us both shot by some farmer.'

Prince and I started across the yard and out on to the road. The freezing air hurt my cheeks and made me feel sort of awake and alive as if I'd swum in the sea. Overhead nude tree branches arched themselves upwards showing off their grace against the indigo sky.

'Pádraig Harrison trees,' I muttered.

Prince looked at me and wagged his tail and then ran ahead. I broke into a slow trot to encourage the circulation in my feet and started to feel more relaxed as I got out of my head and into my body and closer to Mattie's house.

All right, nearly there. Just around the bend was Pádraig Harrison's des. res. and then another couple of minutes and I'd be at Mattie's house. I'd knock hard and run the risk of waking him up. He wouldn't mind. He'd understand that I couldn't go home without a cigarette

I rounded the bend in the road just before Pádraig Harrison's house and was looking up at the starry sky struggling to remember the names of constellations, when I heard the voices. Or maybe it was just Mattie's voice I heard first. It's so hard to be sure.

Anyway, it makes no real difference, I heard voices, or a voice, and when I looked in their direction I saw that up ahead of me on the road – right outside Pádraig Harrison's house – there were two people standing near a car.

As I focused on the two shapes I saw that both men seemed to be holding shotguns and that there was a third man walking towards them with a dog. Even in the darkness I knew the third man was Mattie.

Only Mattie walked like that. Mattie and his dog, Boru. Probably out for a bit of poaching in the clear moonlight with his gun held bayonet-style in front of him.

'Hoy!' Mattie shouted. 'Hoy! You! What are you doing?'

The dark figures – I supposed they were men – turned around towards Mattie's voice.

'Where the fuck did he come from?' one of the men said in a nasal accent I couldn't place.

'Stop right there! What do you think you're doing? Don't move or I'll shoot!' Mattie called loudly in his rasping voice.

The dark people didn't answer. Instead, one of them stepped forward. Was it the one who spoke with the strange accent? Was it the other one? I didn't know who was who or what was what as the action break-necked forward. Before I could think or move or even take a deep breath the man took another step towards Mattie and fired his gun. Just like that. Fired straight at him.

I stood in the road – a stalagmite, rigid and welded to the spot. And Mattie fell to the ground. He didn't call my name like he does in my dreams. He never even saw me. How could he? He was too busy playing the hero. Too busy wading in and almost asking to have a hole blown in his chest.

'What did you go and do that for? Gimme the fucking keys,' I heard a voice say in that same hard accent I'd heard before, and then I heard a car engine roaring away into the night.

The car driving off seemed to snap me out of my catatonic state and I ran to where Mattie lay, spread-eagled on the frost-sparkling tarmacadam.

'Mattie! Mattie!' I shouted bending low over his warm body. 'Oh, Jesus, oh, Jesus, what am I going to do. Oh, Mattie, oh, Jesus.'

'What happened?' Pádraig Harrison's voice said behind me.

'Somebody shot Mattie!' I screamed. 'Can't you see that he's badly wounded? Phone an ambulance, phone the police, phone somebody – anybody, for fuck's sake just go and get help.'

I heard the sound of slipper soles running back towards his house. I didn't turn my head because I didn't care. I just wanted Mattie to be all right.

'Mattie?' I said, whispering this time, as if that was a better thing to do, 'Mattie?'

I put my hand on his back and it didn't seem to be moving. But I told myself that that didn't mean anything. After all it's hard to tell things like that in the middle of the night when you're kneeling on a frosty road and the man in front of you is wearing two pullovers and a tweed overcoat.

I stroked his back gently and looked around. Where was the ambulance? Why did these people have to take so fucking long when they were needed so badly? I saw that Mattie's tweed peaked cap was lying on the other side of him on the road.

'Jesus, look at that,' I said, stretching over him to pick up his cap. 'It'd never do if something happened to your cap, now, would it, Mattie?'

Mattie stayed silent beside me as I stuffed his cap into the pocket of my coat.

'You'll be fine,' I said, returning my hand to his broad,

still back. 'They'll be here in a minute to help you, Mattie, and then everything will be all right.'

I stopped talking and looked up at the sky, and it was clear and full of stars, just exactly as it had been five minutes earlier when the world was still in one piece.

'Hold on, Mattie. It won't be long now. Do you remember what you used to say to me after Jess left? Do you remember that, Matt? I never told you how that helped me, did I? I always meant to tell you that, why didn't I tell you?'

My voice petered out as it lost the battle with the band of fear tightening around my throat. I took a deep breath.

'Nothing lasts,' I said, my voice gathering volume as I spoke, 'that's what you said to me, Mattie, when I was almost at the end of my rope. I was ready to die loads of times, but I didn't because of that.'

I squeezed Mattie's cap in my pocket like a talisman and took another breath. 'You said, nothing lasts, not good things, not bad things. Nothing lasts so just hold on – that's what you used to say – just hold on, Séamus, and everything will be all right. I listened to you Mattie and I did what you told me – I held on and I was grand. You were right. So do that, Mattie. Just hang on and you'll be grand as . . .'

A hand fixed itself around my right arm and gently tried to pull me away.

'Sorry, sir,' a small, dark-haired woman in a white dress and navy Aran cardigan was saying to me, 'we need to have a look at your friend. If you'd just step over here to the side.'

I stood up and walked to a hollow in the road near a ditch with frosted spikes of hawthorn and watched as three people huddled around Mattie in the dark and lifted him on to a stretcher and into an ambulance. I'd never even heard them arrive.

'Come into the house, Séamus,' another woman's voice was saying.

I tried to focus in the direction of the voice. Was it the nurse again?

'They'll take him to hospital, there's nothing you can do,' the voice said, speaking again.

'Chrissie?'

Chrissie nodded and pulled her coat close around her throat. 'Come on, come in. You'll get your death standing out here.'

The ambulance driver slammed the back doors of the ambulance.

'Sounds like a hearse door,' I said, looking at Chrissie. She put her hand on my arm.

'He'll be fine. Come with me, Séamus. The kettle is on.'

I shook my head. 'No. He won't be fine.'

I turned over my right hand, the hand that I'd rested on Mattie's back, and held it towards her and she gasped like I knew she would.

'See?' I said, looking myself for the first time at the blood I knew was smeared all over my palm.

Chrissie's breath formed lots of small, exerted clouds in front of her face.

'Come in out of the cold,' she said, in a gentle voice, 'it won't do either you or him . . .'

'Mattie.'

'Mattie. It won't do Mattie any good for you to stand here and get your death of cold, will it?'

'No,' I answered, like a child.

'Come on, then.'

I nodded and followed her into Pádraig Harrison's house. In the kitchen, Pádraig was pacing the floor like a demented animal. His face was white and stretched looking and there were black rings around his eyes.

He didn't speak when I came in. Chrissie guided me with gentle pressure on my arm until I found myself sitting at the table. She placed a large mug in front of me and filled it with coffee.

'Drink.'

I picked up the mug and held it in my numb hands. I saw that my hands were mottled red and purple and blue. The hot mug made them sting.

Pádraig stopped pacing and stood in front of me. 'Did you see it?'

I looked up at him.

'Did you see it, Séamus? Did you see what happened?'

'Pádraig –' Chrissie began.

'For God's sake, I'm only asking the man a question, Chrissie. What did you see out there, Séamus?'

I shrugged and sipped from the big, white mug. A flower vase of a mug. So big and so thin. Porcelain. Chrissie pulled Pádraig to a corner of the kitchen near the huge range cooker and they whispered loudly. I didn't even try to hear. I couldn't be bothered.

Gradually, my hands thawed and so did my brain. Over and over again I heard the sound of the shot. And, as I heated up and feeling returned, I noticed the stickiness on the palm of my right hand.

I looked at my hand and saw that the lines on my palm that were supposed to be full of my destiny were still full of Mattie's blood instead. Thin, brown-red lines latticed over a dirt-streaked palm.

'Séamus, I know you're upset.'

I looked up to see that Pádraig had pulled up a chair close to mine and was leaning forward towards me. 'This is upsetting for all of us, but if you saw anything – anything at all – perhaps you should tell me, now. OK?'

'Or maybe it might be better if you told me,' an unfamiliar voice said.

We all turned towards the voice. In the doorway stood a

squat, ginger-haired man. He looked to be in his early forties. His face was slapped red by the frost outside and he wore a puffy, orange-coloured, feather-filled jacket buttoned up to his chin.

'I'm Detective Richardson,' the man said, in a soft Cork accent. 'Paul Richardson. You're the man who came on the scene?'

I nodded.

'I wonder if you could tell me a little about it? If you feel up to it.'

'Séamus has had a bad shock,' I heard Chrissie's voice say. 'It's night. It's dark. He didn't see anything. What's the point in hassling him?'

I looked at Chrissie. Her face was as white as Pádraig's, but she had two spots of red on each cheek like the painted face of an old-fashioned porcelain doll.

Why was she so concerned about me? I wondered, though I thought it was nice. Kind. I was hungry for goodness and kindness after what had just happened.

Chrissie looked at me and I smiled at her.

'I'm fine. And I did see some stuff. I don't know if it's any good, but I'll be glad to tell you. Is there any word of Mattie?'

The ginger-haired detective shook his head. 'Sorry. They've taken him away. I'll let you know as soon as we hear anything.'

'He's dead, isn't he?'

'Well,' Detective Richardson said as he pulled out a chair and sat opposite me at the kitchen table, 'he was still alive when they examined him, but he's very seriously injured all right.'

I opened the fingers of my right hand and exposed the bloodstains. The policeman looked at my hand and then back at my face and I could see in his eyes that he knew as well as I did that Mattie was dead.

'If you're up to answering a few questions . . .'

'Fire away,' I said, as I exhaled a sore breath that turned into a manic laugh. 'Jesus! Bad choice of words.'

He smiled as he pulled a small wire-bound notebook from the feathery depths of his jacket. 'If I could see – sorry, I'm not sure of your name?'

'Séamus. Séamus Considine.'

'OK, I wonder if I could speak with Séamus, alone, for a few minutes?' Detective Richardson looked at Chrissie and Pádraig who were standing side by side in front of the cooker. I watched in silence as if I was a spectator at a play.

Pádraig moved as if he was about to object, Chrissie muttered something to him and shook her head and then she pulled his arm. Pádraig creased his mouth closed and followed Chrissie across the room. Chrissie turned in the doorway and smiled at me.

'OK, now,' Detective Richardson said, as the door closed behind Chrissie and Pádraig, 'maybe if you just tell me what happened tonight?'

'Well,' I said, taking a deep breath to try to contain the awful feeling rising from my belly, 'I don't suppose you smoke?'

Detective Richardson nodded and dug into a pocket in his jacket before throwing a packet of cigarettes and silver lighter on to the table. 'Help yourself.'

I lit one of Detective Richardson's cigarettes and inhaled deeply. The fear inside me backed down a little, but my head swam from the nicotine.

'I've been off these things for over a month,' I said, smoking greedily now as if it might save me.

'I know what it's like. Giving them up is fine. It's trying to stay off them is the problem, isn't it?'

'Mattie always encouraged me to give up and stay off them, though he'd been smoking himself since he was a young fella working with his father on the potato farms in Scotland. Every time he lit a Woodbine he used to say the

43

same thing, "Oh another nail in my coffin," and then he'd laugh his wheezy auld laugh and smoke away with total enjoyment. Did you ever know someone like that? Someone who could say the same things, but it was like they were new all the time? Like he meant them? Not boring at all.'

I paused and smoked in silence for a few minutes. My head had stopped spinning and I could feel the fear inside me dribble back into some deep place. I decided there and then that I would never again stop smoking.

'I'm glad he didn't stop smoking,' I said, as I stubbed out my cigarette on the edge of a tiny glass dish that I vaguely hoped wasn't for food. I looked at Detective Richardson. He looked back at me and I wondered, briefly, about all the times he'd had to see horrible things and I felt sorry for him.

'Would you mind if I had another one? Sorry, what's your name again, detective?'

He shook his head. 'Paul Richardson – call me Paul and help yourself.'

So I lit my second cigarette of the evening and told him about the lurking dark shadows who'd shot a hole in Mattie Ahern's chest.

As I spoke Paul Richardson wrote without comment. I finished speaking and he continued to write for a minute then he stopped and looked at me in silence for almost another minute before he spoke again.

'When you say the man you heard had an unusual accent what exactly do you mean?'

I looked at him as I thought about his question and saw that he was watching me with his pale blue eyes, not just looking, but watching, and I realized that he knew it was possible that I'd shot Mattie myself and that all this act of being shocked and horrified was just an effort to pretend otherwise.

And I didn't mind – it just made me feel sad for him. Sad

that he had to live in a world where everybody was a suspect. I closed my eyes, for a minute, and replayed the tape of the incident that was whirring away inside me and listened for the soundtrack.

'I'm not sure,' I said, opening my eyes. 'A hard accent. Hard and clipped – strange.'

'Northern?'

I shook my head. 'Not Irish anyway.'

'Scottish?'

'No, sort of nasal, and I do know it, I just can't place it.'

'American?'

'No. I don't think so.'

'Australian?'

I closed my eyes and listened again. 'Maybe. Maybe.'

'But definitely not Irish?'

'Definitely not Irish.'

Paul Richardson snapped his notebook closed. 'Grand. That's great, now, thanks very much.'

The kitchen door snapped open. We looked up to see Chrissie, with her hand wound into the collar of Mattie's dog, Boru.

'He's just standing in the middle of the road,' she said. 'I don't know what to do with him.'

Chrissie let him go and I whistled and called his name. Boru ran to me, and I rubbed his warm piebald head and tried not to look into his eyes because I knew that he knew Mattie was dead.

'Where's Prince?' I said.

Chrissie shook her head.

'Probably gone home,' I said. 'They're brothers, you know. Mattie got Boru at the same time as he got Prince for me. They're from the same litter, though they don't get on at all. Do you think dogs can suffer from sibling rivalry?'

I looked up at the Detective and Chrissie, and both smiled at me.

'You'll just have to get used to your brother now, Boru, won't you, boy?'

Boru sat at my feet and leaned his warm body against my leg. I rubbed his head and felt his sides move in and out as he breathed.

'You'll take him home?' Paul Richardson said as he stood up.

'For a while, I don't think I'll be able to keep him if Mattie ... if Mattie ... you know, but he can stay for a while. I would keep him – he's a great dog – half retriever and a very well developed half at that with all the hunting he's done with Mattie.'

Paul clicked his tongue and Boru wandered over to him, wagging his tail. The detective hunched down and stroked Boru with long, definite strokes from head to tail. Boru looked like he might smile if he was able.

'He likes you,' I said, 'and in fairness it isn't everyone he likes. He bit the postman. Pity he didn't bite those bastards earlier.'

'He was afraid,' he said, still stroking the dog.

I noticed Chrissie had left the room, though I hadn't heard her go. We sat in silence for a few minutes as the policeman stroked the dog and I tried not to think.

'Can I ask you a favour, Séamus?'

I nodded.

'Could I take Boru home for a few days?' He paused and caressed the dog's head, Boru's long ears slithering through the big, freckled hand. 'Our dog was killed last week – knocked down by a car – and my twelve year old, Tara, is heartbroken. You never saw a child to love dogs more – she'd take very good care of him while Mattie is in hospital. It'd help her to look after Boru even if it was only for a few weeks.'

I imagined a small, female version of the chubby detective hugging Boru. It seemed oddly right.

'What do you think?'

I shrugged. 'If he wants to go with you by all means take him. Prince and himself will have to be kept separately anyway, so I'll probably end up with at least one of them locked in the shed.'

The policeman stood up and pushed the packet of cigarettes across the table towards me. He picked up his lighter and put it in his pocket.

'I'll talk to you soon,' he said, smiling at me, and I thought when he smiled he looked like a slightly anxious, plump teenager. There was something earnest about his smile. Or maybe there was just something desperate about me after what I'd seen as I searched the faces of people who weren't murderers to see if I could find something that would make me less afraid of the world.

Paul Richardson clucked his tongue again and he left the kitchen with a silent wave, Boru following closely behind him. I hoped Tara liked him because I had a horrible feeling Boru was in the market for a new owner.

After they left, I sat by myself for a while, chain-smoking in Pádraig Harrison's stainless steel kitchen and wondering why the floor had fallen out of the world entirely. Because it had most certainly gone. It was just an aberration, I told myself, that was all. A fluke. A one-off. The world was still safe. And true and trustworthy. But then I saw Jessica's green eyes and Mattie's broken body falling to the road with the life shot out of it and I felt the fear begin to unravel in my chest and I knew that there weren't enough cigarettes in the world to stop it overwhelming me.

3

'I Can't Stand Up for Falling Down'
Elvis Costello, 1980

At seven o'clock next morning the telephone rang. It was Paul Richardson to tell me what I already knew. Mattie was dead. Dead on arrival, he said. I'm very sorry, Séamus, I'm really very sorry.

I told him it was all right. I knew. But I kept thinking, *DOA – like the movies, DOA – like the movies.* He must have died en route to the hospital, Paul Richardson said. There was nothing they could do. I said, thanks. How's Boru? Tara loved him already he said and they were glad to have him stay with them. As soon as he hung up I made my way back upstairs and fell back into bed and straight back to sleep.

At eleven, Cassandra woke me to tell me my mother was on the telephone. I groaned and groped my way downstairs.

'Oh, Séamus,' was all my mother said when I came on the phone. I thought she was going to cry and I couldn't bear it.

'I'm fine. Honest to God, Ma, I'm grand. Nothing happened to me.'

'I heard it on the news, this morning and I just knew. When they said those words – *the local schoolteacher* – I knew straight away it was you. I tried to call but I couldn't get through. Was the phone off the hook? I rang your father, he'd gone to work already. He went to work at six this morning – they have a big job on. He didn't hear the news and I needn't tell you that he got an awful fright when I told him. An awful shock. Couldn't get over it. I mean, as your father said, if you lived in New York like your brother we might be expecting something like this – but Castleannery? I don't know, Séamus. I just don't know.'

I winked thanks at Cassandra who handed me a mug of coffee and a pair of woollen socks, then I sat down on the bottom step of the stairs and, cradling the receiver between my shoulder and my cheek, pulled the socks on to my freezing feet.

'I swear to God, Mam,' I said, pausing to sip some coffee, 'I'm totally fine. Nothing at all happened to me. It was a bad shock all right, but I'm not even scratched – poor Mattie, though, now that's something else –'

I stopped speaking and swallowed about half the mug of scalding coffee to force the tears back down my throat.

'God rest him,' my mother's voice whispered in my ear, 'he was that lovely man who lived up the road from you, wasn't he? The man who gave you Prince after Jessica – when he was a puppy?'

'That's him.'

My tongue felt as if it was swelling with the heat. I opened my mouth to let it cool down.

'Anyway, Ma, I have to go. I'm sitting at the end of the stairs in my underwear, freezing to death. I'll call you later, OK?'

'Will I come down?'

'No, I'm grand, Mam. Really.'

'But you've had such a hard time – and now this as well. Why don't you come home?'

'I have work.'

'Surely they can get a substitute teacher? You need to rest.'

'No. Really. I want to go back to work. There are only a few weeks until the Christmas holidays, I can rest then.'

My mother was silent for a minute. I drank more coffee.

'Are you sure I shouldn't come?'

'Honest, Ma. Cassandra is here. I'm fine.' I heard a checked sigh on the other end of the line. 'I'll come home soon.'

'How soon?'

'The weekend Eamon comes home. How about that? Isn't that only the weekend after next?'

'All right. Are you sure you're OK?'

'I'm fine. Tell Dad I was asking for him.'

'I will. Bye, love. Take care.'

'OK, Mam. Talk to you later, so.'

'Take care of yourself, love.'

'I will, I promise. Thanks for calling.'

I finished off the rest of my coffee before I stood up, then I went upstairs to shower and dress. Cassandra was reading a newspaper at the kitchen table when I came back down. She looked up and smiled at me.

'You slept?'

I nodded. 'Surprisingly enough.'

I poured myself a cup of tea and sat at the table beside her. Then I remembered.

'Oh my God! What day is it? Monday? Oh, shit! I need to ring school. Jesus what time is it? There'll be pandemonium.'

'Calm down, I did it already.'

'You did?'

'I did.'

'You're a saint.'

'I know. Now sit down, Séamus, and eat something.'

'I'm not hungry,' I said, as I lit the second to last cigarette in Detective Richardson's pack.

Cassandra looked at me.

'Don't start. I have a lot on my mind.'

'I didn't say a word. Where did you get those?'

'The police. Detective Richardson. The one in the puffy jacket with the gingerish hair?'

Cassandra shook her head.

'Probably gone by the time you came down to Pádraig's

house last night. Anyway, they came in handy. That's why I was there last night, you know. I was on my way down to see if Mattie was up. I couldn't sleep and I thought I might be able to bum a couple of Woodbine off him to get me through until morning. That's why I was there . . .'

My voice became thinner and thinner until it suddenly vanished. For fuck's sake – why did this keep happening? Cassandra folded the newspaper and looked directly at me.

'You told me. Last night.'

'Sorry. Repeating myself at thirty – what'll I be like when I'm as old as Mattie.'

'I'm not complaining. It's just the shock. You had an awful experience.'

'Not as bad as Mattie's.'

'I know that, but still horrible. How do you feel?'

'I feel fine,' I said, because I couldn't even begin to explain how I really felt, and anyway Cassandra might tell her mother who'd tell mine and I couldn't bear to have my mother fussing all over me as well as everything else.

'Jessica rang,' Cassandra said, and I could hear that she was speaking with great care to keep all stray emotions in order and hidden away.

'Oh?' I said, matching her tone.

'Mmm, she heard the news. Wanted to make sure you were OK.'

'That was nice of her.'

Cassandra looked at me for a minute. 'You must be kidding,' she said, at last.

I shrugged and lit the last of the detective's cigarettes.

'Well it was. It was nice of her.'

Cassandra shook her head and twisted her mouth as if she was twisting the top of a bag to stop the contents spilling out. I ignored her, instead I imagined Jessica's face. Jessica hearing the news report. Realizing that they were talking about me.

What was it my mother said she'd heard on the news? *Local schoolteacher*. That was it. That was me. The same Séamus she'd loved and married and left for a bastard of an architect in Dublin last March.

I imagined her looking across the breakfast table at that slimy bollocks and feeling sad and sorry for what she'd done and glad that she had another chance to make it up to me.

'She said they were about to go to Los Angeles, and if you needed anything to give her a ring when they get back next week,' Cassandra's voice said, butting into my dream.

I looked at her.

'Oh, OK,' I said, as disappointment fluttered inside me like a stomach bug.

Cassandra was staring at me.

'What?' I said.

'Are you sure you're OK?'

I stood up. 'Look, I'm fine, really. I'm going to go for a walk. I think I'll go as far as the village and buy cigarettes. Prince! Come on, boy!'

Cassandra opened her newspaper again and fixed a thin smile on her face.

'See you later,' I said, pulling my coat on as I walked out of the kitchen.

'Bye, Séamus.'

Prince and I stepped out into the cold air of the day. I shoved my hands deep into my pockets wishing I'd brought gloves. My right hand found Mattie's cap. It felt soft and damp and like an announcement of what had happened.

Mattie is dead, it seemed to say, as Prince and I walked across the yard and out on to the road. He's dead. This time yesterday he was alive and now he's dead. And not only is he dead, but somebody shot him.

It was too hard to believe. Like something you'd read or hear or see in a movie. Too weird for words. Nobody I knew well had ever died before and I hadn't realized what it was like. I mean I thought I knew, but I didn't really.

Now I was sorry for all the blasé things I'd said. *Sorry for your troubles. He had a long and happy life. Life goes on.* I was truly sorry for the way I'd gone on with my life when other people were feeling this. A quick handshake, a small stab of empathy and then business as usual. Sorry. Sorry. Sorry. I didn't know, I really hadn't realized.

If Mattie could be shot dead in the middle of the night, then anything could happen. Aliens might be real. I might win the Lotto. Jessica could come back and tell me she loved me.

The week before – no, not even that – the day before, less than twenty-four hours before, I might not have forgiven Jessica. But suddenly I could see that life is short, and not solid but like a thin film under our feet ready to tear asunder at any minute. After all that had happened I was willing to move anywhere I could find heat and love and lack of evil.

'Hello, Séamus,' a woman's voice said all of a sudden, and for a split second I thought it might be Jessica, even though I knew it wasn't her voice. I looked up.

'Chrissie.'

I smiled. She smiled back at me. 'How are you this morning? I was just on my way up to see how you were feeling.'

I started to say that I was fine thanks and there was no need to worry. Yes, yes, it was a shock but, what can you do? These things happen. Poor Mattie, God help us, poor old Mattie who never hurt a fly.

But something about the scar near her lip side-tracked me, and I couldn't say anything as my eyes filled with tears. I blinked hard, but I couldn't stop them coming.

'Where is that dog?' I said, turning my head away. 'Prince! Prince!'

Prince trotted up to me and I bent to rub him, blinking

and stretching my face to make my eye sockets widen and absorb the tears.

'Good boy, good boy,' I said, as I stroked and patted, sniffing as quietly as I could manage and attempting a surreptitious wipe of my face with the palm of my hand. 'I'm fine thanks, Chrissie. Not too bad this morning. Not too bad at all.'

But I knew she wasn't fooled.

'Can I walk with you?'

I wanted to say no, go away, leave me be, I can't pretend and I'm not able to show you what I feel. But I didn't. 'Sure,' I said instead, 'I'm just walking into the village to buy some cigarettes.'

Chrissie nodded and fell into step beside me. At first I tried to think of things to say that might distract her from what had just happened. But I couldn't think of anything and as we walked in silence, crunching the frosty road under our shoes, every moment getting closer and closer to Pádraig Harrison's house, closer and closer to where crime-scene tape festooned the ditch like a macabre ribbon of remembrance, it mattered less and less to me that she might have seen me crying.

Fuck it. After all Mattie's body was somewhere miles away being cut up in a police morgue as they tried to find out what killed him when it was clear to all the world that the gaping hole in his chest was the culprit.

Why wouldn't I cry for a gentle old man who brought me eggs every day for six months after my wife left with her easel and her suitcases? Apart from anything else, I knew I'd miss him.

We hurried past the crime scene and I looked the other way – across the fields. I concentrated hard on the bare trees and tried to imagine spring.

'It's very quiet here,' I said, at last, finally unable to ignore the place we'd passed.

'They've been here all morning.'

I looked at her.

'The police. Looking for clues. They only left a little while ago.'

'Oh,' I said, and I wanted to ask questions and say more but I couldn't because the weight on my chest was so heavy I could hardly breathe.

After a while the village loomed ahead on the horizon, the bell-tower of the church climbing higher than the trees and smoke from chimneys drifting into oblivion. Chrissie seemed content to walk in silence. Her red woollen hat pulled down over her blonde hair and a black scarf wound round and round her neck so many times that between hat and scarf only the oval of her face that contained her eyes, nose and mouth was clearly visible.

Prince bounded around nearby chasing real and imagined prey in the hedges. The day was bright and clear. Blue sky. White hoar frost still on the trees and grass. The earth under my feet metallic hard. Not a soft day, anyway. And that was good.

'I didn't know you smoked,' Chrissie said, suddenly, as we approached the outskirts of the village.

'Well, on and off. I have the soul of a smoker and I smoke on and off and I guess this is one of the "on" times.'

'Understandably.'

'Not because of Mattie, I was already back on the cigarettes, I told you that, didn't I? I told you that that's why I was out last night. Looking for Mattie. Looking for Woodbine. There were things – other things, before – before.'

My sudden burst of honesty receded as quickly as it had arrived. I looked at Chrissie's pink nose and she smiled at me.

'That's right,' she said, through her scarf, her breath forming tiny, moist droplets on the fabric, 'you said that last night when Cassandra came. I'd forgotten.'

'Here we are,' I said, anxious to avoid her sympathy, 'I'll buy you coffee and I can buy loads and loads of cigarettes in here and we can thaw out, before we set off back up this freezing road. How about it?'

Chrissie's red hat bobbed in agreement and we walked towards the door of Sheehan's Bar and Lounge and I forced myself to think only about cigarettes.

Mattie's funeral was four days later – after the police released his body. I found I couldn't think about what the police were doing all that time with Mattie's body. Somehow, it seemed almost as much of a violation as the gunshot wound. Not that it was – I knew it wasn't really and that it was necessary and all of that – and still . . .

The funeral itself was crowded, even Paul Richardson and a huddle of obviously plainclothes policemen came along. Funeral or not, the puffy orange jacket was still in evidence. He nodded at me when I caught his eye and I wondered if he was still watching me.

Maybe he really thought I was the murderer? I tried to tell myself that that was a good thing and tried to think positively, but I wasn't too hopeful that they'd ever find the real murderer and it seemed like a waste of time to be watching me.

Not that they weren't trying. They were but I knew from the tone of voice Paul Richardson used every time I rang to enquire how the investigation was progressing that it wasn't. It was at a standstill and all the goodwill and hard work or even resentment on my part that they just couldn't *find* the bastards and make them pay didn't make any difference.

The police would probably keep working – interviewing, investigating, thinking – for a few more weeks and then the investigation would gradually peter out and remain unsolved. I hated the thought of that, it made my insides itch and rage and still I couldn't change anything so I forced my attention back to the funeral.

When I made myself concentrate on my surroundings I was amazed at how many people had come to pay their respects to Mattie. I looked at their faces and at the sadness in their eyes as they listened to the priest. It was remarkable, especially as he hadn't any living family – his two brothers had emigrated, lived and died in America.

And he'd never married – though they say he was engaged once to a woman who went to Boston on a visit and was never seen in Castleannery again. Maybe that was why he was so kind to me when Jessica left?

As I stood amongst the coated, hatted, umbrella-balancing throng at the graveside it was hard to believe that Mattie was once a young man in love. But then again it was also hard to believe he was dead.

Cassandra stood beside me at the funeral. I could feel her shiver in the sleet as we stood at the graveside and listened to Father Finnegan describe how much we'd all loved Mattie. I could feel the assent all around me. Because everybody had loved him – with the exception of the woman who ran away to Boston, possibly.

How had Mattie managed not to close his heart after it was broken? That's what people do when they've had their heart broken. That's what I'd felt like doing since Jessica left. I wished I'd thought to ask him his secret while he was still alive.

I pushed my freezing hands into my coat pockets and found Mattie's cap, still bunched, in one. I didn't think I'd ever seen Mattie without that cap – not even indoors. He probably took it off in church, but I didn't know because I didn't go too often myself.

The priest finished his prayers and stepped back to let the gravediggers begin their work. Nobody else moved. Cassandra shivered again as the clods of earth thudded loudly on the coffin lid and I put my arm around her.

'Thanks,' I whispered.

'For nothing,' she said, smiling up at me.

I shook my head. 'No. It means the world to me that you blocked the wind like that the whole way through the burial.'

Cassandra laughed and hurriedly made herself cough as people around us began to turn their heads. She hung her head and I could feel that she was still laughing.

'You are a pig,' she whispered.

'Then you are the cousin of a pig,' I whispered back. 'Let's get out of here. I see some of those bloody newspaper people are here again and I couldn't bear to have to answer questions.'

Cassandra nodded and we detached ourselves from the crowd and walked quickly towards my car.

'Look, there's that guy from the *Tribune*,' Cassandra said, as I tried to urge the engine to life. 'He saw us. Looks like he's coming this way.'

'Comeoncomeoncomeon,' I muttered as the damp engine sputtered and complained. Then it started. 'Yes!' I said, reversing without looking behind me and driving away just as the reporter reached the cemetery gates.

'Jesus,' Cassandra said, swivelling her head from side to side. 'You nearly hit that red car.'

'Yeah, yeah, yeah,' I said, speeding up, 'nearly never made it.'

Cassandra tutted.

'Home?'

'Home,' she agreed.

We drove in silence through the rainy landscape and I tried to turn my mind away from the pictures of the night Mattie was killed. The falling body. The dark men with masks. The fact that I'd just stood there and watched as they'd killed him. It was no good, I told myself, there was nothing that could have been done. But I didn't believe that. Not really.

'Who owns that car?' Cassandra said, as I pulled into the yard in front of my house.

I shook my head free of pictures of Mattie and looked. A silver Audi was parked outside my front door and as I cut my engine a tall woman with short dark hair stepped out of the driver's seat and slammed the door shut.

Hunching her shoulders against the wind, she pulled her long, black coat close to her body, leaned against her car and watched us as we approached the house. Cassandra was close to my back as we proceeded across the wet and shiny concrete towards the stranger.

'Hello,' the woman said, holding out her hand in front of her. 'Alison Chang.'

I nodded. 'Séamus Considine,' I said, feeling compelled to take the proffered hand and shake it.

The tall woman smiled, and I could see that her eyes were brown and slightly slanted as would befit her name, but truthfully I would never have guessed she had any oriental blood percolating through her veins if she hadn't told me her name.

'Cassandra O'Brien,' my cousin said, stepping out from behind me.

They shook hands. Hundreds of tiny needles of cold, sleety rain began to pelt sideways into our cheeks.

'Do you want to speak with me?' I asked, raising my voice as if the rain was loud as well as cold.

Alison Chang nodded her wet head. 'Please.'

'You're not a journalist?' Cassandra asked.

Alison Chang looked surprised. 'No, I'm not.'

I beckoned and all three of us ran towards the house.

'Great watchdog,' Alison Chang said, as Prince raised his head, sleepily, when we walked into the kitchen. He settled himself on his cushion in front of the range and went straight back to sleep.

'Oh, he's a savage,' I said, filling the kettle and switching it on. 'What can I do for you, Miss . . . Chang?'

'Alison – I wonder if I could ask you a few questions . . .'

Alison Chang rummaged in her handbag and produced a wire-bound notebook.

'No,' I interrupted, rage bursting in my head, 'you couldn't. Out. I'm sorry, but I won't answer any more questions about Mattie. I've had it with you lot, so I'd be very grateful if you'd leave right now.'

Cassandra came to stand beside me.

'Look. Please, hold on a minute. I think you misunderstand –'

'No,' Cassandra interrupted, 'we don't misunderstand. You said you weren't a journalist. Mattie was his friend. Can't you understand what that means? Have you people no respect for ordinary things like love and friendship?'

'But –' Alison began.

Cassandra wouldn't let her speak. 'No. Can't you see that it's bad enough that Séamus had to see what he saw and go through all the – the pain of it, without you lot hovering like vultures everywhere he goes?'

Alison Chang wiped a hand across her wet hair and then held it out, palm up, in front of her, and I had the sudden and ridiculous thought that if there was a tiny, tame robin in the kitchen he might land on her outstretched palm. I dug my fingernails into the back of my hand to keep my attention in reality.

'Look. I don't know what you're talking about,' Alison Chang said, her hand still extended in a bird perch. 'I told you the truth. I'm not a journalist. I just came here to ask you a few questions about William Ormston. If another time would be better?'

'William Ormston?' I repeated.

Alison Chang nodded and put her hand down by her side.

'Why?' I said.

'Who?' Cassandra said.

'He's the man we found across the road a few weeks ago – me and Mattie. You know about it, Cassandra. They were talking about it the other night at Pádraig's house. He died.'

Alison Chang nodded again.

'And why do you want to talk to me about William Ormston on the day Mattie is buried?'

Alison Chang shook her head. 'I'm sorry. Your friend has obviously died and I've come at a bad time. I had no idea. I really am sorry. I'll go.'

I looked at Alison Chang. She was almost as tall as me, nearly six feet tall, which meant she could look straight into my eyes. Which is what she did.

'Maybe you'd talk with me some other time? When you're feeling a bit better. There's no hurry.'

'You know Mattie was the other person who was there when we found William Ormston? I was useless. Mattie talked to him and sent me to ring an ambulance and told him he'd be fine. All that was Mattie's doing. I was there, that's all. He was the one who helped him.'

'Your friend who just died?'

'My friend who was murdered.'

'What?'

'Don't you watch TV or read the newspapers?' Cassandra asked. 'Mattie Ahern — shot dead five days ago just outside the village of Castleannery.'

Alison Chang's eyes widened. 'And he was involved in finding William Ormston?' She took a loud deep breath as if she was going to plunge her head under water. 'I know you're upset, but I wonder if I could talk to you now? I promise you I won't take long and I'll leave as soon as I've told you why I came, and you need never talk with me again.'

'I don't think —' Cassandra began.

'No, it's OK,' I said. 'You may as well stay and have a cup of tea. I was going to make a pot anyway.'

I brewed the tea and Cassandra made a heap of soft, buttery toast, which all three of us started to eat in silence.

'OK,' Alison began, pausing to take a mouthful of tea, 'I work for a firm of solicitors in Dublin called Capel and Williams and it just so happens that at the moment Capel and Williams are doing some work for an American firm called Henderson, Shanahan and Smith.'

Cassandra and I nodded.

'Henderson, Shanahan and Smith are representing William Ormston's children in a case against his estate.'

Alison paused. Cassandra and I looked at her and continued to eat our toast. Alison Chang drank another mouthful of tea and Cassandra refilled her cup from the yellow ceramic teapot my mother had given to Jessica and me one Christmas. Jessica had never liked it.

'William Ormston was a very wealthy man. You might know that.'

Cassandra and I nodded.

'His wife, Stella, is the sole heir as he had no children.'

'But you just said your firm were involved with representing his children?' Cassandra said.

Alison nodded. 'He didn't have any legitimate children. He led an odd life. For the past few decades William Ormston lived part of the year at home in Co. Wicklow and the other part in various locations around the world.'

'Like a movie star,' Cassandra said.

Alison smiled. 'He only married Stella a few years ago and even after he was married he continued this practice for some time. For a lot of the time when he wasn't in Wicklow he seems to have lived in South Dakota in a small town called Winston.'

'With Stella?' Cassandra asked.

Alison shook her head. 'No, seemingly not. He appears to have spent part of every year in Winston on and off for twenty years – right up to six months before his death. While he was there it's alleged that he lived with a woman called Geraldine Lamb.'

'Oh my God!' Cassandra said. 'This is better than a soap on the telly.'

Alison smiled. 'William Ormston and Geraldine Lamb had two children, or so she claims – Chuck, aged seventeen, and Vera, aged fifteen. Geraldine Lamb is making a claim on behalf of her children against the estate of William Ormston.'

Alison Chang stopped speaking and drank her tea. Prince walked over to her and sniffed her legs and then ambled off to search for something interesting to eat off the floor.

'OK,' I said, breaking the silence, 'but what does that have to do with us? Me? Mattie?'

Alison Chang shook her head. 'I don't know. I'm just a minion. I was sent to find out exactly what happened when William Ormston was here, that's all. I wasn't even aware that there was another person present, and I certainly had no idea that this man was dead.'

'You'd imagine your company would know,' Cassandra said.

Alison Chang nodded. 'Yes, you would.'

'Why don't they just investigate the claim and get it over with?' Cassandra said.

'As soon as William Ormston died there were more claims on his estate – not just Geraldine Lamb and her children. To date there have been two more claims, both from young men in their early twenties – one in Samoa where Ormston had a small factory and one in California. Henderson, Shanahan and Smith are representing this group of alleged Ormston offspring. Geraldine Lamb's two children and these two other men have united forces to stake their claim.'

I stood up from the table to get my cigarettes from the windowsill.

'It's the simplest thing in the world nowadays to prove or disprove paternity,' I said, lighting a cigarette and holding the packet towards Alison Chang.

She shook her head. 'Yes, it would be easy to prove if we

had anything to use. There is, literally, as far as we can trace, not one single sample of William Ormston's DNA available to us.'

'And he has no living relatives?' I asked.

'Well, only these would-be children,' Alison said.

'Can't you get DNA from a corpse?' Cassandra asked.

Alison nodded. 'But he's buried and we'd have to have a compelling case to get a judge to allow an exhumation. Which is why I'm here.'

'But tell me,' I said, leaning against the metal bar at the front of the range and trying to blot out the picture that sprung immediately into my mind of Mattie doing the same thing the day William Ormston died, 'if he lived so much of his life in South Dakota with this woman –'

'Geraldine Lamb.'

'OK, Geraldine Lamb – well surely there are witnesses, family photographs, that sort of thing?' I said.

'They lived in quite a remote place – no real neighbours. There are two witnesses who claim to have known him, both related to Geraldine Lamb. She claims that there was a whole album full of photographs in her house, but it burned down just two weeks ago and all of the photographs went with it.'

'And the two men who say they are his children?' Cassandra said.

'They claim to have met their alleged father a couple of times apiece – both of them have photographs of themselves with William Ormston; both taken during visits to the zoo, funnily enough. But having your photograph taken with somebody at the zoo doesn't prove that he was your father. Also he doesn't seem to have had any kind of long-term relationship with either of their mothers. Unlike the relationship Geraldine Lamb claims to have had with him.'

'How about maintenance?' I asked, glad of the distraction. 'Did he ever pay maintenance?'

'They all say he did contribute to the upkeep of the

children – well, the mother of the Samoan man is dead, actually, but he claims she was supported by William Ormston. But we can't find any records of payments. Geraldine Lamb says he always had large amounts of cash on him and that all of the money he gave to her was in cash. That isn't entirely unlikely – he was a very wealthy man and one known, actually, for carrying large amounts of cash.'

'And what does his family say?' I said, stubbing out my cigarette on the top of the range.

'His only legal relative is his wife, Stella. And Stella says that they can't be his children because William had a vasectomy when he was a young man. Never wanted children. Had a miserable childhood himself and swore to never have any children.'

'What age was he?' Cassandra asked.

'Sixtyish,' I said.

'Sixty-seven,' Alison Chang said.

'No wonder they had no children if they only got married a few years ago,' Cassandra said.

'Stella is a young woman,' Alison Chang said. 'Thirty-one or two. They married when Stella was in her late twenties. She claims that she would have loved children and that they even went to see a doctor, but there was no hope of William fathering a child.'

'And there's proof of this?' I said.

Alison nodded. 'Insofar as a report written by a company doctor is proof. We can't find any records of the vasectomy he was supposed to have had, but then again it was common knowledge amongst people who knew him that he'd had a vasectomy. He was adamant about not wanting children. There are at least ten people – all pillars of the community – who can testify to that.'

'And the visit to the doctor with Stella?' Cassandra said.

'Well, nobody except Stella and the doctor seem to know about that, but I'd imagine that'd be fairly normal.'

Cassandra nodded.

'Maybe they're all lying.' Both women turned to look at me.

Alison Chang nodded. 'Maybe.'

Cassandra refilled her cup. 'It seems to me like it'd be more unlikely for them to come together if it wasn't true. How would they even know each other?'

'And I think that makes it more suspicious.' I opened the range and tossed in some empty milk cartons. 'I mean a woman with two young children in Texas.'

'South Dakota,' Cassandra corrected.

'All right, South Dakota. A woman with two young children in South Dakota. A full grown man in Samoa and another one in California, is it?'

Cassandra and Alison Chang nodded.

'But how did they meet?' I continued. 'How did they know each other? It seems like a bit of a bandwagon, if you ask me.'

'Well,' Alison said, 'it did involve a kind of a fluke. Geraldine Lamb approached HS&S in Pierre, the capital city of South Dakota. Willie Henderson, the Samoan man, was studying at the University of Pierre and he went to HS&S's offices as well when he heard William Ormston was dead.'

'That's amazing,' Cassandra said.

Alison nodded. 'Yes, and as if that wasn't enough, the other would-be son – Bill Sullivan – was living in LA and he went to the Los Angeles office of HS&S to seek advice when the news of Ormston's death arrived there. So they all ended up with HS&S, one way or another.'

'But how does this company have so many offices?' I said.

'HS&S is a massive international law firm,' Alison answered. 'We don't really have anything like that here. Anyway, that's what they all did and I'm not sure who saw the connection or how, but that's how they met.'

'And they never knew each other before?' I asked.

'No,' Alison Chang said.

'You can prove that?'

Alison Chang nodded. 'As much as it's possible to prove.'

'It's obvious that they're telling the truth,' Cassandra said, standing up to fill the kettle again. 'Will you have more tea, Alison? Or maybe you'd like coffee?'

'I'd love a cup of coffee.'

'Séamus?'

'Yeah, coffee would be great. How can you say that they're telling the truth, Cassandra? You don't even know them.'

She shrugged and pulled at the short black skirt she'd worn to Mattie's funeral. 'I just believe it. That's all. I believe it. And another thing, Séamus, when you think about all of this don't you think that it must somehow be connected to Mattie's murder?'

'No,' I said, lighting a cigarette. 'No, I don't, Cassandra. How, in the name of God, is there a connection between the claims on William Ormston's estate and Mattie's murder?'

'Well, he found him,' she said.

'So did I and I'm still alive.'

'But maybe there's something in what she says,' Alison Chang said.

'Don't be ridiculous.' I sat back and folded my arms.

Alison looked with great concentration at her empty toast-crumbed plate as I inhaled smoke deep into my lungs and wished I was far away; maybe on that fishing trip Mattie and I used to plan on winter evenings. There'd never be a fishing trip now.

Tears pricked my eyeballs like thistles and I inhaled again. 'Look, I was there. Mattie was shot by people who didn't know who he was. Robbers, obviously, about to rob Pádraig Harrison's house – he's some sort of a big shot software designer. I saw it all. Mattie disturbed them and maybe they panicked, I don't know, but they shot him and ran away.'

'Still,' Cassandra said.

I shook my head. 'I know Mattie is one of the people who found William Ormston, and I believe you when you tell me that somebody is trying to stop claims on Ormston's estate, but it's a total coincidence and that's all. You should tell the police, Alison, really you should, and let them deal with it. I'm sure you'll find it's all just a coincidence.'

'I don't know, Séamus,' Cassandra said, as she placed three clean mugs and a cafetière of coffee on the pine table. 'I see what you're saying and when you say it like that it does sound like coincidence – or maybe misfortune would be a better word. Still, I wonder about it. What do you think, Alison?'

Alison Chang seemed to start awake as Cassandra said her name. 'Me? I don't know. Who did you say owned the house where your friend was shot?'

'Pádraig Harrison,' I said, returning to sit at the kitchen table. I plunged the coffee and poured it into the three waiting mugs.

'And he's a local?'

I shook my head. 'No, he's Irish all right, but not from around here. He only moved to Castleannery about six months ago.'

'Eight months,' Cassandra said. 'He told me last night.'

'From where?'

'London. He used to work in London for some big company and now he's freelance. Works from home. He's some sort of a software genius – or so he'd have everyone believe. It's obvious that's what those bastards were after.'

'Probably, if he's the Pádraig Harrison I'm thinking of – what does he look like? Thirty-fiveish, tall, dark –'

'Handsome,' Cassandra interrupted with a grin.

Alison nodded. 'Looks like that in the photographs I've seen. If he's the guy I'm thinking of he's a bit of a computer whizz, isn't he?'

'Something like that,' I answered. 'Why?'

'I think I know him – well, know of him. He was chief executive of a big software company. He could still be there. The company is called Artemis or Athena – something Greek. Anyway, the thing is that they're Ormston Electronics' biggest rival.'

'Oh my God!' Cassandra said. 'Oh my God! So . . . so what you're saying is that maybe William Ormston and Pádraig Harrison are somehow connected.'

Alison shrugged. 'Possible.'

'How do you know him?' I said.

'My . . . somebody I know was a good friend of Pádraig's brother, Cathal. They used to surf together, that kind of thing,' Alison said.

I nodded. 'OK, but it could be a different Pádraig Harrison.'

'Certainly could,' Alison said.

'But it isn't,' Cassandra said. 'I just *know* that it's the same one.'

'You can't just know,' I said, lighting another cigarette. Cassandra was really beginning to annoy me. Not that she'd noticed.

'Well, I do know, Séamus. Oh my God, I just thought of something. What if – what if William Ormston was visiting Pádraig when he had his stroke?'

'Pádraig was away,' I said, reluctant as I was to let him off with anything. 'I can guarantee you that there was nobody there.'

Cassandra shrugged. 'He might have left before it happened. They could have had a meeting and then Pádraig left, and after he left William whatshisface had his bad turn and died.'

'Even if your mad leaps of imagination are accurate,' I said, 'it's not all that big a deal. It's not illegal to have a meeting with somebody, is it?'

'No,' Cassandra said, 'but it's fairly suspicious behaviour

to pretend not to know anything about William thingie being in the neighbourhood, don't you agree? And, from what Pádraig was saying the other evening, I take it he's singing dumb?'

I nodded. 'Ormston, by the way.'

'What?' Cassandra said.

'William Thingie – his name was Ormston. At least learn his name if you're going to concoct wild theories about him.'

'Shut up, Séamus,' Cassandra said, pouring more coffee into her mug.

'I knew he was something special,' Cassandra said, after Alison had left.

'Who?' I asked, as I watched the rain drizzle all over the kitchen window. 'William Ormston?'

'Pádraig Harrison.'

'Oh. Yeah.'

'I wonder if William Ormston did come here to visit Pádraig?'

I shrugged.

'Will she tell the police, do you think?' Cassandra said, clearing the used dishes off the table and turning on the tap.

'She said she would. We can check in a couple of days, but I don't see how it matters. William Ormston died of natural causes and Pádraig Harrison didn't murder Mattie, I'm pretty sure of that – unless he was able to run away and drive off, turn around, run back into his house and put on his pyjamas and slippers all before he came out to me.'

'I never said he was a murderer,' Cassandra said, squirting washing-up liquid into the steaming running water that filled the sink in front of her. 'He's much too handsome to be a murderer.'

'That's a great defence,' I said, pulling a clean tea-towel from a drawer and grabbing the first soapy cup from Cassandra's hand. 'You must tell Alison Chang that some people are simply too handsome to be murderers. You never know she might be able to use it in court sometime.'

'Ha, ha. Still, you have to admit it's amazing that so many coincidental things have happened, isn't it?'

'I suppose,' I said, drying the plates we'd used for our toast.

The doorbell rang. Cassandra and I both paused and looked at each other.

'I'll go,' she said. 'Send them off with a flea in their ear.'

'Thanks,' I said, ashamed that I wasn't able to do it myself.

Cassandra walked to the door pulling the kitchen door closed behind her. I rolled up my sleeves and washed the cups and spoons and plates that were still immersed in the suds. The kitchen door opened and Cassandra came back into the room followed by Tim Winter.

'It's Tim,' Cassandra said, unnecessarily, smiling at me and trying to check, with a series of semaphore eyebrow signals, if she'd judged the situation correctly.

'Just dropped in to see how you were doing,' Tim said, a wide smile across his boyish face. 'My God, it's bad out there. Really, really miserable. Sleet and wind. Freezing.'

'Yes it is,' I said.

'So?' Tim said, looking closely at me. 'How are you?'

'I'm fine,' I said, folding the tea towel and laying it on the kitchen table. 'Thanks, Tim. I'm grand, really.'

'That's good,' he said, awkward-looking now as he shifted slightly from one foot to the other. He pushed his hands deep into the pockets of his long, padded raincoat and then pulled out his hands and began to remove his gloves.

'Nice coat,' I said.

'I took your advice. I don't think the old linen jacket was up to it.'

I smiled and lit a cigarette.

'Great turn-out at the funeral,' he said, as he extracted one finger after another from their leather sheaths.

'Everybody loved Mattie.'

Tim nodded. 'It's such a shame.'

'Mmm.'

'I was just telling Tim about Alison Chang,' Cassandra said, walking past me to the sink. 'Tea, Tim? Coffee?'

'Anything. Thanks, Cassandra,' he answered, but he was looking at me.

I smiled at him.

'So, Séamus, tell me, are you recovering at all?' Tim said, scrutinizing my face.

'Ah, I'm fine,' I said, reluctant to talk about it all. 'Tired. But I'll be fine.'

'Such an awful thing,' he said, still looking at me. 'Mattie shot like that and nobody even has a clue who shot him. Unbelievable.'

'Well, I think they'll catch them,' Cassandra said, making coffee.

'Do you?' Tim said, smiling widely at her.

Cassandra blushed. 'I do . . . if they keep at it. Detective Richardson was at the funeral.'

Tim nodded. 'I saw him.'

'That detective is in charge of the investigation,' she said, 'and he looks to me like a man who won't give up easily. Have you met him?'

Tim nodded again. 'Yes, I'd say he's met everyone around here by now. They seem to be taking it all very seriously, all right.'

'They should,' I said. 'Mattie was murdered. It *is* very serious.'

'Of course. I didn't mean –'

'I think these things just take a bit longer to get going than they do in the movies,' Cassandra said. 'You know how in the movies and on TV everything is fast and all fits together neatly and easily? Real life is never like that.'

'That's for sure,' Tim said.

'I mean – who were those men that killed Mattie? I bet they didn't know Séamus was there – but he was and he can tell you that they weren't Irish. Now that's a clue, isn't it? And there might be other clues that we know nothing about, but that the police are pursuing as they say.'

'Where do you think the men were from, Séamus?' Tim asked.

'No idea,' I said, a feeling of exhaustion sweeping over me. 'Listen, Tim, I hope you don't mind but I'm completely whacked and I was just off to bed before you arrived.'

'I didn't mean to disturb you. I know you've had more than enough with all of this. Look, I just called in for a minute. I'll head off straight away.'

'No, no. Why don't you stay and have a cup of coffee with Cassandra?'

'Do. I've already made the coffee.'

Tim looked at her and they exchanged smiles.

'I'd love that.'

I left Cassandra and Tim together in the kitchen and felt my way up the dark staircase to my bedroom. I could have turned on the light, but I didn't want to. I wanted the darkness. I was tired of being able to see things. But it made no difference. I climbed in between my wintry sheets and lay down and immediately the darkness all around me filled up with pictures of Jessica's face contorted with some emotion I'd never seen before as she was telling me she was leaving.

It was March. The birds were singing in the trees. I know because I remember the sound of their singing. There were probably daffodils and succulent unfurling buds on the trees as well, but I couldn't swear to it because I didn't notice those things. Just the birds and Jessica's face. Her eyes as she looked at me without really looking. Her mouth as she said the words.

'I'm leaving.'

Such a small sentence. Tiny, like a deadly microbe that has the capacity to dissolve your innards.

I tried to understand what she meant.

'When?' I said, hoping I was misreading the signals.

'Now.'

'When will you be back?' I said.

She shook her head. 'Look, I'm sorry. It's not you, it's me and this – all of this, and I just can't do it any more. It's not working. You must see that, Séamus. For the longest time it hasn't worked and now – well, now I'm leaving. It's better.'

'In what way?' I whispered, because I knew it wasn't better.

She shook her head again and picked up her bag. 'We'll talk later. When we've had a chance to –'

Her eyes were full of tears and I wanted to say, don't go, don't go, see, you don't want to go, Jess, you know you don't, it's making you sad. But I just stood there, holding a maths copy in my left hand and the red pen I'd been using to correct it in my right.

She walked towards me and kissed me on the cheek, pushed her easel under her arm, picked up a suitcase and gathered a handful of bags and that was it. Six years of marriage finished in a few minutes and I hadn't even seen it coming – not really.

I lay in bed listening to the murmur of voices wafting up from downstairs. Then, just as I was about to embark on the usual trail of destruction that led to my heart I fell suddenly, unexpectedly and mercifully, fast asleep.

4

'There's a Guy Works Down the Chip Shop Swears He's Elvis'
Kirsty MacColl, 1981

When I told my school principal that I wanted to go back to
school two days after Mattie's funeral, he was worried about
me and tried to persuade me to take another week's leave.
But I didn't want to be at home.

I was high on trying to survive. Running in my head,
scheming and planning and plotting ways out of the painful
place I was in. A rat in a trap. Now one thing seemed like
the best idea I'd ever had. Ten minutes later the opposite
course of action was screaming its suitability at me.

As I drove into school that morning I regretted it. I could
have taken more time off. I *should* have taken more time off.
Too late now. But the air of the classroom was filled with
the clean, new energy of thirty-two children and as the day
progressed with maths, Irish and English, recorder music
and rivers and tributaries, and details of Howard Carter and
the tomb of Tutankhamen, a mist of innocence descended
on me and made me feel better.

Cassandra was sitting on the bonnet of my car at a quarter
to four when I came out of school, her short legs swinging
and her heels rhythmically bumping the tyre below her.

'You look better,' she said, jumping on to the ground.

I smiled at her and meant it for the first time in days.

'Yeah, well, I don't feel too bad,' I said, opening the car
and throwing my loaded schoolbag on to the back seat. 'In

75

fact, I feel a good bit better. How are you? What did you do with yourself all day?'

'I went walking with Prince and I took some great pictures. Do you ever bring your phone with you, by the way, Séamus?'

'Yes, of course I do.'

Cassandra put her hand into her pocket and held my mobile phone towards me. 'Why do you have one if you never use it?'

'I do use it, actually, but what's the point in bringing it to school? I can hardly leave it turned on during class now, can I?'

Cassandra looked at me.

'OK,' I said, rolling my eyes. 'Jessica bought it for me and I can never remember to bring it with me when I go out.'

'Try. It's very annoying to have to come and find you when I could just call or text.'

'OK,' I said, as I started the engine.

'Alison Chang rang. She wants to know if she can come and meet you again. Asked me to ask you to ring her. Her card is on the fridge and it has her number on it.'

'OK. Thanks. Do we need milk and bread?'

Cassandra nodded as she flicked down the visor and looked at herself in the fogged-up mirror.

'Both,' she said, applying something from a purple enamel tin to her lips.

I stopped the car in front of Carr's Supermarket. 'Do you want anything?'

She shook her head. 'No, I'm grand. By the way, Séamus, I won't be home for dinner. I'm going into town for a meal and a movie. I won't be late.'

'By yourself?'

'With Tim – Tim Winter,' she said, opening the door and getting out of the car and then leaning down to look through the open door, briefly, at me. 'See you later. Thanks for the lift. Bye.'

I climbed out of the car and watched Cassandra's small form hurrying down Castleannery's single street. As she reached the bend at the end of the street she turned and waved at me before she disappeared up the narrow path to the doctor's surgery.

I was tired and hungry after my day at school and sort of amused at this unexpected turn of events. I grabbed a random selection of groceries from the supermarket and made my way home through the closing-in evening. I wondered if maybe I might manage to pass an entire night without being haunted by the departed in one sense or another.

I didn't think that that was very likely so I was relieved to find Chrissie standing outside my door as I drove into the yard.

'I was just about to leave.'

'I'm glad you're here,' I said, before I could help myself. Chrissie smiled at me.

'It's just that it's my first day back at work – Cassandra's gone out –'

'Yes,' Chrissie interrupted, patting her gloved hands together, 'I know. To town with Tim.'

'You know Tim well, do you?'

'Very well,' she replied, following me into the kitchen. 'He's my brother.'

I turned and looked at her.

'We don't look alike, but I swear it's true. Tim is my brother.'

'Is he older or younger?'

'What do you think?'

I looked at her and a smile slid across her mouth. 'Older,' I said, smiling in return.

'Flirt – I'm two years older than Tim. He's my baby brother.'

'So that's why you're in Castleannery?' I said, filling the kettle. 'I thought you were –'

'Pádraig's girlfriend?'

I shrugged.

'No. Just a friend. We were a bit of an item once a couple of years ago, but not any more. Now we're just friends.'

'But last night?'

Chrissie smiled. 'Sometimes I stay over.'

'None of my business,' I said, smiling. 'Sorry. Didn't mean to be nosy.'

'No problem – it'd be a natural assumption, I suppose. So how was it being back at work?'

'Fine. I'm not too bad.'

Chrissie smiled again and I could smell her perfume, which reminded me of florist shops.

'Mind if I take off my coat?' she said.

'Make yourself at home.'

The kettle switched itself off with a loud click.

'Tea?'

Chrissie nodded as she shrugged out of her coat. 'It's nice here,' she said, strolling slowly around the kitchen with Prince following behind sniffing her flowery trail. 'Pretty.'

'I like it, but a lot of people don't.'

'Really?' Chrissie said, fingering the crocheted cover on Prince's favourite cushion.

Jessica hated it, for example. 'I was suffocating there,' Jessica had said, when she eventually phoned me a week after she left. 'I feel as if I'll just suffocate in that house. That village.'

I wasn't able to answer because I could hear the words she wasn't saying. I knew what she meant. Houses and villages can't suffocate you, but maybe a husband could. I let the telephone receiver fall from my hand and went slowly upstairs to bed. As I climbed the stairs I could hear Jessica's voice, like a receding echo in a tin can, calling my name from the dangling receiver.

'Well, I like it a lot,' Chrissie said, cutting through my memories. 'It's bright and warm and cosy.'

I looked at her and as usual was drawn to the scar by her

lips. Why would you have a scar there? She flicked her sleek blonde hair behind her ears and then pushed her hands deep into the pockets of her jeans.

'Are you making tea?'

I started, aware that I'd been staring. 'Yes!' I said, with too much emphasis. 'Sorry! How do you like your tea?'

'Any way is fine, I'm not fussy.'

Turning away I made the tea and carried the pot to the table. Chrissie came towards me, but instead of taking a seat as I'd expected, she walked right up close to me and stood in front of me.

'Are you all right?' she asked in a voice that was almost a whisper.

I nodded and made a fair effort at a half-smile. 'Grand.'

'You've had a hard time, haven't you?' she said, reaching out a long-fingered hand to touch my arm and then retracting it as soon as I could feel its weight.

I shrugged. 'I'm fine.'

She smiled and reached out the same hand to touch the side of my face. Her hand was soft like velvet. I was hardly breathing.

Slowly Chrissie leaned forward and stretching herself upwards kissed me on the lips. I felt the touch of her mouth and the heat of her body in front of mine and I thought it might be better than getting drunk if I could lose myself in my body with Chrissie. And then I saw the scar near her mouth and it was such obvious evidence of pain that it made me, suddenly, see that she was real.

'The tea,' I said, stepping just far enough away from her so that she was out of my reach. 'It'll be freezing.'

Chrissie looked at me for a minute and I shot an embarrassed look at her. She didn't react.

'Great,' she said, as if she was resuming the conversation we'd been having before she'd kissed me, 'pour it quickly before it gets cold.'

Chrissie and I sat down at the table and as I poured the tea I wondered if maybe I'd imagined what had happened. She had moved so seamlessly back to where we were before she kissed me that it seemed more likely that it hadn't happened than it had.

But even as I sipped my tea I could taste the unknown flavour of her on my lips and, occasionally, if I looked closely enough, I could see something odd in her eyes.

'So do you like teaching?' her voice said all of a sudden, disturbing my introspection.

'Well, I suppose I do. The pay isn't great, but I like the work. I like the kids. What do you do yourself, Chrissie?'

'Oh, this and that,' she said, placing her mug on the table and rubbing its patterned side with her long thumb. 'I think I want to leave London and I suppose once I make a decision about that I'll be able to settle down to something specific.'

'Are you thinking of moving to Castleannery?'

'No. I originally just came to visit Tim and Pádraig.'

'Pádraig seems to like it here. And Tim has been here for years, so I guess he must like it as well.'

'Yes, he does. Tim does like it and Pádraig says he's glad he came here.'

'So how long's Tim been here? He was well established as the local GP and hurling coach by the time I arrived five years ago.'

'I think pretty much since he qualified. He was in Boston for a while – a year, maybe – and then he moved to Castleannery.'

'So, where will you live, do you think, if you move back to Ireland? Dublin?'

She inclined her head and looked at me before answering, and I was sure I could see that unnameable something in the back of her blue eyes again. But then it faded and I wasn't so sure any more.

'Well, I thought I might prefer Cork. Not the county –

definitely not the county – but the city maybe. I come from County Cork originally, and I think I'd like to go back there now.'

'Whereabouts in Cork?'

Chrissie smiled. 'It's a tiny place. You won't have heard of it.'

'Try me. I am a teacher, you know. You'd be surprised at the obscure places I've heard of.'

'Ballyintra,' she said, raising a single eyebrow.

I laughed. 'OK, you were right, I've never heard of it.'

She smiled back. 'It's not even a village. A shop and a signpost. Probably a petrol pump by now.'

'Don't you go back there to visit?'

Chrissie shook her head and the unnameable something flitted across her clear-skinned face. 'My parents are dead. I haven't been back since I left. Anyway, enough about me. Tell me more about the children you teach. Have you any hilarious school stories?'

'Let me think,' I said, willing to be led away from whatever it was she didn't want to talk about. 'Though I can't think all that well on an empty stomach. How about I cook you dinner? Not that I'm a great cook, mind, but there are a couple of lamb chops and some spuds there, if you'd eat that.'

'That would be great. I'll just run up to your bathroom and then I'll give you a hand.'

As soon as Chrissie left the room I stood up and cleared the cups off the table. Then I scrabbled through the bottom of a sack of potatoes for enough unshrivelled potatoes for two people and chucked my findings into the sink. The doorbell rang.

'Hello?' I said in surprise, as I opened the door to find Alison Chang standing in a red parka in the gloomy evening light. She smiled at me as she pulled down the fur-trimmed hood of her jacket.

'Hello. I rang earlier. Spoke to your wife. I wonder if I could speak with you? It won't take long, I promise but I decided it might be better not to telephone –'

'My wife?' I said, letting my hands fall to my sides.

'Cassandra?'

I laughed. 'Oh, Cassandra. I was wondering how you'd spoken to my wife. Cassandra's not my wife – my wife ran away. Cassandra's my cousin.'

Alison Chang's mouth dropped slightly and my heart flipped at the stupidity of what I'd said. We stood looking at each other as the rain beat against her back.

'Look,' I said, moving away from the door and wishing I was somewhere far, far away, 'come in for a minute. You can't stand out there.'

Alison Chang and I walked almost side by side to the kitchen.

'Lovely and warm in here,' she said in a high, cheerful voice as soon as we walked into the room.

I stood in front of the sink. 'Would you mind if I continued washing the spuds while you talk to me?'

'Not at all,' Alison Chang said, unzipping her parka. 'I just need to ask you a few questions, that's all, and then I'll leave and let you have your dinner in peace.'

I turned on the tap and began to wash the mud-encrusted potatoes. Was Alison Chang afraid of me now? I wondered, as my hands started to freeze in the stream of cold water.

Did she think I was a wife-beater? A Bluebeard, from whom my poor wife had had to escape? She must see men like that every day in her practice and have to help them in court to make a convincing defence for why they hit their wives and didn't bother maintaining their children. Now she'd think I was one of them. I looked at her over my shoulder. Did I care? I didn't know.

'So, what is it you need to ask me?'

She smiled at me. 'Mind if I take a seat?'

I shook my head. She sat down and took out a notebook and a purple-coloured pen. 'OK. I wonder if you wouldn't mind telling me two things – exactly what happened the day you and your friend found William Ormston and also exactly what happened the night your friend Mattie was shot?'

I was piling the washed potatoes into a pot that stood on the draining board just as Chrissie walked into the kitchen. She had brushed her hair and seemed to have put some sort of make-up on her eyes.

'Chrissie. This is Alison Chang. She's just called to get some information from me, we won't be a minute.'

Chrissie looked at Alison and Alison nodded.

'Nice to meet you, Chrissie.'

Chrissie coughed. 'Oh, hello . . . listen, I just remembered – I've some work that I have to have finished and sent off by later this evening, so would you mind if I didn't stay to eat? You haven't prepared the food yet, have you?'

I shook my head.

'Maybe some other time?'

'That would be great,' I said.

Chrissie pulled on her coat and leaned down to give Prince a quick pat. 'I'll be off, so,' she said, scanning the entire kitchen with a quick glance. 'Don't bother coming to the door with me, it's too cold. Nice to meet you, Alison. I'll see you later, Séamus.'

I leaned against the sink and waved a silent goodbye and watched as Chrissie disappeared out the door. I used to have a quiet life, once, I thought. Where had that gone? In that life everybody was alive and mostly happy. Even me.

Alison was looking at the door that Chrissie had closed behind her. I looked at her profile. It was a handsome profile. Noble looking, like a statue with an upward curve of the lips. She turned and looked at me as soon as we heard the front door slam. I saw that she was rolling her purple pen between her fingers.

'May I ask you a question?'

'That's what you're here for.'

'What's that woman's surname? Chrissie what?'

I thought for a minute. 'Winter. Her brother is Tim Winter, the local GP, so her name is probably Winter as well.'

Alison nodded and looked back at the doorway as if Chrissie might re-appear.

'Why?'

'Well,' Alison said, tipping back in her chair, 'I was just wondering that's all. Is she Chrissie Winter the actress?'

I shook my head. 'I haven't a clue.'

Alison continued looking at the doorway.

'I bet she is,' she said, softly, almost to herself. I could see that she had sketched a tall, weeping tree along the side column in her notebook.

'Maybe she is. But what about it?'

'Well, I suppose I'd just never think a place like this . . . as small as this, I suppose, could have so many rich and famous people knocking around.'

'Not to mention dead people and unknown gunmen.'

Alison looked at me. 'Sorry. I'm really sorry. I didn't mean –'

'It doesn't matter. Now that you're here you may as well tell me a bit more about William Ormston. It's funny being involved with somebody in a crisis like that.'

I looked at Alison who nodded, so I continued. 'There's something – I don't know what it is – maybe something personal, about it. I'd like to know more about him.'

'No problem. What do you want to know?'

'Anything. Everything.'

Alison nodded and paused to flick through her notebook. 'There isn't an awful lot known about him, believe it or not. He was born in Carlow and seems to have had an unremarkable life until sometime in the sixties when he started an import–export business. Not sure what that was, but he began to make money. Sometime in the early seventies he married Anna Brennan – she was from Carlow as well.'

Alison paused and looked at me as I set the pot of potatoes I had been washing on to the range to cook. I sat down at the kitchen table and lit a cigarette.

'OK,' Alison continued, as I sat back in my chair. 'Anna was killed in a car crash in South Africa in about 1977 and they say that William was heartbroken after her death – they had no children, of course.'

'Of course.'

Alison smiled. 'Then a few years ago he married Stella Franklin.'

'Took him a while to get over Anna.'

'Unless you consider that he was supposedly fathering children around the world all that time.'

'Well, there is that, I suppose,' I said, stubbing out my cigarette.

Alison smiled and tucked her black, bobbed hair behind her left ear. 'He set up his software company in the late seventies and it went from strength to strength, expanding until it became what it is today.'

'Who inherits the company?'

'Stella. Stella inherits everything – unless we can prove paternity for some or all of the claimants and even then she'll inherit the lion's share.'

'But it's quite a big share, isn't it?' I said, remembering the distress on William Ormston's face and Mattie's rough hand on the back of his tailored jacket. 'I mean, he seems to have been very wealthy – plenty for the whole lot of them.'

Alison smiled. 'People tend not to want to share in these cases. And, anyway, if they're not telling the truth then they're not entitled to any of his estate and Stella is right to resist.'

'Are they telling the truth? Your company is helping them – do you believe they're telling the truth?'

Alison shrugged. 'I think they are. But you can never tell.'

'Why do you want to know about his death?' I said, suddenly, only half meaning to ask the question.

'I was sent to find out. I didn't ask why.'

'So, why do you think your bosses want to know the details?'

She shook her head.

'After all, it was just one of those things. He died of natural causes – not like Mattie. Nobody ever suggested anything else, did they?'

'No.'

'So?'

'I'm not sure. All I can say is that maybe they're trying to find out why he was here when he died. See if there's some connection. I honestly don't know.'

'You should speak to Pádraig Harrison. Ask him if William Ormston visited him.'

'I did. I telephoned him this morning from the office.'

'And?'

'He said no.'

'It doesn't make that much difference anyway, does it? He still died.'

Alison smiled a thin, tired smile. 'Yes. Yes. He did.'

'No matter who he was or what he was or how much money he had, he died anyway,' I said. But I wasn't thinking of William Ormston. I was seeing Mattie falling to the ground in the cold darkness.

'Look,' she said, standing up and reaching for her red parka, 'I've taken up more of your time than I intended. I'm sorry about that, Séamus. I really would like to make an arrangement for us to meet so I could get the details of William Ormston's and Mattie Ahern's deaths – if you're still willing?'

I nodded. 'Grand.'

'OK. When would be a good time for you? I understood

from – Cassandra – that you're back at work, so you're probably busy. If you can tell me a day and a time I'll try and fit in with whatever suits you. How about that?'

'OK. The sooner the better, I guess. How about tomorrow? After school, maybe you wouldn't mind coming here again?'

'That'd be fine,' she said, writing on her small wire-bound notebook. 'Time?'

'Evening? Maybe eightish?'

'Great. OK, thanks very much.'

'One thing, Alison.'

'Yes?'

'Would you eat a lamb chop and a few spuds?'

Alison laughed. 'Now?'

I nodded. 'If you'd like to. Chrissie was supposed to stay for dinner, but I think you must have frightened her away.'

'I don't see how I did.'

'I'm only joking. But I still have a couple of lamb chops and a pot of spuds if you're interested.'

Alison returned her red jacket to the back of the chair. 'To be totally honest,' she said, running a hand through her silky, black hair, 'I haven't eaten all day and I'm absolutely starving, so I'd be delighted to eat your food. Thank you very much.'

Alison and I were in the sitting room, half asleep in front of the television news when Cassandra arrived home.

'Alison!' she said as she walked into the room, dropping coat and handbag and keys in a trail behind her.

'Cassandra,' Alison said, sitting forward in her chair.

Cassandra threw herself on to the couch beside me.

'Well? Alison, how are you? I'm surprised to see you here at this hour of the night.'

Alison smiled. 'I need to be leaving actually. What are the roads like? Icy?'

Cassandra shook her head. 'They're fine,' she said, looking at me.

'Alison came to ask me some questions.'

'Which we didn't get around to just yet,' Alison interrupted.

'No, we didn't. So I fed her your dinner.'

'I hope he didn't burn it.'

'I never burn food.'

Cassandra looked at me.

'Well, not often.'

'It was very nice,' Alison said, smiling.

'See. Not "delightful" – just very nice.'

Cassandra made a face at me. 'Your food will never be delightful, Séamus, face it.'

'So? What about yourself? Where did you go?'

'We went to town because we thought we might see a movie, but there wasn't anything decent on so we just had dinner at that new Italian restaurant.'

'And?'

'And it was lovely. Very nice,' Cassandra said, in a quiet voice. She paused for a minute and then looked at me.

'Did you know Chrissie is Tim's sister?' I said.

Cassandra nodded.

'Thanks for telling me that, by the way.'

'Jesus, Séamus, it was fairly obvious if you just paid more attention to what was going on around you.'

'No it wasn't. Anyway, that's a different point. Alison thinks she's an actress.'

Cassandra nodded again. 'She is.'

'You never told me that either.'

'Well, I only just found that out myself. Tim told me tonight. She isn't acting any more, but she was quite well known in England for a while. TV, plays and even a couple of movies. But she's retired from acting for the past few years. Now she's a writer. Writes novels – kind of trashy ones, but very successful according to Tim. Writes under the name Samantha Forrest.'

'I never heard of her.'

'That's not too much of a surprise,' Cassandra said, curling her feet under her body. 'You know absolutely nothing about things like that.'

'That's not true.'

Cassandra laughed.

'I was right, though,' Alison said, standing up. 'She is Chrissie Winter the actress. So, tomorrow, Séamus? Is that OK? Eightish?'

'Eightish. Grand.'

'Great. See you then. Bye, Cassandra. I might see you then.'

'Sure,' Cassandra said, sitting up straight. 'Bye, Alison. Nice to meet you again.'

I walked Alison to the door and waved goodbye as she drove into the dark, rainy night.

'Nice woman,' Cassandra said, as I came back into the sitting room.

'Yes, she is.'

'Very pretty, isn't she? All cheekbones and that shimmering blue-black hair and almond-shaped eyes.'

I laughed. 'Almond-shaped eyes? Bit corny, Cass.'

'Well, they are,' Cassandra said, stretching out on the couch. 'Obviously that's why the expression was coined, because there are people in the world who really do have almond-shaped eyes. Do you have a date with her on tomorrow?'

'Don't be ridiculous. She's coming to ask me questions for her investigation.'

'Why didn't she ask them tonight?'

'We were having dinner. She was leaving and I asked her if she wanted to stay for dinner.'

'Sounds like an excuse to me,' Cassandra said, closing her eyes. 'She just wants to see you again.'

I sat into an armchair and looked at the flames consuming the last few pieces of wood in the fireplace.

'I doubt that,' I said, wondering if I should tell Cassandra about Chrissie and the kiss. But maybe it hadn't really happened? Maybe I'd imagined it? I'd wait a while before telling Cassandra.

'Naw, she looks like she's interested,' Cassandra said, sleepily. 'I'm a woman, we can tell these things.'

'Well,' I said, leaning forward to poke the fire, 'I doubt that very much as she probably thinks I'm a wife-beater or something.'

'Why would she think that when it's obvious that you are a poor – though respectable – primary school teacher?'

'Well, it might have something to do with the fact that when I was explaining that you weren't my wife I blurted out that my wife ran away.'

'What?'

'Oh, Jesus, what a night, Cass,' I said, rubbing my aching head with my hands. 'Alison thought you were my wife and I was explaining to her, but I think it kind of upset me when she said, 'Your wife said' or whatever it was she said, so I said it couldn't have been my wife because my wife ran away.'

I looked over at Cassandra who had propped herself up on one elbow. 'Did you say it like that?'

I nodded.

'"My wife ran away"?' she said.

I moaned.

Cassandra looked at me and then burst out laughing.

'So, you can see that it's very unlikely that Alison would like to have anything to do with a man whose wife had no option but to run away.'

'Mmm. I'm not so sure about that.'

'Anyway tell me about your night. Dinner with Tim the doctor? When did this happen?'

'Last night, I suppose. We just seemed to get on so well when he called here, and then he rang me today and asked me out.'

'I thought you liked Pádraig Harrison?'

'Well, I do,' she said, lying back down on the couch. 'But I suppose if I was truthful I'd have to say that I like the look of Pádraig – even you must admit that he's pretty beautiful – but there's something about Tim. I don't know, I just like him.'

'He's a nice guy. Did you have a good time?'

Cassandra let out a long, deep sigh. 'Brilliant.'

'Delightful?'

She smiled. 'Now you have it.'

'Well, I'm exhausted,' I said, standing up from my armchair. 'I'm going to go to bed while the going is good and maybe I'll even sleep. Night, Cass. Don't fall asleep on the couch – you'll freeze.'

'I won't. Night, Séamus.'

I walked across the room and turned the old-fashioned round, brown Bakelite doorknob.

'Séamus?'

'Yeah?'

'Jessica is an idiot.'

'What?'

'You heard me. Jessica is an idiot. She always was. A silly little girlie who wants everything her own way. What do they call it? *Puella eterna* – is that it? Like Peter Pan only female.'

'Look. Don't. She wasn't. Isn't.'

Cassandra sat up and put her feet on to the floor. 'She was and she is, and nobody in the family wants to say it, because they're all trying so hard not to upset you. But it's what everybody thinks.'

'Cassandra –'

'No, listen – you're a good man and, God knows, you're a handsome man. That's why women – like Alison – and I'd say even the sophisticated Chrissie herself, are giving you the eye. Sooner or later you have to face up to it. Jessica treated you badly, and you deserved better treatment.'

'Well, anybody is entitled to leave a marriage if they're not happy. You can't force yourself to love somebody.'

'I don't mean that. I mean she always treated you badly. Long before she ever left and set up house with that architect guy.'

'That's not true.'

'Yes it is. Nothing you ever did was enough for her. Your job. Your house. Your clothes. Castleannery. All I ever heard that woman do was complain.'

'No.'

'Yes.'

'You're only saying that because you love me.'

'Well, what do you know?' Cassandra said, standing up and jamming her feet into her shoes. 'I rest my case.'

5

'Hey, Joe'
Billy Roberts, Third Story Music Inc., 1962

I picked up the ringing telephone as I walked in the door from school next day.

'Séamus?' a voice said into my ear as soon as I said hello. I dropped my car keys out of slack fingers on to the hall floor.

'Jessica?'

'I'm glad I managed to get you at last. I've tried loads of times and you never seem to be there when I ring.'

'Sorry. I'm sorry. I thought you were in Los Angeles?'

'I was. I came back a few days early. I have an exhibition next month and I need to do some work for it.' Jessica gave a long, low sigh. 'I really, really tried to put it out of my head while we were in the US,' she continued. 'Did my absolute best to get into the spirit of the holiday. Just couldn't do it. I was distracted all the time. Eventually Vin said, look, the hell with it, why not come home, change the ticket, it's only money –'

'Oh, I see. Where is the exhibition?'

'The Mark's Gallery. Great break for me really, but the work is hell. I feel as if I'll never be finished. Anyway, how are you? Are you OK? I was worried about you. You could have phoned to let me know you were all right, Séamus. It was on the news, for heaven's sake.'

'I know. I'm sorry, Jess – Jessica.'

'Still, you *are* all right and I suppose that's the main thing. Who was the man who was killed?'

'Mattie Ahern.'

'Do I know him?'

'Yes, he lived quite near to us . . . me. Lovely old guy.'

'The man who delivered the milk?'

'No. That was a woman, Jessica. Mattie. He used to bring us down eggs sometimes. You said he reminded you of Groucho Marx.'

'Oh, yes, now I think I know him. Mattie. I forgot his name. Poor man. Still he was old, I suppose.'

'I don't think age would make much difference to getting a bullet in the chest, Jessica, do you?'

'That's not what I meant.'

'It's what you said.'

'You're twisting my words. I called out of concern for you and now you're twisting my words.' Jessica's voice swelled with tears.

'Oh, Jessica, look, I'm sorry. I'm tired. I've had a hard day.'

'I know how you feel,' she said, letting out a small sigh. 'I thought I was never going to get home. We spent almost four hours hanging around Kennedy waiting for the flight to begin with. Then I was sandwiched on the plane between a fat woman chewing something hideous and a man who snored for the entire flight. I'm completely exhausted.'

'Sorry for snapping, Jess, I do appreciate you calling. Especially as you're so tired.'

'My pleasure,' she said, and her voice was like a balm that was flowing into me, making me feel better than I'd felt in weeks. 'I was really, really worried, Séamus. Anything could have happened. It might have been you who was killed.'

I laughed. 'They'd need a silver bullet,' I said, and I heard Jessica sigh again.

'Are you OK?'

'I'm . . . well, I wonder if we could meet sometime?'

'Sure,' I said. 'Sure, Jess. I'd like that.'

'Maybe you'd like to come to the opening of my exhibition? I'll get them to send you an invitation if you'd like to come.'

'That would be nice,' I said, though I had absolutely no intention of going anywhere I'd be required to watch Jessica and the architect all evening.

'There is one other thing,' she said, her voice dropping almost to a whisper.

'Yes?'

'If you're coming up to Dublin maybe you could bring my old carriage clock? I can't find it in my stuff anywhere so it must still be in Castleannery. It may be in the spare bedroom. My grandmother gave it to me when we got married and my mother is starting to give me a hard time about it.'

Jessica paused for breath. I didn't say a word.

'In fact,' Jessica went on, 'she was on the phone just twenty minutes ago asking if I found it. Don't trouble yourself about it, now. Just if you're coming up to Dublin.'

'No problem,' I said, lighting a cigarette and inhaling the disappointment with the smoke.

'Séamus?'

'Yes?'

'Are you smoking again?'

'Yes.'

'Really! I thought you'd quit that disgusting habit.'

'Ah, well, I had, but things sort of got away from me over the past while and –'

'For goodness sake, Séamus, you need to stop smoking. Honestly! It's so bad for you.'

'I know, I will – maybe in the New Year.'

'Do that. Listen, I have to go, forty million things to get underway for the bloody exhibition. Glad you're all right. Talk to you soon.'

'Thanks for calling.'

'My pleasure,' Jessica said, pausing for a minute. 'It's nice to hear your voice again.'

'Yours too.'

'Bye, Séamus.'

'See you, Jess.'

I held on to the receiver after she was gone, reluctant to hang up on what had at least been a connection with Jessica. I told myself not to put too much store by what she'd said. We'd been together one way and another for more than seven years. It was a long time to be with somebody. You were bound to miss them when you were no longer together.

I certainly missed her. My head felt as if it might explode. Fuck. Life really was way too fucking annoying for words. Maybe if I talked to Cassandra she'd be able to think of something that might help.

'Cassandra?' I called, remembering that she should be there. That was good, I'd talk to Cassandra. Tell her what Jessica had said, put it all out there and see what somebody else thought.

'Cassandra?'

The house was silent. I picked up my car keys and the cake I'd bought for entertaining Alison Chang and walked into the kitchen. Maybe she was out for a walk or something. It was almost dark in the house. Navy sky filling up every window.

I flicked on the light and saw a huge sheet of paper held in place on the fridge door by a magnet shaped like a strawberry. Cassandra had bought the magnet. And the banana-shaped one beside it.

Séamus – gone out with Tim.
Back later.
Love, Cassandra

I read the note out loud to myself. Fuck it. But maybe it was just as well that she wasn't there. What would I have said anyway?

I foraged in the fridge for leftover pasta and when I found it tipped it on to a plate and set it to reheat in the microwave and all the time my telephone conversation with Jessica replayed in my head. It was so weird to hear her voice. So totally fucking weird.

Inside me echoes of Jessica's words ricocheted like bullets. Snippets of words precipitating the regulation avalanche of questions. Was it really good for her to hear my voice? Did that mean she missed hearing it? Or even that she missed me? Was she sorry she had hurt me? Sorry she'd left me? Anything was possible.

It was even possible that she was trying to find a way to tell me she still loved me. Imagine that. Maybe she'd just come back out of the blue. Pull her car into the yard and tell me she was coming home. I'd help her bring in her bags and we'd talk about everything that had happened and decide to move on, and in twenty years' time we'd look back on this and say it had enriched our relationship.

I lit a cigarette as the microwave beeped, but I needed to smoke more than I needed to eat. I didn't really feel hungry any more. I felt full and the thought of trying to push food into my body nauseated me. So I made myself a cup of coffee, opened the back door and walked into the dark yard. Prince strolled past me in the doorway and straight into the warm, bright kitchen.

I leaned against the wall of the house and looked into the night. The steam from my coffee, the smoke from my cigarette and the heat of my breath mingled into the clouds around me. It was cold, but I wanted to be cold because I wanted to think clearly. If only I could think clearly and not feel too much – it seemed as if the cold air might help me to do that.

But the night air wasn't strong enough to cut through the fog I was living in. Mattie's face appeared in front of me as if I could really see it. He seemed to be smiling, but I started to cry because he wasn't really there and neither was Jessica – or even my stupid cousin Cassandra – and I didn't know if I could bear the rawness of being so alone.

Alison Chang was late.

'Does nearly nine count as eightish?' she said, as I opened the front door. 'I'm really, really sorry. I had a flat tyre and seem to have left my phone at home, so I couldn't even ring you. May I wash my hands? I'm a bit mucky after changing the wheel.'

'Straight up,' I said, pointing, 'the door facing you at the top of the stairs.'

'I really do apologize,' she said, as she hurried past me.

'I wasn't going any place anyway,' I said, to her tall, straight back. 'Will you have a cup of coffee?'

She turned at the top of the stairs and smiled at me. 'Any chance of a cup of tea?'

'Every chance,' I said, smiling at her, suddenly calmer than I had been since Jessica's phone call. 'Go straight into the sitting room when you come down and I'll go get some tea.'

When I arrived in the sitting room ten minutes later with a tray of tea and carefully sliced carrot cake, Alison was looking at photographs, framed in silver and wood and brass and grouped together on a table by the window. She turned and smiled at me when she heard the door open.

'Rogue's Gallery,' I said, putting the tray on to the coffee table. She smiled again and put down a big, wooden-framed photograph and went to stand in front of the fire.

I saw that the picture Alison had been holding was one of Jessica and me on our wedding day. It was my favourite. It wasn't the posed and formal kind – though there was one of those too. Instead we were laughing uncontrollably when my brother, Eamon, fell backwards over the stone wall he was standing on trying to get a shot of the entire wedding group. Cassandra had taken the shot and I loved it because I could hear the sounds of happiness that went with it.

I poured two cups of tea and handed Alison a slice of carrot cake on a plate.

'Thank you,' she said, sitting down in an armchair, 'this is great.'

We sat in silence, eating cake and drinking tea. It was funny that Alison and I seemed to be able to sit in silence. I'd noticed it before. Strange, considering we hardly knew each other. As she finished her cake she put the plate back on the tray and then knelt down in front of the coffee table to refill her teacup.

'Tea?' she said, looking up at me.

I smiled and nodded and she filled my cup. She looked away for a moment and then looked back at me. 'That really is a fabulous photograph.'

I swallowed some carrot cake. 'It was our wedding.'

She nodded. 'I can tell.'

She paused and adjusted her kneeling position to pour milk in her tea.

'You look so . . . happy.'

I lit a cigarette. 'We were,' I said, exhaling, 'we were actually very happy.'

'Do you want milk?' Alison asked holding up the jug.

I shook my head. 'No, I'm fine. Thanks.'

'No problem,' she said, standing up and then sitting back down into the armchair. 'Long line of geishas.'

I looked at her, imagining her face painted white. 'Really?'

Alison laughed. 'No. Wrong country, but it sounds good.'

I laughed. 'Tapping into the old Western prejudice, eh?'

Alison smiled and sipped tea. We slipped back into silence for a few minutes.

'These things happen, you know,' Alison said, all of a sudden, putting her cup back on to its saucer. 'I'm divorced myself.'

'Are you?' I said, filled with disbelief. 'Sorry – that's a stupid thing to say. Obviously you are if you said you were. Just sometimes, I know it's dumb, but it's as if I'm the only one – not that we're divorced – but, you know.'

She nodded. 'I do know. I think it probably always feels as if you're the only one it ever happened to. I felt the same.'

'And now?'

She looked into her teacup for a few moments, then looked at me and I could see that there was no other description for her eyes except almond-shaped. 'Well –' She stopped and took a deep breath. 'Now, it's not as bad. Things pass, you know. Everything passes.'

'That's what Mattie used to say.'

'He was right.'

A Jessica-flavoured feeling broke loose and floated free inside me, but somehow it was all right. 'What did you want to ask me?'

She put her cup on to the coffee table and flicked open the wire-bound notebook. 'I'm not sure I want to ask you anything specific. Maybe if you tell me about it?'

'About what?'

'Finding William Ormston. What happened to your friend. Anything you think of.'

So I began to tell her, and while it might have been better for her to have me tell her everything, I discovered that it was also better for me. It made me feel lighter. Freer.

Maybe it was because she was writing it all down and for some reason I trusted her to keep the information safe, which meant that I wouldn't have to keep remembering it over and over. Or maybe it was just straightforward catharsis.

Alison left with a full notebook and as soon as she'd gone I walked straight up the stairs to bed and fell into an immediate, dreamless sleep. I woke at six o'clock in the morning and when I awoke my first thoughts were about Alison Chang. Who was she? Where did she come from?

She was clearly Irish – spoke with an Irish accent, moved around as you do when you're on your own turf, but she also obviously had family connections outside of Ireland. If not Japan then China? Maybe I'd ask her if I ever saw her again.

I was up and showered and breakfasted and collecting books from the couch in the sitting room when I noticed Jessica's carriage clock standing on the floor behind the couch. Jessica was looking for that, I thought. I must send it up to her, because no matter what I had told her I'd no intention of going to her exhibition. I pulled the front door closed behind me, and as it closed I realized that that had been my first thought of Jessica. Ordinarily I thought of her as soon as I opened my eyes.

I arrived home from school that day after six, covered in mud having refereed two hours of hurling in the rain. Alison Chang's silver car was parked in the yard and she stepped out of it as soon as I pulled in. She was wearing the same long black coat she'd been wearing the first day she arrived.

I climbed out of the car, the mud caked to the side of my face stinging like a burn as she looked at me. I scrubbed at my cheek with the sleeve of my damp jacket, which was a mistake because it just made it sting some more.

'A match,' I said, reaching into the car boot for my bags.

'Did you win?' she asked, leaning against her car with her arms folded. A thick mist was falling which made the air between us visible. I slammed the boot closed.

'Well, if by winning you mean none of the under-tens were hospitalized, then, yes, we won.'

'That's good.'

'Come on in,' I said, as I walked past her. 'We can't talk out here.'

Alison followed me across the yard.

'What are you doing here?' I asked, as I turned the key in the lock and glanced over my shoulder at her.

'I just need to ask you a couple of questions that I forgot last night. Details.'

I nodded and dropped my bags on to the floor of the hallway. 'I have to have a shower. Cassandra doesn't appear to be here, but make yourself at home and I'll be down in a minute.'

Then I turned and rushed up the stairs. As I showered and dressed I wondered why I was acting like a schoolboy – embarrassed and sad and glad all at the same time.

It couldn't be Alison because I knew that she was a nice woman, but I was still in love with Jessica. Still saw Jessica's face when I closed my eyes. Maybe there were other explanations. Hormones, for example?

Alison was sitting on an old fireside chair by the range, her head resting against its high back and her eyes closed, when I came into the kitchen. She sat upright as soon as she realized I was there. I made a pot of tea and put some cups on to the table.

'So. What do you need to know? I thought I told you everything.'

'Well,' Alison began, taking a cup of tea from me, 'I just . . . I thought that maybe you might have remembered something about the men who shot Mattie – what did they look like, stuff like that. I'm not sure what it might tell us, but just if you did . . .' Her voice trailed off.

'I didn't see them properly,' I said, pulling out a chair and sitting down. 'I didn't know them. They were men. Both very tall. One maybe six two, the other at least six four. And somebody shouted. I think it was the bigger one. He shouted three things. "Where the fuck did he come from?" "What did you go and do that for?" and "Gimme the fucking keys." And I don't know where they – or he – were from but he was definitely not Irish. Which just leaves the entire rest of the world to search. And that's about it. I'm sorry I can't help you more.'

Alison shook her head. 'No problem,' she said, still not looking at me. 'I just thought I should have all the details as you remember them.'

'I thought I told you that much last night, but probably not.'

'No. You didn't say anything before about the men not being Irish.'

'Didn't I? Well, I don't know. Maybe they were Irish, maybe they live here, but that man I heard definitely originated someplace else. I keep trying to place his accent. The policeman who interviewed me said maybe Australian, but I just don't know.'

'Was it accented English? You know, like a German person speaking English?'

I shook my head. 'No. It wasn't like that.'

'And it wasn't Australian?'

'I don't think so.'

'New Zealand?'

'Maybe. I wish I'd paid more attention, but at the time it just wasn't the most important thing that was happening.'

'I know, it couldn't have been with everything else. Unless . . . Séamus, could it have been South African?'

'Could what have been South African?'

'The accent – the man who shot Mattie. Could his accent have been South African? It's not a million miles away from an Australian accent.'

I looked at her and something inside my head slid into place like a gear. 'Yes,' I said, slowly, then everything erupted. 'Jesus Christ, you're right, Alison! That is what it was – he had a South African accent – that Afrikaner accent, I'm sure of it. Jesus, you're a genius. I never thought of that. I have to phone the police and tell them.'

I left the kitchen still talking to myself and went into the hallway to search through the drawers in the telephone table for the phone number Paul Richardson had given me. I found it on the floor under the table. With shaking hands I dialled the number and asked the pleasant-voiced woman who answered to put me through to Detective Richardson.

'May I say who's calling?' she trilled.

'Séamus Considine.'

'Hold just a minute, Mr Considine.'

Almost immediately Paul Richardson's soft Cork accent filled my ear. 'Séamus! How are you?'

'I'm all right. Not too bad. Look, I know where that accent was from. The accent of the man who was there when Mattie was shot, I mean.'

I paused.

'Go on,' he said.

'South African. Afrikaner. I know it's not much, but I just remembered it and I thought I should tell you.' I stopped, feeling foolish all of a sudden.

'You did the right thing,' Detective Richardson said, as if he could tell that I felt a bit of a fool. 'Often, you know, shock can sort of freeze you and gradually as time passes you remember things.'

'OK. Right.'

'So, feel free to call me any time. If you remember anything at all. Even if it seems insignificant to you, Séamus. You can't tell what it'll lead to.'

I listened to his voice and I believed him. 'Paul?'

'Yes?'

'Have you made any progress in finding Mattie's killer?' I suddenly felt overwhelmed with a need to know the answer.

'No, Séamus. I'd like to tell you that we have, and that we know who and why, but I can't. So I'm delighted to get any information at all.'

'And do you think you'll ever find out?'

'Well, I can't promise you anything,' the Cork voice said. 'I wish I could. But I can tell you that we are working on it day and night.'

'And if you can't find out who did it, what then? Won't you just have to leave it?'

'Maybe, but that'll be an awful long time from now – if ever. And meanwhile I'm doing everything I know how to do. If I can't find the men who murdered Matthew Ahern it won't be from lack of trying, I can promise you that much.'

'Thank you. I appreciate that. One more thing.'

'Go ahead.'

'Boru. How's he doing?'

'He's doing great – Tara adores him and he never leaves her side. Walks to school after her every day. You don't want him back, do you?'

'No, but you did me a favour taking him home the night of Mattie's murder and we never talked about it being a long-term arrangement. I feel responsible, I guess.'

'Well, all I can say is that if there were any favours done you were doing them. Tara was devastated by Trixie's death and now – well, she's herself again.'

'That's great.'

'So we can keep Boru?'

'I'd never take him from a happy home.'

'Why don't you drop in and see him next time you're in town?'

'I might – thanks. And Paul?'

'Yes?'

'Thanks for everything.'

'No problem. Take care of yourself.'

'You too,' I said, before I hung up.

I wandered back into the kitchen, desperately trying not to feel the feelings that went with the memory of the night Mattie was shot.

'Look at the time,' I heard Alison's voice say. 'I'd better go and let you have your dinner in peace. Sorry to disturb you.'

Alison stood up and pulled on her black coat. I watched her in silence. Her face seemed to be unsettled somehow, as if she was saying something with her face that she wasn't saying with her mouth. Tiny droplets of mist still glittered on the shoulders of her coat.

'Thanks again,' she said, looking straight at me this time. 'You've been a great help.'

'No problem.' I lit another cigarette. 'It was nice to see you and you've been an even bigger help to me, helping me pin down that accent.'

Her brown eyes grew wide and she smiled. 'You're welcome. It was nice to see you too.'

I looked at her tall, slender frame as she filled my view.

'Alison?'

She looked at me.

'Would you eat an omelette?'

'What?'

'An omelette. I haven't eaten yet and I was wondering if you'd like to stay a while and have an omelette with me?'

Alison took a deep breath and then a wide smile crossed her face. 'I'd like to, but I feel bad about it.'

'Why?'

'Well, you seem to be feeding me a lot recently. First lamb chops, now an omelette.'

'Where will it end? It could be Irish stew next for all you know.'

Alison laughed. 'Still, it isn't right. I come in here disturbing you and you end up having to feed me.'

'It's not a disturbance, I swear. Especially since Cassandra started running around with the local GP. I mean, all day long I have only the company of nine year olds and they're fine, don't get me wrong, but they are only nine. At night all I have for company is Prince. So, you've been doing me a favour agreeing to eat my food.'

'Then I'd love to stay,' Alison said, slipping off her wet coat. 'I hadn't realized I was being so selfless.'

I stood up and pulled a carton of eggs from the fridge and began to break them into a glass bowl.

'Can I help?'

'No, thanks,' I said, as I cracked eggs, 'you can entertain me while I slave over your dinner, how about that? Maybe you'd sing me a song – anything at all will do, I'm not fussy.'

'I'm pretty sure you won't want me to sing, Séamus.'

'Then just tell me stories.'

'Stories?'

'Tell me everything about yourself. Who you are, where you're from, your most embarrassing experience – that kind of thing.'

Alison laughed. 'OK,' she said, walking over to stand by me as I whisked the eggs. 'I was born in America thirty-one years ago. My father – who was Irish – was long gone by the time I could become conscious of having a father. My mother is actually an American, but her family, as you may have guessed, come from Hong Kong.' Alison paused and hooked the curving front of her bobbed hair behind her ear.

'You don't sound like a Yank,' I said, chopping onions and mushrooms.

'I grew up in Dublin. My mother came here because she was offered a job in UCD – she's a sociologist.'

'Did she think she might find your father?'

Alison laughed. 'Well, I think that she probably did, though she'd never have admitted such a thing. I'm not sure what she was doing except that that's the most likely reason she took the job. But I don't know for sure. She never talked about him. Wouldn't. As you can see by the fact that I'm called Chang, she didn't even let me use his name.'

'Were they married?'

'Supposedly, but my mother would never let me ask her anything about him or her time with him.'

'Is his name on your birth-cert?'

'Yes,' she said, in a whisper.

I stopped chopping for a minute and looked at her.

'What was his name?'

Alison sighed a long, sad-sounding sigh. 'O'Rourke.'

'Have you ever met him?'

'No, no, never.'

'I suppose it might be hard to find him after all this time.'

Alison nodded and smiled.

'Maybe if you ask your mother again?'

Alison shook her head and blinked fast.

'Surely she isn't still angry with him after all this time?'

'Well,' Alison said, after she took a deep, deep breath, 'I'm not sure what she feels now, she may well have forgiven him in some other realm. But I have to tell you that, unfortunately, she hated my father's guts until her dying day.'

'When did she die?'

'A long time ago. I was twenty-four. Just finished college.' Alison stared at something invisible over my head.

'I'm sorry.'

She adjusted her eyes to look at me. 'It's fine, really, totally fine. But it's probably a mistake to get married three months after your mother dies. Anyway, life goes on.'

I picked up the whisk and busied myself with beating eggs to cover the silence in the kitchen.

'Surely that's not everything,' I said, as I turned around still holding the glass bowl in my hand.

Alison looked at me. 'What do you mean?'

'You're keeping something from me,' I said, leaning an elbow on the tiled worktop.

Alison's eyebrows separated in a look of dismay and a slow blush crept up along her face from her neck. She shook her head in silence. 'I don't know what you mean. Really, I don't.'

'Your most embarrassing incident?' I said, tripping over my words as I tried to speed up and save her. 'You never told me your most embarrassing incident.'

I lit the gas under the frying pan and trickled a tiny amount of oil on to it. I looked at her. 'Well?'

Alison smiled and sighed. 'Oh, OK, let me see, there are just so many.' She paused to think and I could see the blush recede and her composure return and I wondered, as I poured egg on to the sizzling pan, how I'd upset her so badly.

'College,' Alison said, all of a sudden, 'my absolutely most embarrassing incident was when I was at college. I was going out with this guy and his sister hated me. Anyway, she told me I was invited to a party. A really, really cool party – you know the sort – intellectual, cool people, invitation only type of thing.' Alison paused.

'Go on,' I said.

She took a deep breath. 'Well, I was never one of those super-cool people, so, I was thrilled. She said she was going too and she'd meet me there. Just turn up, she said. So I did. At nine o'clock like she'd told me. Some guy I never saw before opened the door and I just walked in past him. They were all sitting around – including Sheila, that was her name – looking at me. It was obvious that they hadn't been expecting me and had no idea who I was. Sheila just ignored me. Pretended not to know me. Finally, the guy who owned the flat asked me what I wanted. It was horrible.'

'What did you do?'

'I just laughed and said, "Oh there must be some mistake, sorry about that" – and then I left.'

'That's horrible,' I said, sliding a cooked omelette on to a plate and pouring more egg on to the hot pan. 'Bloody bitch. What did your boyfriend do? Was he furious with his sister?'

Alison smiled and shook her head. 'No, he was furious with me.'

'With you?'

'Yes. Sheila told him it was a joke and he said I should have known she was only joking and that I should have known I'd never be invited to one of those parties.'

'You can't be serious.'

Alison smiled. 'Honest to God.'

'Bastard,' I said, sliding the second omelette on to a plate and carrying both plates to the table. 'Grab the bowl of salad out of the fridge, will you, Alison, and let's eat.'

I collected cutlery and glasses and a jug of water and dropped them on to the table and then I cut some brown soda bread into slices. We sat down opposite each other at the table and began to eat.

'So?' I said, swallowing a mouthful of omelette. 'Did you finish with him after that?'

Alison chewed and looked at me. Her eyes looked like they might be able to see more than other eyes. I wondered if it was their shape.

'No, I didn't finish with him after that, it took a while actually. Believe it or not I married him.'

'No way!'

Alison nodded.

'And his sister? What did she say when you got married?'

'Well, do you know something – this sounds terrible, but sometimes I wonder if I married George to get back at Sheila. She was furious when we got married and really didn't seem to cheer up until we were divorced.'

'A bit extreme, don't you think? Maybe you should have emptied a glass of wine over her or called her names.'

Alison laughed. 'You're right. But we all make mistakes. How about you? Why did you marry your wife?'

I tried to swallow a mouthful of bread, but it stuck in my throat. Taking a deep breath I forced it down and then had a long, gulping drink of water.

Alison was still looking at me, waiting. I noticed that her face was a long, slender face and I remembered that Jessica's was round, like a cherub, and that she had never liked the shape of her face. I looked down at my empty plate.

'Because I loved her,' I said at last.

Alison seemed to emanate stillness as the words floated over the table towards her. I fixed my eyes on a sliver of mushroom that was stuck like a crescent moon to the edge of my plate.

'I'm sorry,' she said, after a minute, 'that was a stupid question. I didn't mean anything by it. Not everybody makes as big a mess of their lives as I do.'

'Yeah, they do,' I said as I looked up, she was staring at me. 'Or at least I do.'

'Sorry.'

I tried a smile and it worked. 'That's OK. Would you like some coffee?'

'No, thank you. Thank you for the lovely meal but I'd better get going. I think there's a storm forecast and if that's the case there may be floods and I'd like to miss those.'

I watched as she shrugged into her coat and buttoned its brass coloured buttons all along its length. I must appear pathetic, I thought. This beautiful woman wants to stay and chat and I'm slipping into some horrible puddle of self-pity. But I couldn't help myself. I was already immersed.

'Well, thanks again,' Alison said, interrupting my thoughts.

'You're more than welcome,' I managed to say, as I stood up.

'Stay where you are,' Alison said, smiling at me and collecting her notebook and handbag, 'I'll let myself out. Stay here. It's miserable outside.'

It's miserable inside as well, I thought, but I didn't say it. Instead I said, 'Drive safely.' And, 'I hope you miss the storm.'

Alison waved and left the room before I could follow. I stood by the table looking at the debris of our dinner and heard the front door close gently. I needed to wash the dishes and clean up but I couldn't. I was paralysed and all I could do was to stand right where I was standing.

After a few minutes I heard the front door. Cassandra. I was relieved. Cassandra would shift me out of this place. Cassandra would know what to do. The kitchen door opened and Cassandra and Tim Winter came in. Both buttoned into heavy woollen coats, both red-cheeked from the wind.

'Jesus! Séamus!' Cassandra said, ignoring the mess and the fact that I was standing like a moronic statue in the middle of the floor. 'You'll never guess what happened.'

I looked at her in silence. Tim caught her by the arm, but Cassandra was already in full flow.

'Tim had a visit today – didn't you, Tim? Some guy from Dublin, enquiring about William Ormston and all that and guess what?'

Cassandra paused and I shrugged.

'You won't believe it. He showed Tim a photograph – look, I brought it, here it is.'

On to the kitchen table Cassandra tossed a photograph of Alison Chang. A younger Alison in a pale-blue sweater and jeans holding a golden retriever by a long leash and smiling, demurely, at the camera. But it was, without a doubt the same Alison. Our Alison Chang. I looked at Cassandra.

'And?'

'And,' she echoed, 'this guy who called in to Tim says that she's claiming to be William Ormston's daughter.'

6

'Everybody's Got Something to Hide Except Me and My Monkey'
The Beatles, 1968

I focused on Cassandra's face as if that would make it easier
for me to understand what she said. But I still couldn't get it.

'But that couldn't be. She was just here and she worked
out that the man who shot Mattie, his accent was South
African.'

'Sorry?' Tim said.

'The man. I heard one of them shouting, I told you that.'

'Oh, right. And?'

'And I couldn't place his accent and just a while ago when
I was talking to Alison she suggested it might have been a
South African accent and it was. I don't know why I never
thought of that, but she was right. Afrikaner.'

'You're kidding?' Cassandra said, coming to stand in front
of me.

'No. Afrikaner. That was it. I rang Detective Richardson
and told him.'

'And what did he say?' Tim said.

'Oh, just that he was glad I rang and to ring again if I
remember any more details.'

'And will you, do you think?' Cassandra said. 'Remember
more?'

I shrugged. 'Paul Richardson said sometimes as the shock
wears off it's possible to remember things that happened.'

'Is it, Tim?' Cassandra said.

Tim looked startled. 'Is what?'

'Is that true?' she said, grinning at him. 'You must know about shock and things like that, you're a doctor.'

Tim wrinkled his forehead as if he was concentrating. 'It probably is true, I couldn't say.'

'Still,' Cassandra said, turning her attention back to me, 'Alison may have worked out part of the puzzle, but she's still the woman in the picture, isn't she?'

I nodded and sat down. 'Yes,' I said, suddenly exhausted, 'unless she has an identical twin sister.'

'Well?' Cassandra said. 'What do you think she's up to?'

I shook my head and found I couldn't speak because it was all just too hard to understand. Tim made coffee and I began to sip from a green mug and still I couldn't speak.

'But Alison Chang is working for the solicitors who are representing the alleged children of William Ormston, isn't she? She couldn't do that if she was one of them, could she? It would be conflict of interest or something like that, wouldn't it?' I said.

Cassandra sighed. 'She lied.'

'What?'

'Lied, Séamus, she lied. It's not that hard to understand, for God's sake. People lie all the time. She lied.'

'And did she – is she – is that her name? Is Alison Chang her name?'

'Yes,' Tim said, 'it is her name and, actually, she *is* a solicitor and she is from Dublin. Or that's what the man who visited me said.'

'And how do you know he wasn't lying?' I said, unreasonably cross with Tim. 'He might be lying. Jesus!'

I stood up abruptly from my chair, and it rocked, noisily, on the tiled floor. Walking to the draining board I grabbed my cigarettes and lit one in shaking confusion.

'He could be lying as well. Everybody could be lying. How can you tell any more? People lying, people shooting. What the fuck is going on in the world?'

I looked out of the window at the night and concentrated on smoking my cigarette. I didn't know what to make of any of it. Alison Chang was a liar. Jessica left me. Somebody shot Mattie Ahern.

I didn't believe I could cope with life in Castleannery much longer. I wasn't robust enough. Maybe I might volunteer for one of those remote teaching jobs in Africa? It couldn't be more hazardous.

'Sit down and finish your coffee, Séamus. There's probably a rational explanation for all of this. She seems like much too nice a woman to just go around flogging lies hither and yon without a good reason.'

'To get information,' I said, pacing up and down behind Cassandra's chair as I smoked. 'That would be a good reason, wouldn't it? Fool those nice people to get what you want.'

'That's not what I mean.'

'But let's face it,' I said, and I laughed a manic laugh like a cartoon villain, 'it probably is the case.'

'Look, I'd better be off,' Tim said standing up, quietly. 'I'll see if I can find out anything tomorrow, Séamus. I didn't know anything about this till Cassandra saw the photograph. It was on the desk in my office. I never even met Alison Chang myself.'

I looked at his narrow, white face.

'OK,' I said, shrugging, and flicking my cigarette into the coal bucket. 'Thanks, Tim.'

'See you, so, Séamus.'

'See you, Tim.'

Cassandra and Tim disappeared out of the kitchen and into the hallway. I could hear their voices murmuring softly as I lit another cigarette. I remembered that feeling. The feeling that you'd found somebody you already knew.

A recognition and a relaxation. A feeling of coming home. A feeling that the only time you could let your breath out properly was when you were with that person.

I could see that something like that was happening for Cassandra and Tim – or I thought it was – and I felt like a black cloud on their sunny horizon. I smoked yet another cigarette and listened to the tiny noises of their leave-taking, then I heard the front door close.

'Well, what about that?' Cassandra said, coming into the kitchen, a smile plastered in place.

'What about it?'

'Aren't you amazed? She seems so nice.'

I shook my head. 'No, unfortunately I'm not amazed. I'm beginning to realize that people can do anything.'

'Don't be so cynical. It doesn't suit you.'

I laughed. 'Too bad. You'd better get used to it.'

'Look, you're upset about Alison and all the other stuff and that's understandable.'

'I'm not upset. There was a time when I would have been upset but not now. Now I'm used to it and I'm finally getting the picture – and that's not a bad thing, everybody needs to change.'

'But . . .'

I held up my hand. 'Listen for once in your life, Cassandra. I'm different than I used to be. Life happens to you and it makes you different. Makes you change. Isn't that what's supposed to happen?'

Cassandra shrugged.

'It is,' I continued, 'and even if it isn't, it's what's happening to me. I'm changing from being a fucking eejit who trusts everybody and juggles life like it's a set of bowling balls when it's really a whole load of glass spheres – to becoming – well, I don't know what the fuck I'm becoming but I do know that – that eejit is dead and gone and that's a good thing.'

Cassandra looked all over my face for a minute as if actually searching for something. 'I wish I could say something useful. Something that would make you feel better.'

'No need,' I said, and inside me I could feel a sort of armour forming under my skin and I liked the sensation because it made me feel safe. 'Really, don't worry, I am absolutely fine.'

Cassandra rubbed her head again. 'Goodnight, Séamus. Tim might find out something about Alison Chang tomorrow and then maybe we'll have the whole picture.'

'Yeah,' I said, wanting her to go to bed and leave me alone. 'Yeah. Goodnight, Cassandra.'

Cassandra walked silently out of the kitchen and up the stairs. I hunched down in front of the range and rubbed Prince who snored his appreciation as he wriggled under my hand.

'Poor old boy,' I said, as I stroked his black and white coat. 'Poor, poor boy.'

Alison Chang was waiting outside the school the next day when I emerged with my arms full of copybooks. She smiled as I approached her and I found myself automatically returning her smile until I remembered.

'Alison,' I said, and my voice was cold and brittle like a breath of ice. She looked like I'd hit her.

'Just passing through – thought I'd see how you were,' she said, recovering from my tone and carrying on as if it hadn't happened. I looked at her.

'Oh, right. I see. Excuse me, I need to put these copies into the car before I drop them.'

'Oh, sorry,' Alison said, stumbling as she moved out of my way. 'Here, let me help. Give me the keys and I'll open the car, shall I?'

'No thank you,' I said, leaning against the car and fumbling at the lock. 'I can manage just fine.'

I dropped the copies on to the back seat and closed the door. When I turned around Alison was still standing there, looking at me as if I'd slapped her in the face.

'I'd better be off,' I said, walking past her and around the car to the driver's door. 'Lots of work.'

'Oh, OK.'

I unlocked the door.

'Séamus?'

'Yes?'

'Are you still angry with me for what I said last night, because I didn't mean anything about you – or anyone, I was really only talking about myself, you know how it is . . .'

I looked at her over the roof of the car and the chinks in my new internal armour began to warp as I noticed the quiver in her lips and the blotches of red on her cheeks. Then I remembered.

'No, Alison, I'm not angry about that. But I am angry with you, because I just discovered that you lied to me.'

Alison shook her head and frowned.

I nodded slowly. 'Yes, indeed. All that stuff about working for the solicitors that are representing William Ormston's alleged children? Lovely story. Pity it wasn't true.'

'But it is true.'

I looked at her. 'OK. Fine. So how about the fact that you're one of the people claiming William Ormston was your father? Forgot to tell me that little tidbit of information, didn't you?'

'Oh,' Alison said, in a tiny voice. She closed her eyes and took a deep breath. 'Oh.'

'You should have told me the truth,' I said, as a geyser of anger welled up, suddenly, in my chest, 'I just wish people would tell me the goddamn fucking truth. I mean, Alison, they don't even have to tell me the fucking truth *all* of the time. I'm a reasonable man, but I think it would be good if I was told the truth just once in a while. Is that too fucking much to ask?'

Climbing into the car, I started the engine and drove off

without even looking in Alison's direction, much less looking again at her bruised and shocked face. I was home and parked outside my house before I realized it. Prince was yapping at the car.

'OK, OK, boy,' I said, as I got out and collected my books and bags and copybooks, 'at least I told her. At least I told her.'

I was pacing restlessly around the kitchen waiting for the kettle to boil when I heard the doorbell ring. I stopped, frozen by the sound of its tinny chime reverberating in the hallway. Was it Alison? I didn't want to see her. Ever. But maybe it wasn't. Where was Cassandra? Why was she never around these days when I needed her?

The doorbell rang again and I decided not to answer it. Why should I bother? She'd see the car and she'd know I was home and not answering the door on purpose and that was good because it meant she'd get the right message and in the unlikely event that it might be somebody else they'd come back later if it was important. Just then the back door swung open.

'Jesus!' I shouted in fright, leaping about a foot in the air.

Jessica stood in the doorway. 'People are getting murdered in Castleannery and you're still leaving the back door open while you spend the day out of the house.'

'Jessica?' I said, not really sure if I was dreaming.

Jessica looked at me. 'Yes?' she said, in her soft and lovely voice that felt to me like being wrapped in a warm blanket. 'Yes, Séamus? What is it?'

I looked at her, muffled into a cherry-coloured, woollen coat, standing in the light of the doorway and the armour inside me shattered and fell into ashes.

'Nothing. Nothing at all. It's just so great to see you. Come in. Sorry for not getting the door – I thought you were somebody else.'

Jessica looked at me quizzically as she pulled off her cream, leather gloves and deposited them on the kitchen table.

'Who?' she said, walking towards me.

'Nobody. Nobody important. So, how are you?'

Jessica laughed. 'Do you really want to know?'

'Yes,' I said, and it was true, I did.

She walked past me and the smell of her wafted by. That Jessica smell that was soap and shampoo and perfume and something that was none of those things, something that was just Jessica.

'Sit down. And tell me what's happening. Would you like coffee?'

Jessica shook out her long, slightly curly, blonde hair and pulled a chair out from the table.

'That would be just lovely. I'm absolutely shattered after the drive. Well, it's not really the drive. I mean, it's a lovely drive from Dublin to Castleannery, isn't it?'

I nodded.

'Truthfully, what has me exhausted is the exhibition. I'm drained from it. I can't even begin to decribe it to you, but I'm totally drained. I really and truly wonder if it's going to be worth it, but Vin says it will be and I know he's right. Oh, thank you – real coffee, delicious! You remembered I never could stand instant . . .'

She paused to take a mouthful of coffee.

'Well, I should remember.'

Jessica smiled at me. 'So,' she said, sitting back in her chair, 'tell me – how are you, Séamus? Have you recovered yet?'

'Recovered?'

'From your trauma – the shooting business?'

'Oh, that. Yes, I suppose. I'm fine.'

'And did they ever catch the people who shot that poor man?'

'Mattie? No, not yet.'

'Police!' Jessica said, throwing her green eyes up to heaven. 'So bloody inefficient.'

'Well, I don't think it's that. They have very little to go on when you think about it. No motive. No real evidence. No clear description of the killers.'

'I can't get it out of my head that you might have been shot as well.'

I shrugged.

'I brought you a present.'

Jessica reached into her handbag and brought out a small, green, fabric-covered box and placed it on the table between us. I looked at her and then at the box and she smiled, and it was her real smile and not her strained ex-wife smile.

'I saw it when I was in LA and I just knew it was meant for you.'

I opened the box. Inside a tiny wooden horse – perfect in every detail – lay on a bed of white tissue paper.

'Ebony,' she said. 'Isn't he amazing? It was made in 1849 for an English Baroness who commissioned it as a birthday present for her husband.'

I lifted the tiny horse out and held it in the palm of my hand. She was right, it was amazing, and I did love it. Jessica traced the horse's carved flanks with the tip of a slender finger.

'This sort of close work often made artists blind,' she said. 'Did you know that? This same artist could also write whole sentences on single grains of rice. Isn't that unbelievable?'

I looked at Jessica as she traced the horse's features.

'Thank you so much,' I said.

She looked up. 'You're welcome.'

We sat in silence for a minute, both looking at the tiny horse.

'Séamus?'

'Yes?'

'You know that – well, even with the other stuff that happened you are – well, if anything had happened to you –'

'Nothing happened.'

'I wish the police would find those murderers and then maybe I wouldn't be as worried about you.'

'They're trying.'

'Still. They should try harder. Anyway, look, I know you're probably busy but I needed to come here and sort something out.'

'I'm not busy,' I said, ignoring the vision of thirty-two Maths copies that sprung into my mind's eye. 'I'm delighted to see you.'

'I'm happy to see you too,' Jessica said, reaching for my hand and squeezing it gently. 'You remember when we spoke on the phone?'

I nodded.

'Well, I've been thinking since we spoke,' Jessica said, absent-mindedly stroking the back of my hand instead of the horse. I closed my fingers over the tiny ebony horse and stayed very still in case she stopped or discovered her mistake.

'I've been going over and over things in my head since we spoke and I think I've worked something out.'

'Really?'

My heart stopped beating for an interminable moment and I was afraid to breathe. Was it now? Would everything be all right from now? I remembered a time she made me fresh chicken soup from scratch when I was ill and how it made me feel so much better. Jessica was always able to make things better for me.

I didn't care about the architect, I could forget him, I could forget anything – everything – if she'd only come back to me. We could move – if she wanted. Even emigrate. Whatever would make Jessica happy would make me happy.

'Really,' she repeated, breaking into my thoughts, 'I've

spent a long time thinking about it and I'm sure that carriage clock is in the sitting room behind the couch.'

Jessica smiled broadly as if I should be overjoyed by her statement.

'I mulled it over and over – nothing. Then out of the blue when I was driving to town it came to me in a flash – I could sort of picture it there. I suppose it's because I'm an artist and I have a very strong visual sense. Would you mind if I ran into the sitting room to have a look? I need to get on the road as soon as possible. Vin worries if I drive long distances.'

My mouth filled with the taste of vomit, but I swallowed hard and even managed to pull my lips back over my teeth as if I was smiling.

'No,' I said, in a shaky voice, 'no, help yourself. It's in a bit of a mess.'

Jessica jumped up from the table and left the kitchen. My hand felt as if she'd gouged channels in it with her nails. Inside me the dust of my armour reconstituted and slid itself under my skin, but not fast enough to stop the tears that were collecting in my throat.

'Found it!' I heard Jessica's jubilant voice shout from the distance. My head jerked slightly at the sound of her voice. A few seconds later she was back in the kitchen.

'Here we are!' she announced, plonking the rusty clock in front of me. I wanted to slide it on to the floor with my hand and listen to it crash to pieces on the tiles.

'I was right,' Jessica was saying, 'that old visual sense, comes in handy now and then! My grandmother is coming to stay.'

Jessica buttoned up her coat. 'She's been living with my Aunt Freda in France for the past two years and she's coming home on holidays and this clock was originally hers – she gave it to me. I told you that on the phone – so my mother warned me. "Jess," she said, "get that bloody clock before Nan comes or we'll all have to pay the price."'

Jessica brushed her hands through her hair and smiled. 'I'm so relieved to have found it. Anyway, I'll be off. Thanks for the coffee, Séamus. I'll be expecting you at the exhibition, now, mind. You are coming, aren't you?'

I swallowed hard. 'I'll see. Depends on a few things.'

'No, do come, Séamus. I'll be so, *so* disappointed if you don't come.'

She stood in front of me with a mock pout. 'I'll just expect you there and I won't take no for an answer. OK? Oh, my God! Look at the time!' Jessica bent to kiss my cheek. 'Take care.'

''Bye,' I managed, as I stood up on wobbling legs and followed her to the door. I watched as she climbed into a black Saab I'd never seen before. She waved to me before she drove away. Away from me. Back to Dublin. Back to Vin. Vin the architect. Vin the wife-stealer.

Just as I was about to close the front door a silver car drove into the yard. For a second I thought it was Alison Chang, but as soon as the car stopped I could see that it was Chrissie.

'Hey!' she said, as soon as she opened the door of the car. 'I'm looking for my brother and I was wondering if he might be here with Cassandra? I rang but there seems to be something wrong with your phone.'

Chrissie was the most definite-looking blonde person I'd ever seen. Jessica, by contrast, for all that I thought her the most desirable woman on earth, was like a photographic negative with her pale face and hair and sea-water coloured eyes. Chrissie, on the other hand, had dark skin and dark eyes – maybe brown, maybe dark-blue, I wasn't sure. Maybe she was really a brunette with her hair dyed blonde? I had no idea.

'He's not here,' I said, glad to be distracted from my thoughts, 'but come in anyway and have a cup of coffee.'

'Great,' Chrissie said, climbing out of her car and following me into the house.

'So,' I said, sitting down in the chair next to Chrissie as I handed her a cup of the coffee I had made for Jessica and lit a cigarette, 'how have you been?'

Chrissie smiled and lifted her cup.

'I've been fine,' she said, looking at me with those dark eyes. I saw now that her eyes were navy, with flecks of greenish yellow. 'Just fine.'

'You never told me you were an actress,' I said, leaning back in my chair.

Chrissie blinked. 'No. No, that's true, I didn't.'

'But you are?'

She nodded, closing her eyes in assent.

'Why didn't you say?'

Chrissie sighed and opened her eyes. 'I'm not an actress any more. Mostly I write now.'

'I know, romantic novels – or so Cassandra said.'

'Don't knock it. They sell.'

'I'm not knocking it. Far from it. But how come you never told me any of this?'

Chrissie shrugged. 'I don't know. It's a difficult thing to drop into casual conversation.'

I dropped the legs of my chair back on to the floor and my eyes fixed on the scar by Chrissie's lip.

'Where did you get that scar?' I asked, reaching out to touch it with the tip of my right index finger.

'An accident,' she said, not moving as I traced the faint crescent line, 'when I was little.'

'Do you remember it?' I asked, looking into her navy eyes. She looked back at me, not moving, hardly breathing.

'Yes, I remember it well.'

'Were you afraid?'

'Terrified.'

'Poor Chrissie,' I said, before I leaned across towards her and kissed her mouth, just skimming the scar with my lips.

Chrissie kissed me lightly and then pulled away to look at me. Her eyes were wide and she moved her mouth as if to speak, but I couldn't take listening to words.

My head was full of a thumping noise and I didn't know what it was and the only thing that seemed like it might make it stop was kissing Chrissie. So I kissed her again. I pulled my chair close to hers as I kissed her and I could feel her turning towards me. I reached out and touched the curve of her cheek and laid my hand along the side of her face.

The thumping noise in my head was receding, and all of my senses were beginning to fill up with Chrissie. The raw feeling that seemed now to be permanently inside me, felt soothed. I felt so grateful I could have cried.

Deep inside me a debate was raging. Was I using her? Was she using me? What the hell did I think I was up to? Where would all of this lead? But I didn't care, so I refused to listen. As far as I was concerned the parts of me that wanted to debate could debate away, while I concentrated on the warmth that was growing inside me and burning away everything in front of it like a forest fire.

Then the door opened.

'Shit!' I heard Cassandra say as she dropped her handbag on to the kitchen floor with an enormous clatter. Chrissie and I pulled apart and looked around. Cassandra was crouched on the floor retrieving a rolling-away lipstick and handfuls of loose change. She looked up at us.

'Oh, hi, Chrissie. Tim has just left. He dropped me off. He said that was your car, but I thought it belonged to Alison Chang,' she said, cramming everything into her brown leather sack bag and standing up. 'Bloody handbags, I hate them, don't you? And still I keep everything in this – as you can see – and I wish . . . where is Prince? I haven't seen him all day and I thought he'd be here by now. Is he here? Have you seen him?'

I stood up from my chair and grabbed my jacket. 'Out. He must be out, I'd better look for him – he could be worrying sheep.'

'In what sense do you think Prince would worry them, Séamus?' Cassandra said. 'Would he talk to them about money maybe? Because, let's face it, I love Prince but he's too stupid to chase them.'

'Very funny,' I said, not looking at Cassandra. I was angry with her and I knew it wasn't her fault and that she didn't know and hadn't intended to come home at such a bad time – and still I was angry. Where was she all day? Why wasn't she here when Jessica came? And why turn up now that I didn't want her? Typical. I pulled on my coat.

'Well, thanks for dropping by, Chrissie. It was great to see you. Sorry to dash off but –'

'No problem.'

I looked at her and tried a smile. She smiled back at me.

'Don't worry about it, Séamus. I'll see you later.'

I waved at the women in the kitchen and left immediately, lighting a cigarette as I walked out the back door. It was getting dark and the rain had stopped. I walked out of the yard, stopping every now and again to whistle and call out Prince's name. There was no sign of him.

Turning left at the gate, I walked along the road surveying the darkening countryside. There were houses dotted across the fields and up the side of the hills and I could see that their lights were all on and I could imagine that they were all warm and cosy and happy.

Happy families, eating and doing homework and feeding calves and doing whatever happy families in Castleannery did at that time of day. I noticed that some of the people seemed to have added coloured lights to their houses. It seemed odd but looked pretty. Like Christmas.

I stopped walking. It *was* Christmas – or almost. Of course it was, how could I have forgotten? School was closing in a week's time – I knew that and still I'd forgotten. Everything else seemed to be clogging up my mind like a dammed river. Dammed, I thought. Damned? I laughed at myself and started to walk again.

It began to rain and I pulled Mattie's cap from my pocket and jammed it on my head. The feel of the tweed against my neck and the smokey smell reminded me of Mattie and made my chest hurt. But that was OK. I wanted to remember him. And I was glad it hurt.

The rain got heavier as I walked. Covering the field ahead of me in a sheet of grey and a northerly wind began to rise, slicing my cheeks with the freezing raindrops. What a fucking miserable climate. Why couldn't it be all snow and blue skies like Christmas cards?

Which reminded me. I needed to do some Christmas stuff with the kids at school. I hadn't done anything – they probably thought I was losing my mind. And maybe I was. It wouldn't be the first time, would it? And if it happened once then it could happen again or at least that's what everybody thinks, isn't it? That's what I used to think.

Poor Mr Considine. Had to have that leave from school after his wife left. Mattie was very good to poor Mr Considine at that time. Very good entirely. Poor Mattie, God help us. Poor Mattie.

And it was true. Mattie was very good. He gave me Prince and he visited me every day and he was never afraid of my sadness. The rain stopped as suddenly as it had started and the wind grew stronger. Mattie's cap was soaking wet and felt as if it might weld on to my head with ice so I removed it and shoved it back into my coat pocket.

Why are people so frightened of sadness? I wondered, as I walked on in the dark. Are they afraid it's contagious? Afraid that if they tip off your sadness their own sadness will split open like a ripe fruit and spill all over them? I could understand why people might be afraid of madness or anger. But sadness? And yet it seemed to be the scariest of all.

But Mattie wasn't afraid of it. He'd make some tea and tell me about his animals – maybe about a cow that calved or a sick sheep. And then he'd tell me all sorts of other things like snippets of politics from the radio and who was sick in the parish and who was dead and who was getting married and who had recently been married or born.

Mostly I'd just sit and listen to him talk. He didn't seem to need me to respond to him, he'd just keep talking, rubbing his leathery hands together when he laughed and smoking his Woodbines down to tiny stumps.

All the time he spoke he looked straight at me, straight into my sad eyes. Or at least I suppose they must have looked sad if they were reflecting what I was feeling inside. But whatever he could see in them he didn't turn away from it or seem to be afraid of it. He wasn't even afraid to listen to me talk about Jessica leaving.

Whenever I wanted to talk about it he would listen. Nodding at my words, never telling me to stop or making me feel like it wasn't the worst thing that had ever happened to anybody and I should buck up and get on with it. Pull myself together and be thankful for my health and my permanent, pensionable and incremental job and all the other blessings I'd had in my life.

Mattie never said that. All he ever said was, 'I know, I know,' and, 'It'll pass. I know it doesn't feel like it, Séamus, but it'll pass. Everything passes.' It was funny that, when I thought about it.

Mattie didn't try to cheer me up or stop me feeling sad and, in a funny way, as a result, I felt less sad around Mattie.

Around other people I was sometimes consumed by sadness as if in protest to their urging onward and upward.

My mother did that. Tried to stop me feeling sad with protestations of luck and smothering sympathy. And I knew she genuinely wanted me to feel better, but somehow it made me feel worse as if the sad part of me was insisting on having its sadness.

Mattie didn't do that; nor Cassandra – in fairness. She may have managed to destroy my chance for a slice of blissful forgetfulness with Chrissie, but she wasn't one of those who tried to stop me being sad. Cassandra wasn't afraid of sadness. She was a lot like Mattie in that respect. In fact, Mattie hadn't seemed to be afraid of anything, which is probably what got him killed.

I climbed up on to a ditch and whistled for Prince. I could see some sheep grazing up on the hillside. He certainly wasn't there. I called out.

'Prince! Here, boy! Prince!'

But all I heard in return was a cow lowing softly and, for no reason, the sound made my eyes fill with tears. A sudden wind gusted around me and cold rain began to fall on to my face. I climbed off the ditch and sniffed the stupid tears furiously back up my nose and turned towards home.

Prince was surely at home by now. Had I looked upstairs under the bed? No. Had I looked in the sitting room? No. They were Prince's favourite places. Why hadn't I searched there, I wondered, as I wrestled my way home against the wind and freezing rain.

Because I'd wanted to escape. When I was interrupted I hadn't wanted to face Cassandra or Chrissie or anybody. I hadn't wanted to sit around talking and drinking coffee and acting like life was . . . was . . . something it wasn't.

Well, they'd surely be gone. I could go home and correct my homework and go to bed. Jessica's face came into my head and I pushed it away and tried calling Prince again.

'Prince!' I shouted. No answer. So, I walked on, hands in pockets, head down, rain-stung face and water dripping down the collar of my jacket to form tiny freezing pools near my collar bone.

When I reached the yard I was happy to see that Chrissie's car was gone and Cassandra's bedroom light was on; which meant that she was probably upstairs painting her toenails or super-cleaning her already clear skin with some caking concoction or other.

I'd go to my room if Cassandra was around, I thought, as I let myself into the house by the front door. I didn't want to have to talk to anybody and, at the moment, especially not to her.

But downstairs was quiet. I walked through the dark hallway into the sitting room and saw that somebody had left a bottle of whiskey on the coffee table. An unopened bottle. And I knew it wasn't mine and I couldn't have cared less. Grabbing the bottle by the neck I took a short detour to the kitchen to find a glass. Then I climbed the stairs, hurrying all the time in case Cassandra appeared on the landing and I had to talk to her.

Once in my room, I relaxed a little and tore open the bottle, pouring myself a glass full to the brim with whiskey. Then I sat on the end of my bed and, looking out the window into the night, began to gulp big mouthfuls. I had no interest in having a drink. No interest in relaxation or enjoyment. I wanted only oblivion.

Nobody could be expected to stay conscious when they were having their leg sawn off or major heart surgery, I reasoned. This was much the same. I was in the middle of a heart by-pass of sorts. Searching for a way to be in the world that didn't tear my heart asunder. And I was halfway through the operation and in desperate need of an anaesthetic.

I drank like that, swamping my innards to try to drown the pain. Mostly I don't remember what I was thinking, or trying not to think. Pretty soon the alcohol took hold and blurred the world, which felt more bearable. I don't remember too much after that.

I have a vague memory of walking along dark roads to Mattie's grave and of lying on the wet earth talking to him. And I know I fell asleep, not because I remember falling asleep but because I remember waking up, half frozen, with a searing headache and stiff legs, huddled against the wall beside Mattie's grave. Dragging myself off the wet ground I tried to remember if I had driven to the graveyard.

'Fuck,' I said, in reaction to the pain that was like a million bee-stings all over my frozen feet as I stood up. I banged my feet against the ground to try to encourage the blood to return faster. Every time I stamped my feet my head exploded with pain and I muttered more curses.

'Sorry, Mattie,' I said, as the blood began to circulate in my feet and the pain abated. I looked at the silent earth. 'No disrespect. I'd better go home.'

Digging my hands into the pockets of my coat I made my way out of the graveyard, walking as briskly as I could manage in the hope of warming up. I looked at my watch. Four a.m.

The village of Castleannery was like a cardboard outline of a small Irish village. Dark. Silent. A row of houses, huddled together asleep. A wide sweep up to the church with its bell tower. The school. Big, blank, dark windows and tall basketball posts standing guard at each end of the play-ground. Some shops. More houses. Sleeping silhouettes.

As I walked through the village I began to both sober up and wake up and I thought about Mattie and it all seemed a little bit less sore than it had been. Suddenly, I heard the sound of a car door slamming somewhere along the street in front of me.

Instinctively, I stepped into the dark shadow of a hedge and tried to see where the noise originated. I couldn't really see anything from where I stood. Stupid choice of hiding place and, anyway, why was I hiding? What was happening to me?

'All right. Dublin. Eleven forty-five,' a voice said in the night. My heart jumped. I knew that voice, I fucking did, I knew that voice. My alcohol-laden stomach turned over.

The Afrikaner.

A car door slammed again and I stepped away from the hedge so that I could see better, but by the time I stepped out I was just in time to see the taillights of a car disappearing from view. I ran down the street after the car, but it was too late. They'd gone and all I could make out was that the car appeared to be red and that the last two numbers of its reg were 1 and 2.

7

'I'm So Lonesome I Could Cry'
Hank Williams, 1949

I ran back up the street and looked at the quiet houses and tried to think what the murderous bastards could have been doing here in Castleannery, but there wasn't any obvious answer. Everywhere was closed. Everywhere was dark. There didn't seem to be anybody awake in the whole village so all I could conclude was that they had stopped in the village on their way to some other place. But why?

I stopped and leaned my hands on my knees and struggled to get my breath and lessen the pounding in my head and when I looked up I saw that I was outside Tim Winter's house. Before I could think about it I walked up to his front door and rang the bell.

As soon as I heard the ringing in the dark house I was sorry. What point was there in that? Disturbing people unnecessarily. What did I expect him to do? It was too late, they'd already escaped again. The sound of the doorbell inside the house faded and I turned to walk away just as the door opened behind me.

'Séamus?'

I turned around. Chrissie was standing in the doorway of Tim's house. She pulled her pink dressing gown tightly around her and blinked sleepy eyes.

'Oh, Jesus. Look, Chrissie. I'm sorry, all right. I didn't mean to wake you, I wasn't really thinking. Go back to bed. It's a mistake. It's fine. Sorry.'

I rubbed my stubbly chin with my hand and looked at her. She seemed to be trying to focus on my face.

'Come in.' Chrissie stood aside to hold the door open.

'No, look, I'm sorry. Go back to bed.'

'Just come in, Séamus,' Chrissie said, as she walked back into the house leaving the door open behind her. She paused at the end of the hallway. 'Come on,' she said and then she vanished.

I stood on the doorstep looking into the dark hallway for a moment before following her into the house. Fuck it, it was too late now to be sorry and she *had* invited me in, after all, and even if she hadn't I might have asked her because I didn't think I could bear to be by myself.

At the end of the long, dark hallway I could see a light so I walked towards that. Opening the door that ended the hallway I found Chrissie already sitting at a small, circular, white, table-clothed table in the centre of a startlingly white kitchen. White cupboards. White wall tiles. White floor tiles. White cooker. White fridge. White sink. White net curtains at the window. White glass lampshades overhead. Everything was as white as a snowstorm except for a terracotta bowl full of blue hyacinths standing on the draining board.

'Chrissie,' I said, suppressing the impulse to shade my eyes from the glare around me.

'You're drunk,' she said, quietly, looking straight at me, 'that's why you came. You're drunk.'

I looked back at her and there was something different about her, I couldn't say what. But definitely something.

'No, I'm not. I mean you're not completely wrong, I *was* drunk – I don't know, maybe "drunk" doesn't even properly describe the state I was in I was so far gone – but I'm not now and that's not why I'm here, anyway.'

Chrissie shrugged. 'OK,' she said, folding her hands on the tablecloth.

I looked at her again. Why did she look the same but different? Was it because I was drunk? I was so confused I felt as if I was being spun and it made me want to puke.

'I saw him,' I said, taking a deep breath to suppress the regurgitation, 'the man who killed Mattie. Well, I didn't see him but I heard him – out there on the street just now. That voice, I heard it and that's how I knew who it was and now he's gone and there's nothing I can do about it – I shouldn't have come here. Impulse. Pure stupid impulse and –' My voice gave out. 'Sorry,' I whispered.

'So you keep saying,' Chrissie said, smiling at me. 'Sit down. It's hurting my neck having to look up at you.'

I pulled a white metal chair away from the table and sat down beside her.

'Glasses! You're wearing glasses, that's what it is.'

Chrissie laughed. 'I usually wear contacts, but it's the middle of the night. I might lose an eye if I tried to put them in right now and I'm blind as a bat without them.'

'They suit you.'

'Charming devil. You stink of whiskey. Do you want coffee?'

'No, I'm fine and I swear to you I'm sober now. I'm just a bit shaken by what happened. Why would he still be here, Chrissie?'

'Maybe it wasn't him.'

'Wasn't who?' a voice said. We turned around to see Tim standing in the back door.

'I thought you were in bed,' Chrissie said.

'House-call. Who was who or wasn't who?'

'Séamus thinks he saw – heard – the man who shot his friend, Mattie.'

'Did you?' Tim asked.

I nodded. 'Outside on the street not ten minutes ago.'

'Did you get a look at him?'

'I didn't see him, I heard him, Tim. I wouldn't recognize him if I saw him but I heard his voice and that's how I'm so sure that I'm right.'

'The accent,' Tim said, closing the door and throwing his brown leather bag on to the white worktop. His face, normally pale, was grey with exhaustion.

I nodded.

'You're sure?'

I nodded again.

'Why can I smell whiskey?' Tim said, looking around him.

'Séamus,' Chrissie said, standing up, 'I think I will make coffee. Do you want some, Tim?'

'Why not,' Tim said, sitting down beside me in Chrissie's chair. 'Jesus, I'm exhausted.'

'Hard night?' I asked, needlessly.

Tim sighed. 'You could say that. Phil Hanly had an asthma attack. Gina Shandon went into labour and Harry Fitz died.'

'Harry Fitz from over near Newport?'

Tim sighed and nodded. 'Heart attack.'

'He must have been old.'

'Eighty-three. Still, he wasn't the worst of them.'

I nodded and then Tim nodded, and then we sat in silence as Chrissie made the coffee and jumbled cups and plates and biscuits and milk jugs on to the table in front of us. Neither Tim nor I moved to help her. Chrissie poured herself a cup of coffee from the aluminium percolator and motioned towards Tim and I.

Tim poured two cups and handed one to me. I picked it up and started to drink it immediately. It scalded the inside of my mouth, but after the whiskey it didn't make much of an impact.

'I wonder why that guy was here?' Tim said, after a while, resting his elbows on the table and sipping from his cup.

'I should have tried to catch him,' I said, ignoring the question.

'Maybe it wasn't him,' Tim said, 'maybe it was just a coincidence.'

'I didn't even try. I was surprised – but that's not really an excuse is it? I'll be ready the next time,' I said, pausing to take a mouthful of burning coffee. 'I'll never let him go again.'

'I mean, a South American?' Tim said. 'What business would a South American have in Castleannery, for God's sake.'

'South African,' I said, tuning in to what Tim was saying.

'South African. That's right. Afrikaner?'

'Afrikaner.'

Chrissie sighed loudly and Tim and I looked at her.

'You could sleep here, Séamus. There's a spare bed and I'm sure Tim wouldn't mind, would you, Tim?'

'No problem,' Tim said, yawning loudly and then smiling at me. 'No problem at all.'

'No thanks,' I said, forcing my legs to stand up. 'I'll head on home. Thanks for the coffee.'

'Stay, Séamus,' Tim said, looking up at me. 'You're probably not sober enough to drive yet.'

'No, it's fine really. I haven't a car with me, anyway. The walk will be good for me.'

Tim sat back in his chair and observed me. His face was remarkable in the way it had the features and appearance of a boy with the exhaustion and care-worn look of an adult.

'I'll drive you,' he said. 'Don't bother to argue. If I don't drive you home and you get knocked down or something on the way out the road I'll never forgive myself.'

'But –'

Tim held up a hand and shook his head. 'Ah! I have the energy to drive you home, but not the energy to argue. Come on.'

Tim stood up and my aching, dead-legs made me nod in

thanks because they knew what I was too stubborn to admit
– I'd never have made it the whole way home.

'Thanks, Chrissie.'

Chrissie smiled.

'I appreciate it. Sorry I woke you.'

Chrissie shook her head. 'No problem. More entertaining than sleep, anyway.'

'Thanks again,' I said as we left the kitchen.

Chrissie waved a hand at me. 'See you soon.'

I followed Tim out the back door and through the silent garden to where his car was parked. We drove out of his driveway and through the village in silence. Everything looked asleep as we travelled out of the village and into the countryside. You'd wonder how buildings could look asleep but they can. And fields and gates and even the animals and the plants.

Tim put the radio on and it filled the car with the chatter and noise we hadn't the energy to make ourselves. The heat and the motion of the car made me drift in and out of consciousness. I forced my eyes open just as Tim rounded the last bend before my house. And that's when I saw it right outside Pádraig Harrison's house.

'Stop!' I screamed, banging the dashboard. 'Stop the car.'

Tim skidded to a stop. 'What is it?'

I opened the car door and ran back towards Pádraig Harrison's house. There it was. Parked under the huge horse-chestnut tree that grew beside Pádraig's front wall. The Afrikaner's car.

My heart was beating erratically and everything had a sudden sheen of surreality. The house, the car, the shape of Tim trotting down the road towards me. None of it seemed to be substantial.

Had I really found Mattie's murderer? Was it possible that I was actually standing by his car? And what now? Any second he could walk out of Pádraig Harrison's house and then . . . and then what? Would I throw him to the ground and tie him up while we waited for the police?

Maybe I'd wait for him, calmly, in the shadows of the receding night and call to him as he emerged and quietly announce my intention to drag him to the police? Maybe he'd be taken by surprise when he saw me. Or maybe he'd just murder me like he'd murdered Mattie when Mattie unexpectedly got in his way?

I bent down and scrutinized the dirty number plate in the weak moonlight – 99 D 18612. I was confused. I didn't even know if I was afraid. How do you know which of those swirling, liquid gut feelings are fear and which ones are joy and, even, which ones are alcoholic poisoning?

Right then, though, I couldn't have given a shit what I was feeling. All that seemed important to me was that I was being presented with a second chance. Or, more correctly, a third chance. An opportunity to effect retribution where I'd failed to offer protection.

Somehow the murderer hadn't escaped and I had him and soon he'd be sorry for what he'd done to Mattie. I bent to look at the number plate again. 99 D 18612. It had to be him hiding in Pádraig Harrison's. But why here? I turned it over and over in my head until suddenly it all clicked together and I could see the connections as bright as day and only wonder why I'd never seen them before.

Pádraig Harrison and the Afrikaner. As I straightened up I remembered all I'd heard about William Ormston and software designers and multi million pound companies and I could see that they were all in it together.

Maybe even Alison Chang was part of it and had been sent to suss me out. The swirling and shifting in my gut stopped, and my head cleared like a mist that's burned away by hot sun.

It was time for action, time for me to stop dithering. *Will I, won't I, could I, should I.* I'd just go up and bang – hard – on

Pádraig Harrison's door and insist that he hand over the murderous scum he was harbouring. Now. This fucking minute. Let him take his chances with me. I looked around and saw that Tim was standing beside me.

'What are you doing?' he said.

'It's his car,' I said, surprised at the calm in my own voice. 'The Afrikaner. He's here in Pádraig's house. I might have known. That's where he was the first night, isn't it?'

'Séamus?'

'No, I can see it now, Tim. I have to do something. See here?' I pointed all around like a tour guide. 'They've taken away the plastic crime scene tape.'

'They obviously have all the evidence they need from here.'

I shook my head. 'They could have tried for longer. But, fuck it, now it doesn't matter, now I have him.'

I walked away and Tim grabbed my arm. I turned back to find him looking straight into my face. His long, thin face was calm – almost serene – belying the tight grip he had of my arm.

'Where are you going?'

'Guess, Tim.'

Tim tutted loudly. 'For God's sake, Séamus. You're still half pissed. Go home.'

I shook my head.

'No way. Not this time. I keep letting that bastard escape, but it won't happen this time.'

'And what will you do?' he said, his voice quiet and even, but his grip on my arm as steady as ever. 'The house is in darkness – Pádraig is probably asleep, so what excuse will you give for waking him up? Oh, there's a car parked on the road outside your house? For God's sake, surely if the murderer was in there he wouldn't leave his car out on the road like this?'

'Maybe he would.'

Tim tutted. 'Don't be stupid – Pádraig has a big house and a long driveway – why not drive it up and hide it behind the house?'

'I don't know. I just know that I'm not walking away again. I'm going up there to find out what's going on.'

'And what'll you say?'

'I'll say I know he's involved with that murdering bastard. I'll make him come out. Ah, fuck it, Tim what do you want? A pre-prepared speech? I don't know what I'll say, but I can't keep letting that bastard get away.'

Tim rubbed his face with his long, thin fingers. 'You're sure this is the right car?'

'Positive.'

Tim looked at me. 'OK. I believe you, but, even so, I don't think it's a good idea to go barging in there in the middle of the night.'

'If I don't he'll get away.'

Tim shook his head. 'And what's the alternative? What's your plan? That you bang on the door and order Pádraig to hand over the murderer?'

I shrugged and looked at my feet. 'Better that than doing nothing, again. Look, I know he's your friend so why don't you leave? I understand how it is – don't mind at all –'

Tim groaned loudly, cutting off my sentence. 'He's not that close a friend. And, anyway, do you seriously think I'd let him harbour a murderer? Mattie's murderer? I was very fond of Mattie myself, you know.'

We looked at each other.

'I know. Of course you wouldn't help a criminal. But it's the only thing I can think of and, Tim, honest to God, I can't go away again and let him escape. I just can't.'

'No,' Tim said, walking around the car, 'I know you can't, and I'm not asking you to do that.'

'I have to do something.'

'I know, but there's a good chance that if you do as you're

planning. Pádraig Harrison will tell you to get lost and slam the door in your face and if the man who killed Mattie *is* actually inside then he'll be alerted and escape anyway.'

Tim stopped speaking and completed his circuit of the car and then he came to stand in front of me.

'A burgundy Ford Mondeo, 99 D 18612,' he said. 'Write it down.'

'With what?'

'Come back to my car a minute.'

I shook my head.

'Come on. I promise I won't drive you away.'

Reluctantly, I followed him back to his car and sat in the passenger seat. Tim was already writing when I got into the car.

'Now,' he said, handing me a prescription pad with his name and address printed across the top and the registration and model of the car scrawled in black pen across the bottom. 'Open the glove box.'

Obeying Tim, I slid open the latch on the glove box in front of me. Tim leaned over and pulled a mobile phone from the dark compartment.

'Call the Guards,' he said.

'What?'

'Call the Guards.'

'Why?'

'Because you can't just barge in there and demand that the Afrikaner – if it is him – accompany you to the Garda station. I mean whoever owns that car either isn't the murderer and he'll have you arrested for harassment or he is the murderer in which case he probably won't be all that co-operative.'

'But he might get away.'

'We're sitting here watching the car. We'll follow if he tries to get away.'

'OK,' I said, patting my pockets. 'I have a phone.'

Tim watched as I patted and searched. No phone. Bloody phone. Why couldn't I remember to bring it with me, for fuck's sake? It was probably at home in the kitchen as usual. Tim raised his eyebrows and handed me his phone.

I looked over my shoulder at the dark house and stationary car as I took Tim's phone. 'Will I try 999?'

Tim nodded. 'Why not.'

I dialled the number and asked to be connected to the police. A tired sounding woman's voice eventually identified herself as police and I explained my problem.

'OK, we'll try to send somebody out,' she said.

'No,' I said, panic rising in my throat, 'trying to send somebody won't do. You *have* to send somebody out. Is there no way I can speak to Detective Richardson? I thought there was an incident room or whatever you call it. Don't you have some facility for taking messages in the middle of the night?'

'Yes, sir, that's correct, we do have a facility for taking messages in the middle of the night – that's what I'm doing. It's the middle of the night and I'm taking a message.'

'That's not enough.'

'Look. I promise you we *will* get on to it as soon as we can and there *will* be a full report for Detective Richardson in the morning.'

I wasn't happy, but didn't know what else to do. 'OK, I suppose. Goodbye.'

I told Tim what the dispatcher had said.

'OK,' he said, starting the engine of his car.

'No! No. Hold on. Let me out. You go home and get some sleep, Tim. I'm going to stay here until the police arrive.'

Tim shook his head. 'Why?'

'In case he tries to leave, obviously.'

'But he won't and even if he does the police have the registration number of the car so they'll find him.'

I thought about what he said. How much chance did I really, *really* have of stopping a murderer? I'd probably freeze again when it came right down to it. Probably fuck it up as usual and he'd get away again and I'd have made it harder to find the bastards.

Tim was right. I didn't want to alert the Afrikaner to the fact that we knew about him. Or at least not until the police arrived. I wished I knew something else to do, but my head hurt and I felt as if I was going to throw up and apart from puking on the murdering bastard . . .

'Are you sure?' I said, looking at him in the dark. 'Are you completely positive that they'll be able to find him?'

'Positive. It's a brilliant lead. Every car in the country is registered – the police will easily identify the owner. Look, go home and get a couple of hours sleep and phone that detective guy in the morning. They'll surely have picked up our friend by then.'

I looked over my shoulder again at the sleeping house and car. Maybe it'd be best. Better than doing it wrong, anyway. I was no match for professional killers. I was a schoolteacher. I liked folk music.

'OK. OK. Maybe you're right, Tim. I'll go home and they should be able to catch that bollocks without my help. In fact, they'll probably have a better chance of catching him if I don't interfere.'

Tim started the engine and a few minutes later we were outside my house.

'Thanks, Tim.' I said, getting out of the car. 'Sorry to keep you up half the night.'

'Don't worry about it. I'm used to it,' he said, waving at me as he pulled out of my yard and disappeared into the night.

I let myself into the house and wandered towards the kitchen where I saw that it was still only five in the morning. I couldn't bring myself to go to bed and it was too early to phone Paul Richardson.

I made coffee and saw that Prince had come home some-time while I was drinking myself senseless and wandering the countryside. I wondered who had let him in to sleep in his favourite spot in front of the range. Probably me before I left for my pilgrimage of reparation.

Pulling an empty notepad out of my school bag I wrote 99 D 18612 and then the words, 'Burgundy Ford Mondeo'. Then I slowly began to write down an account of everything I'd seen and heard that night. It had to be important. It had to mean something that that man was still around and I knew my head was fuzzy and I wanted to make sure I remembered to tell everything.

As I wrote my head filled with questions that swarmed through my thoughts like killer bees. Why hadn't I con-fronted Mattie's murderer back there on the street when I'd the chance? No wonder Jessica left. No wonder I was stuck in a dead end job in a village school.

I should have gone into Pádraig Harrison's house. But I didn't. I shouldn't have listened to Tim. But I did. I listened because he was saying what I wanted to hear because I'd been afraid, that was the truth of it.

I was just afraid. And it wasn't something noble – like being afraid that I'd tip off the killer and let him escape – no matter what I tried to tell myself. It was simpler than that – I was afraid he'd kill me. Shoot me like he had Mattie. And so I'd jumped at the first suggestion of escape. OK, Tim, sure Tim, you're right, Tim, three fucking bags full, Tim.

I tried to ignore the battle in my guts and wrote as furiously as if I was being chased. When I finished writing I trudged upstairs to the shower in the hope that it might make me feel human.

By the time I was showered and dressed it was eight a.m. I decided to try ringing Paul Richardson, but a gruff man told me he wouldn't be in until nine o'clock, so I stuffed my scrawled account of the night's happenings into my school bag. Then, because I couldn't bear the sound of my own thoughts one minute longer, I went back upstairs to wake Cassandra.

'Why are you drinking at this hour of the morning?' Cassandra groaned as I leaned over her and poked her shoulder to wake her up. 'It's disgusting. You smell like a wino. Are you drunk?'

'No, not any more,' I said, sitting down on the bed. 'Wake up. I have to talk to you.'

'Jesus, it's the middle of the night,' she said, propping herself up on a pillow. 'Hey – did you drink the whiskey that was in the sitting room?'

'I'll give you the money for it, for fuck's sake.'

'Shit, that was a present for my parents from Tim.'

'OK, I'll give Tim the money for it. What's the big deal?'

Cassandra dropped her arm and sank back down into her pillows. 'What's wrong?' she said, rolling on to her back and blinking her brown eyes as she rubbed her face awake.

'The man who shot Mattie. I saw him again.'

Cassandra sat straight up in the bed. 'What? Where?'

'In the village.'

'And what was he doing?'

I shook my head. 'I don't know, but I heard him shouting to somebody. Clear as a bell in that weird accent – *All right. Dublin. 11.45.*'

'And how do you know it was him and not somebody making a date with his girlfriend?' Cassandra said, sitting upright in the bed and reaching for a cardigan to pull on over her pyjamas.

'Because there aren't that many Afrikaners in Castleannery and even fewer on the street at four o'clock in the morning.'

'Four o'clock in the morning? What the hell were you doing in the village at that hour?'

'Nothing.'

Cassandra looked at me.

'Visiting Mattie's grave,' I rushed, not meeting her eye. 'But it's not important why I was there. I'm not a murderer like that bastard, so I can go where I like.'

'Séamus,' Cassandra interrupted, putting her hand on my arm.

I pulled away. 'What I was doing doesn't matter. What was *he* doing? Why is he still here?'

'But four o'clock in the morning? I have to say –'

'Forget about that and concentrate on what I'm saying.'

'No, I won't forget about it. You have to promise me something.'

'What?'

'For God's sake, stop going out in the middle of the night. Get drunk if you want but stay in the house – you're worse than a tom cat – and you meet *way* fucking weirder people around here at that time than you'd expect.'

'Cassandra, pay attention. Why was he here? What does it mean?'

'I don't know. But if you're right and it was him –'

'I am right. I went into Tim's – Chrissie was there and Tim came in from a housecall and drove me home and then we saw it again outside Pádraig Harrison's house.'

'Saw what?'

'The Afrikaner's car. We rang the police on Tim's phone and they said they'd send someone, but they wouldn't put me in touch with Paul Richardson. I can't get through to that man. I've been trying for hours now. You'd think they'd take murder investigations more seriously.'

'It's still early,' Cassandra said, squinting at her watch. 'Jesus! Very early. You'll get him after nine.'

'I suppose,' I said, standing up and pacing up and down beside Cassandra's bed.

'Maybe the car belonged to somebody else,' Cassandra said, plumping her pillows and then settling back to watch me pace.

'I doubt it,' I said, pausing for a moment, 'but maybe. Tim said the Guards'll be able to trace it. But whatever about the car, the voice was definitely his. I'll never forget that voice even if it did take me a while to pin down where it was from. I'll still never forget the sound of it.'

'OK. What was he doing in Castleannery then? That's the real question, isn't it?'

'Or one of them.'

Cassandra swung her legs out of bed and pushed her feet into her tattered sheepskin slippers. 'Come on down to the kitchen and we can talk about it there. I need tea.'

Cassandra enveloped her small body in a huge yellow, fleecy dressing gown and I followed her downstairs.

'I wonder if we should try to find out ourselves what's going on,' Cassandra said, as we sat in the dim kitchen listening to the kettle boiling.

I looked at her. 'The police can do that. That's why I rang them.'

'Yes, yes,' Cassandra said, responding to the sound of the boiling kettle by making a pot of tea, 'but just say that they don't have any success – then maybe what we need to do is to start looking ourselves. In some ways it'd be easier for us to find a stranger around here than it would be for some Guard from town. And it'd certainly be easier for us to keep an eye on Pádraig Harrison.'

I looked at Cassandra – asymmetrical brown eyes, thick black eyelashes, slept on cropped, black hair, sleep-crease marks on her bright face – and the sight of her annoyed me.

'It's not a game,' I said, picking up my school bag.

'I didn't say it was a game. I said we should try to look for that man ourselves. That's all I'm saying.'

'Well, I'd better get going or I'll be late for school,' I said, suddenly so annoyed with Cassandra that I couldn't bear to be in the same room.

'I might ask around,' Cassandra said, sitting down at the kitchen table and tucking her feet up under her. 'You should keep trying to get hold of that detective and tell him what you saw.'

'Your help has been invaluable,' I said, grabbing my coat and my school bag, as I struggled to hold on to my temper.

'Oh yeah – one other thing – your mother rang yesterday. Said to remind you that Eamon will be home on Friday.'

'And?'

'And that you promised you'd go home this weekend.'

'I know,' I said, 'I hadn't forgotten. Why did she ring?'

'I dunno. I'm just reminding you. I think I'll stick around here for the weekend if you don't mind.'

'It's your own decision.'

'I can look after Prince.'

'Whatever you like. I'm off. See you later. If you're home.'

'Bye,' Cassandra said, largely ignoring me as she sank into some sort of a reverie. 'Don't worry, you will see me. I'll be home later if not sooner.'

I slammed out of the house and into my car and as I drove to school I thought about how annoying Cassandra was being and I was sorry I'd bothered my arse to wake her to tell her what happened.

As soon as I walked in the classroom door I was confronted by a fist fight. Jamie Fitzgerald, a tall, blond angular boy and Richard Neulon a short, dark, bullish boy, were rolling on the floor in front of my desk.

The air in the room was filled with a combination of noises. Grunts and growling sounds from the fighters, jeering and encouragement and squeals of distress and excitement from the spectators.

I dropped my bag inside the door and grabbed both boys by the back of their uniform sweaters and pulled them apart.

At first they resisted, still blind with fury and frothing a foam of vengeance from their mouths.

'Give it over!' I shouted as they strained against me to reach each other. Gradually, the resistance subsided as their overwhelming instincts ebbed and they realized it was me and that I was the law in their world and that they had no choice but to obey.

'This is ridiculous!' I said, shaking each boy a little to emphasize my words.

'Yes, sir,' they muttered in unison.

Neither boy looked at me. They both stared in sullen silence at their shoes and I knew in my heart that behind those drooped eyelids a million plots were being hatched to consummate the fight as soon as I was out of view.

'No more fighting.'

'No, sir.'

'Get back to your seats and behave yourselves, for God's sake.' I released my grip, suddenly, so that both of them staggered slightly before returning rapidly down the aisles of the classroom to their seats.

The physical exertion of breaking up the fight seemed to help me to snap into the now and made it possible for me to teach my class. At eleven o'clock, while the children were on their break, I persuaded Ann Ryan, the sixth-class teacher, to take my yard duty and walked out of the school grounds and punched the number of the Limerick Garda station into my phone.

'Séamus,' Paul Richardson greeted me as he came on to the line, 'how are you?'

'Did you get my message? Did somebody go to the house? Did you find him? Arrest him? Did you –'

'Séamus. Hold on a minute. We did. We did. A car went there early this morning – before seven and there was nobody there but an elderly lady – an aunt of the man who owns the house.'

'Pádraig Harrison.'

'Yes. Pádraig Harrison's aunt. Even he wasn't there himself. And there was no other man there. Certainly no Afrikaner man.'

'And the car? What about the car? Because I did see him – or at least I heard him – last night in the village and I know he was there.'

'Are you sure?'

'Positive. And if Pádraig Harrison wasn't there then maybe he brought him somewhere before I arrived. Maybe he abandoned his car and Pádraig drove him.'

'The car was stolen yesterday afternoon in Dublin. It's registered to a Betty Phillips from Blackrock in Dublin.'

'I know it was the same car,' I said, my stomach knotting. 'I'd swear it was and I'd swear it was that murdering Afrikaner bastard that I heard last night.'

There was total silence on the other end of the telephone for a few seconds.

'I believe you,' the soft Cork voice said, at last, 'but there isn't anything we can do for the moment. We did fingerprint it but –'

'Nothing.'

'I'm afraid not.'

'But if Pádraig Harrison is involved –'

'We have no proof. Nothing. You didn't even see the suspect at the Harrison house last night, did you?'

'No.' Fuck it. I knew I should have gone in.

'So we'll just have to keep our powder dry for the moment.'

I didn't answer.

'Séamus?'

'Yes.'

'Do you agree?'

'I suppose.'

Then silence for about a minute.

'You took away the tape,' I said then, breaking the silence.

'The tape?'

'The crime-scene tape – from outside Pádraig Harrison's.'

'Oh, that. Yes, we did. But it doesn't mean we're not still working on it. We still have to analyse everything we found at the scene.'

'Did you find much?'

He paused and I could hear him inhale a cigarette. 'I can't say. Not at the minute.'

'You didn't find anything.'

He sighed. 'No. No, not a lot.'

'Ah, well,' I said, pretending a philosophical disposition.

'Look, I'm sorry about this, but that's often the way of it, Séamus. If you can just be patient for a little while. I know it's hard. Listen, don't forget to call in and see Boru next time you're in town.'

'I'll do that. All right, thanks for your help. I'd better get back to class. See you.'

I disconnected without waiting for him to say goodbye. My chest hurt with anger. Did nobody else care that Mattie Ahern was murdered? I rolled my tattered account of the night before into a cylinder-shape. Everybody seemed to be full of other things they had to do and I knew that people had lives, but still I wanted it to be important to them that someone had shot Mattie dead.

I walked, blindly, back into the school and down the corridor to my classroom, bumped every few seconds by anxious children trying to contain the high spirits they'd been allowed to release for fifteen minutes and were now required to push back inside them for the rest of the morning's lessons. My class tumbled back into our room and I stood at the top trying desperately to push my own half-released ragged parts back inside so I could continue teaching for the rest of the day.

*

When I returned from school the house was empty, as usual. For fuck's sake, I thought, as I dropped my bags in the hallway, was Cassandra ever around any more? Even if she was out taking photographs and trying to make some kind of a living that might be something. But she wasn't. She was just arsing around the countryside with the local GP.

I opened cupboards and the fridge looking for something to eat. The whole thing was totally out of hand, I thought, as I threw bread and butter and an assortment of ham and salad on to the worktop.

And what if somebody needed a doctor? Did they ever think of that? What if somebody got sick and there was no doctor around because he was otherwise occupied with my cousin? I bet they never thought about things like that. Oh, no, just did what they wanted and to hell with everybody else.

The whole parish was probably ailing and in danger of death because my cousin was leading the only doctor in the region astray. I made myself a sandwich and opened the back door, whistling for Prince.

I'd watch TV, I decided, as I chewed a mouthful of sandwich. Fuck her – fuck Cassandra – at least if she wasn't around it meant I could do as I pleased. Eat when I felt like it – my stomach was still a bit delicate after its recent feed of whiskey – and just watch TV with Prince. That way I might even be able to avoid thinking without having to get drunk and Cassandra could just fuck off for herself.

I whistled for Prince again. At least Prince was loyal. He'd snuggle his snout into my leg and go to sleep as I watched TV and make me feel as if I had some sort of contact with another living creature. But there was no sign of him. I closed the back door and, picking up my sandwich and the newspaper and a mug of tea, made my way into the sitting room.

'Prince?' I called, whistling softly as I opened the sitting-room door and switched on the light. Everything was still. No Prince. Only a patch of clear floor surrounded by a rectangle of dust where Jessica had removed her clock. Fucking clock.

Maybe Prince was asleep somewhere else in the house? I switched on the TV and walked back to the bottom of the stairs, calling his name and whistling. Silence.

Bloody dog. I went back to the sitting room and sat on the couch and closed my eyes. Where was he? I listened to the sound of the newsreader's voice receding into the distance. Where could Prince be? And where was that Afrikaner bastard, now? Where was Jessica? Gradually all the questions begin to merge together and I fell asleep.

When I awoke, a man was hammering a gazebo on TV and I could see through the uncurtained window that it was night. My mouth tasted of the remnants of last night's whiskey and my head was reverberating to the sound of the hammering.

Sitting up, I ate the remains of my ham sandwich and drank my cold tea. Still no sign of Prince. I listened to see if I could hear his whine. Maybe he'd been locked out in the rain – he hated that. Silence. For the first time I began to feel a cold nub of worry in my gut. Had he been knocked down by a car? Had he acted against all our expectations and worried sheep and been shot by a farmer? Where the fuck was he?

I stood up, painfully, and made my way into the kitchen. After swallowing two paracetamol I opened the back door and looked out at the rainy night.

'Prince!' I shouted, pausing to whistle. 'Prince! Here, boy! Come here, this minute, Prince!' I whistled again and then stopped to listen. Then I whistled yet again. Still no Prince. I stepped out the door.

Maybe he was behind the shed. Sometimes he went there searching for rats. The rain seemed to be getting heavier as

I walked across the yard. It wasn't like Prince to stay out in the rain. He didn't like to get wet. He liked to sleep on his cushion in the kitchen in front of the range. Other than that he liked to eat and chase a ball, and that was about it for Prince.

As soon as I approached the shed I saw him. Before I ever reached him I knew he was dead. But knowledge, at the beginning, is really only so much information. Just like every other event of significance in my life, at the start the reality of what it meant was as far away as China, as foreign as eating beetles and as distant and unconnected as the tiny planets that twinkle at us as stars.

So, without a pause for thought or examination, I bent down and picked Prince up in my arms, walked across the dark yard and laid him, gently, on the back seat of my car. Then I sat in and drove the five miles up the road to the nearest vet.

I banged on the door of the vet's house and led Billy Ryan, the vet, through the pouring rain to my car. Without speaking I opened the back door of the car and pointed to the dark, motionless shape. Billy bent into the car and leaned over Prince for a few seconds, then he straightened up and looked at me.

'He's dead, Séamus.'

The rain pounded on Billy's hatless, bald head and he blinked as he looked at me.

I shook my head. 'But he's young,' I said, slicking my wet hair away from my face, not liking the sound of the words as they were spoken outside me. 'And there aren't any marks on him, are there? At least I couldn't find any, are there, Billy? Can you see any marks on him?'

'No,' Billy said, his middle-aged eyes full of sympathy and I noticed that they were crinkled at the corners from too many years squinting into the sun while talking to farmers. 'No marks that I can see, but I'd need to examine him properly. Can I bring him into the surgery and look at him? I'd need to bring him inside if I was to be able to tell you what happened.'

I didn't answer. Billy put his hands into the pockets of his pants and sat back on his heels as if we had all night to stand beside my car in the pouring rain.

'My guess is that he was poisoned,' Billy said, as it became clear that I wasn't able to answer. 'A lot of farmers poison their land and he may have eaten something, but I can't be sure till I examine him. Will I take him inside?'

I looked at the shape of Prince lying there on the seat and I didn't want to think about Billy Ryan poking him and cutting him open.

'It won't hurt him,' Billy said, as if he could read my mind. 'I promise you.'

I looked at him and nodded and then I leaned in and scooped the stiffening dog up in my arms and followed Billy into his warm house. In the hallway we met a teenage boy in a torn T-shirt.

'Mr Considine,' the boy mumbled, pausing at the foot of the stairs.

I looked at him. 'Ricky?'

The lanky boy smiled and nodded.

'I'd hardly know you. How are things?'

The boy shrugged his thin shoulders and I could see underneath the acne and the burgeoning man's shape the eleven-year-old that I'd taught only three years before.

'OK,' he said, looking at Prince in my arms. 'What happened?'

'We don't know, yet,' the boy's father said. 'Poor old boy seems to have been poisoned.'

Ricky looked at Prince and then he looked at me. 'I'm sorry. That's sad.'

The suddenness of the sympathy made me catch my

breath and the accuracy of the statement swamped me. Ricky was right. It was sad.

I nodded.

Ricky bit his bottom lip and then sighed deeply. 'What can you do?' he said, then, as if he knew what it meant. Maybe he did. I hoped he didn't.

'Well, that's life, I suppose, Ricky,' I said, to cover up my feelings. 'You're right. What *can* you do?'

The boy shook his head and turned to climb the stairs. I watched him for a second and then I followed his father into his surgery.

Billy Ryan turned on the lights and motioned me towards the examining table. I laid Prince gently on to the disposable sheet that covered the table. He seemed asleep. A bit stiff and his eyes were closed, but Prince spent so much time asleep that it didn't look like an entirely unnatural posture for him. Billy Ryan caught me by the arm.

'I'll get at it straight away and I'll ring you as soon as I know anything,' he said, gently propelling me back towards the door. 'I may have to send some stuff off to the lab to get exact results, but I should have a good idea once I have a chance to look at poor Prince and I'll let you know straight away.'

He paused to look at me. But I wasn't able to work out what he wanted from me so I just looked back at him in silence.

'OK, Séamus?'

'OK,' I said, as I realized he wanted my permission. 'OK, that's fine.' Even I could hear that my voice sounded flat.

Billy Ryan motioned me towards the door and led me back through his house into the night.

'Get some rest, Séamus,' he said, as we walked. 'A good night's sleep always makes things better. Go on home and I'll ring you in the morning.'

I stepped out Billy Ryan's front door into the night and

walked straight to my car without stopping. Sitting into the car, which still smelled of Prince, I started the engine, lit a cigarette, found a loud rock station on the radio and drove home. As soon as I pulled the car into the yard in front of the house the door flew open and Cassandra ran out, dressed in a long, white nightshirt.

'Séamus!' she shouted as she ran through the rain in her bare feet. 'Séamus!'

I jumped out of the car and caught her just as she slid on a patch of mud near the car.

'What?' I shouted, pulling her upright and holding on to her bare arm. 'What's wrong with you?'

'Oh, Séamus, oh, Jesus – somebody was in the house. The back door was open and everything was thrown on the floor and all the dishes were broken and the floor was all wet because the rain came in.'

I dropped her arm and look at her.

'Come on inside. I'm soaking wet,' I said, turning away and walking into the house.

I felt so tired that I could have just laid down on the wet concrete and slept right there and then.

'You were asleep in the sitting room when I came in,' Cassandra was saying, as she trotted behind me across the dark, wet yard and into the warm bright house.

'I didn't want to wake you so, I decided that I'd leave you alone for a while. I went upstairs and had a bath. I was doing my nails when I heard you drive away. I didn't come down immediately – I had a face pack on so I read a magazine for a while. I didn't hear anything, that's the weirdest part. Anyway, after a while I came downstairs to make some tea and when I walked into the kitchen I found this.'

Cassandra and I had reached the kitchen by the time she'd finished her litany and she waved her hands at the mess on the floor. The floor was still wet and the butter dish lay upturned, but unbroken in the middle of the debris.

Cassandra picked up the sweeping brush and began to brush at the shards of porcelain sprinkled on the floor. I took the brush from her.

'Put something on your feet, for Christ's sake. How stupid can you get?'

'All right! All right!' Cassandra said, disappearing into the hallway and reappearing in her tattered slippers.

'I can't believe you walked around in this without putting on your shoes,' I said, sweeping furiously. 'What kind of an idiot –'

'OK, OK, I get the point. I was upset. You're right, what can I say but it's all right. I'm not cut, am I?'

'Dumb luck,' I said, scooping the remains of the dishes on to a plastic shovel and into the dustbin. I bent down to pick up the butter dish. How had this happened? I wondered, as I scraped butter off the floor. Who had been in my house? What the fuck was going on?

'Will I make tea?' Cassandra said, standing in front of me.

I looked at her, having somehow forgotten that she was there, but then I thought, that might be because she was never there when I needed her, mightn't it?

'Tea? Or do you want coffee?'

'Sure,' I said, walking to the dustbin and stamping on the pedal. 'Whatever you're making, I don't care.'

I dropped the laden butter dish into the bin and let the lid snap shut.

'Why did you throw that away? It wasn't broken.'

'I wanted to,' I said, wiping the damp floor with an old towel. I wiped and wiped at the tiles on the floor until they were almost dry. Behind me I could hear Cassandra making tea.

'It's all a bit scary, Séamus, isn't it?'

I stood up and washed my hands at the kitchen sink and didn't answer.

'Do you think that somebody came into the kitchen?' she said.

I sighed and lit a cigarette.

'You're smoking way too much,' Cassandra said, putting two mugs of tea on to the table and sitting down.

'Just leave me alone, all right?'

Cassandra gave an indignant snort and took a mouthful of tea. 'Well?' she said, swallowing her tea. 'Do you? Do you think somebody was here and broke all the dishes and stuff?'

'Obviously.'

'Obviously?'

'Everything was broken so *obviously* something happened.'

'Yeah, but did – did someone, you know, come in and do this?'

I shrugged. 'Who knows? I might have left the back door open and a wild cat or a ferret or something could have come in.'

'OK. That sounds good. A wild cat. I like that. If it was a cat Prince'll get him. Where is he I wonder? It's not like him to stay out in the rain.'

'Prince is dead,' I said, too tired to cushion the blow.

The colour disappeared from Cassandra's face and her eyes became huge coloured mirrors.

'What?'

'Prince is dead. I'm sorry for telling you like this, but I can't think of how else to tell you and it's no worse anyway than finding him like I did – he's dead.'

'Where is he?'

'Billy Ryan's. I found him at the back of the shed and I took him there . . . Billy said he thought he'd been poisoned, but he'd examine him and find out.'

'Poisoned?'

'Poisoned.'

'But why poison poor Prince?'

'I have no idea, but somebody did. I'm going to bed. I can't stand upright another minute.'

'Now? You're going to bed now? You can't go to bed now. We should ring the police? What about Prince?'

'Prince is dead,' I said, walking towards the hallway. 'And there's nothing I can do about it and I have to sleep.'

'I can't believe you're going to bed. I'll never be able to sleep.'

'Then stay awake,' I said, walking through the doorway and up the stairs.

'Cassandra?' I called from the top of the stairs. There was no answer. 'Cassandra?' I called again.

'What?'

'Do you know it's almost Christmas?'

Silence.

'Well? Do you?'

'Obviously.'

'I didn't. Goodnight.'

I walked into my bedroom, not waiting for her to reply. Not caring. I didn't care about anything at that moment. I didn't care if Cassandra was scared, or who killed Prince or Mattie, or why, or if we were in some sort of mortal danger – all I cared about was lying down. The bed seemed to call to me. Seducing me into it. I pulled off my boots and climbed into bed, fully clothed, and fell asleep immediately.

8

'Fattening Frogs for Snakes'
Sonny Boy Williamson, 1957

I left the house next morning before Cassandra even woke and I was glad to be leaving because I didn't know that I could actually bear hanging around the house for a whole weekend without Prince. What kind of a bastard would poison a dog? It wasn't worth thinking about it. None of it was worth thinking about.

It was a bright morning, for a change, and as it was still only nine o'clock by the time I arrived in town, I surprised myself by deciding to visit the market before going home. I parked my car by the courthouse and walked the short distance to the market.

The stalls were set out with the usual array of fruit, vegetables, cakes, cheap clothes and, in deference to the time of year, Christmas decorations and electronic Santas that laughed and bent at the waist. I found myself looking into the faces of the throngs around me and wondering what was going on in their lives.

Did those women with the headscarves bartering with the stall-keepers really have dark secrets that haunted their sleep? Did that man in the baseball cap selling carpets have a past he couldn't escape? Who was the woman with the streaked blonde hair selling lace and lavender sachets? Could these be the kind of people who would poison a dog? Betray their husbands? Shoot an old man?

I bought a fruitcake and a dozen apples before giving up

the delaying tactics and setting off for my parents' house. My mother answered the door when I arrived.

'Well,' she said, hugging me and kissing my cheek. Then she smoothed my hair and hugged me again. 'You're here.'

I nodded and we walked together to the kitchen. My father was making scrambled eggs.

'Will I put your name in the pot?'

'That'd be great.'

I sat at the kitchen table and looked around me. It looked the same as usual. Oak presses. White walls. Green tiles on the floor. The carved, dark-wood African mask that they'd brought home from a holiday in Tenerife. How could it all look pretty much as it had looked all my life when so much was different now? Stop all the clocks, as the man said.

'Seamie, boy!' My brother Eamon threw open the door to the kitchen. I stood up. We hugged, briefly, and then he stepped back and looked at me.

'Heard you almost got shot,' he said.

'Eamon!' my mother said.

'Not really,' I said. 'They didn't even see me.'

'Sorry about your friend. I remember him from when I was home at Easter after . . . do they know who did it?'

I shook my head and thought of Prince, but I couldn't make the words come out. Couldn't take the sympathetic looks. Sym Pathetic. Pathetic. That was me.

'Or why?' he asked.

I shook my head again. 'An attempted robbery they think. Mattie was in the wrong place at the wrong time.'

'God. And in Castleannery of all places,' Eamon said. 'Who'd have thought?'

'I know,' I said.

'And apart from that?' Eamon said, pausing to look straight into my face. The Jessica question. I smiled and it made my face hurt, but I didn't care.

'I'm grand. Not too bad at all.'

'Well, you're lookin' good on it,' Eamon said, thumping my shoulder.

'Which is more than I can say for you. That stubble makes you look like an IRA fugitive.'

'Very funny, Séamus, very funny. You obviously know nothing about fashion. Is Cassandra with you?'

'Still in Castleannery. How's New York?'

'Good enough, good enough. New job – did I tell you that?'

'No.'

'Yeah, that old bastard Franklin left.'

'The guy from Mayo who was head of your department?'

Eamon nodded. 'Fucking won the lottery last month! Can you believe that?'

'Eamon!'

'Sorry, Ma. Anyway, he won the lottery and retired. And guess what?'

'You got his job?'

'No. Tom Mangan – remember him from school? He got it, but then I got Tom's job – head of marketing.'

'Well done.'

'Thanks. Is that scrambled egg for me Dad?'

'Yes,' our father said, winking at me. 'Maybe if we give you food you'll stop talking for five minutes. You Yanks – all the same, never shut up!'

'Yeah, yeah, yeah,' Eamon said, laughing as we all sat around the kitchen table. 'It'd take more than a plate of scrambled eggs and toast to shut me up, Da.'

Eamon and I were together for most of the day before he said anything else to me about my shit life.

'So tell me. Really, Séamus. How *are* you doing now?'

I looked at him and listened to the din from the Roman epic we were watching on TV as we waited for the football match to begin. Eamon glanced quickly at me and smiled before turning his attention back to the living Technicolor lion wrestling.

'Now there's a real man for you,' Eamon said, laughing as a gladiator snapped the lion's neck and strode victoriously from the sandy arena. 'They don't make them like that any more, do they?'

'No,' I said, and suddenly I wanted to tell my big brother everything. Tell him how I was really doing. Explain how I was failing. Maybe if I asked Eamon he'd know what I should do? How I should act. Eamon laughed again as two leather-clad gladiators leaped around wielding heavy swords.

'Can I ask you a question?' I said.

'Sure. What time is the match kicking off?' Eamon asked.

I leaned over and looked at the newspaper. 'Three. Coverage begins at two.'

'Thank God for the Premier League,' Eamon said. 'I don't think I'd survive too many more Roman epics.'

I nodded again. Eamon turned his head to have a look at the TV screen. Advertisements were flashing across my peripheral vision. I stared as a tall, blonde woman, who reminded me of Chrissie, twirled in a field of long grass. 'So? What was it you wanted to ask me?' Eamon said.

I didn't answer. He sat up and looked around the side of his armchair at me.

'What?'

'No,' he said, 'that's *my* question. What? You said you wanted to ask me something so go on, go ahead and ask.'

I leaned back into the couch and closed my eyes. Eamon, I wanted to say, Eamon tell me how to be in the world. You're my brother and you're older than me and you have a good life – or at least it looks good – and I'm lost and abandoned and fucking completely at sea and don't know what to do or how to be . . .

I could have puked with the pressure of how much I

wanted to ask him and I thought that maybe I could ask him, maybe it would be a good thing because, well, because he'd want to help me. I knew he loved me and was glad I was alive and not shot by the bastards who killed Mattie.

But I was afraid to ask because it just seemed like more weakness on my part that I *needed* to ask him in the first place. And yet I didn't know what else to do or how to continue with my life if I didn't get some answers. And I didn't know who else I *could* ask. I couldn't ask Dad – he'd be upset or tell Mam or generally not be able to bear hearing what a failure I was.

So that left Eamon and I could ask him but, if I did, what would happen then? I felt like a man standing on the windowsill of a burning building trying to psyche himself into jumping to safety.

'It's just –' I began, teetering on the edge. 'I don't know what I –' and just as I was forming the words in my mouth and preparing to spit them out, the door opened and Jessica walked in.

'Séamus!' she called, running towards me and throwing herself on to the couch beside me. She put her arms around my neck and pulled me close and kissed my face at least a dozen times. I was so surprised I didn't even move, just sat like a dummy in her grasp.

'Séamus,' she said again, when she'd finished her kisses. She pulled away and smiled at me. 'Séamus, Séamus, Séamus – it's so good to see you.'

I looked over her shoulder and saw that my mother was standing in the doorway, her cardigan pulled tightly around her as she watched the tableau in her sitting room. Then I heard Jessica's name and the voice that called it was so similar to mine that I wasn't sure it wasn't me speaking out loud.

Jessica looked around, still holding my hand with one hand as she brushed tears from her eyes with the other.

'Eamon?'

She jumped up from the couch and rushed to exchange kisses with my brother.

'Jessica. Well, well, well, how the hell are you?'

'Oh, you know how it is,' she said, returning to sit beside me and picking my hand back up in hers. 'Busy. My sister Janice had a baby and we thought we'd pop down and see her.'

'That's nice,' my mother said. 'A girl or a boy?'

'A boy. Ultan. I rang Castleannery this morning to tell Séamus about Janice's baby and Cassandra told me you were here. I couldn't believe it, so I thought I'd pop in just to say hi.'

'Will you have tea, Jessica?' my mother said in a voice like crushed ice.

'No, Helen, thanks. I'm really just paying a flying visit, I'm very, very '

'Busy,' my mother interrupted.

Jessica nodded. 'Yes, busy, you know how it is.'

'Jessica,' another man's voice said, and in the doorway behind my mother I saw my father.

'Tom,' Jessica said, in a descending tone, 'great to see you.'

My father didn't answer and also didn't come into the room, which left both of my parents positioned in the doorway like bouncers. The thought made me smile and I looked away for a second and tried to compose myself. Silence descended in the sitting room and I hoped nobody thought I was going to be able to progress the situation because I hadn't a clue what to say.

'Well, I have to fly,' Jessica announced, suddenly, solving the problem. 'Just dropped in for a minute to see Séamus. I really can't stay.'

'That's a pity,' Eamon said, standing up, 'maybe we'll get together some other time, eh, Jess.'

Jessica stood up as well. 'Yes, that would be good. Well, great to see you all, see you soon.'

I smiled at her, but stayed sitting.

'Goodbye, Séamus. Maybe we could get together over Christmas? I'll be home for most of the holiday. How about we have a drink. Catch up. What about it? You come along as well, Eamon. How about Stephen's night? Sevenish?'

'Oh, Jess,' Eamon said, rubbing his stubbled chin with the tips of his fingers, 'what a pity – I've promised the world and his mother to meet Christmas week. And you're not around either Séamus, are you?'

I looked at Eamon and he returned my look with a disagree-with-me-and-you're-dead look I remembered from our childhood.

'No. Sorry.'

Jessica looked at me.

'I'd forgotten that. Séamus is off to Dublin straight after the Christmas dinner to see Maura, aren't you, love?' my mother suddenly said. Everyone in the room looked at my mother then and she pulled her cardigan closer to her body.

'Did I tell you that, Tom?' she continued, looking around at my father.

'No. You didn't. Who is Maura?'

My mother laughed a high, tinkling laugh like wind-chimes. 'Tom, for goodness sake! Maura? Séamus' girl-friend?'

'Oh *that* Maura,' my father said, grinning at me, and now he looked like he might wink. I wondered if he was at all bothered by how proficiently his wife could lie. 'Lovely girl, Maura. Have you met her yet, Jessica?'

Eamon coughed loudly. 'Excuse me,' he spluttered.

'No,' Jessica managed, but even I could see that she was knocked sideways by this turn of events.

'Well, we must try to get together some other time, Jessica,' Eamon said as soon as he'd recovered his breath.

'Yes,' Jessica said, still clearly stunned. Though not much more stunned than I.

'Well, there you go now. Funny old world. It's a pity you have to rush off,' my mother said, her body so far out the door she was almost ordering Jessica to leave. 'Perhaps we'll see you again soon. Give our best to your mother.'

Jessica took the rather loud hint and walked towards the door.

'Bye, Séamus,' she said, turning back to give me a watery smile. 'Have a nice time in Dublin.'

'Thanks,' I said, still sitting down.

'No more wild and dangerous escapades now,' Jessica said, raising her hand to wave.

'No. I'll try. Bye, Jess.'

I stayed sitting on the couch and watched as my brother, mother and father shepherded Jessica out the door. Eamon came back into the room and threw himself sideways on to the armchair, his long legs dangling over the arm.

'Is it starting?' he asked.

'Just about to.'

And then we both watched as lines of men filed out on to a football pitch in the driving rain and the game began. My mother's head appeared around the door.

'Anybody need anything?'

Well, maybe an explanation, I thought, but I said, 'No, thanks, Mam.'

'Eamon?'

'No, Mam, thanks.'

Two minutes later my father came into the room and the three of us watched the match. It was insane and I knew it was insane. We should be talking about what had just transpired in the room. But we weren't and we weren't about to, and I thought it might be mad but then again it was no madder than everything else that had happened and at least the football was better.

*

Eamon never asked me who the fictitious Maura was so I presumed he asked Mam and she'd admitted what she had done. I couldn't believe that my mother had lied to Jessica. I'd never known my mother to do something like that and I couldn't understand this sudden change. I could have asked her, I suppose, but I didn't know what I'd say, so I just left it.

The rest of my Saturday at home continued as if nothing untoward had happened and Sunday was much the same. Every so often I'd catch my mother looking at me as if she wished she could see through my skin and find out what was going on inside. But when I caught her eye she'd just smile and carry on with what she was doing.

As the weekend wore on I moved further and further away from the idea of talking about what was going on in my life. Or even what was going so badly wrong in my life. What was the point in talking about it? What the fuck would I say? Where the fuck would I start?

I just needed to get on with it.

I waited as late as I could before leaving Limerick for Castleannery. I didn't want to have to deal with Cassandra. I needn't have worried. By the time I arrived back it was eleven o'clock and my house was in darkness and reverberating with the lack of Prince to welcome me home. I slammed the front door and went straight up to bed, annoyed with myself for being disappointed. What had I expected, anyway? I might have known she'd be out.

I slept fitfully all that night. Waking every couple of hours to look at the clock and wonder why my dog had been poisoned. I vaguely heard Cassandra come in at some point, but I was half asleep and mixed up the sound of her footsteps with a dream of drums and being chased by a herd of angry elephants.

Eventually it was morning and I could get up and get on

with the day. I was exhausted and confused. I felt as if I'd slipped down into a black hole and I wasn't sure there was ever going to be any way out for me. I hadn't the first idea of where to begin to solve my problems or what they meant or why things were happening.

So I just decided to let the whole big shit-heap that was my life alone. I was sick and tired, and fucking useless at solving the problems anyway, so I let it all sit on the edge of my consciousness, like a paddler trailing his feet in a river.

The good news was that at least it was almost holiday time. All I had to do was survive until Wednesday and then we'd have our holidays. Then I'd be free. Though I wasn't sure what I wanted to be free for – to brood? Mope? Reflect on how my life was slipping out of my control? It didn't make much difference. I'd been doing versions of that for weeks anyhow, and at least once I was on holidays I wouldn't have to try to educate a roomful of children at the same time.

I struggled through the last few days at school. The Nativity play was on Monday, and the school resounded with the noise of small people running back and forth along the corridors, with tea towels on their heads and dressing-gown costumes to make them look like Middle Easterners. This year the cast was drawn from the younger classes so thankfully I wasn't involved. Just as well really considering that I'd only recently realized it was Christmas time.

Tuesday we had the concerts and the children sang and danced with tinsel-glistening hair and faces shiny with excitement. My class were lucky to be presenting anything at all as their teacher was having a nervous breakdown. But I hid all the madness away and scraped together all the songs we'd learned since September – including a rousing chorus of YMCA. The parents loved it. And nobody saw that I was unravelling – which was the main thing.

So I survived the concerts – glad of the diversion really –

and smiled at the Christmas cards and presents that were left on my desk. All the time eyeing the clock, counting down, waiting for those last three days to pass. And eventually they were over.

Finally, it was Wednesday. I made my excuses to avoid the annual teachers' dinner, waved goodbye, wished dozens of Happy Christmases and left for home. When I arrived home, still clutching my cache of presents, Cassandra was sitting at the kitchen table, pale faced and half-heartedly reading a magazine.

'You're here. That's unusual. Tim busy?'

'Billy Ryan rang.'

'Oh?' I said, as I filled the kettle.

'Prince was poisoned.'

'Well, I think we might have figured that out.'

'Maybe. I called the police.'

'About?'

'About their Christmas card list. I was worried I mightn't be included.'

'Oh right,' I said, refusing the bait.

Cassandra slammed her magazine on to the table. I looked at her.

'Don't you care? Doesn't it bother you at all that Prince was poisoned?'

'I can't see the point in ringing the police. If they can't find who killed Mattie they'll hardly find who killed poor Prince.'

'I think you're wrong. All of these things might be connected and, anyway, they're crimes and you have to report crimes to the police. I rang them this morning and they seemed to take it quite seriously.'

'Really? Do you want tea?'

Cassandra shook her head. 'No, thanks, I have some. They did, Séamus. That detective you spoke to when Mattie was shot – he's in charge of the investigation.'

'I know that. I told you that ages ago.'

'Well, I suppose I forgot. Anyway, when I rang he actually came out here to the house and spoke to me and took a statement.'

'Paul Richardson?' I said, pouring myself a cup of tea.

Cassandra nodded. 'Yeah, he said that it was probably a very frightening experience having stuff broken in the kitchen like that and the dog killed and that he'd look into it. He'll be calling back.'

I sipped my tea.

'What do you think?'

'Nothing. I don't think anything about it.'

I looked around the kitchen, reflexively, for Prince and though I knew he was dead, somehow I was still surprised not to see him snoring on his cushion in front of the range. I drank more tea.

'Séamus what is *wrong* with you?'

'Nothing,' I said, putting down my cup and lighting a cigarette. 'No, that's not strictly true, there is something wrong with me. Why didn't he come here when I saw the Afrikaner's car? He barely spoke to me on the phone. Barely sent someone to investigate. Why was that?'

Cassandra rubbed the top of her head. 'I don't know. I thought you said he did send someone out and that the car was stolen?'

I blew out hot, angry breath between my lips.

'Yes, yes, I did say that and they did do that, but I'm telling you that car was driven by the man who murdered Mattie Ahern and if they took me seriously then they'd have kept pursuing that line of enquiry until they found the Afrikaner.'

'Maybe. But he might be harder to find than you think. I must have asked fifty people about him after you told me you thought he was around and not one of them had ever heard of him or anybody like him anywhere in these parts.

In fact, to be honest, hardly any of them even knew what an Afrikaner accent was –'

'What?' I interrupted.

'Nobody saw him or heard him or really even knew what I was talking about. Old Mrs Morrissey in the cottage at the end of the hill was absolutely hilarious. She made me tea and told me all about her brother – Cedric – imagine, that was his name. Anyway, Cedric was a priest and he lived most of his life in Africa working on the missions. It was like *Dancing at Lughnasa* without the dancing.'

'Christ. Mrs Morrissey is bats by the way. I don't think she ever had a brother so she probably *was* telling you the plot of *Dancing at Lughnasa*. She does that. She told me once that she'd been a spy for the Americans during the Second World War.'

'Well, maybe she was. Spies exist so somebody has to be a spy, don't they? Why not Mrs Morrissey?'

'Forget that. Who else did you ask about the Afrikaner?'

'Everybody. I was thinking after you left for work and I thought why not ask around – if I'd found out anything I could have told the police, couldn't I, and it'd help them in the long run to have somebody asking questions for them, wouldn't it?'

I shook my head and lit another cigarette.

'What?' Cassandra said.

'Nothing.'

'No, Séamus it's not nothing. What are you thinking? Was I wrong to go around asking questions?'

I sighed as I exhaled. 'Bit late now.'

'What do you mean "late"?'

I shrugged.

'Séamus – if you have something to say just say it.'

I shrugged again. 'Prince is already dead.'

Cassandra's eyes widened. 'What are you saying?'

'Nothing.'

'Yes you are, you're saying I had something to do with Prince being killed. That's what you're saying, isn't it?'

I stared at her and didn't respond.

'Isn't it?'

'I'm not saying anything, Cassandra. You're doing most of the talking around here as usual.'

'Yeah, but you're implying that Prince being poisoned had something to do with me. But even you told me that Billy Ryan said he probably ate some poison put down by a farmer.'

'Maybe,' I said, 'it makes no difference and we'll never find out. I think the whole thing is a waste of time, frankly, but if you want to get all hot and bothered trying to solve the crime, go right ahead with your Nancy Drew impersonation. It's just that, personally, I don't think we'll ever solve anything and I'd advise you to be a bit more careful with your actions from now on. OK?'

Cassandra's lips quivered and she looked as if she might cry. She put down her cup and stared at the table for a while and when she looked back at me her face was more composed.

'I think you're wrong,' she said.

I shrugged. 'Maybe.'

'No, definitely – but, well, you might be right about Prince . . .' Cassandra's voice tapered off and her small frame shook for a moment. I watched as she drew in long, deep breaths. 'I think you're wrong about the rest of it,' she said, as soon as she'd stopped shaking. 'I think we should all work together to try to find out what's going on and I think we'll eventually find the murderers and know why all of this is happening.'

'Do you?' I said. 'Do you really?'

Cassandra straightened her shoulders and took a deep breath. 'Yes, I do.'

'Oh.'

'I have a theory, actually.'

'Really? Do tell. I'd love to hear it.'

'Alison Chang.'

'Alison Chang? Is that your theory? You think Alison Chang killed my dog? Maybe you think she killed Mattie as well?'

Cassandra shrugged.

'You can't be serious.'

Cassandra fiddled with a corner of the discarded magazine.

'I'm completely serious,' she said, not looking at me. 'I'm not saying she killed Prince or Mattie but I am saying she might be involved in some way.'

I tutted loudly.

'She's a liar. She told you – and me – lies about who she was and why she was here. We know nothing about her. She could be anyone.'

'Yes. But that doesn't make her a murderer or a dog killer.'

Cassandra flipped the magazine open and leaned forward as if she was reading it. 'I know that. That's what I just said but I thought we should look for her. See what she knows. Even if she didn't do anything bad she might be able to help us. It is a lead, after all. Mattie was murdered. Prince was murdered. Somebody or something came in and broke up our kitchen. Alison Chang lied. All I'm saying is that it's a lead . . .'

And that was it. Something that had been battered by Jessica and murderers and dog killers exploded inside my head.

'*My* kitchen,' I said, slowly.

Cassandra looked up at me.

'Not *our* kitchen Cassandra,' I said, '*my* kitchen.'

'OK. Your kitchen.'

'Good. I'm glad that much is clear.'

'Clear but not the point,' Cassandra said, sitting back in her chair.

'Oh? Exactly what is the point so? Maybe you'd bestow some of your great wisdom on me, Cassandra.'

'The point is that we have to try,' Cassandra said holding my eyes with hers. 'We can't just sit here and be threatened and beaten and not even try to defend ourselves. Not even try to find out who is doing this and to make them stop.'

'Oh, *that* point,' I said, lighting a cigarette. 'I already understand that particular point, Cassandra, and I'm sure you'll be glad to hear that I have every intention of defending myself and as for sitting here, well, you don't need to sit here at all, as it happens, do you?'

'What do you mean?'

I took a deep breath. 'You can go home, Cassandra. There is no need for you to put yourself at risk any longer by staying here and, frankly, I didn't want to say it but now we're on the subject – well, I'd be happier if you did leave. I think I prefer living alone at this stage in my life.'

Cassandra stood up with a noisy scraping of her chair. One emotion after another skittered across her face. She stared at me as if looking to see if she could find an explanation.

'You want me to go home, Séamus? Is that what you're saying?' she said at last, in a soft voice.

'Yes,' I said, through tight, thin lips, 'that is precisely what I'm saying.'

Cassandra pulled herself up straight and smoothed down her hair. 'Fine. That is completely fine. I have no intention of over-staying my welcome. I'll go home immediately.'

'Whatever you like,' I said, folding my arms and leaning back against the range. Cassandra bent to pick her handbag off the floor and walked towards the door. 'I'll go upstairs and pack and then I'll be out of your hair as soon as I can arrange a lift to the bus.'

'I'll bring you to get the bus.'

'Don't bother. I'll telephone Tim, and don't worry about the phone call. I'll pay you for the call.'

'Have it as a Christmas present,' I said in an even, controlled voice.

'Shove it,' Cassandra said, disappearing through the door.

I stayed where I was standing, listening to the low murmur of her voice on the telephone and then the sound of her feet pounding up the stairs and around the first floor of my house. Good, I thought. Go. Get out of my house.

You're never here when I need you, anyway. If you'd been here they couldn't have killed Prince in the first place and if you'd been here then you'd have helped me with Jessica and all the other things. Pretending to be my friend. Pretending to be here for me when all the time you're here to make cow-eyes at the bloody stupid doctor. I punched the wall beside the range.

'Fuck, fuck, fuck, fuck, fuck.'

The red-hot pain in my knuckles made me look. They were covered in matching red blood. I could still hear Cassandra pounding around and I wanted to be gone before she came down. I'd take Prince for a walk across the fields, that'd get me out. My heart dropped. I couldn't. No more Prince. No more nuzzling, idiot dog. No more walking companion. I'd have to go by myself.

Grabbing my jacket I slammed out the back door and across the back of the yard to the fields behind. As I climbed over the rusty gate that separated my yard from McCarthy's field, I heard a car pulling into the yard. Tim Winter coming to save his damsel in distress. Well, let him. Let him save her. In fact, let him save whomever he wanted. I'd had it with the whole fucking lot of them.

I walked across the empty field and climbed a second gate and sat on its slightly warped top, watching the cows graze their way slowly around the field. It was almost completely dark but it didn't seem to be that long since I had come home from school.

What date was it anyway? December what — twentieth?

Yes, the day before the shortest day of the year. The Winter Solstice. I wished it was summer. I wished it was even spring. Anything but this black, endless twilight. Nothing clearly visible and nothing properly hidden.

I thought about Jessica's visit and how I'd allowed myself to hope. I'd promised myself I wouldn't do that. I wouldn't hope any more and still, when she was there in front of me, every one of the ordinary pauses in her conversation was being filled in by the tumbling words in my head.

Words I wanted to hear more than anything. *I love you. I want you. I want to come home. I'm sorry I left.* But she didn't say any of those things, no matter how many times I hoped to see her lips form them and hear her voice curl around them, it didn't happen.

I just had to face it, be a man, for once, and face it. I had to see why she didn't say those words and look it in the eye and not be afraid. She didn't say them because she didn't want those things. She didn't want me. Why would she? All she wanted was her clock. Her stupid, broken, ancient clock was what she wanted – not me.

But I never seemed to learn. Why was that? Why was I so stupid that I couldn't learn? Why was I always hoping, always being stupid? Leaving myself open. It had to stop, it just had to stop. I couldn't survive much more of it.

I was a man, for fuck's sake. A man and, surely to God, as a man I should be tougher? Men were tough. I knew it wasn't politically correct any more to say it out loud but everybody knew it was still the case. And even if they were expected to be nurturing and caring and in touch with their feminine side – they were still expected to be tough. Still expected to be men.

How had it happened that I'd never learned to be tough? Was it my father's fault? Was Eamon tough? Or did he just seem tougher than me because he was my older brother and he used to hit me a thump whenever I annoyed him?

I thought he probably was fairly tough. Tougher than me anyway – which wouldn't be hard. Well, I'd had it with being a fucking fool. I was fucking damned if I was going to carry on the same way – it couldn't be done. I wouldn't survive if I kept going the same way.

I was just going to have to get my shit together I decided, as I hopped down off the gate and walked across the wet grass. Once and for all I was going to learn how to be in the world. Maybe I'd change my job?

Teaching children – what kind of a job was that for a man? And sure I liked the job but the money was shit and maybe if I'd gone and taken a different job to begin with – like Pádraig Harrison – then maybe everything would have been different.

I was clever. You have to be clever to be a teacher – and I was resourceful and imaginative and innovative, or at least as much of those things as Pádraig Harrison. Or Jessica's architect.

I climbed another gate and walked towards a small copse at the edge of the field. Every cow I passed took a small glance at me and then continued chewing.

'Maybe I'm not as harmless as I look,' I said aloud to a Friesian cow. 'I've eaten a lot of burgers in my time, I'll have you know.'

She looked at me with her big, liquid eyes and then turned her head away.

'And I wear leather shoes,' I said, as I moved further away. 'Be afraid of me, can't you. Be afraid.'

As I reached the trees it occurred to me that there might be a bull somewhere in the field that I hadn't noticed. I hoped there was. Wrestling a stampeding bull would be as good a start for my life as a tough guy as any other.

Or maybe there might be murderers waiting in the copse of trees. That was the kind of place murderers waited. But the copse was empty except for the scurrying noises of small animals. I found that I very quickly became bored of walking without Prince, so I soon gave up and went home.

Cassandra was gone when I got back. I knew she would be and now that I'd cooled off I was sorry she'd gone and sorry about the way I'd treated her. So I had to talk myself back into a state of righteous indignation with her as I made my dinner and read the newspaper in the silent house.

I turned on the TV to dissolve the silence but by half eight I was almost as exhausted as I had been the night Prince died so I made my way, slowly, up to bed.

As I drifted off to sleep I heard the telephone ring and decided to ignore it and let whoever it was go away or leave a message or ring back later. Which is why I awoke at seven thirty in the morning to the sound of my mother calling me and banging on the front door.

For a minute I thought I was at home and that my mother was calling me for school. The sound of a stone pinging against my bedroom window, however, eventually woke me up properly. I opened the window and from all that distance I could see the top of my mother's head.

'There you are,' my mother said as I opened the door, 'and you're all right. Thanks be to God. Séamus, where were you? I was worried about you.'

My mother hugged me and kissed my face and then marched past me to the kitchen. I followed like a small child.

'Nice to see you, Ma,' I said, leaning against the worktop and lighting a cigarette.

'And you, Séamus,' my mother said, looking at me from under her eyebrows as she took off her coat and hung it neatly on the coat hooks in the hallway just outside the kitchen door. I never used them. I hung everything on chairs. My mother came back into the kitchen.

'I see you're still smoking.'

'Yes,' I said, and I inhaled deeply as if to prove I wasn't

just pretending. 'Didn't you notice that last weekend when I was home?'

My mother smiled. 'Well, you gave them up before, I thought maybe you might have gone again.'

I shook my head.

'OK, so,' she said in her organizing voice as she looked at the sink that was overflowing with dishes, 'we could start by getting these washed, couldn't we?'

She rolled up her sleeves and filled the sink with suds and steaming water. And as she worked and I smoked, I marvelled at how I could hear all the unspoken words, the reproaches about health and wealth, the worries about where I'd been and if I was all right. I imagined the conversations she and my father might have had after Jessica left and I had haunted the world like an empty wraith trying to survive having my innards ripped out.

'He'll be fine,' my father might have said. 'Really, Helen, he'll be fine. These things take time.'

And my mother might have shaken her head or it's possible that her eyes might have filled with tears. 'No,' she might have said, 'no, Tom, he won't. Look at him, you can see he's not all there as it is. Séamus is soft. He isn't able for it – not for any of it. See how sad he looks? Can you really tell me that he'll ever not be sad?'

But none of this was visible on my mother as she washed dishes and hummed 'Bridge Over Troubled Water'.

'So,' she said, as she clapped the last cup on to the draining board and let the sudsy water gurgle down the drain. Drying her hands she turned to look at me. Her hazel eyes looked into mine and I unaccountably remembered handing her a homemade card when I was about six and how her eyes had sort of twinkled as she looked at it.

'So?' I repeated.

My mother smiled. 'I thought I'd just pop down for the day. Your father is away for a couple of days – London –

'and I was off work and I thought, sure I'll go see Séamus.'

'And what about Eamon?'

'Eamon is fine. He's gone to Dublin for the day as it happens. Martin Phelan is home from Australia and I think they've gone up to see some other friend.'

'Willie Healy,' I said and lit another cigarette. 'He said something about it at the weekend all right.'

'When are you getting your holidays?'

'Yesterday.'

'Good. You're very pale – you could do with a rest. And what day are you coming home? Maybe you should come home today altogether. Have a bit of a rest before Christmas. I'm sure Cassandra will want to go home early, unless of course she wants to come and stay with us and she'd be more than welcome, though Lucy'd go mad if she didn't come home.'

'Cassandra has already gone home,' I said, trying to keep all expressions off my face while knowing that my mother was capable of accurately reading the back of my head.

My mother looked at me. 'Just now? This morning before I arrived?'

'Yesterday. I . . . we . . . she decided she wanted to get out of here for a while, things haven't been great . . .'

'Home?'

I nodded.

'It's just that I stayed with Lucy last night and I could have been mistaken but I'm fairly sure neither of the girls were there.'

'She may have gone somewhere with Tim first. That's always possible.'

'Tim?' my mother said, predictably.

'Her new boyfriend. The local GP. I haven't seen much of her recently, to be honest. She and Tim have been spending a lot of time together.' I paused, hoping that my mother would be appalled that Cassandra was running around with some local guy instead of keeping me company.

'Oh, right,' she said, absentmindedly, tapping the worktop with the index finger of her right hand. 'That's nice. Why didn't she tell you if she was going on holiday first I wonder?'

'She doesn't tell me everything,' I said, staring down into Prince's empty basket.

'Oh,' my mother said. I glanced up and she was looking at me, so I looked back at the chewed tartan blanket that still smelled of Prince even from the distance. 'I heard about Prince. I'm very sorry, love.'

'Who told you?'

'Lucy. Cassandra told her on the phone. She was very upset.'

I nodded and crushed out my cigarette. Fucking Cassandra. Couldn't keep her mouth shut if she was paid.

'Séamus?'

'Yeah'

'Why didn't you tell us when you were home? About Prince, I mean.'

I shrugged. 'I don't know.'

'I'm so sorry, love.'

I nodded and my mother stepped forward and hugged me. The minute her arms went around me my eyes filled with tears and I longed to be a small boy and slide into her embrace and let her sort out the world for me. But I couldn't. I was trying to grow up. Trying to be tough. So I pulled away and swallowed three or four times.

'What can you do?' I said, remembering Ricky the adolescent. 'What can you do?'

It seemed like a good thing to say. I could see why Ricky might like it. Philosophical and manly at the same time. Not a Neanderthal reaction and not a wimp's reaction. Perfect. I was in much the same place as Ricky, if the truth be known – we were both tough guys in training. My mother squeezed my arm and moved away.

'Toast. I'd love a slice of toast. Will you have some,

Séamus? You can't have nicotine by itself for your breakfast, you know, they say it's bad for you.'

I looked up at my mother and she smiled at me. 'I'll make toast. It's the least I can do considering that you just washed all the dishes.'

'Grand. Let me fly upstairs and powder my nose while the toast is on.'

I put bread in the toaster and made a pot of tea, piling plates and cups on to the table while I waited for my mother. I wondered about Cassandra. Where could she be? Why hadn't she gone home?

She must still be at Tim's. She spent all her bloody time with him anyway while she was in Castleannery, she might as well stay there altogether. That was probably it. Tim's house. Unless . . . A tiny fibre of worry took root inside me but I stamped on it.

Yes, I said to myself buttering toast, that'd be about right. She should marry Tim altogether and just become the GP's wife, forget about work, forget about her photography. She could dust sideboards and polish silver and give tea parties to polite women in twin-sets.

'So,' my mother said as she came back into the kitchen, 'upstairs looks lovely. Have you painted?'

'No,' I said, tossing toast on to a plate. 'Here, Ma, eat before it gets cold. Would you like something else? A boiled egg or something.'

'Not at all, not at all,' my mother said, smiling at me as she sat down at the table. 'This'll be lovely. Any bit of jam in the house?'

I opened the fridge and took out a jar of homemade blackberry jam that Cassandra had bought. Then I sat down opposite my mother.

'Lovely,' my mother said, unscrewing the jar and smothering her toast in the jam. I couldn't eat so I drank tea and resisted the urge to smoke.

'Are you positive Cassandra wasn't at home?'

My mother chewed a mouthful of toast and nodded.

'Positive. I have an Aran cardigan in the car that Lucy asked me to bring down to her.'

'Right,' I said, fiddling with my teaspoon, 'probably at Tim's.'

'The boyfriend?' my mother said.

I nodded. We sat in silence. When my mother finished her toast she laid the knife neatly across her plate and reached for the teapot to pour herself more tea.

'I suppose it wouldn't be any harm to give her a ring,' my mother said.

I shrugged.

'I mean is she going home? Is she staying there? What am I to do with her cardigan?'

I stood up and took my mobile phone from the dresser and handed it to my mother.

'Call her,' I said. 'Her number's in the phone. I have to go take a piss.'

'Séamus!'

'Sorry. Sorry. I thought you were Eamon.'

I climbed the stairs two at a time and made good my excuse by using the toilet. Fucking typical of Cassandra to cause even more hassle. When I returned to the kitchen my mother was looking at my phone as if it was about to do something.

'Did you ring?' I asked.

She nodded. 'No reply. It's ringing all right but there's no reply. Does she usually use her mobile phone or is she like you?'

'She loves that bloody phone.'

'OK. Well maybe we could give her boyfriend a ring?'

I sighed. I really didn't want to talk to Cassandra, but I also didn't want to explain why to my mother.

'What did you say his name was?' my mother said.

'Tim. Tim Winter.'

'Do you have his number?'

'Of course. He's the local GP and, anyway, I know him.'

'Great. Maybe you'd give him a ring so, if you wouldn't mind, love. I'd hate to drag that cardigan the whole way home again.'

'OK, if you like,' I said, standing up, immediately anxious to get it over with.

'No, love, there's no need to do it now. In a little while will be fine.'

'Look, I'm standing up now, I may as well ring,' I said, as I walked towards the phone in the hallway. 'Nothing as heavy on the suspensions of a car as an unplaced Aran cardigan.'

I walked into the hallway and dialled Tim's number and wondered if he'd even be there. What time was his surgery? Maybe he'd be in bed? What time was it anyway? I looked at my watch. Ten o'clock. Chrissie's voice answered the phone.

'Hi Chrissie, Séamus Considine here. Sorry to disturb you.'

'Good morning, Séamus. I hope you're OK after your adventure the other night.'

'Oh, fine, fine, you know yourself. I didn't think you'd still be around.'

'Neither did I. I don't know what's wrong with me. I can't seem to face up to leaving Castleannery. I must be getting fond of the place.'

'You'll have to stay here altogether.'

'Maybe I will, you'd never know. Anyway, what can I do for you, Séamus? Are you looking for Tim?'

'Well, yes and no. I'm looking for Cassandra more than Tim, and I thought Tim might know where she is. She's not staying there with you lot is she?'

'No. I don't think so. I haven't seen her around, though it's possible that she's here someplace and I don't know about it. Hold on, Tim is in the kitchen, I can hear him, he'll know. I'll get him for you.'

I listened to the sound of Chrissie's shoes receding and then the softer noise of Tim's shoes approaching and somewhere in the background a radio was playing 'Lola'.

'Séamus,' Tim said, 'what can I do for you?'

'Sorry to disturb you, Tim. I know you're probably up to your eyes but I was wondering if Cassandra was around. My mother is here and she has some stuff that Cassandra's mother asked her to deliver to Cassandra.'

'No,' Tim said, slowly and thoughtfully, 'no, Séamus. Cassandra went home yesterday. I drove her to the bus. I thought you knew that. She told me . . . well, that you knew.'

'That we had a fight and I asked her to leave? Well, that's true. But are you sure she went home, Tim? My mother seems to think she isn't there. She didn't go anywhere else, did she? She has a friend in Dublin – Sheila is her name, I think – she often stays with Sheila.'

'No,' Tim said again, and I could hear a new note in his voice. 'I put her on the bus yesterday evening. I wanted to drive her home but she refused. Said she wanted to think. Where could she be? Unless, as you say, she changed her mind and went to see her friend after all?'

'Maybe,' I said, trying not to respond to the rising worry in Tim's voice. 'That's it, I'd say. You know Cassandra, as capricious as they come. Look, I'll get on to Sheila and see if she's there. Thanks, Tim.'

'Séamus?'

'Yes?'

'Maybe you'd get back to me when you locate her?'

'No problem. I'll either ring you or get her to ring you herself as soon as I locate her. Thanks, Tim.'

'Talk to you later, Séamus.'

I hung up and stood in the hall trying to fit the pieces together. Tim brought her to the bus. She was definitely homeward bound. It was unlikely that she'd have been able to get a bus or train to Dublin; by the time she got into Limerick it'd be too late to make the connection.

That meant that even if she was planning to go and stay with Sheila she'd have had to go home first and travel to Dublin next day. I began to lose hold of the fear that'd been growing inside me.

'Well?' my mother said as I walked back into the kitchen.

I took a deep breath. 'Well, she doesn't seem to be there. Not with Tim, anyway. He put her on the Limerick bus yesterday evening and presumed she was going home.'

I picked up my mobile from the kitchen table and tried Cassandra's number. It burred in my ear and I waited. Eventually a woman's voice told me I'd reached Cassandra's number and to leave a message.

'Call home,' I said. 'Everyone is looking for you.'

Then I hung up and tried ringing the number again.

'These bloody mobile phone networks,' I said to my mother who was watching me, 'very unreliable. It's always worth trying to get through a few times.'

My mother nodded and cleared dishes off the table. I tried Cassandra's number yet again, aborting the call halfway through the dull burring noise and throwing the phone back on to the table.

'She's probably gone to Dublin to Sheila for a few days,' I said, as an idea formed. 'Christmas shopping or some such girl thing. Would you ring Aunt Lucy and get Sheila's number and I'll call her and see if I can talk to Cassandra? I don't want to ring Lucy myself and worry her unnecessarily.'

My mother adjusted her pink, lambswool cardigan and took a deep breath.

'Good idea,' she said smiling, but I could see that she was worried. 'I'll do that straight away.'

I poured myself a cup of lukewarm tea and lit a cigarette while waiting for my mother to get the number. Two minutes later she came back into the kitchen and handed me a slip of paper.

'Great. What did you tell her?'

'Nothing,' she said, helping herself to the same lukewarm tea.

I looked at her and she paused in her pouring.

'OK. I told her lies. I thought that was best, don't you?'

'Excellent idea,' I said, making my way back to the phone.

As Sheila's phone rang I imagined Cassandra answering and how I'd be angry and aloof and bark out orders for her to phone her mother and her boyfriend. How could she be stupid enough to worry everybody like this – especially considering everything else that had been happening? But the phone rang on and on and just as I was ready to give up a sleepy voice answered the phone.

'Hello?'

'Hello? I wonder if I could speak to Sheila, please?'

'Speaking,' the sleepy voice drawled. 'What can I do for you?'

'Hello, Sheila, I don't know if you remember me. I'm Séamus Considine, Cassandra's cousin . . .'

'Séamus! Hi, how are you? Sure I remember you, what can I do for you?'

'I was wondering if you'd seen or heard from Cassandra at all?'

'No, not for a few weeks. The last time I heard from her I thought she said she was down staying with you for a while.'

'That's right. Are you sure, Sheila? You haven't been out or away or anything?'

'No. I've had a bit of a flu so I haven't been outside the door in a week. Bloody thing. Is everything all right?'

'Just a bit of a mix-up here at this end. We've managed to get our wires crossed. Nothing major.'

'OK, that's good. Will I get her to ring you if she turns up?'

'Please,' I said, listening to the increasing tempo of my heart as it pounded in my ears. 'Thanks, Sheila.'

'No problem, see you.'

I hung up and turned around to find my mother standing behind me, arms folded, face closed. I shook my head in answer to her unasked question.

'There's only one thing for it,' my mother said, pausing to take a deep breath and straighten her not even slightly out of place cardigan, 'we must telephone the police.'

9

'All Day and All of the Night'
The Kinks, 1964

We didn't telephone the police immediately, though I suspected that my mother would have preferred if we had. Instead, all the rest of that day and all that evening we called everybody we could think of who might possibly know of Cassandra's whereabouts. But nobody had seen or heard from her for weeks. Apart from Tim, I was the last person who seemed to have seen her and I hadn't a clue where she could be.

In between these phonecalls we tried Cassandra's mobile number over and over and over again. By early evening it wasn't even ringing, just going straight to her voicemail and I was beginning to develop a serious aversion to the voice that kept telling me to leave a message.

'She can't have just vanished,' my mother said, late on Thursday night when we'd exhausted our list of possibilities and given up on Cassandra's own phone.

'No. She can't.'

I poured tea and we sat in silence at the kitchen table. My mother's face was lined with anxiety and she pulled her cardigan so closely around her it was almost stretched enough to button at the back.

'You cold?' I asked, wondering if that was why she was hugging herself so tightly in her cardigan. She shook her head and sipped tea from her mug.

'No, I'm grand.'

'Oh, OK,' I said, sipping some of my tea, 'good. That's good.'

My mother smiled again and we returned to silence. We couldn't talk because if we were to talk someone would have to say things neither of us wanted to hear. It would be unavoidable that we would have to mention the possibility of Cassandra meeting some – literally – unspeakable fate.

So we drank the tea. The fridge hummed and the clock ticked and in a field nearby a cow lowed but we didn't speak.

'OK,' I said, standing up as soon as I finished drinking my tea, 'will we go to bed? There isn't much left that we can do tonight and, who knows, she might turn up by morning.'

My mother stood up as well. 'Good idea. I can hardly see I'm so tired.'

We walked together, in silence, and on the upstairs landing I bent to kiss my mother goodnight. As my lips touched her cheek she caught my head between her hands and kissed me on the forehead.

'Goodnight, love.'

I looked at her and her eyes were full of tears and I couldn't bear it because it meant she was as frightened for Cassandra as I and that might mean I wasn't mad but actually, horribly, right.

'Night, Ma,' I said, ignoring what I'd seen, 'sleep well.'

I went into my room and closed the door in case my mother tried to say aloud the thoughts that were floating in the air between us. My body ached from exhaustion and tension and I was sure that I'd fall fast asleep immediately. I was getting good at that – sleep escape. But even though I was exhausted almost to the point of pain, every time I closed my eyes the horror thoughts inside my head swirled like a bad 1960s movie effect.

I turned on to my stomach. No better. Flipped on to my back. Gave up and sat up and tried to read. No use. The words jiggled on the page and made my eyes water. I turned off the light and lay down on my back. No go. I flipped on to my side and tried deep breathing and imagining calm and pleasant places. Still no luck.

I sat up in the dark, lit a cigarette and tried to make myself think about Jessica. It was ironic – distracting myself from one pain with another. But I couldn't think about Jessica. All I could think about – no matter where I hid or what I tried to do – was Mattie being murdered and how if Cassandra was dead it'd be all my fault.

I eventually fell into a raw and fitful sleep shattered by the ringing of my alarm clock at seven o'clock. But I was happy it was morning even if I was fit to puke with exhaustion. What day was it? Friday.

I got up and went downstairs to find my mother already up and dressed and finishing her breakfast. She looked much the same as she had the night before and I guessed that she'd probably had about as much sleep as me. But I didn't ask.

'Will I make you some breakfast?' she asked, looking up from the *National Geographic* she was reading as I came into the kitchen.

I shook my head. 'Tea will do fine and I'll eat some of that brown bread in a minute.'

My mother nodded and continued reading her magazine. I ate some breakfast, smoked a cigarette, drank four cups of coffee and went into the hallway to telephone the police. It was still only 8.15 a.m.

'And what age is your cousin?' a young-sounding woman asked me.

'Twenty-nine.'

'I'm sorry, sir, but I'm afraid we can't consider an adult woman you haven't seen for two days as a missing person.'

'But she *is* missing. Look, I understand that there are rules, but there are also exceptional circumstances. Will you do me a favour?'

'If I can.'

'Would you call Detective Paul Richardson and tell him Cassandra is missing?'

'I don't –'

'Please. Look, what harm will it do? If I'm just a mad crank then – so what? You won't have given me his number and he can just ignore this. On the other hand, if it's important he'll be glad you called.'

'I . . .'

'Please. Please just do that much and I promise I won't bother you again. Tell him I rang – Séamus Considine is my name – and tell him Cassandra is missing since Wednesday.'

'All right.'

'Thank you,' I said and hung up.

I told my mother what the policewoman had said and she decided to go to Limerick to tell her sister Lucy in person.

'It'll be all right,' I said to her as I kissed her goodbye.

She smiled. 'Ring me if you hear anything.'

I nodded and then she took her handbag and left. I watched her walk across the yard to her car and her hopelessly deformed cardigan flapping around her like a sail.

I waved goodbye and then went into the kitchen and tried to read, but my mind hopped like a flea so I cleaned the kitchen instead. At eleven o'clock the doorbell rang and I was glad to be interrupted. I opened the door to find a haggard Tim Winter standing on the doorstep.

'No word?' he said, walking straight past me into the kitchen. I closed the front door and followed him.

'No.'

'Fuck it, Séamus, where can she be?' he said looking at me, his eyes glassy with fear.

I shrugged. 'I rang the police.'

'And?'

'And nothing. She's an adult, she's only gone since Wednesday, she can't be considered a missing person yet.'

'Fuck it,' Tim said, bending in two as if I'd punched him in the stomach.

'Look, Tim. She's fine. I know she's fine.'

'Then where is she?' he said, straightening up and looking at me.

A thin line of saliva joined the corner of his mouth to his chin, but he didn't seem to notice. I wondered if I should tell him. Not that I gave a shit and it certainly didn't even get on to the same scale of importance as Cassandra's disappearance, still, maybe I should tell him.

Maybe the deal with the universe was that one should observe the social niceties even when the sky was falling down? Maybe there are rules for these catastrophes? Rules of engagement with disaster. I couldn't decide, and then I didn't have to because the doorbell rang again.

I opened the door to find Paul Richardson smiling at me. He offered me his hand as soon as he stepped into the hallway.

'Séamus,' he said, grasping my hand in both of his, 'good to see you again. I was here only the other day with Cassandra – she was telling me about what happened to Prince. And now they tell me she seems to have gone off somewhere herself?'

I nodded, not able to speak and motioned him to follow me into the kitchen. His puffy jacket rustled as he walked and I tried not to associate him with the night of Mattie's murder. I was irrationally glad my mother had already left to be with her sister because I didn't want her to meet Paul Richardson. Even though I knew she wouldn't have the same associations as I – it didn't matter – I was still glad.

Tim was pacing the floor smoking one of my cigarettes when we walked in. I introduced the men and they shook hands.

'Grand and warm in here,' Detective Richardson said, taking off his coat and pulling out a chair. 'May I?'

'Please. Do you want tea or anything?'

Paul Richardson smiled his round-faced smile at me and shook his head. 'No, thanks, I'm grand. But maybe we could get started if you're ready?'

'No problem,' I said, sitting opposite him. 'What do you want?'

'Just tell me what happened,' he said, neatly laying a notebook and pencil side by side on the table in front of him.

So I told him. Tim continued to walk around the kitchen and smoke as I gave the details of the last time we'd seen Cassandra.

'We can't officially consider her a missing person, yet,' Paul said as I finished my account. He wrote something indecipherable in his notebook, suddenly stopped writing and looked up, as if he'd thought of something else.

'I know. They told me.'

'Not that she is a missing person, either mind,' he said as he arranged his pencil diagonally across his open notebook. 'I'm not saying that. Mostly these cases are false alarms and it'll turn out that she's off someplace doing her Christmas shopping and just forgot to tell anybody.'

'Do you really think so?' Tim interrupted, standing, shoulders hunched, behind the detective's chair.

'Sure,' Paul Richardson said, smiling and looking around at him, 'that's usually the case, anyway, thank God.'

Tim nodded as he listened to the policeman and then began pacing again. Suddenly, as if he needed to concentrate on the long-ashed cigarette in his hand, he stopped walking and just stood there smoking, carefully tipping the ash into his cupped hand and staring into space over my head.

Paul Richardson finished speaking and turned around in his chair and looked directly at me and I could almost hear the worried thoughts that were rattling in his head. Where was she? Why had she disappeared? What happened? Had somebody hurt her?

I wasn't surprised. It stood to reason that he was concerned about Cassandra in the light of everything that had happened. I was.

'Cassandra went around the other day asking questions, did you know that?' I said, as much to distract myself from the tortuous medley playing in my head as to inform the police.

'About?' Paul said.

'The Afrikaner,' I said. Tim leaned across me to take another of my cigarettes from the packet.

The policeman's ginger eyebrows shot up so high they almost disappeared into his matching hairline.

I watched Tim attempting to light his cigarette. His hands were shaking so violently he couldn't make the lighter flame come into contact with the cigarette for long enough to achieve anything. His face was grey and his shoulders so stooped that his long, thin body was bowed. Eventually the cigarette ignited and he stuck it in his mouth, sucking hungrily. Then he rubbed his hands together rapidly so that the skin on his palms made a fast swooshing sound. I felt so bad for him I couldn't bear it.

'Shopping,' I said, smiling the lie at Tim, 'that flake has probably gone Christmas shopping.'

And I knew it wasn't true, but I couldn't see the point in increasing Tim's distress. It wouldn't help Cassandra. My lie worked. Tim's face cleared slightly and his eyes seemed to focus for the first time since he'd arrived.

'Séamus is right,' the ruddy policeman said, suddenly, standing up and pushing his arms into the sleeves of his puffy jacket. 'I don't think I'll even call on Cassandra's family just yet. Did you tell me your mother is there, Séamus?'

I nodded.

'Great. By the way, we found her bag.'

'Her bag?'

'I had one of the lads go and check at the bus station in

Limerick and right enough there was an unclaimed bag that arrived at the station off the Wednesday evening bus from Castleannery. We opened it and there was the usual clothes and toiletries and stuff and also a camera with her name printed inside the case.'

'So it's Cassandra's.'

Paul Richardson nodded. 'It's at the station. Maybe you'd drop in and have a look at it the next time you're in town? Just to make sure that it belongs to Cassandra – though we'd like to hold on to it in the meantime, if that's all right?'

'OK,' I said, not wanting to imagine strangers delving into Cassandra's bag in a police station. 'I suppose.'

'Mind you she'll probably be collecting it herself before you get as far as it.'

'Probably.'

Paul Richardson zipped the jacket zipper right up to his chin and put his notebook and pencil into a pocket with a loop fastener.

'There's a mobile phone in her bag as well,' he said.

'Fuck,' I said, 'why did she do that? She busts my balls for not remembering my phone.'

Paul smiled. 'She must have packed it into her luggage and forgotten it. Probably packed in a hurry.'

I nodded remembering her face as I asked her to leave.

'OK, look,' Paul said, 'maybe you'd give Cassandra's family – I mean the rest of the family – give them my number if they want to talk to me?'

I nodded.

'And hopefully I won't have to call on them at all. Hopefully she'll turn up wondering what all the fuss is about?'

I stood up. 'Hopefully,' I said, continuing with my echoing act.

Tim stood behind the detective.

'Hopefully,' he said, as well.

'I'd better be off so,' Paul said, shaking hands with both of us.

'Thanks,' I said, as we shook hands and I felt the power in his hand and, somehow, the sympathy as well. 'Thanks for everything and thanks especially for coming all the way out here.'

'No trouble.'

'I'd better go too,' Tim said, squinting his eyes as if struggling to remember something important.

I squeezed his arm. 'Talk to you later. I'll keep you posted.'

Tim nodded and smiled and then the tall, lanky doctor and short, well-padded policeman left my house together. The silence in the house after they left was overwhelming, and so irritating that it was like an itch all over me.

I made more tea and a ham sandwich, but I couldn't eat and could barely manage to push tea down my constricted throat. Taking my cup, I walked outside and sat on the broad windowsill outside my sitting-room window.

The sky was clear and wintry blue and the sun was shining, though it was cold. I smoked and sipped my tea and looked around me and inhaled the smell of winter, hoping to be distracted by the world.

I knew Cassandra wasn't shopping, or visiting or taking photographs or sightseeing. She was a flake all right, but not that kind of a flake. She'd never go missing like that and not tell anybody where she was going.

The pictures of Mattie's falling body covered the inside of my head like wallpaper, so permanent I'd stopped trying to get rid of them. Where was Cassandra? I turned the question over and over in my head, as if it were an object that I could scrutinize for answers.

Alison Chang.

I thought of her, suddenly, and almost fell forward off the windowsill. Maybe she'd know something that would help?

It couldn't hurt to find out. I jumped on to the hard, frosty ground and walked quickly into the house.

How could I find Alison Chang? Did I have a telephone number for her? I half-remembered her giving me a telephone number once. But when? And was it a card or a piece of paper? And what the fuck had I done with it?

I threw my empty cup into the sink in the kitchen and went to the hallstand and rummaged in the tiny, packed drawer that somehow smelled of mothballs even though I'd never used one in my life. Bills and payslips and receipts and old birthday cards tumbled up towards me in a heap, but no phone numbers. I closed my eyes and made myself think.

I could see Alison Chang in the kitchen with me and Cassandra after Mattie's funeral. Hair shiny with rain, face interested and attentive. I saw her hand me a card and then . . .

In the kitchen cutlery drawer.

I pulled open the drawer and there it was underneath a nest of tablespoons. Alison Chang's telephone number. What a dumb place to keep a telephone number, I thought, as I tried not to run to the telephone.

Stupid, idiotic place. Ridiculous, insane place. But, still, if I was organized enough to file away her telephone number then I'd have been organized enough to throw it away when I was angry with her. Swings and roundabouts.

I dialled her home number. Alison Chang's telephone rang and I listened and listened and listened. No answer. I looked at the card again and found a mobile number and I dialled that. The phone rang again and I waited. Then there was silence and my heart thumped and leapt like a salmon when her voice answered.

'Hello,' she said. I could hear the sounds of an engine and car radio in the background.

'Alison? Séamus Considine here. Look, don't hang up, I know you probably don't want to talk to me but I need to talk to you. Cassandra is missing.'

The telephone beeped in my ear as she disconnected.

'Fuck,' I said, dialling her number again. It was engaged. 'Fuck, fuck, fuck.'

I punched the life out of my re-dial button for about five minutes. Her telephone was obviously switched off. Now what would I do? Maybe she'd kidnapped Cassandra or had had something to do with it? Maybe Cassandra was right after all and Alison Chang was slap bang in the middle of this whole mess?

If that was the case then what had I done by calling her? Had I alerted her to something? No, that was nonsensical. If she'd kidnapped Cassandra or had her kidnapped then it'd hardly be a surprise to her that Cassandra was missing.

But what if it was? What if I'd jeopardized Cassandra in some way? I hadn't meant to but that didn't make any difference – I hardly ever meant to do damage and still I managed it. If I hadn't had that fight with Cassandra none of it would ever have happened.

What *was* the fight about? I couldn't remember. Stupid bastard, I thought as I chainsmoked and prowled around my house. Stupid, stupid bastard can never leave well enough alone.

I went into the sitting room and switched on the TV. Perching on the edge of the couch I pointed the remote control at the television. Nelson Eddy and Jeanette McDonald. Flick. A motor race. Flick. A football match. Flick. News. Flick. An advertisement for yogurt. Flick. A gardening programme. I couldn't watch them. Moving, smiling, singing, talking, laughing. Fuck's sake.

The telephone rang. I dropped the remote control on to the floor and ran to the phone.

'Yes?'

'Séamus?' a woman's voice said. Cassandra? Was it Cassandra?

'Cassandra?'

'No, Séamus. It's me. Jessica. Hope I didn't disturb you doing anything important.'

'Jessica. Sorry. How are you?'

'I'm fine, I'm fine. And you?'

'Well, not great really. Cassandra seems to be on the missing list and we're all a bit worried about her.'

'Oh, really? That's awful, but I'm sure she'll turn up. I know you're very fond of her, but, let's face it, she's always been a bit scattered.'

'I suppose, I suppose.'

'Anyway, I'm sitting here trying to finalize the guest list for the opening of my exhibition. I can't tell you how depressing it is, but I have no choice, I have to do it – or so they tell me. Part of the package. Anyway, can you confirm that you'll definitely be coming?'

My head swam with the details of what she was saying. 'Sorry?'

Jessica tutted. 'My exhibition? Remember I told you? I invited you. Will you be coming?'

'Oh,' I said. I had no intention of going but I also had no intention of discussing why I didn't want to go with Jessica. Especially now. 'Sure. I remember. Yes, all things being equal I'll be there.'

'Sure?'

'Yep.'

'Positive?'

'All things being equal.'

Which meant that I wouldn't have to go because the truth was that things were never really equal in the world, were they?

'Great. Anyway, better rush. I've a load of people to get

on to and already half the day is gone. Hope Cassandra turns up soon. Talk to you later, Séamus.'

'Bye Jessi –' I managed before the phone was hung up.

My stomach tightened. I must have upset her in some way to have her hang up so abruptly. Typical. I couldn't do anything right it seemed. I heard the crunch of tyres in my front yard as a car pulled hastily to a halt. I waited for the customary bark, remembered with a twist in my gut and then walked to the front door. Just as I opened the door Alison Chang was raising her hand to knock.

'You live in Dublin,' is all I could say.

Alison shrugged. 'I was in Limerick. You called my mobile.'

'But you hung up on me,' I said, still struggling with surprise at the sight of her.

'Because I had to get here, Séamus, it required me to drive not talk.'

'But I thought you were mad at me for . . . for . . . you know, what I said that day.'

Alison Chang shrugged. 'People have said worse things than that to me. I even told you about some of them if you recall. What happened to Cassandra?'

I shook my head and my limbs felt heavy with fear. 'I don't know. She left to go home. Tim brought her to the bus. He even saw her getting on to the bus and then – nothing. She's nowhere to be found.'

'And have you told the police?'

I nodded. 'And the worrying thing is that Paul Richardson took it seriously, even though technically she hasn't been gone for long enough to be a bona fide missing person.'

'Lovely expression that – bona fide missing person.'

I looked at her. 'What do you think might have happened to her?'

Alison shook her head. 'Any chance I could come in?'

I opened the door fully and stepped back. 'Sorry.'

Alison and I walked into the kitchen and stood looking at each other for a few seconds. I saw that her face was paler and thinner than I remembered and that her eyes were still almond shaped as Cassandra had described.

'Do you mind if I sit down?' Alison asked, motioning to a chair.

I shook my head. 'Tea? Coffee?'

'No, I'm fine. OK, just tell me what happened.'

'Nothing. Nothing much anyway. Cassandra went looking for the Afrikaner. I think myself that that might be relevant and, to be truthful, I think our friendly detective thinks the same. He can't say that, though, can he?'

Alison shrugged and widened her eyes.

'No. He can't because then he'd have to admit that they should have done more when I saw him . . .' I paused. 'Am I making any sense?'

Alison shook her head and smiled. 'Not much.'

'OK. I'll try to explain, but stop me if I start talking gibberish, OK?'

'Fine.'

'Right, I was out one night recently in the middle of the night and I saw him – or more like heard him – the Afrikaner, I mean. I heard his voice at about four o'clock in the morning in the village, right here in Castleannery. Then he drove away and I thought he'd escaped again but I got a look at the car. Are you following me? Does it make sense now?'

'I think so. You heard the Afrikaner in the village at four a.m. and you saw his car?'

'Yes,' I said, wondering why I couldn't have said that. 'OK, well anyway, to cut a long story short, I saw the same car outside Pádraig Harrison's house on my way home and I reported it to the Guards but they said the car was stolen, so, basically, he got away. Are you with me so far?'

Alison nodded.

'OK. Cassandra then took it into her head to ask around

to see if anybody knew anything about an Afrikaner being in the vicinity – it being an unusual enough accent, etc.'

'OK, go on.'

'Right. Well, then she left and was supposed to be going home and that was Wednesday, this is Friday, and nobody has seen or heard from her since.'

I stopped talking and Alison looked thoughtful as though she was assessing what I'd said.

'Why did she go home so suddenly?' she said, after a few moments. 'I mean had she some commitment or other? It seems odd that she should go home like that.'

'We had a fight. No, that's not true. I was mean to her and basically kicked her out – or at least suggested she leave. It's not that odd.'

Alison didn't speak for a minute.

'I can be pretty mean. Especially if my feelings are hurt.'

She looked at me and raised both eyebrows but still didn't speak. I wondered if I should apologize, but she didn't seem to be holding it against me – otherwise she wouldn't be here, would she? Not that it was all my fault, anyway. After all she was the one who had lied.

'Where is Prince?' Alison said, suddenly, interrupting my thoughts.

I laughed and she looked at me enquiringly. 'Dead. Prince is dead. He was poisoned.'

Alison caught her breath and reached a hand out towards me. I was standing at the other side of the table so it was too far away to make physical contact but funnily enough I could almost feel the heat of her hand on the back of my arm.

'Poor Prince. Was he poisoned on purpose?'

'No idea, I think probably, but I could be being paranoid. I have to admit that I think it had something to do with Cassandra going around questioning people like that.'

'Maybe. And now Cassandra is missing.'

'Tim is worried out of his head.'

'Tim?'

'Cassandra's boyfriend, the local GP – Tim Winter – Chrissie Winter's brother.'

'Oh, right. Tim. I'd forgotten that. And did you say you saw something outside Pádraig Harrison's house?'

'The Afrikaner's car. I don't care what the police say. I know it was the car he was driving.'

'Have you looked for Cassandra?'

'Just made phone calls and things like that.'

Alison stood up. 'Have you any idea where you could look for her?'

I shrugged.

'Have you tried her friends?'

I nodded.

'And her family haven't seen her?'

'No.'

My head raced. 'Pádraig Harrison's house?' I said, suddenly. I couldn't believe I hadn't thought of it before.

Alison looked at me.

'We could look for Cassandra in Pádraig Harrison's house,' I said.

She didn't contradict me but also didn't agree. Which made me nervous.

'It might be mad but if we were to go there – you and me – we could pretend we were going to ask him if he's seen Cassandra, tell him she's missing and stuff and try and have a look around, see if we can find anything.'

I looked at her impassive face. At last she nodded. 'Not a bad idea.'

'Great,' I said, as an unexpected burst of adrenaline whooshed inside me. 'Great stuff!'

At least it'd be movement. I was sick of sitting and worrying and glad to be making some movement – any movement. Then I remembered.

'Will he recognize you? Didn't you say you knew him or is it that you met him before when you were going around asking questions about William Ormston?'

'I never met him. Just spoke with him on the telephone and I never knew him. My ex-husband was a buddy of his brother. What difference would it make anyway, even if he did know me?'

'None. OK. Right. You're right. Let's go and see Pádraig Harrison. The bastard.'

Alison and I hurried out of my house. I didn't know why she was hurrying but I knew I was hurrying in case I changed my mind.

'We can take my car,' she said, sitting into the driver's seat of her silver Audi without waiting for an answer.

I sat in beside her and she pulled out of the yard before I'd even buckled my seat belt.

'Jesus,' I said, impressed at the pick-up and luxury of her car, 'are these seats leather?'

Alison shrugged without turning her head. 'What difference does it make?'

'None, I suppose. Unless you have to drive my car.'

Alison smiled and before I knew it we were outside Pádraig Harrison's gate.

'This is where your friend was killed, isn't it?' Alison said, indicator flashing as she stopped in the centre of the road.

I nodded and pointed to the spot where Mattie had fallen. 'There was a sort of vague stain there for a few weeks after he died, though I think they wash the road after things like that.'

'They do.'

'My imagination, so.'

Alison shook her head. 'In a way there'll always be a stain on that part of the road, won't there?'

And that was the thing I liked about Alison Chang. She seemed to understand things in a way that hardly anybody else understood. Cassandra, maybe. Jessica, never. Not that that mattered because it was different with Jessica. Everything was different with Jessica and Alison might be good at some things but at least Jessica hadn't lied to me.

Though that wasn't true either. She obviously had lied to me during our marriage when she was mixed up with that architect and before she left me. But at least she hadn't lied to me recently. Maybe that was something. Fuck, fuck, fuck. Life.

Alison walked in front of me to the front door of Pádraig's house while I was tying myself into internal knots and rang the doorbell. We stood in silence outside. I surveyed the garden, searching for signs of the Afrikaner or Cassandra, but all I could see were bare-branched shrubs and a smattering of snowdrops.

The door opened.

'Séamus!' Pádraig said, clearly surprised to see me but immediately reaching out to shake my hand. He looked at Alison.

'Pádraig. I wonder if we could come in? This is a friend of mine, by the way – Alison Chang.'

'Pleased to meet you, Alison,' Pádraig said, tilting his handsome head to one side as he shook her hand.

'And you, Pádraig,' Alison said, smiling broadly as she returned his handshake.

Pádraig stepped back from the door. 'Come right in. Pardon my manners, you must be frozen. Please come in. Come into the sitting room, actually. I've a big fire there.'

Alison and I followed Pádraig to his sitting room where he did, indeed, have a huge fire burning in the grate. Papers were strewn on the floor in front of the couch and he bent to pick them up.

'Sorry about this,' he said, grinning up at us as he hastily stuffed the papers into a leather briefcase. 'I'll just throw this lot into the study and then we can chat.'

Pádraig took his overflowing bag out of the room and returned almost immediately.

'Now,' he said, standing in front of the fireplace, 'can I get you anything? Tea? Coffee? A drink?'

Alison and I both shook our heads.

'No. We're fine, really, thanks anyway,' I said.

'Alison Chang?' Pádraig said. 'I know that name. Have we met before?'

Alison smiled. 'No, but I called you a couple of weeks ago. I was doing some work for Capel and Williams – background on the Ormston death a little while ago?'

'That's right, that's right – I remember now. And you know my brother, don't you?'

'Well, not personally – a friend of a friend kind of thing.'

'It's a small world,' Pádraig said. 'So? What can I do for you?'

'The thing is, Pádraig,' I said, losing patience with the social banter. 'Well, it's just that I was wondering if you'd seen Cassandra recently?'

Pádraig smiled. 'Actually, I did. I met her yesterday. In the village. She seemed in good form.'

'Yesterday? You're sure it was yesterday?'

Pádraig rocked a little on the leather heels of his highly polished, black brogues, as he considered my question. 'It could have been the day before. Let me think. I was in Dublin yesterday – yesterday was Wednesday, wasn't it?'

'No,' I said, my heart sinking, 'Thursday.'

'Then it *was* Wednesday because I had a meeting with the bank in Dublin and that was on Wednesday. I met Cassandra as I was coming home. I think she said she was going back home, now that I come to think about it.'

'She was. That was her plan. Was Tim there?'

'No. Should he have been there?'

'No, no. I just wondered, that's all.'

'So, that's it? That's what you wanted to speak with me about?'

I looked at the floor and tried to overcome my intense natural dislike of Pádraig Harrison and the suspicion that was welling inside me making me want to throttle the truth out of him. Alison coughed and we both looked at her.

'We haven't heard from Cassandra in a couple of days,' she said in a quiet voice, leaning forward in her seat towards Pádraig, 'and . . . well, truthfully, Pádraig, we're a bit worried. Cassandra can be a little depressed sometimes. You know how it is . . .' Alison let her voice trail off like a silk scarf disappearing around a corner.

Cassandra, depressed? I was surprised. I hadn't known she was depressed and I thought I knew pretty much everything about Cassandra. How the hell did Alison know? She didn't even know her.

I looked at Pádraig and saw that he had latched on to Alison's energy like a trailer. Nodding in understanding. Face a picture of handsome concern. I turned my attention to Alison. And then I realized. Jesus, I thought, how dumb can you be Séamus Considine?

'I do know,' Pádraig was saying, nodding gently. 'Really, I do. Depression is a dreadful, dreadful affliction and on the increase all the time, I believe. Poor Cassandra. Who would have thought?'

Pádraig and Alison did some more silent head nodding. Pádraig looked at me and I nodded my head as well and tried a rueful smile. He smiled back at me.

'I wish I had spoken with her for longer, now,' Pádraig said, directing his words at Alison.

'You couldn't know,' Alison said.

'Yes, yes, but maybe if I'd taken the time to speak a little longer with her I'd be able to help you now. I hope she's OK.'

'Pádraig?' Alison said, reclining right back into her fashionably shabby armchair.

Pádraig raised a shapely eyebrow. Did he pluck them? Is that what successful, handsome computer whizzes do? Do they pluck their eyebrows? And if they do are they still tough guys? Probably.

'I wonder if it would be a lot of trouble for me to have a cup of coffee. I hate to ask but I seem to have a headache coming on and I find that coffee is marvellous to keep a headache at bay.'

'No sooner said than done,' Pádraig said, running a hand through his well-cut and slightly long hair. And that was another thing – Pádraig's hair always looked to be exactly the same length. How did he manage that? Callipers?

'I hope it isn't any trouble,' Alison repeated, rewarding his response with a smile.

'Not a bit. If you can just excuse me for a few minutes I'll get you some coffee. Séamus? You'll have some too, won't you?'

'If you're making some,' I said, trying to work out what was happening.

'Great!' Pádraig said, walking towards the door. Alison stood up from her chair and walked towards him. He stood still watching her tall, leisurely approach. I could see that he appreciated it. And I wasn't happy about that, but I also wasn't surprised as, in spite of everything, I was enjoying the view myself.

'Pádraig. Could I use the bathroom?'

'By all means. Upstairs. You can't miss it.'

Pádraig turned and walked out the door into the hall-way. Alison returned to pick up her handbag. 'Go out to the kitchen and keep him occupied for ten minutes,' she whispered as she walked past me.

I looked at her in confusion.

'Come on, Séamus. Do it.'

I stood up and followed her out of the room.

'Upstairs so, is it Pádraig?' Alison called.

'That's right,' Pádraig called in return.

Alison set off up the stairs taking them two at a time but making no noise. I made my way in the direction of Pádraig's voice. Opening a door at the end of a long hallway I saw the kitchen of the night of Mattie's murder and for one moment it literally took my breath away as I was flooded with remembering. But I pushed away the feelings with a thought of Cassandra.

'Can I help at all?' I announced in a voice as bright as the glint off a sequin.

Pádraig looked up from his coffee-making in obvious surprise. 'Séamus?'

'Just thought I'd see if I could give you a hand.'

'Well, let me see now. Maybe you'd put cups and stuff on that tray?'

He pointed to a silver tray already laid out on the worktop. 'Cups and saucers – there in that cupboard in front of you.'

'Great,' I said, reaching up to open the frosted-glass door to reveal stacks of white cups. I took down three cups and three saucers and put them on to the tray. Then I remembered what Alison had told me to do.

Having a quick look to satisfy myself that Pádraig couldn't see what I was doing, I picked up all three cups in my left hand and dropped them on to the terracotta-tiled floor.

'Oh, my God!' I shouted as the porcelain smashed around my feet.

Pádraig's head shot around from what he was doing.

'I am so sorry! Oh my God, Pádraig, what can I say? Look, I'll replace them. Where did you buy them? Tell me and I'll go straight into town first thing tomorrow.'

Pádraig, who had moved to stand beside me, surveyed the damage.

'Is there a sweeping brush anywhere?' I said, walking away from him and opening a door at the end of the room. 'Great. I'll sweep it up. Stand away there, Pádraig, in case you get cut. Tell me, where did you buy them? I am *so* sorry. I suppose it's the strain I've been under with Cassandra and . . . and her problems and all that . . .'

I swept shards of white porcelain from around Pádraig's feet and I imagined that in his head he was trying to convince himself not to scream at me, which I have to admit made me smile to myself.

'Dustpan?' I said, as I collected the smashed crockery into a pile.

Pádraig walked, silently, to the utility room and came back and handed me a spotless blue plastic dustpan and matching brush. I bent down and swept up the breakage and then followed Pádraig's pointing finger until I found an aluminium pedal bin.

'So?' I said, laying my tools side by side on the floor next to the bin. 'Tell me where you bought them, Pádraig, and I'll replace them.'

Pádraig smiled a wide, even-toothed smile. 'Absolutely no need,' he said, swinging back into his usual suave mode. 'It could happen to anyone. Look, I have plenty more where those came from.' He paused, reaching up to get three more cups and place them on the tray. 'Now. And the coffee and a few biscuits . . . OK – now some milk and sugar. There we are – all set. Let's go. Alison'll be wondering where we've gone.'

Pádraig started off towards the door carrying the tray. I hoped Alison was back, but I didn't think I could stall him any longer unless I faked a heart attack and even that probably wouldn't have worked as he had already gone through the door.

I followed Pádraig down the hallway and into the sitting room. Alison was sitting in her chair, calmly flicking the pages of a glossy magazine. She looked up and smiled as we came into the room. Pádraig laid his tray on to a blonde-wood coffee table and poured three cups of coffee.

I looked searchingly at Alison, but she kept her eyes fixed on the magazine on her long lap. 'I have to admit that I love architecture magazines.'

Pádraig handed her a cup of coffee and smiled. 'Me too.'

'Did you see the Tom de Paor on the front of last month's issue?'

'Amazing,' Pádraig said, as he handed me a cup of coffee while still looking at Alison.

I wondered if there was any way we could leave without drinking the coffee. I could hardly bear the thought of having to wait to discover what Alison had found while I was smashing dishes in the kitchen. I looked at my watch.

'Look at the time. I hadn't realized. We need to get back soon, Alison, I'm – um – expecting a phone call. About Cassandra. My mother or the police. Well, both actually – maybe even Cassandra's mother – sorry to hurry you.'

Alison looked in my direction without meeting my eye. 'Of course,' she said, taking a long drink from her cup, 'Delicious coffee, Pádraig. Sorry we can't stay longer.'

Alison stood up and placed her almost empty cup back on the tray. I put my still steaming, still full cup beside it. When I turned around Pádraig and Alison were shaking hands.

'I'm sorry too,' Pádraig was saying as he held on to her hand, even though the handshake was obviously well finished.

Alison smiled into his eyes. I found it very annoying that she didn't seem to be avoiding his eyes.

'Maybe another time,' Pádraig said.

'Maybe,' Alison said.

'Soon?'

'Hopefully.'

They let go hands as if they were reluctant to separate. I wanted to push the slick bastard into the fire.

'Thanks a lot, Pádraig,' I said, through my teeth, as we walked to the front door.

'No problem, Séamus,' he said, as he opened the door. 'You will let me know if I can help in any way, won't you?'

'Of course,' I said, waving and walking ahead of Alison to the car. Alison pressed her key ring to unlock the car and we sat into our seats and both waved to Pádraig who stood watching as we drove down the driveway.

'Well?' I said, as soon as we were out of view. 'Did you find anything?'

Alison shook her head and kept her eyes on the road. 'Damn twilight. I hate twilight, you can't see anything properly and that would be bad enough except that it sort of tricks you and you think you can see but it's all out of sync.'

'Twilight? Jesus, Alison, you're as bad as Cassandra talking about mad stuff. Are you saying you found nothing? Where did you look?'

'Everywhere upstairs. All the rooms were empty except for one – which was obviously Pádraig's bedroom.'

'Then he must be keeping her somewhere else. It would be dumb to keep her in his own house.'

'Maybe he doesn't have her. By the way, where are we going?'

'Back to my house, I suppose.'

Alison pulled into a gateway and turned her car in the opposite direction.

'What do you mean, maybe he doesn't have her?'

'I think that's fairly obvious. Maybe he didn't kidnap her.'

'But what about the Afrikaner's car?' I said, struggling to

keep my feelings of annoyance under control. Bloody, fucking marvellous, I thought. Now she'd seen him she'd changed her mind. I obviously had to do everything myself. You'd think a solicitor could be trusted to be professional and objective, for fuck's sake.

'You told me that the police said the car was stolen,' Alison said, pulling her car to a halt in front of my house.

'But it was outside his house. What would a stolen car – a stolen car driven by a murderer for that matter – what would it be doing outside his house if he wasn't involved? I saw the car with my own eyes, Alison. And I know that the man who got into that self-same car in the village of Castleannery was the man who murdered Mattie. I know that as well as I know anything.'

Alison turned off the engine. 'OK.'

'I suppose you think he's too handsome to be involved,' I said, before I could stop myself.

'What?'

'That's what Cassandra said about Pádraig Harrison,' I said, scrabbling for cover. 'She said he was too handsome to be a murderer.'

Alison laughed. 'Well, he certainly is handsome.'

'I suppose,' I said, my stomach tightening. 'Do you want to come in?'

'I need to get back. But I'll just come in for a minute and use your bathroom, if you don't mind. I never got a chance to actually use Pádraig Harrison's bathroom. By the way, tell me something, did you break dishes in his house?'

'Cups,' I said, stepping out of the car.

'Nice work. Very nice.'

We walked in silence towards my house and I wondered who the hell this woman was. Coming into our lives out of nowhere, lying to me, helping me, flirting with Pádraig Harrison.

I had just reached my hand into my pocket to find my keys when the front door flew open.

'Christ!' I said, as I recognized the white face in the dark hallway. 'Cassandra, what the hell happened to you?'

10

'Life's a Long Song'
Jethro Tull, 1972

'Oh, Séamus, where were you?' Cassandra said, pulling me by the sleeve into my hallway.

'Where were *you*, more to the point? We've been looking for you for the past two days, Cassandra. Call your mother. Call Tim. Call the police. They're all frantic looking for you.'

'I called them. Or at least I called my mother and I tried to call Tim but he wasn't there so I left a message for him with Chrissie. I didn't call the police, but then I didn't know they were looking for me. Why are they looking for me?'

'Paul Richardson is looking for you more than the whole of the police force. He was here. They aren't officially looking for you yet, it's too soon, but under the circumstances – with everything that happened.'

Cassandra nodded and her eyes filled with tears.

'I'll call him later,' I said.

She nodded again and the tears spilled down her face. I reached out and hugged her. Her small body trembled with silent sobs as she hugged me back.

'I'm sorry, Cass.'

'Me too,' she whispered.

'Where were you all this time?' I said, as she pulled away and blew her nose.

'I followed the Afrikaner.'

'What?' I said, and I tried to pull her away from me so that I could look at her face but she just hugged me tighter.

'I followed the Afrikaner,' Cassandra repeated into my chest, 'and I got stuck and I thought they'd catch me and I had to walk and walk and I lost my handbag and my money . . .'

'Hold on. Slow down. Let's go and sit down and you can tell me what happened. I don't know about you but I'm whacked – all this high drama and investigation really takes it out of you, doesn't it?'

Now Cassandra pulled away from me and grinned.

'Would you mind if I came and listened too?' Alison said.

Cassandra and I turned towards her voice. I'd forgotten Alison was still there. I looked at Cassandra.

'No problem,' she said.

'Could I run up to the loo first?' Alison said.

'Help yourself,' I said.

Cassandra threw herself on to the couch as soon as she walked into the sitting room and pulled her knees up to her chin as she wrapped a paisley-patterned throw around her small body. 'Oh, God. I have had such a weird time.'

'Well, I'm just glad you're back and you're OK.'

Alison came into the room and sat on the arm of the couch near Cassandra.

'That was fast. You obviously didn't search the upstairs of my house,' I said.

Alison smiled.

'Séamus!' Cassandra said. 'That's a terrible thing to say.'

Alison and I grinned at each other.

'Private joke,' I said. 'You tell us your story first and then we might tell you about it.'

Cassandra lay back into the couch and closed her eyes. I could see a vein in her temple throb and her lips quivered as if the words were queuing inside her mouth afraid to come out.

Then her eyes opened, she sat forward and smiled at us. 'OK – here it is – I caught the bus on Wednesday – Tim brought me into the village.'

She stopped and looked at Alison. 'Séamus and I had a fight and I decided to go home.'

'She knows.'

'OK. Good. Anyway, I got on the bus and we took off and everything was fine. I read my book, fell asleep, tried to ignore the sound of ten different Walkmans humming around me – the usual stuff. That was all fine. Then we stopped at a restaurant.'

'Where?'

Cassandra shook her head, 'Don't know, I never remember seeing it before, but then I usually sleep all the way to Castleannery. It wasn't in a town or anything, it was out in the middle of nowhere. A garage with a restaurant and a shop.'

'Carragh?' I asked.

'Dunno. The driver said he was having a small problem with the bus and we should go and get a cup of coffee while he went into the garage to try to sort it out. So, I did that. Bought a newspaper, had some coffee and I was just about to leave the restaurant when I heard the voice.'

'The Afrikaner?' Alison said.

Cassandra nodded.

'But he could have been anybody,' I said. 'Even I'm not paranoid enough to think every South African is mixed up in Mattie's murder.'

'Well, I must be. I stayed put and listened as hard as I could to try to catch what he was saying. I thought he said something about Dublin and I even thought I heard him mention Castleannery, but I couldn't be sure.'

'And his companion?' I asked.

'Sounded Irish.'

'But they could have been anybody,' I repeated.

'Yeah, but they weren't. And I just knew it.'

'How?'

Cassandra shrugged. 'No idea. I kept listening and I heard him say something about the van – "Go in the van" or "Be in the van". Something like that. So I waited and followed them out of the restaurant and sure enough they walked straight over and climbed into a blue Ford Transit van.'

'What did they look like?' Alison said.

'Well, she was shortish and dark, not much taller than me. But he was tall – very tall. Dutch looking. Maybe early thirties.'

'When you say very tall, what do you mean?' I said.

Cassandra thought. 'It's hard to tell – everybody looks tall to me – but I'd say he was six foot four at least.'

Alison looked at me and raised her eyebrows, but I wouldn't let my face respond.

Cassandra nodded. 'Very, very tall. Anyway, they got into the van and I went up to the back of the van and saw that one of the doors wasn't completely closed.'

'Don't tell me you opened it and got in,' I said.

'I won't tell you so,' Cassandra said, laying her head, tiredly, against the back of the couch. We sat in silence for a moment.

'Cassandra,' I said, menacingly.

Cassandra grinned up at me. 'OK, OK, calm down. I did get in. I couldn't resist. I pulled the door, it opened and I just jumped in before I could think of anything one way or another and then suddenly the van started up and drove away from the restaurant before I could get back out.'

Cassandra paused.

Alison groaned and covered her face with her hands. 'Oh, God.'

'That's the way it happened. It was all fairly undramatic.'

'What did you do?' Alison said.

Cassandra yawned and rubbed her closed eyes. 'I stood there for a minute being pitched around the place as the van drove along and then, as it became obvious that they weren't about to stop any time soon, I sat down on a bunch of sacks that were thrown in the corner of the van.'

'And was there anything else in there?' I asked. 'Anything beside sacks?'

'A shovel, some McDonald's wrappers, a petrol can, a small holdall with some underwear, a washbag and a smell of dog.'

'That was it?'

'That was it.'

'So, where did they go?'

'I don't know. All I do know is that they drove for ages. There weren't any windows, which meant that I couldn't see out. I eventually gave up hoping they'd stop at a set of traffic lights so that I could jump out.'

'Christ,' I said.

Cassandra grimaced. 'I must have fallen asleep because, next thing I knew, the van had stopped. I heard them talking outside and I knew they were about to open the door, so I covered myself with some of the sacks and tried not to breathe.'

Cassandra stopped.

'Very scary,' Alison said.

Cassandra nodded and swallowed a few times. 'Very. Not to mention smelly. It was the sacks – they were responsible for the dog smell. I thought I was going to give myself away by throwing up.'

'And did they see you?' I said.

She shook her head. 'No, I don't know how, because the sacks weren't exactly great cover, but it was dark and they seem to have been just taking the holdall. At least that's all that I could see was missing when they'd gone and, I suppose, they didn't expect somebody to be hiding in the back of their van, so they weren't very observant.'

'Jesus,' I said.

'Shut up, Séamus,' Cassandra said, automatically. 'I think I was lucky as well, though. I was pretty sure I could hear a deal of snogging going on before they opened the door, so

I was hoping that they had other things on their minds. And that was it. After they went away, I listened and waited until all was quiet for ages and ages and then I got out of the van.'

'And where were you?'

Cassandra shook her head again. 'No idea at the time, but it turned out that we were in Tipperary – up in the Silvermines somewhere, I think – so I couldn't have been asleep for very long. All I could see was that we seemed to be parked outside a small house of some description. A rent-an-Irish-cottage kind of job, do you know them?'

Alison and I both nodded.

'Wherever this place is, anyway, I promise you it's the middle of nowhere. I never saw darkness like it – you could bite it, it was so thick.'

'Wax lyrical, why don't you, Cassandra?' I said.

Cassandra glowered at me. 'Shut up, why don't you, Séamus.'

'So? What happened then?' Alison said.

'OK – it was dark – the only light came from the house. And as it was the only option other than the freezing woods, I assumed that the lovers had gone inside.'

Cassandra stopped again for a minute as if collecting her memories. 'Could you hand me that big cushion, Séamus?'

I threw her a big, soft, green cushion and she put it on to the arm of the couch and laid her head down on it. I stood up and took the matching green throw off the armchair under me and threw it over her. She pulled it around her so that she was wrapped in multiple swathes of fabric like a mummy.

Cassandra smiled at me and I felt, momentarily, like crying, because at least she was back and she was alive and relatively unscathed. Instead I asked another question.

'So you had a look around, I presume?'

Cassandra grinned 'Naturally. I could hardly leave without looking around, but I couldn't see or hear much. The curtains were closed. Not many streetlights in the middle of nowhere. I crept around for a few minutes and then I figured that the Afrikaner and his girlfriend had gone to bed.'

'What time was it?' Alison asked.

'Twenty to ten.'

'Early to bed?' I said.

'Very funny, Séamus. Anyway, I could have broken in, I suppose, but to be honest I was scared.'

'Good,' I said.

'Yeah, I was thinking, Jesus this is the guy that killed Mattie and here I am in the middle of nowhere and nobody even knows I'm here and if he catches me he'll shoot me too and they'll never even find my body.'

'Unless he was an innocent South African tourist that was just travelling around Ireland,' Alison said.

'He wasn't.'

'How do you know?' I said.

'Because they hadn't locked the cab of the van.'

'That's hardly incriminating.'

'Well, if you'd just shut up and let me tell you what happened, Séamus,' Cassandra said, rearranging the green cushion higher on the arm of the couch and then settling herself back down with a loud sigh.

I sighed as well and sat back in my chair.

'Anyway, where was I? OK, they didn't lock the cab of the van – I suppose they didn't think there would be any-body but themselves around. Once I was certain it was safe I crept in and opened the glove box and had a good look inside.'

'And?'

'And I found a paper bag with bars of chocolate and guess where it was purchased?'

'The Champs Elysées?'

Cassandra threw a withering look at me. 'Carr's super-market in Castleannery.'

'Coincidence,' I said. 'What difference does it make if they were in Castleannery on their way someplace else? They're probably just two innocents. Maybe they're on their honeymoon? Maybe they were just touring around. Seeing the sights?'

'They weren't.'

'OK. If not tourists then, I don't know, let me see — maybe he's a diamond merchant. There's a lot of that in South Africa, I believe.'

Cassandra sighed.

'A tiny bit stereotypical,' Alison said.

I shrugged. 'Well, we don't know that they weren't doing something ordinary, that's all that I'm saying.'

'I do.'

'Because you found a few bars of chocolate?'

'No,' Cassandra said, taking a deep breath, 'because I found a shotgun under the driver's seat.'

'Jesus,' I said.

Alison gasped.

'And what did you do?' I said.

Cassandra sat up, discarded the lengths of fabric from around her body and pushed her feet into her shoes. 'I took it. It's in the kitchen on the table.'

I jumped out of my seat and ran to the kitchen. Even as I was running I didn't quite know why. It wasn't as if I thought the gun would escape or even be stolen.

But there's something about being told that there's a gun in your kitchen that makes it impossible to walk. So I ran through the house until I reached the kitchen and there it was. In the middle of my discarded dishes and food scraps – a long, deadly looking shotgun.

'Fuck,' I said out loud as soon as I saw it.

'Pretty much what I thought myself,' Cassandra said behind me.

I turned around and Cassandra and Alison were standing

in the kitchen doorway. One short and dark, one tall and dark. Both staring at the gun. Both frightened looking.

'How did you get it here?'

'Well, first I took it out of the cab and then I wrapped it in one of the sacks from the back of the van.'

Cassandra pointed her finger. Alison and I both looked where Cassandra was pointing. A dirty jute sack lay crumpled in the corner of the room near the range.

'And then?'

'And then I walked. I had to walk. The first night – Wednesday night I suppose it was – I walked for as long as I could manage. I was wrecked. Very hilly country in that part of Tipperary.'

'Why didn't you call someone?' Alison asked.

'I couldn't find my phone. I figured I must have left it behind me here.'

I shook my head. 'Forgot to tell you that part, Alison. The phone was in Cassandra's suitcase. The Guards have it in Limerick.'

'The Guards have my case? Who gave it to them?'

'You left it on the bus, you idiot. Paul Richardson has it and he said your phone is in it.'

'I can't believe I packed my phone. Mind you I was in a bit of a temper.'

'Sorry,' I said.

Cassandra grinned. 'At least they found it, that phone cost me a lot of money. I can't afford to replace it.'

'Materialistic bitch,' I said, laughing. 'Tell us what else happened.'

Cassandra leaned against the wall and folded her arms. 'OK. I walked and walked and walked all night – I told you that. I wanted to put some distance between the murderers and me. It was bright and I was still walking and, at maybe eight in the morning, I found a hay-barn and I hid in that and went to sleep.'

'You're joking,' I said.

'No, I'm deadly serious. That's why I was gone for so long. I slept most of the day on Thursday. It was past four in the afternoon when I woke up and it was dark.'

'You must have been freezing,' Alison said.

Cassandra shook her head. 'No, hay is pretty warm.'

'All right, you didn't have a mobile, but surely you could have found a village and phoned somebody,' I said, suddenly angry as I remembered the interminable hours of waiting. 'We were out of our heads worrying about you.'

'Yeah, surely I could. Get off my case – do you think I'm a fucking eejit? That's what I was planning to do. I walked from that barn, along the main road for about an hour and then I saw a village and I was going to find a telephone and call you. That was the plan. I was delighted to see the village, and then, guess what?'

'What? An alien spaceship landed? There was an earthquake? A tidal wave? You left your tux in the cleaners?'

She put her hand up in the air like a traffic cop. 'Don't start. I was tired, starving, damp, smelly and carrying a fucking shot-gun wrapped up in a fucking sack that smelled of fucking dog and if I wasn't so fucking put to the pin of my fucking collar I might have thought of a better plan. Or even . . . even if the blue van with the Afrikaner hadn't driven by, maybe then I'd have thought of a better plan. But right then –'

'OK. Sorry. Sorry.'

Cassandra took a deep breath and blinked away tears.

'Sorry. Look, I didn't mean to give you such a hard time it's just . . . it's just I was so worried.'

Cassandra nodded. 'I know.'

'Can I ask you just one thing?'

'What?' she said, warily.

'Does your mother know you curse like that?'

'Oh, shut up Séamus,' Cassandra said, but she smiled.

'Tell us what happened,' Alison said.

'Well, I was afraid to stay outside when I saw the van. I know they hadn't seen me or anything, but I did have the gun and I sort of panicked. I saw a place that I thought was a warehouse or something like that and the back door was open so I ran in there and hid.'

Cassandra looked at Alison as she spoke. 'But it wasn't a warehouse it was a garage. There were a few cars up on those hoist thingies and a few with open bonnets, but there didn't seem to be anybody around. All the lights were off and the place was silent. Eerie, really, but I didn't want to go back out and I thought it might be a good place to stay for a while. Plus I was starving.'

'Yeah,' I said, 'I was thinking that. What did you eat all that time?'

'Nothing. I'd eaten the evening before in the restaurant when the bus stopped, but not a thing after that. And I lost my handbag as well. I forgot to tell you that.'

'Where?' Alison asked.

'I think I left it in the bloody hay-barn, but I'm not positive, anyway it meant I had no money. I was ready to eat my own hand. Once I saw that there wasn't anybody around in the garage place, I had a nose around to see if I could find any food.'

'Did you find any?' Alison said.

'Yeah. There was a small room at the back with a kettle and tea and sugar and stuff and two packets of Lincoln Cream biscuits. So I ate half a packet of biscuits and drank some tea and then I had a sit down on a battered old armchair.'

'Made yourself at home, didn't you?' I said.

'Shut up, Séamus, I was wrecked. There were a couple of newspapers there so I had a read – thought it might be better if I let the Afrikaner put a bit of distance between us and, well, I must have dozed off.'

'Jesus, Mary and Joseph,' I said.

'I'd had a hard day.' she said. 'I don't really remember falling asleep but I must have because when I woke up and went out into the garagey place, well, the door I'd come in was locked and I couldn't get out.'

'Oh, dear,' Alison said.

'Oh, fuck,' I said.

Cassandra nodded.

'And weren't there any windows?' I said.

'No, just those up really high Perspex panel things. Jesus, Séamus, don't you think I looked?'

'If it was a garage they'd have had a phone, wouldn't they?' I said.

'Yeah, they would and they did – in their tiny, weenchy little back room with the kettle and the biscuits, but, guess what?'

I shook my head.

'It was broken?' Alison asked.

Cassandra nodded. 'Dead as a doornail.'

'I don't believe it,' I said.

'Makes two of us,' Cassandra said. 'There I was, locked into this garage in God-knows-where, it was freezing, smelly and I was pretty sure I heard mice, and all I had to eat and drink were Lincoln Cream biscuits and black tea – the milk was sour. And the phone was broken. I wanted to cry.'

Cassandra sighed and closed her eyes for a moment. When she opened them again she was looking directly at me.

'What did you do?' I said.

'I banged on walls and shouted and walked around and read *The Star* and *The Mirror* and found some overalls to use as covers and eventually went back to sleep.'

'Poor Cassandra,' Alison said.

'Yeah, poor me,' Cassandra said. 'I resorted to eating the knobbly bits off the biscuits one by one so that they'd last longer.'

'So, how did you get out?' I said.

'I got out this morning, when Georgie Harris – the owner as it turns out – came into work.'

'And you just walked up to him and said, "Hello, I'm Cassandra, I've been locked in your garage since yesterday,"' I said.

'Something like that. I told him I got off the Dublin bus by mistake. I said I thought we had to change for Limerick and I got off and went into a pub to go to the loo and when I came out the bus had left – I was pretty convincing, if I say so myself. The poor lost girl, got off at the wrong stop, left her bag on the bus, alone and forlorn – I could nearly hear the violins myself.'

I rolled my eyes. 'Did he ask you what the hell you were doing on his premises?' I said.

'No, because he was too polite. But I told him anyway.'

'You told him you were hiding from the Afrikaner?' I said.

'No. Idiot. I said I'd been sheltering from the rain – luckily it poured rain most of yesterday. I said I ran inside and must have been accidentally locked in. He was so surprised to find me he didn't seem suspicious. I mean – why would he be? For God's sake, unless I was going to drive out in one of the cars there wasn't much I could have stolen.'

'That's a good idea,' I said, leaning over and tapping her on the arm. 'You could have rammed through the doors like in the movies.'

'Ha, ha,' Cassandra said.

'So this man,' Alison said, 'he let you out?'

'More than that. He drove me home. All the way from the village of Doire to Castleannery. That's how I got here.'

'And the gun?' I said. 'Didn't your new friend wonder why you had a gun?'

'Everybody doesn't have as suspicious a nature as you,' Cassandra said. 'Anyway, he didn't know what it was. I found one of those woven plastic fertilizer sacks in the garage and I wrapped it in that. He never even asked what it was.'

'Good old Georgie,' I said. 'Did he have a bit of a notion of you, do you think?'

Cassandra grinned. 'What can I say? He's a nice man. Middle-aged. Unmarried. Nursed his ancient parents for years when all his brothers and sisters went to England.'

'How do you know all this?' I asked.

'It's a long way from Doire,' Cassandra said.

'So you let the poor man think you were in the market for a husband?' I said.

'Well, technically I am, and I suppose I did sort of hint it would be all right with me if he telephoned.'

'Cassandra!'

'Get over yourself, Séamus – it's a long way home from the back of beyond when you've lost your handbag and are dodging murderers.'

'I suppose.'

'Anyway, I'd say poor old Georgie was probably more afraid that I'd sue him for the trauma of being imprisoned in his premises than he was enamoured of me. Anyway, that's my story and here I am.'

'Amazing,' Alison said.

I rubbed my face with my hands as I tried to process all she'd said, but all I could think of was that Cassandra might have been killed and I couldn't digest that so I moved on.

'What will we do with it?' I said, looking at Cassandra. 'The gun, I mean. What are we supposed to do with it now?'

'Well, I didn't lose my handbag and spend the night with rats –'

'Rats?' I said.

'OK, mice, but what difference does it make? It's still the same principle – I didn't suffer all of that for nothing.'

My head swam with the confusion of relief and nothing

seemed to make much sense or present itself as an obvious course of action.

'So why did you?' I said.

'Now who's thick, Séamus? I bet it's the murder weapon. That – obviously – is why I took it.'

'We'll give it to the police,' Alison said.

'Exactly. Go right now, this minute, Séamus Considine and telephone your friend the detective and we'll give it to him.'

I nodded and went to the telephone as I could see – once they told me – that it was the obvious course of action. But the policeman in charge told me Detective Richardson was off duty and wasn't going to be contactable until tomorrow. I tried to wheedle a mobile number – to no avail. Eventually I gave up and asked him to tell Detective Richardson that Cassandra was home and that I'd ring later. He agreed and I went back to the kitchen.

Cassandra and Alison were drinking tea and leaning against the worktop. Neither of them looked as if they were sharing a room with a murder weapon. What a title. Murder weapon. Weapon of murder. Life finisher. Man killer. My head was speeding up. I forced myself to focus.

'No luck. He's off-duty and they won't give me a number. He'll be back tomorrow at ten so I'll ring then.'

'Why didn't you ask to speak with somebody else?' Alison asked.

I shrugged. It had never even occurred to me.

'It doesn't make much difference,' Cassandra said. 'It isn't going anywhere.'

Just then the doorbell rang. All three of us started slightly.

I walked along the corridor towards the front door before I could stop and think. The bell rang again, making my skin tingle with the noise, which in turn made me angry with myself. I barrelled my chest to contain the fear and threw the door open, ready to take on all comers.

'She's back?' Tim said, rushing past me. 'Chrissie said she rang – is it true?'

'In the kitchen,' I said to his back.

By the time I reached the kitchen Tim and Cassandra were kissing the frenzied and hungry kissing of the terrified and Alison was rinsing her cup under a running tap. She smiled at me.

'Well,' I said, 'the young lovers reunite, how sweet.'

Tim and Cassandra stopped kissing and held each other tightly as they turned to look at me.

'I was so worried,' Tim said.

'He was,' I agreed.

'I thought something terrible had happened to you.'

Cassandra beamed and snuggled her head into his chest. 'Well, as you can see I'm perfectly fine. A little tired and worn out, but basically fine.'

Tim stroked her spiky hair with his bony fingers and smiled. 'We looked everywhere for you. Everywhere we could think of, anyway.'

'We even visited Pádraig Harrison,' I said, suddenly remembering, 'and Alison searched the upstairs of his house for clues to your whereabouts.'

'Did you?' Tim said. 'When?'

'I met him, actually, on Wednesday,' Cassandra said.

'He told us. He said he met you in the village.'

'Did he, really?' Cassandra said, making a circle of her mouth and opening her eyes wide in amazement. 'But it wasn't in the village.' She adjusted herself to better fit into the loop of Tim's arm.

'What wasn't?'

'I met him in that restaurant place where the bus stopped. He was putting petrol in his car. I met him just after we arrived, before I even went in to the restaurant.'

'You are joking! And then you found the murderers inside?'

'You found murderers?' Tim said. 'What do you mean that you found murderers?'

'It's a long story.'

'She got into their van and they drove off and she found their gun and had to walk back from high up in the Galtees or the Silvermines or the devil knows where . . .' I said.

'Stop!' Tim said, pulling back to look at Cassandra. 'What is all this?'

'I'll tell you all about it later. I promise.'

'No. Now. Tell me now,' Tim said, his voice edgy and insistent.

Cassandra shrugged. 'I'm exhausted. Can't it wait?'

'No,' Tim said, stepping away from her entirely. 'I want to know what you found and what happened.'

We all looked at Tim. His eyes were wide and his mouth was held in a thin, tight line that quivered unsteadily at the corners as he stared at Cassandra. She looked right back at him, and I could see her pull herself up to the full extent of her five feet and half an inch. I knew her well enough to know that she was about to tell him to fuck off and I was simply too tired for another drama.

'Tim has been out of his head with worry all weekend,' I said. Everybody turned around to look at me. 'You have no idea what it was like waiting here afraid something had happened to you.'

Cassandra looked back at Tim. His face melted and his mouth slackened and he looked as though his long, thin legs were about to fold underneath him. 'I'm sorry,' he said in a whispery voice, 'I didn't sleep a wink last night. I just wondered – just wanted – '

Cassandra reached out and took his hand in hers. 'It doesn't matter. I'll tell you anything you want to know.'

'Why don't you two go into the sitting room? Alison and I have some note comparing to do. Go on – we'll bring in tea in a while.'

Tim looked at me gratefully and then he and Cassandra disappeared out of the kitchen. Which left me alone with Alison and it struck me that was how we started out earlier in the day.

Alison boiled the kettle and made tea and I buttered bread to make sandwiches. And suddenly, now that Cassandra was back and even though there was a gun wrapped in sacking in the hallway of my house where I put it, I wanted to know why Alison had lied to me.

I sliced tomatoes and the inside of my head was ringing with questions. Alison moved, silently, around my kitchen, never asking me where anything was, but somehow seeming to find everything she needed. Her face was tired and her shoulders stooped a little and I knew she probably wouldn't be able to face an interrogation right then. And anyway there was no need. I could always ask her some other time.

We sat down together at the table and ate our damp tomato sandwiches and drank our tea in silence. After I finished eating I sat back in my chair and stretched my neck trying to relieve the pain in the muscles of my shoulders.

I lit a cigarette and gulped down a full cup of tea. Then I leaned over the table, refilled my cup, sat back into my chair again and looked at Alison. She was looking at me and she smiled as we made eye contact. I smiled back.

'Why did you lie to me?' I said, the words tumbling out of my mouth without permission.

Alison didn't move her gaze or even stop smiling. 'I thought we might get to discuss Pádraig Harrison's upstairs décor or something else trivial tonight,' she said, dropping her eyes for a minute and then looking straight back at me.

'Sorry. I know it's bad timing, but I can't seem to be able to forget about it.'

Alison shrugged and sighed. 'I did lie, but I don't know how to explain it to you.'

'Try.'

Alison sighed again. 'That's not really true either. I do know how to explain it but I – I'm afraid, I suppose, that you won't believe me.'

'Try,' I said again, stamping out my cigarette on the edge of a saucer.

Alison pushed her chair back from the table and stretched her legs. 'William Ormston was my father. I never knew that until about a year ago and even when I found out I didn't do anything about it for a while. Eventually I wrote to him and . . .' she paused and touched her mouth with her right index finger.

Alison got up, looked at me, briefly, and then walked out of the kitchen. I could hear her walking through the hallway and opening the front door. She was leaving. Well, what did I expect?

Maybe I should follow her and ask her to come back? She could always tell me about it some other time, it didn't have to be right at that minute. Or did it? I thought about that, because maybe it wasn't true, maybe it did have to be right at that minute.

After all she *had* lied and even if it wasn't a great time to look for an explanation I didn't think I could take it back now that it was said. Which was a pity. She had been there when I needed her after all. The kitchen door opened and Alison walked back into the room.

'I thought you'd left.'

She sat back down in the chair she had vacated and placed a sheet of paper on the table in front of me. I looked at her and she motioned to me to read it. The letter was written on heavy, good quality, plain white paper, watermarked with a cursive blue logo that said '*Ormatronics*' and it was dated 15 September.

Dear Alison

Thank you for your letter of 25 August and the photographs
enclosed therewith. I do remember your mother well and I am sorry to
hear she has passed away. I would very much like if we could get
together for a chat. I will, however, be out of the country for a couple
of months. I am due to return in early November, so perhaps if I get
in contact with you as soon as I return we might arrange to meet?

I look forward to our meeting and wish you all the best.

Yours truly,

William Ormston

I finished reading the letter and folded it in half and
handed it back to Alison.

'I know,' she began, pausing to pick up the letter in her
hand, 'I realize it doesn't prove that he was my father, but I
know that he was.'

'You told me your father's name was O'Rourke,' I said.

Alison looked at me. 'I lied.'

I lit another cigarette and we sat in silence for a few seconds.

'Anyway,' Alison said, breaking the silence, 'what this does
prove is that Ormston did have a relationship with my
mother and was willing to meet with me and I think that has
to be significant.'

She stopped speaking and looked down at the sheet of
paper that she smoothed and placed flat on the table in front
of her.

'You're probably right,' I said.

She looked up at me. 'But it doesn't explain why I lied
does it?'

'You told me your father's name was O'Rourke,' I said
again, because somehow I couldn't let go that part of the lie.

Alison took a deep breath. 'I know. But most of what I
told you was the truth. It's even true that my firm is involved
in investigating the Irish end – it's just that I'm not. Or at

least not officially. I'm pretty new there – I spend my time dealing with the smaller cases.'

Alison paused and looked at me and I looked away.

'They'd never let me investigate something as potentially big as this,' she said. 'Anyway, truthfully, there wasn't much to investigate at the Irish end. The American lawyers were just making sure to cover all bases. But when Capel and Williams were engaged to investigate, I heard about it, as you do – office gossip – and I suppose the simple truth is that I just couldn't keep away.'

'So you're investigating this off your own bat?'

Alison nodded.

'Didn't they guess at work?'

Alison shook her head.

'How come?'

'I left. I tried not to leave for a while but it began to consume my whole life. At first, I took a few days off here and there to follow things up. I was on a day's leave the first day I came here, for example. But then I found out about what was happening here and it just took me over, I suppose.'

'So you quit your job?'

Alison nodded. 'Two weeks ago. I decided I'd always be able to get another job, but that I needed to spend my time working on this until I got it out of my system. Does that sound mad?'

'Yes. But as I haven't exactly got a great track record in relation to sanity myself, I don't believe I can judge.'

Alison smiled and I smiled back and I wished that the world was just an ordinary place where everybody wasn't carrying scars and armour and terror deep in the tissue of themselves. I wished she hadn't lied so that I didn't have to have it proven to me over and over again that anybody any time can be the person to betray you. As if she heard my thoughts the smile faded from Alison's face.

'I'm sorry I lied to you.'

I held my breath to control the knife-pain in my guts. I nodded and picked at the skin around my thumbnail and began to hum a series of unconnected notes. 'So why? Why did you lie?'

'Well, firstly, I needed a cover to ask questions. But then, I don't know, I just couldn't seem to find a way to tell you that didn't sound as if I'd been dishonest.'

I looked at her and raised an eyebrow.

'I know, I know. I *was* dishonest, but I didn't know how to explain it to you so that you wouldn't . . . I wouldn't –'

'What?'

'I did it so that you wouldn't think badly of me, I suppose,' Alison said, taking a long breath in and out.

Alison looked away from me and I fiddled with my tea-spoon. Why would she care what I thought of her? Life was a lot more complex than I'd been led to expect. People love you and betray you and shoot your friends and lie to you, while worrying what you think about them. It all sat like an indigestible lump in my brain.

'Are you taking a case against William Ormston's estate as well?' I asked to change the energy in the air.

Alison looked up at me and shook her head. 'No. I don't want any of his money.'

'So what have you been doing since you left your job?'

'Investigating the case.'

'But why if . . . ?'

'To know. I just want to know.'

Her eyes filled with tears and it looked like she was about to cry and I was afraid she would. I didn't know if I had it left in me to look at her being vulnerable, so I asked another question.

'What did you discover?' My stomach hurt as I spoke, because I didn't really care about what she had discovered. I just wanted her not to cry.

Alison tilted her head back and closed her eyes for a minute. 'Quite a lot, actually,' she said, suddenly opening her eyes and looking straight at me.

And I could see something in those eyes that I didn't want to know. Disappointment? Pain? I avoided the question in my head as if it was a rock in my path.

'Tell me,' I said, to keep the subject changed.

'Well, William Ormston's first wife – Anna Brennan – was killed in a car crash in South Africa. I told you that already, didn't I?'

I nodded.

'OK, well, I always knew that, but I did some research into the newspapers around the time of the crash. I couldn't find much detail. The crash happened just outside a place called Annburg. There were two vehicles involved – a car and a schoolbus. It isn't clear exactly how many people were involved. All I can be sure of is that William and Anna were there, because they were named. And the bus driver – a Fred Smith – he was named because he was killed as well.'

'How did you get hold of the papers?'

'On the Internet.'

'I suppose it might be an idea to go to South Africa,' I said. 'You might find someone who remembers something. I mean, if you're interested in following up this clue and trying to find out what happened there.'

'I went last week,' she said. 'I decided I'd never find out what I needed to know unless I went there myself.'

I laughed. 'And the weather?'

'Hot. It's summer there, you know.'

'What did you find?'

'Well, it was worth my while going. I met the man who was the local chief of police at the time, for example. He's retired now, but alive and pretty compos mentis. He was the first to arrive at the accident. Said Anna Brennan was dead at the scene and they had to cut Fred Smith out of the cab of the bus because it'd ploughed into a wall.'

'But he was alive?'

'Just. Died on the way to hospital.'

'Anybody else hurt?'

'Doesn't seem to be. There were loads of kids, of course, because of the school bus, but they weren't badly injured. Neither was Ormston.'

'What exactly happened?' I said.

'There doesn't seem to be a good explanation for the accident – it wasn't even a dangerous stretch of road. The police chief blamed Ormston.'

'Why?'

'He said he could smell alcohol from him at the accident scene. He tried to follow it up, but he told me that he got a phonecall from his superiors saying all William Ormston's blood tests were clear and there was no need to pursue the matter any further.'

'So he didn't,' I said.

Alison nodded. 'I suppose he figured there was no point and, anyway, William Ormston was gone.'

'Bastard,' I said.

Alison nodded.

'You might change your mind about suing his estate. People often do.'

Alison bit her lip and her eyes filled with tears. She stood up, put on her coat and fixed her hair behind both her ears. 'I don't think so.' She focused her attention on buttoning her coat and then looked at me for a moment. 'Thanks for the sandwich.'

I nodded, and though I was sorry for her I was glad she was leaving now that she was upset. I hadn't the energy for it any more. Pathetic but true.

'OK,' I said, going to stand up, 'take care. Thanks for your help.'

'No need to get up,' Alison said, in a high, snappy voice. Was that her court voice? 'I'll let myself out.'

I shrugged, annoyed now with her sudden change of mood. I was just too fucking tired to be putting up with this shit. She was upset? Big deal. We were all upset.

'Fine,' I said, sitting back into my chair. 'See you.'

Alison walked to the kitchen door and opened it. 'Séamus,' she said. Her voice was softer and quieter.

I turned around in my chair to see her. She looked young, suddenly, and scared. I felt bad for abandoning her, but what could I do? And, anyway, she'd get over it. It had happened to me lots of times – especially recently – and I'd gotten over it, hadn't I?

'What?'

'Don't forget to make tea for Tim and Cassandra. We said we would.'

Then she turned and left the room. I was jelly brained and angry and ashamed and frustrated as I listened to the front door close. Fuck it, anyway. Really and truly, why did everything happen to me?

I didn't need any of this grief after all the things that had happened to me, and there was the fact that she'd lied. There was always that. Brought it on herself, really. I was busy swirling the facts into a thought-path that would prove to me that I hadn't done anything wrong when Tim came into the kitchen.

'She's asleep and I'm whacked. I've had practically no sleep for the past few days – too little even for a doctor. I covered her with a coat. Maybe you'd see if you could get her up to bed?'

'No problem.'

'See you tomorrow.'

'See you, Tim,' I said, not even attempting to stand up. I listened to him leave and then went into the sitting room. Cassandra was asleep, curled in a ball on the couch covered with the throws and Tim's coat. Which meant that he'd gone out into the December night without a coat. Very chivalrous.

I shook Cassandra, gently, by the shoulder, but she was so deeply asleep there wasn't any response. The house was chilly. I fetched a quilt and covered her, turned off all the lights and started up the stairs to bed.

I could hardly wait to hit the bed. Somehow I had moved from being an insomniac to some version of a hibernating creature. I never seemed to want to do anything except sleep any more.

Just as I reached the top of the stairs the telephone rang. Fuck, I thought. Let it ring. I stood and listened for a minute and then I remembered that my mother had come the whole way to Castleannery the last time I hadn't answered the phone. So I went back down the steps of the stairs, my legs screaming with tiredness.

'Hello?' I said, as I picked up the receiver.

Silence.

'Hello,' I said again.

More silence. I moved to hang up. Somebody coughed on the other end of the line.

'Séamus? It's me, Alison. I need your help.'

11

'Running On Empty'
Jackson Browne, 1977

For some insane, exhausted, perverse reason, I almost laughed when I heard Alison's voice on the phone. Luckily, for once, I didn't obey my impulses.

'What's wrong?'

There was a short pause.

'I have a flat tyre,' she said, her voice echoing in that enchanted otherworldly way of mobile phone networks. 'Which would be fine, except that, with everything that's been going on, I forgot all about the fact that I also had one a few weeks ago.' She paused. 'So I don't have a spare.'

'I'll come get you. Where are you?'

'Just the other side of Castleannery.'

'Near the graveyard?'

There was no answer for a moment, then I heard a loud sigh. 'Yes. Just in front of it. I didn't realize.'

'Don't worry about the dead. In my experience it's the living that cause all the problems. See you in about ten minutes.'

I checked the sleeping Cassandra in the sitting room, grabbed my keys and left. As usual my car was reluctant to start and as I coaxed it I suppressed the rising embarrassment bubbling inside me at the thought of Alison Chang sliding her elegant form out of her leather seated car into my copybook-littered crock. Shit, I thought. Too bad if she doesn't like it.

I drove through the night, listening to a classical music station on the car radio and not really thinking of much. Or at least not in a focused way. There were so many things to think about that they were jostling each other for room in a mostly closed down brain.

I saw Alison's car as soon as I passed the last lamppost on the one and only main street of Castleannery. The light inside the car was turned on and I could see that she was sitting back in her seat. I stopped my car behind hers and as soon as I turned off the engine she got out of her car and locked it.

Alison walked towards me turning up her collar against the damp cold of the night. 'Thanks for coming out,' she said, in measured tones as she sat into my car. 'I appreciate it. I'm sorry for calling you so late, but I didn't know what else to do.'

'No problem,' I said, searching her face for some clue as to what exactly was going on inside her. But her face was unreadable, and I wasn't sure that I wanted to know anyway. 'At least your car will be safe enough there. The dead people will guard it.'

Alison nodded, but didn't answer.

I started the engine of my car. 'OK. Where do you want to go?'

'Well,' she said, continuing to use a voice as formal as a bow tie, 'if there's a hotel nearby, you might drop me there.'

I laughed.

'If it's not too much trouble. Or even if you know of a taxi service . . .'

I laughed again. 'It's not that. It's just that there isn't a hotel within twenty miles of here and the taxi has to be booked a day in advance. You are more than welcome to stay at my house. We'll have somebody come and fix your car in the morning. Or I'll drive you until we find an hotel, if you prefer. Whatever you like.'

'It's too far to drive,' she said, her voice getting quieter and quieter as she spoke.

'I don't mind,' I said, in a voice that wanted to match her quietness. 'Whatever you want to do.'

'Well,' she said, pausing to have a quick look at me with her all-seeing eyes, 'maybe if I stay at your house – if you don't mind. I'll be gone first thing in the morning.'

'That's settled, so. Seat belt?'

'On.'

'OK.'

I did a three-point turn in the middle of the dark road and began the silent drive towards my house.

'Sorry that it's not as comfortable as your car,' I said, in spite of my resolutions. I pulled the car to a stop in front of my house.

'Well, it has four working tyres. Which is more than you could say about my car at the moment.'

Alison and I went into the house and I tried to think of things to talk about, but the air between us was full and I was just too tired.

'Cassandra is asleep on the couch,' I said, standing at the bottom of the stairs, 'and I'm totally exhausted so I hope you don't mind if we go straight up to bed?'

Alison shook her head. 'Of course not.'

'There's a spare bedroom upstairs. The bed is made up I think, and it should be all right. If you come with me, I'll show it to you.'

I led the way upstairs to the spare bedroom. I reached my hand into the dark room and turned on the light.

The room used to be Jessica's studio and a guest room when things were different. A lot of Jessica's stuff had still been there in boxes the last time I looked, but I saw that they seemed to have disappeared. Cassandra, probably, clearing away the traces to try to make me feel better. Now the room was empty except for an old iron bedstead covered in a rose-patterned quilt and a small pine dressing table.

'It's lovely,' Alison said.

I looked at her.

'It is,' she said. 'Thank you very much for your help.'

I smiled. 'You're welcome. Look, the bathroom is just there and that's the hot-press – please help yourself to towels and whatever else you need. OK, that's it. I'm off to bed. Goodnight. Sleep well.'

'Goodnight,' Alison said, holding the edge of the bedroom door in both hands. 'Thanks again.'

'No problem,' I said, turning to walk away.

'I want to tell you something and I can't think how to say it properly, but I really want to say it anyway. Can I tell you?'

'Go ahead.'

'Well, I truly have no interest in William Ormston's money and I'm not making a claim against his estate because it would be unethical to be involved like this if I was.'

'Look, Alison, it's none of my business why you're doing it.'

'Still. I just want to know about him. I don't know why, but I do and, anyway, I couldn't care less about money. I don't need it. That's why I could just give up my job. My mother was very wealthy and she left me all her money, so I have plenty. Thanks for everything. Goodnight.'

She stepped into the spare bedroom and closed the door before I could speak. All I caught was a flash of brown eyes and her pale face as she disappeared. I stared at the closed door for a minute and then walked to my room, undressed and got into bed. My body was grateful to find itself lying down, but suddenly my brain had woken up.

I looked at the dark bedroom ceiling and thought about what had just happened. Alison Chang was rich. How rich?

Sort of rich? Really, really rich? Inbetween rich – if such a thing is possible.

Rich is such a relative term. I knew I was rich relative to most of the population of the world, and I also knew that relative to, say, the architect now living with my wife, I was quite poor. So how rich was she? Rich enough to quit work and hare off to South Africa searching for her roots? That was definitely richer than me.

I flipped on to my stomach and tried to fall asleep. As usual, pictures flicked around my head every time I closed my eyes. Tall men with shotguns, Jessica, the ditch outside Pádraig Harrison's house, my mother, Alison's tired, sad eyes as she closed the bedroom door.

I rolled on to my back again. Well, if she was rich then that explained the car with the leather seats. And if she was rich did she live in a beautiful, tastefully decorated house? Probably. And now she was sleeping in my guest room with the bare floorboards and lumpy-mattressed bed? I mostly didn't care.

Gradually, I fell into a fitful sleep. I was so tired and strung out that I would gladly have sold my soul for a couple of hours' sleep-oblivion. But I couldn't seem to manage to let myself relax quite to the point of unconsciousness.

Every half hour or so I woke and sat up and looked at the clock. Two o'clock. Two forty. Three o'clock. Four fifteen – that was almost a sleep. Five o'clock. By six ten I was more exhausted than I had been before I went to bed.

I lay there – wide awake – and for the first time let myself feel the full extent of the terror that'd been rattling around inside me all the time Cassandra was missing. But at least she was home safely – even if she had brought a gun.

Jesus, the gun! I sat up in the bed. I'd forgotten about the gun. Where was it? In the kitchen or had we moved it? I'd meant to move it, but had I? I couldn't remember.

I remembered Cassandra holding it – but where had she put it?

I sat up in bed and tried to visualize the gun and see Cassandra moving it – or not – but the inside of my eyelids were like a blank TV screen now that I wanted some pictures. Which was bloody typical. I had no choice but to go downstairs to have a look. I forced my aching body to get out of bed and walk through the dark house and down the stairs.

I'd smoke a cigarette as soon as I got to the kitchen, I told myself. And make a cup of cocoa. That might help me get to sleep for a couple of hours. I pushed open the kitchen door and flicked the old-fashioned switch upwards. Brightness exploded all around the room and I blinked.

'Hello, Séamus,' Tim said.

I blinked again. Maybe I'd fallen asleep after all and I was having a dream of being awake and not able to fall asleep?

'Tim?'

Tim nodded and shifted the bundle he had in his right hand into his left hand. 'Sorry to disturb you at this hour of the night. I let myself in – the back door was open. You're an awful man for leaving that door open.'

I listened to his calm and normal-sounding voice and tried to reconcile everything. His words. His tone. The fact that he was in my house in the middle of the night and was holding the dog-smelling, sack-wrapped gun.

'Tim?' I said, and that was it. Something hit me hard on the back of my head and I reeled around falling in a heap on the floor. I didn't completely lose consciousness, but voices seemed to float back and forth around me like water. Tim's voice. A woman's voice. A man's voice. Cassandra's voice? An angry voice.

I felt myself being pulled by the arms and lifted on to a chair and felt the jolt as my head fell forward and my forehead banged against something hard. The kitchen table? I didn't know.

Then I think I might have been unconscious for a while because everything was floating in my head like pictures and sounds in a pond and my head ached with a pain that seemed to scream its way around the perimeter of my skull. I heard Cassandra again.

'Bastard,' she said, and I knew that wasn't an hallucination and I tried to make myself wake up properly. I thought I said her name and heard her say mine. Next I felt a hand on my arm and a hand lifting my head, very gently.

'Séamus?' a woman's voice said. I was glad. Cassandra was still here, they hadn't hurt her.

'Séamus?' a soft hand lifted my head and I opened my eyes. Alison.

'Jesus,' I muttered as I tried to sit up. I rested my head on my hands and somebody – Alison? – put something cold on the top of my head. It felt a lot better than the fire that had been there.

I couldn't lift my head so I tried to focus on the table. If I could make myself see one thing then I'd be able to see everything else. Pine grain. Wavy lines. Were they always wavy or was it just me? Gradually, the world stopped moving and I looked up. The walls of the kitchen wobbled for a moment and then stopped.

'Alison. Someone was here. They hit me. They hit Tim too I think and Cassandra. Jesus! Cassandra! Where is Cassandra?'

'It was Tim.'

'I know!' I shouted. 'I saw him. They took him and Cassandra. The bastards who hit me took them and I think they took the gun as well.'

'No, Séamus, no – listen to me. It was Tim. Tim took the gun, some other guy hit you over the head and then they took Cassandra.'

I shook my head. It was all too ridiculous. I tried to stand up but my legs folded. Alison grabbed me and sat me back on the chair.

'I heard Cassandra after they hit me. Heard her cursing. Did they hurt her? Where is she?'

'They took her.'

I stood up, knocking my chair to the floor. My legs wobbled wildly and I grabbed the edge of the table. 'And you let them? Why didn't you stop them?'

'I couldn't stop them. There were two of them. Tim and another man.'

'Tim?'

Alison nodded and I remembered but it made no sense. 'Tim Winter?'

'Yes. He took the gun and there was another man.'

'Who?'

'I don't know. But I think he was probably your Afrikaner.'

'Fuck it. Tim? I can't believe it.'

Alison shrugged.

'And they took Cassandra and you didn't stop them?'

Alison sighed. 'Did you?'

I didn't answer. Instead I tried to think as I forced myself to remain standing by leaning heavily on the table.

'They also took the gun and Tim seems to have left you a note.'

Alison handed me a sheet of paper.

~~*Don't call the police or I'll kill Cassandra. I'll be gone soon and then*~~ *I'll set her free if you don't follow us. You know I mean business, Séamus.*

    Tim

I read and re-read the note, proof that once again I'd made a mistake in picking the people I should trust. 'Fuck, fuck, fuck, fuck, fuck.'

Alison watched me.

'Why didn't they take you?' I said, suddenly suspicious of

tall, oriental women with beautiful faces and whispering sadness surrounding them.

'Because they didn't know I was here. I hid on the stairs and tried to listen, though I couldn't hear much. It was all over fairly quickly. It was your shout that woke me in the first place.'

'Your car is down by the cemetery,' I said, forcing the pieces to make sense. 'That's why they didn't know you were here.'

Alison nodded. 'I looked out of the landing window as they drove away and I managed to get the number of the van.'

I pressed the ice pack against my throbbing skull and listened.

'We should phone the police and see if they can find it. I'd imagine it's the same van Cassandra hid in so there seems to be a good possibility that at least this one isn't stolen. Maybe the police can trace it.'

I shook my head and the inside of it exploded like glass.

'He'll kill Cassandra,' I said, resisting the urge to vomit.

'Not if the police catch him first.'

'No. It's too much of a risk,' I said. Abruptly, I let go of the kitchen table and tried to walk but my legs refused. I sat back on to the chair and I wanted to cry. Everything was wrong in the world and it was all my fault. I broke everything. Maybe if I sat still nothing else would go wrong?

The bad guys would escape, so what? It made no difference whether or not they escaped. Mattie was already dead and there was no hope of justice. All that mattered now was that nothing happen to Cassandra.

My head pounded like horses and I wished I could slip into unconsciousness and wake up to find Cassandra back home and everything solved.

'Séamus,' I heard somebody say, but I was concentrating on stillness and the pain inside my head and heart.

'Séamus,' the voice said again.

I looked out of myself and saw Alison sitting on a chair in front of me.

'We'd better go,' she said as soon as we made eye contact.

'No,' I said, closing my eyes so that I didn't have to look at her, 'it's too dangerous for Cassandra.'

'We have to try to follow them. They can't have gone far. Call your friend the detective and see if he can help.'

'They'll kill Cassandra,' I said, opening my eyes.

'They might kill her anyway,' Alison said, locking her eyes on to mine so that I couldn't slip away.

'But – but –' I held out the note that was still in my hand.

Alison shook her head. 'She'll be too dangerous to leave alive. I mean, think about it, Séamus. They killed your friend Mattie with less reason.'

I caught my breath at the sound of Mattie's name and how it triggered the picture of him as his body exploded in the frosty night. And how I hadn't been able to save him either.

'Let's go,' Alison said, and her voice seemed to echo around my head.

'No. He'll let her go if we don't try to stop him.'

Alison closed her slightly slanted eyes and pressed her white lips together. I watched her as if she was a kaleidoscope, with academic interest as to the next configuration. Her eyes opened.

'Get up and let's go. We can't just sit here, he'll kill Cassandra. Go telephone your friend the Guard and leave a message if you can't get to speak with him – here, give him your mobile number.'

'I don't know where I left my phone and anyway I think it mightn't be charged. I keep forgetting to charge it, and I can never remember to bring it with me. Cassandra goes mad. Always giving out.'

'Well give him my number then.' Alison began to pace. 'Where could they be, Séamus? They can't have gone too far, yet, can they? Think.'

I shrugged.

Alison bit her lip. 'Think,' she repeated.

'We can't follow.'

'We'll be careful. We won't let them see. Now, think, Séamus. You must be able to think of a place we can start to look.'

My head was a jumble of thoughts and I could see what Alison wanted and why, but I knew she didn't realize how much of a danger I'd put everyone into if I moved.

'His house,' some obedient part of me said in spite of myself. 'I suppose we could see if Chrissie is still there.'

'Good idea,' Alison said, standing up. 'Come on.'

I thought of refusing. I thought of saying what was in my head, but I knew she wouldn't believe me. Alison picked up my car keys and I stood up and followed her towards the door. It was easier than arguing and anyway I knew we wouldn't find Chrissie or Tim or Cassandra. I knew it wouldn't work out.

Just inside the front door Alison turned and looked at me and a slow smile spread across her face.

'Séamus,' she said and I wondered if I kissed her would it stop her in her tracks and make Cassandra safe?

'Yes.'

'Maybe you should put on a pair of trousers before you go out.'

I looked down to find myself clad in a t-shirt and a pair of shorts.

'Shit.'

Alison laughed. 'Wait here.'

I stood in the hallway like a dazed child until Alison returned and handed me a pair of jeans, a pair of socks and a green ribbed sweater. Without a word I put on the clothes and then looked in the hallway until I found my discarded boots.

'Jacket,' Alison announced as soon as I was dressed, and then she handed me a green oilskin jacket. I put it on and we left the house. Alison buttoned her coat up to the chin as we stood outside my front door in the early morning light.

I could hear a donkey braying and a dog barking and I knew that all around me in the countryside people were rolling over in bed, groaning at the day, and I wished that I was one of them.

'You know where he lives?' she said.

I looked at her in the dusky light and nodded, and the broken bits inside my head clanged a warning. 'Yes. On the main street in the village.'

'I'll drive.' Alison walked towards my car and unlocked the doors.

I shrugged and sat into the freezing car as Alison started the engine and I noticed that it started first time for her. We drove to the village in a silence broken only by the occasional sound of my voice giving directions. Turn left, next right, down here. Like a holiday adventure.

Alison stopped the car outside Tim's house on my instruction. The house was in total darkness. I knew it would be and I was glad. Inside of me the terror mixed with hope and shame. Hope that Cassandra would be all right after all. Shame because if she wasn't I prayed that at least I wouldn't have to see her being destroyed.

Alison ran up the frosty pathway to Tim's front door and banged on the door. I climbed slowly from the car and leaned against its slightly warm metal and watched Alison. Imagine I'd banged on that door myself when I was looking for help finding Mattie's killers. How unreal that all seemed.

I'd gone to them for help. Drank tea in the kitchen with Chrissie. Taken lifts and advice from Tim and all the time they were the bad guys?

Tim's front door stayed closed. No sign of Chrissie's tired face behind the door tonight. For fuck's sake – not only Tim but Chrissie as well. One part of me couldn't believe that she was involved as well but another, new part, welcomed it as making sense. She'd let me think she liked me. Kissed me. Seemed to want me. The perfect formula for betrayal. All the time plotting to run away. Why not?

I watched Alison as she banged again on the door and then peered in the darkened windows. Why was she doing this, anyway? What was in it for her? Who the fuck was she anyway and if Cassandra was killed how much would it matter to her?

Alison didn't have a lifetime of knitted together experience with Cassandra. She didn't have all the secrets and games and adventures and hopes and dreams and aspirations that we'd shared. She didn't love my cousin like I did. At worst Cassandra's death would make a tiny rip in Alison's life while it would tear the bottom out of mine.

I noticed then, that Alison seemed to have disappeared. Where was she? I strained my eyes in to the cloudy light and lit a cigarette. Where the fuck was that woman? As I smoked I realized I hadn't smoked since Tim's friend hit me on the head.

The trickle of smoke and nicotine made me feel nauseated and comforted me at the same time and I wished I'd thought of smoking earlier. I watched the front of Tim's house, searching for Alison's reappearance. But all I could see were the trees and the shrubs in the garden as they came more and more into focus with the morning light. I ground out my cigarette and considered lighting another, but there was still no sign of Alison.

Reluctantly, I walked up the path to Tim's door and followed a narrow strip of concrete around the house until I arrived outside the back door. I looked all around in the garden. No Alison. Not that I'd expected to find her. I knew in my heart that she'd gone inside. The place looked empty which was probably disappointing for her but at least it meant there was nobody there to hit her over the head.

I pushed open the back door and found myself in the glaring white kitchen. All the main lights were turned off but a small striplight under a cupboard had been switched on. Alison. Looking around in the dimly lit kitchen I could see almost everything as a result of the whiteness of its operating theatre-type décor.

I stood still and listened. The house seemed to be asleep except for the usual building noises – humming fridges, creaking walls, breathing wood. I made my way, slowly, through the kitchen and into the hallway, standing still every few steps to listen. Silence.

Maybe I'd been mistaken. Maybe Alison hadn't come in. But I knew she had. I could feel her in the house, I just couldn't find her yet. I opened doors and looked into rooms – a sitting room, a waiting room, the room that was Tim's surgery. I opened a narrow door at the bottom of the stairs and found a toilet and wash-hand basin. But no Alison.

She couldn't be upstairs, could she? I mean, why? Why look upstairs when it was obvious that there wasn't anybody here. No Tim. No Cassandra. Not even Chrissie. She must have left, I thought. I must have missed her as I came in.

She was probably waiting out at the car. There wasn't much point in looking upstairs. I stood at the bottom of the dark staircase and looked up. I really, really didn't want to go up the stairs.

'Shit,' I whispered, beginning to climb. As I reached the top of the stairs a white painted door opened and Alison appeared in front of me on the landing. In her hand she held a bundle of papers and she motioned to me to go back downstairs. I turned my exhausted body and complied.

We walked like ghosts until we reached the kitchen and then Alison hurried to the small light and examined the papers. I watched her and wondered what she'd found but mostly I didn't care, mostly I just wanted to lie down on the floor and sleep.

'I think I might know where they are,' she said, excitedly turning around to look at me. 'I bet I know where they've taken Cassandra.'

'South Africa?'

'I don't think so. At least not yet. I think they've taken her to Lahinch.'

I tutted and laughed.

'No, really, Séamus. Call that policeman friend of yours.'

'He's not my friend.'

'All right, but call him.'

I shook my head. 'No.'

'But why? It's worth a try. If I'm right we'll find Cassandra and if I'm wrong we can look somewhere else.'

I shook my head again. The pain had decreased. I fumbled in my pockets for a cigarette and put it in my mouth. No lighter. No matches.

'But –'

'But nothing,' I said, suddenly angry with Alison as well as the rest of the world. 'I'm not doing anything. That's the trick, obviously. I do nothing and then everything will be fine.'

Alison and I looked at each other in Tim Winter's kitchen. A tall, wealthy, self-possessed Oriental woman. A tall, destroyed, battle-weary, battered Irishman. I found a large box of kitchen matches and lit my cigarette.

'Why in the name of God do you think they're in Lahinch, anyway? Why not Johannesburg or Durban or someplace like that?'

Alison shook her head and tapped the sheets of paper she'd been reading. 'They have to hide Cassandra someplace.

And Tim has a new holiday home in Lahinch. A Section 23 – look.'

'So he bought a house,' I said as I exhaled. 'So what? Big deal. Doctors make a lot of money, he probably wanted to invest some of it.'

'I'm not disagreeing with that. But he only just bought it – look at the date, it was all finalized three weeks ago.'

'So?' I said.

'Well, if it's such a recent purchase then he'd be pretty sure nobody knows about it. How far is Lahinch from here?'

'Sixty miles – something like that – less maybe.'

'OK. Let's go and have a look, that's all I'm saying. We have an address and he could be there and we might be able to get Cassandra and –'

I suddenly felt as if I was made of liquid. Tim – who I'd thought was my friend – was a murdering bastard and he had Cassandra. He'd probably kill her or have her killed like he had with Mattie. I felt myself move as if I really was liquid, as if I was flowing and everything around me was dark and black and I had no idea where I was flowing.

Something sharp pulled at my hand, but I flowed on along the river of terror where I could see Cassandra's body falling to the road like Mattie's. Where I could hear the shots that opened his chest and closed his life. Where I could see the taillights of Jessica's car and then Cassandra was dying again and so on and so on like a horrible reel of life.

'Séamus. Séamus look at me.'

A hand fitted itself around my cheek and tried to move my face but I resisted. I wouldn't do it. I wouldn't look. I couldn't look. I couldn't bear to see any more. I pulled away from the hand and fell against a wall of some kind. I was vaguely aware that I was, somehow, outdoors.

'Séamus,' the voice whispered again and the hand moved and stroked my head and it hurt like hell where the bastards hit me, but it wasn't the pain that finished me off. It was the lightness of the touch, like baby-breath, on my head. The gentleness of it cracked my heart open and I began to cry.

A crying with no prelude. No building from sadness to despair. No growing anguish. This was a crying that plunged straight into the pain. One moment I wasn't crying, the next it was all hot tears and snot and gasping for breath. Waves of terror and despair and aloneness. Crying to the point of dissolution.

How was I supposed to do it? How was I to live in the world when it was so fucking hard? Why hadn't that bastard missed Mattie and shot me and then none of this would have happened? Gradually, I became aware of the hand outside me, again. Still stroking my hair. I opened my eyes and turned my head and saw Alison's face.

'Do you know something?' I said in a voice that was as wobbly as a new-born calf's legs.

Alison shook her head and her hair swished over her face. I sniffed loudly and she handed me a bunch of tissues, so I blew my nose. I composed myself and looked again and I still had to say it.

'Do you know something?'

She shook her head and this time she smiled a small, curling smile.

'You are unbelievably beautiful,' I said, because it was true and I couldn't seem to stop the words coming out.

Alison laughed then, and took her hand away from where it still rested on my head. 'Charmer,' she said, pulling away from me.

I turned my head and looked down into my lap. 'Sorry.'

'No,' she said, and her voice came from someplace close and in front of me but I wasn't able to look at her. 'No, it's OK.'

I closed my eyes and took a deep breath and gradually became aware of my surroundings. Grass underneath me.

Cold, hard earth. I opened my eyes and looked around. A bare-branched tree beside me. I lifted my head and the weak sunlight hurt my eyes and I saw that Alison was sitting in front of me and that her cheeks were pink from the frosty air.

We were still in Tim Winter's garden, I realized. Stand up, I told myself. Stand up and be a man. Stand up and don't disgrace yourself like that any more. Pass it off, blame it on the trauma of recent times. Put it back together. Shove the pieces back in place and move.

But my body wasn't moving. I couldn't look at Alison, because I was too ashamed that she'd seen the inside of me like that. Now she knew and there wasn't any helping it, but it was still excruciating.

'Lahinch,' her voice said. And then there was silence for a few seconds. I could hear her breathing and a thrush sang overhead. 'Lahinch, Séamus,' her voice said again.

I couldn't help, then, but look at her. She stood up and put out her hand to help me up. I didn't think I should take it. I should be able to stand up by myself, surely? But I wasn't able and I couldn't keep sitting on damp freezing grass forever.

My hand closed around Alison's hand and a surge of heat spread over it as if I'd plunged it into warm water. She pulled and I forced my legs to lift me up.

'Now. Now we're ready. Let's go.'

But I knew I wasn't going anywhere near the eye of the storm. I shook my head. 'No, Alison.'

Alison looked into my face in that searching way she had and I tried to guess what she might be looking for. A sign that I might cry again? A trace of a man that she might get to do something brave and heroic and save-the-dayish? She didn't know that there was nothing there, but I did and the sheer emptiness of it made me feel almost free.

But she'd stayed with me while I was cracking up. Good Samaritan that she was. She'd stayed and I owed her some explanation. I didn't know how to say it all or really how to begin to explain any of it.

'I'm no good to Cassandra,' was all I could say.

Alison didn't say anything for a minute and never stopped looking into my eyes until I felt that maybe I didn't have to explain anything. Those oval eyes could probably see the tattered pieces inside me flapping like ugly plastic bags blown onto trees. Entangled with themselves until they weren't good for anything except to blot the landscape.

We stood in silence in Tim Winter's garden, our breath visible between us and I realized that I was still holding her hand and I thought I should let it go but I couldn't bring myself to lose the warmth of it.

'Do you really think you're no good to Cassandra?' Alison said, eventually.

I nodded slowly and continuously, like a car ornament.

Alison took some small breaths and pressed her lips together. Then she sighed, quietly. 'Well,' she said, pausing as if she was determined but afraid, 'well, Séamus, maybe you're right. Maybe you are no good to her.'

She looked away and then looked back, gathering me with her eyes. Her words were like nettles on my skin as I heard them from outside me. *Maybe you are no good to her. Maybe you are no good to her. Maybe you are no good to her.*

I wanted to look away because I felt so ashamed, but her eyes still gathered me to her. Maybe I'm no good to anybody, I thought, even though she hadn't said it and my stomach clenched as Alison took a breath and I was sure that those were going to be her next words.

'But you're all she has,' she said, quietly.

I saw Cassandra then, standing behind Alison in the frosty morning and I heard the echoes of her fighting words as they dragged her out of my kitchen and I thought that what Alison said was true. I might not be any good at any of it, but I was all that was available.

A sudden surge of heat travelled up my arm and I looked down at it and saw my hand holding Alison's hand and saw also that there was a sheaf of paper sticking out of the pocket of her red coat.

'Lahinch,' I said. 'I think I know where those houses are, if they're brand new.'

Alison smiled at me and reached her free hand up, briefly, to touch my face, then she let go of my hand and walked out of the garden to my car. The weak, winter sunshine was glistening on the dew-covered silver paint of the car and I sort of ached for its oldness and its efforts to keep going against the odds. Stopping in front of the car, Alison held the keys enquiringly towards me, and I nodded as I took them.

'I've never been to Lahinch,' Alison said, as we sat into the car and I started the engine.

'Really?' I said, pulling away from the kerb.

'No, though I've often thought of going. My ex-husband used to surf and he went there a few times, though I never went with him. He liked it though.'

I nodded as if this was a normal conversation about west-coast seaside resorts and not a harebrained, almost hopeless wild goose chase.

'You'll like it. Especially now. I always like it best in winter when there aren't many people around.'

Alison leaned forward in her seat and turned the car heater on to full power. Warm air circulated around my feet and blew into my face and I felt my body relax against the odds.

'What's it like?' she said, sitting back.

I turned my head, briefly, to look at her. 'Wild seas and wild winds.'

Alison nodded. 'Good. Noth~~ing~~
blow away the cobwebs.'

'I suppose,' I said, as I indicated to turn on ~~the~~
road that'd bring us west.

I 2

As we drove along the country roads we didn't speak much. Alison slept some of the time and I fiddled with the radio until I found a station that played music loud enough to fill my head. In the air between us was the inevitable question as to whether or not Tim and his Afrikaner henchman had taken Cassandra to Lahinch.

Maybe he hadn't. Maybe he'd gone to Donegal or West Cork. Maybe he'd immediately left the country, having killed Cassandra and thrown her body in a ditch before he left Ireland. Or maybe he was in his new holiday home and Cassandra was looking out the window at the Atlantic waves hoping we'd be able to guess her whereabouts and find her.

The early morning traffic through Limerick and Ennis was reasonably light as it was Saturday morning. Even so, it still felt as if it was taking forever. I queued, impatiently, for access to the final roundabout in Ennis and at last swung into the correct exit.

'Lahinch Road,' I muttered aloud as I drove out of Ennis as fast as I could manage, past the huge green sign that announced that our goal was 25 km away.

'Mmm?'

'Sorry. I was talking to myself. I didn't mean to wake you.'

'No, no, it's fine. What did you say?'

'Nothing. Just the name of the road. The Lahinch road. It never seemed important what it was called before.'

I glanced at Alison. Her head was still leaning back ag... st the headrest of the seat, but was turned towards me and she was smiling. I looked back at the road.

'Maid of Erin?'

I nodded.

'How terribly, terribly De Valera,' she said, in a high-pitched English accent. 'He simply couldn't resist a cross-roads, could he?'

'Obviously not,' I said, as I turned my head, briefly, to smile at her and then returned my attention to the road.

We drove through a couple of tiny villages and past houses and overtook cars and tractors and fields of cows. As we whizzed past them all I thought about how it was the case that they all had a reality of their own and an existence of their own but that for us, right at that minute, they might as well have been waxworks. All of them nothing more than scenery on our way to where we were going.

We drove in that silence for half an hour or so. Then it started to rain, so I turned on the wipers. Grey rain coated the windscreen as we drove and I tried to remember the location of the holiday homes.

'What is the address of that place?' I asked, as I drove through Ennistymon, passing one old-fashioned wooden storefront after another and ignoring the tightness in my chest at the sight of the Lahinch 2 km sign.

Alison pulled the sheaf of papers from ....where. I
read from a page. 'Thirteen, Cois Farraig.....
   'Thirteen.'
   'Lucky for some. Do you kno..... ...e last time I was
   I nodded. 'I think so, it'.....
seem to remember no.....
here. Nice house.....
   'We'll find i.... ..ilence between us as a series of unidenti-
   I nodd....ngs rolled around the car. And then, as suddenly
fiable ... always happens, there it was, right in front of us. The
sea.

'Lahinch,' Alison said.

'Lahinch,' I confirmed, driving closer and closer to the
houses and shops and hotels and pubs that were all snuggled
up together as if for protection against the Atlantic.

'Séamus?'

'Yes?'

'I worked something out while we were driving.'

'OK. What?'

'I know who Tim is.'

'So do I.'

'No, not like that. You know the car crash in South Africa
when William Ormston's wife was killed?'

'Yes.'

'I bet that Tim and Chrissie were involved somehow.'

'On the school bus?'

'Maybe, I don't know. But there's a South African connection I'm sure of it. Anna Ormston was killed there, and then
there's the Afrikaner, and as Tim came for the gun he must
be mixed up with him. I could be wrong but –'

'I bet you're right. Chrissie has a scar – on her mouth –
she told me she got it in an accident. Fuck it.'

'You're so eloquent, Séamus.'

'I know,' I said, slowing down as we entered the outskirts

of Lahinch. Should I turn right tow... worth a try. I drove into the empty road and p empty golf course on my left, an army barracks an house after house after house on my right.

Driving around bend after bend. In my head I turned over what Alison had said about Chrissie and Tim. I pulled the car into a lay-by and turned to look at Alison.

'Why have we stopped?'

'Well,' I said, pointing to the left, 'observe the mighty Atlantic ocean.'

Alison turned her head and we looked at the grey silk sea, heaving close to the shore.

'Very impressive.'

'And, behold,' I said as I pointed to a huddle of houses across the road from where we were sitting. 'Cois Farraige. *Beside the Sea*. It's a bit of a give-away, the name of it, isn't it?'

Alison turned her head to look at the houses.

'Though I guess that usually people want it to be easy to find their holiday homes,' I rabbited on, increasingly nervous now that we had found what we were looking for.

'OK, we're here,' I said. 'Now what the hell do we do?'

Alison leaned across me and looked at the small development of white-painted dormer houses. The whole of the small estate was surrounded by a high stone wall so that, even though there were probably not more than twenty houses grouped there across the road from the Atlantic Ocean, we couldn't see well enough to work out whether or not Number 13 was occupied.

'Not bad,' Alison said 'Good investment.'

I frowned at her and she smiled.

'I'll go,' she said, opening the car door before I could object. 'I'll have a quick walk around and see if I can find anything.'

Alison stepped out into the drizzling rain and buttoned up her coat. She took one long look at the sea and then strode across the road and disappeared in the gateway of Cois Farraige. I watched her walk away and my heart thumped with fear and mish-mashed emotions. Why was she here? Why was she helping? What would I do if she left?

I watched the silent white houses and wondered if they hid Cassandra. And I tried not to think of what might be about to happen as I waited for Alison to re-appear. I smoked a cigarette and fiddled with the radio. Where *was* she? It seemed to be taking an inordinately long time.

I strained in my seat to see if I could see anything of her, but all I could see were the houses close together as if they were whispering secrets, and some tall trees dancing wildly in the wind.

Where the hell was she? How long did it take to see if there was anybody in Number 13, for God's sake? All she had to do was have a quick peek and see if she could find their van or a car or something. Lights maybe. Open curtains.

What if they'd seen her? Maybe Tim had seen her and captured her as well. Maybe he'd shot her? The last thought made me open the door of the car and jump out into the rain myself. I ran across the road and was just about to enter the estate when Alison came through the gateway, her red-clad shoulders hunched against the wind and rain blowing in from the sea.

'For God's sake,' she muttered grabbing my arm, 'what are you doing here? Someone will see you.'

'I thought – I was – you were gone a long time,' I said, as we hurried back to the relative shelter of my rusting car.

'They're here,' she said, stopping beside me as we reached the car.

'How do you know?'

'I saw the van and the lights were on and the house is obviously inhabited. I'd say he's very confident that nobody knows where he is – I told you the ink is scarcely dry on that contract.'

'Dear God,' I whispered, as we sat into the car and slammed the doors on the elements, 'what'll we do now?'

Alison was looking away from me out of the window at the sea. Her almost black hair was wet and sleek against her head and I could see her long, dark lashes sweep up and down as she blinked.

'I love the sea,' she said.

'Me too. But right now I'm more interested in what we should do.'

'OK. I'm interested in that too, the only problem is I have no idea what to do.'

'Me neither,' I said.

We sat in my car in silence. I turned on the engine to keep the car warm and we listened to the sea crashing around outside. If we did the wrong thing Cassandra would be dead and there was no going back from dead. Maybe I'd been right. Maybe the best thing was to do nothing? But even if that was the case it was too late. I was already there.

'Séamus?' Alison said, interrupting my rat-run of terror.

'Yes.'

'Phone the police.'

I shook my head.

'We have to. We don't have any weapons and they do, and we'll never be able to stop them if they try to leave.'

'He said not to do anything. He'll hurt her if we do.'

Alison took a deep breath. 'I hate saying this but you know as well as I do that he'll probably kill her anyway. How can he leave her alive? And especially now – he hasn't got a lot to lose, he can be connected with Mattie's murder.'

I shook my head again.

We sat in silence.

'How about this,' Alison said, touching my arm with her hand. 'How about if you call your friend the detective and ask him to come here to meet you. He'll probably be armed and he'll help us if we ask him. Just don't tell him the story on the phone. Have him come alone and then we'll see if we can come up with a plan between us.'

Thinking made me want to smoke again. Rolling down the car window I fumbled in my jacket pocket until I found my cigarettes and lighter and then I lit a cigarette.

'Sorry. I need to smoke.'

'That's OK. What do you think about my idea?'

I thought again about Paul Richardson. His round face and puffy down-filled jacket. What was his life like? Who was in it apart from his daughter Tara and Mattie's dog? Did he have a wife who reminded him to take the jacket with him when he was going out in the cold?

'OK. I'll call him,' I paused. 'But I don't think I have a phone.'

Alison reached into her coat pocket and handed me a small, silver, phone. 'Use this. Do you know the number?'

'Yeah. That's actually something I'm good at, believe it or not. I'm good at remembering numbers and stuff.'

Taking the phone from Alison I dialled the number of the police station and asked to speak with Detective Richardson. After an interminable session of *Greensleeves* I heard his familiar voice.

'Séamus? Is that you?'

'It's me.'

'How's Cassandra? I heard she turned up, there was a message waiting for me when I got into work this morning. I tried calling your house but there was no answer.'

'She's OK.'

'That's great. I told Tara you'd be calling in some day to visit Boru. She's dying to meet you.'

'That's nice. Paul, I need a favour.'

'OK,' he said, his friendly voice slowing down, 'fire away.'

'I wonder,' I said, the words flying around inside me like dust now that I had to say them aloud, 'I wonder if you could do me a huge favour and come down to Lahinch?'

'Lahinch?'

'Lahinch.'

'Jesus, it doesn't look like the best day for the seaside here in Limerick I have to say. Is that where you are?'

'Yes.'

'And you want me to come down there?'

'Yes. Please. If you could.'

'It's a different jurisdiction, Lahinch. It isn't in my jurisdiction.'

'That doesn't matter.'

'But why, Séamus?'

I took a deep breath. Because you're the cavalry, I thought. But I didn't say it in case he thought I meant it literally and he decided to bring the troops. 'I need to show you something. That's all. If you could come, I'd really appreciate it.'

There was a pause on the other end of the telephone line. I could hear another telephone ringing and a man's voice speaking in the distant Limerick police station.

'OK. Where will I meet you?'

'On the seafront. Across from that water-world place.'

'Grand. What time is it now?'

I looked at my watch. 'Eleven o'clock.'

'OK. See you sometime after twelve. Is that all right? Can you wait for me?'

'No problem. See you then.'

I pressed the button on Alison's phone, disconnecting us from the forces of law and order and leaving us stranded on the seashore with evil bastards. 'He'll be here in just over an hour.'

'Good. What'll we do until then?'

'Surveillance,' I said, unable to stop a grin. 'Like the movies. Pity it isn't dark. We could drive without headlights.'

'Well, if it's going to be like the movies then I wish there were some doughnuts and coffee in the car. I'm starving.'

'Me too,' I said, leaning back against the headrest and wincing as I tried to find a comfortable way to accommodate the huge bump on the back of my head.

'Is your head sore?' Alison asked.

'It'll be fine.'

'You should go to a hospital and have it looked at as soon as all of this is over.'

'I mightn't have to,' I said. 'The state pathologist can swab it out during the post-mortem.'

'Séamus. Stop it.'

'Seems to be the style around these guys. Somebody always ends up dead.'

'Well, it won't be you,' Alison said, tucking her dried hair behind her ear so that it curled forward on to her cheek.

'How do you know?'

She smiled and leaned back into the passenger seat. 'Oriental wisdom.'

'Bullshit. You're Irish.'

'OK. Ancient druidic wisdom, so.'

'Well, you're wrong because I think I may starve to death even if that lot don't gun me down first.'

'I know. I'm sure I saw a shop just back there around the corner, one of those tiny petrol stations, it probably has a shop to cater for the holiday homes,' she said, looking out of the car at the sky. 'The rain has stopped, I think the sun may be trying to come out.'

'Do you know that today is 23 December?'

'I only want a doughnut or a packet of crisps or something. I don't expect the turkey and ham just yet.'

'I'm locked in a car with a comedienne. I'm only saying it because it came into my head.'

'Do you say everything that comes into your head?'

I looked at her and my stomach squeezed and I wasn't sure if it was hunger or the memory of telling her that she was beautiful or even the fact that she *was* so beautiful and so warm and so close to me inside my car that smelled of chalk and copybooks. But I don't actually always say everything that comes into my head and so I held on to myself.

'Often.'

'That's a good quality,' she said, blinking her amazing eyes open and closed.

I lifted my hand and touched her hair and she didn't move but just looked straight at me. Then I remembered Cassandra locked in a house or dead or beaten and frightened and I dropped my hand on to my lap and turned to look across the road at the silent holiday homes. When I looked back at Alison she seemed to be composing her face.

'No move there anyway,' I said.

'No,' she said, looking over my shoulder and then in my direction but not straight at me. 'No. Will I walk back to see if I can get some food?'

'Town is too far away to walk.'

'Not to town. To that small shop a little bit back the road? I just told you about it.'

'Sorry, I forgot. Good idea.'

'What will I get?'

'Anything as long as it's edible.'

She opened the car door and stepped out on to the tarmac. Cold sea air filled the car.

'Money?' I shouted leaning across the car towards where she stood.

'I have some. See you in a few minutes.'

The car door slammed and she was gone and I was left with the sound of the wind and the ocean and the vista of the white houses. I fiddled with the car heater to make the temperature more comfortable and then sat back and focused on the Cois Farraige holiday homes. Beside me in the car I could feel the gap in the space vacated by Alison as if it was a breeze around me.

Bad timing, I thought, to be letting this woman get under my skin. Not to mention the fact that she'd lied to me. Though she had apologized and explained. And I did believe what she told me. Maybe I shouldn't. For all I knew, she wasn't at the shop at all but over in 13 Cois Farraige tipping off the murderers inside.

She wasn't, though, I was sure she wasn't. Though, then again, I'd liked and trusted Tim and he'd turned out to be up to his neck in this whole catastrophic chain of events. And I'd trusted Chrissie. What kind of fucking faulty radar did I have? I'd really liked Chrissie as well. For fuck's sake, I would have had sex with her if we hadn't been interrupted. I'd trusted her that much.

That thought made me laugh. There I went fooling myself again. Calling things by the names I wanted them to have. My relationship with Chrissie was nothing to do with trust or love or any of those things. It was way simpler than that. Simple uncomplicated body contact. Sex as a distraction and comfort. An antidote to all the pain around me.

Still I hadn't thought she was mixed up in murder. But maybe she wasn't. Then again, maybe she was. That's what the world seemed to do. Mix and mash up every part, until everything was a confusing concoction that nourished and poisoned at the same time.

I leaned forward and turned on the radio. Christmas songs with jingling bells and forced gaiety filled the confined space of the car but nothing seemed to quell the thoughts ricocheting inside my head. Maybe I was making yet another mistake. Maybe all her help and soft touches were aimed at lulling me into trusting her?

But the truth was that I did trust her and even if it was a mistake well, fuck it, what could I do? I couldn't spend my whole life being suspicious of everybody. Well, maybe I could, but I was probably too lazy for the effort it would take.

Bing Crosby and David Bowie began singing about little drummer boys and I knew that at that moment Alison was walking along the road looking for a shop where she could buy some crisps and not betraying me to Tim. The car door suddenly opened.

'Back already, my God!' I said, half-shouting to detract attention from what I'd been thinking. As if she'd know. What an idiot. But then she looked at me and there was something indefinable in her eyes that made me feel as if she did know what I'd been thinking in her absence.

So I unhooked my eyes from hers and instead took in the general picture of Alison. Hair blown to confusion. Face flushed and the smell of the sea from her clothes.

'Well,' I said, again too loudly, 'what did you get for us?'

'No move from the house, I suppose?' she asked as she settled into her seat.

I shook my head. 'Are you sure they're there?'

'They're there all right,' she said, trying to catch my eye, but I slid out of her grasp each time.

'So, tell me,' I said, and my voice still sounded too loud though I was consciously trying to make it quiet, 'what did you get?'

'Let's see,' Alison said, opening the plastic bag on her lap. 'OK. No doughnuts and no coffee, I'm afraid. Coke, crisps, Seven Up, chocolate and' – she paused, smiled broadly – 'and I couldn't resist these – look.'

Alison produced a small box containing six Christmas crackers and laid it on the dashboard. 'Tomorrow is Christmas Eve after all. See. Two for you, two for me and two for Cassandra.'

Tears welled in my eyes and my heart – that was like a piece of glass, anyway – heaved and rattled as if it would break. But I was determined to stay in one piece. So I picked up the box and pretended to examine the green and red and gold crackers inside until I had enough control of myself to speak. 'Great idea. We'll keep them for later.'

'What would you like?' she said, and she sounded as if she didn't notice I was upset.

'Coke,' I said, trying to be a man and make a fast decision. 'Coke and crisps and chocolate. If they're there.'

Alison handed me a bottle of Coke, a packet of crisps and a bar of chocolate and I proceeded to eat and drink without a pause. I was actually starving and my stomach made loud appreciative noises as it welcomed the food.

Alison sat beside me eating and drinking as well and, gradually, in spite of my churned up feelings and tortured speculations, the atmosphere inside the car began to calm me down like a soothed child. By the time I'd finished eating I felt as if I was on a picnic instead of a wild, dangerous and impossible escapade. I looked at the clock on the dash and saw that it was ten past twelve.

'We need to go back into town to meet Paul Richardson.'

'I'll stay here,' Alison said, gathering the detritus of our brunch into the plastic bag. 'I can sit on the wall and watch the house.'

'There's no point. Really. What will you do if they come out? Run along the road behind them?'

Alison laughed. 'At least I'd know they'd left.'

'We can easily find that out when we come back,' I said, putting on my seatbelt. I looked along the road to see if it was safe. I looked across the road one last time before we took off and then, suddenly, there it was. A blue van was at the entrance to the tiny estate indicating to turn in the opposite direction to town.

'Fuck. Is that the van, Alison? Is that it?'

'Yes,' Alison whispered as if they could hear us. 'That's it.'

We watched in silence as the van pulled out on to the

road and turned right. I waited about a minute and then drove after it. The road was winding and I was afraid of catching up in case they saw us and afraid of losing them down some side road if I stayed too far behind.

Every time I saw the flash of blue on the road ahead of us in the distance my heart allowed a triumphant beat. Every time I lost sight of it altogether for more than a few seconds my heart seemed to seize.

'Paul Richardson,' I said, as I struggled to maintain the correct position behind the van, 'he'll be waiting for us.'

'I'll call,' Alison said, scrabbling in her pocket and producing the phone. 'Number?'

'Hit the redial button,' I said, seeing the van ahead and slowing down.

Alison did as I suggested. 'Hello?' she said after a short pause. 'My name is Alison Chang, I'm with Capel and Williams solicitors in Dublin and I need to speak with Detective Richardson urgently.'

There was a short pause as she listened. 'OK, that's fine, give me his mobile number, then,' she said in a new, louder voice. 'Sorry? No, I have to speak with him right now, it can't wait. May I ask you your name? OK, well then, Sergeant O'Keefe, I need to speak with Detective Richardson and I need to speak with him now. Yes, yes, that would be fine. Hold on,' Alison fumbled with buttons on the keypad of her phone. 'Now, go ahead.'

Alison's telephone made sharp beeping noises as she punched in the list of numbers being spoken into her ear.

'OK, thanks a million, Sergeant,' she said, this time in a soft, slightly amused sounding voice. 'Sorry? Do I know Pierce Sheehan? I do, I know him well. He's fine. Still arguing with everybody, you know yourself – a born solicitor, you're dead right. Of course I'll tell him you were asking for him, I will. Look, I have to go. I really appreciate your help, Dermot. Thanks a million. Bye now, take care.'

I steered the car around a bend as Alison hung up and I caught sight of the blue van ahead of us on the horizon.

'Where do you think he's going?'

'Maybe Galway. I think this is the coast road along by the Cliffs of Moher. Ring Detective Richardson, he's surely in Lahinch by now.'

Alison punched the numbers the Guard had given her into her phone as I spoke.

'I need to ask him to – to –' I said, pausing to find the guts to say the words out loud.

'To check 13 Cois Farraige to see if Cassandra is still in the house?'

I nodded, glad I hadn't had to say it. Alison handed me the telephone, propping it between my shoulder and head. 'You talk to him. It's easier than me trying to explain who I am.'

The small phone burred in my ear, making an echoing noise that was telling even a techno-idiot like me that the coverage wasn't great. Suddenly there was a loud click.

'Hello?' a man's voice said. I could hear radio news in the background.

'Paul?'

'Séamus! Where are you? I was just about to leave. Are you all right?'

'Well, no. No we're not. Look I know who shot Mattie. I know who did all of the stuff. It was Tim Winter or one of his henchmen.'

'The doctor?'

'Yeah.'

'Cassandra's boyfriend?'

'Yes. But look none of that matters right now. They have Cassandra, they took her when they came to get the gun and they knocked me out –'

'The gun?'

'Yes, yes, I'll tell you about that as well when I see you.'

'OK. Who took Cassandra?'

'Tim Winter, I told you.'

'OK. And where is she?'

'Well, they were in a house in Lahinch – which was why I asked you to come down, but just as we were going to meet you they left and we're following them.'

'And where are you?'

'Just coming into Liscannor on our way towards the Cliffs of Moher, I'd say.'

'OK, I'll follow you.'

'No. No, please, I don't know if Cassandra is with them or not. They're in a van. A blue van and we can't tell. I want you to look in the house, first. See if she's there. If she's all right.'

'OK. Where is the house?'

'It's on the way out of town on the Liscannor road. 13 Cois Farraige. New white dormers. Small estate, stone wall in front.'

'Fine. I'll go look and I'll call you back.'

'I'll give you the number.

'No need,' he said, 'it's here on the phone. Just one thing, Séamus.'

'What?'

'When you say "we"?'

'Me and Alison Chang.'

'Alison Chang?'

'Yes.'

'OK. Look, Séamus, if you're right about these guys you need to be careful – so stay away from them until I get there.'

'I will. And one more thing. Please don't call more police – he said he'd kill Cassandra if I tried to follow him.'

'OK.'

'Promise?'

There was a short pause. 'I promise. Talk to you in a minute.'

The phone went silent. I handed it to Alison who looked enquiringly at me.

'He'll look in the house and call us back.'

Alison nodded.

'And if she's there and all right, well, then we can stop worrying and let the Guards chase Tim and his henchmen.'

Alison nodded again.

'She might be there,' I said. 'He may just have tied her up and left her behind while he makes his escape.'

'He might.'

I swerved the car around a narrow bend as we came into Liscannor village.

'Who am I trying to kid?' I said, driving along the quiet main street. 'He took her or he killed her. He'd never take the chance of leaving her behind in case she escaped. She's such a cranky bitch she'd follow him and I bet he knows that by now.'

Alison didn't say anything.

'What do you think?' I said, desperate for an outside view.

Alison took a long, breath. 'I'm certain Cassandra's all right.'

'You can't be.'

'I am. But I think he probably took her with him. I think you're right about that.'

'We'll know in a few minutes anyway. One way or another we'll know.'

Alison nodded and the telephone rang. We looked at each other and then at the phone.

'Already?'

Alison shrugged and pushed a button on the phone.

'Hello?' she said.

I waited, hardly able to see the road.

'Julian? Look, I can't talk to you right now. I'll call you later, OK. Bye.'

'Julian?' I said, adrenaline pumping down my arms into my hands.

'A guy I know.'

'What a time to call, though,' I said, furious with the invisible Julian.

'He couldn't know.'

'Hmm. I suppose not.'

We continued to drive in silence, along the narrow road lined with low stone walls and the sea to our left. The road began to climb and dip, climb and dip, and we passed a tall stone monument and a statue of St Bridget dressed like a nun who taught me when I was eight. Suddenly the sea was on our left. Huge and expanding. I strained my eyes for a sight of the van.

It felt as if it had been an age since we left Lahinch and an age since I spoke with Detective Richardson. Where was he? How long could it take to find the bloody house and search it? There wasn't anybody there, for Christ's sakes, how hard was it going to be to look around a small holiday home? What could be taking so long?

I should never have let Alison persuade me to call him in the first place. It was stupid. We'd endangered Cassandra for nothing. The phone rang again. I looked at Alison, but she kept her eyes fixed on the road as she picked up the phone.

'Hello?' she said, then she handed it to me. 'It's for you.'

I reached for the phone with my left hand and held it to my ear.

'Séamus?'

'Yes?'

'No sign.'

'No sign,' I repeated to Alison and she nodded and smiled.

'Absolutely no sign of her,' Paul Richardson said.

My stomach squeezed. 'There wasn't – isn't – any sign that they might have hurt her?' I said, wanting to gag as I said the words.

'No. Nothing.'

'You're sure? You're sure you have the right house?'

'Yes, yes, 13 Cois Farraige – I found it and there have been people here but there's no sign of Cassandra. Does she have a green fleecy sweater?'

I thought for a minute and tried to picture Cassandra, but all I could see in my mind's eye were her big eyes and all I could imagine was the fear on her white face. 'I don't know. Maybe. Why?'

'Just that I found a woman's sweater in the house and I wondered if it was Cassandra's.'

'It could be. I don't really know. I suppose it might also belong to Chrissie.'

'Chrissie?'

'Chrissie Winter. She's Tim's sister.'

'I remember her. She was staying at Pádraig Harrison's house the night Mattie was shot wasn't she?'

I listened to his words. *She was staying at Pádraig Harrison's house.* She was. Of course she was. Why had I never seen that before? Another black mark against Pádraig Harrison.

'Yes. Yes, she was. That's her.'

'And she's Tim's sister?'

'Yes.'

'Jesus, Séamus, did it ever occur to you to tell me any of this before now?'

'Well, a lot of it didn't seem important before last night. Look, I'm having trouble keeping that van in sight without letting them see me. I can't keep talking.'

'OK, OK. I'm on the road behind you. Where are you exactly?'

I looked out at row after row of low, stone walls. I drove past a galvanized metal shed. A white-washed cottage with a caricature plume of turf smoke that filled the car with its fragrance as we sped past, a field with three donkeys and half a dozen black and white Friesian cows. Then more fields with bare trees and low, dry-stone walls.

'Exactly in the middle of nowhere,' I said.

'Helpful.'

'Well, I'd say we're almost at the Cliffs of Moher.'

I narrowed my eyes and caught a glimpse of a blue van up ahead, my body relaxed.

'Can you still see the van?' Detective Richardson asked as if he could read my mind.

'Just.'

'OK. I'll catch up. Stay with them if you can, but try not to let them see you or confront them or anything like that until I get there. OK?'

'Fine. One thing.'

'What?'

'Don't call in loads of Guards.'

'Why?'

'I told you already.'

There was a long pause.

'Fine. See you in a while.'

The phone beside my ear went dead and I handed it to Alison.

'Did you get most of that?'

'Yes. No Cassandra. I told you. She's in the van. She's fine.'

'Yeah. I hope so.'

Gradually the road began to widen. The sea was dark and topped with waves that looked like icing as it crashed and rolled in the distance on our left. Up ahead of us I could see a brief flash of the brake lights of the blue van and my head slipped into over-drive. They'd killed her. They'd killed Cassandra and they were bringing her body here to throw it off the Cliffs of Moher. Nobody would ever find her then, crushed into a million pieces on the rocks and washed out to sea.

It was a good plan. But then we were there at the Cliffs of Moher, and the van continued to drive along the road and didn't turn left towards the cliffs. I almost screamed with relief. Thoughts flipped around and around inside my head, and I felt as if I was a TV receiving a hundred transmissions all at once. Snippets of pictures and sounds, real and imagined. Dead Mattie. Dead Cassandra. Dead Prince.

'Look at that beautiful view,' Alison said, slicing through the middle of my madness, as we rounded a bend just past the Cliffs.

'What?' I said, in disbelief.

'Look. Isn't it magnificent?'

I looked. Spread out in front of me was the sea. Large and wild and mingling with the sky so that it wasn't obvious where the sea ended and the sky began. And it was truly one of the most spectacular things I had ever seen. But right at that moment it didn't matter a shit to me how beautiful it was. Right then it was water and rocks and air and I didn't care about it in the slightest.

'I can't believe you're admiring the scenery.'

'A beautiful coastline is still a beautiful coastline no matter what else is going on.'

'Still.'

'Still. What's true is true.'

'Not really.'

'No, Séamus, really. It's like being at sea and looking to the horizon – something level and even – otherwise you'd be lost.'

I laughed. 'For fuck's sake, Alison. We're chasing a load of bastards along this fucking windy dangerous road and you're getting philosophical all of a sudden.'

Alison looked away.

'You're serious aren't you?'

She nodded.

I swerved around a hairpin bend. 'OK let's get philosophical so, if you like, it'll pass the time.'

Alison's face flushed and she looked annoyed for the

first time since I'd met her. 'I'm not philosophizing, all I'm saying is that I think reality always makes a pretty good horizon.'

'Really? I think reality is shite. This is reality. Those cold, cruel, murderous bastards up ahead of us in the van. And you're telling me we should look at that in order to maintain our place in the world?'

I screwed up my eyes and glared at the blue van, which seemed to have speeded up some. I pressed my foot hard on the accelerator and my poor car sort of whined before speeding up.

'Well, I hate reality,' I said, 'and I'm sick of the sight of it.'

'It's not always like this. But it's true that sometimes you have to look at the parts of reality that are cruel and cold as well as the other parts.'

'The other parts?'

'There are lots of other parts. Good things. Good people. Kindness. Love. Magnificent scenery. They're all reality as well, aren't they?'

'It's the *as well* part that gets me. What the fuck is that about? I mean OK I can see cruel or kind, good or bad but good *and* bad? Cruel *and* kind? Fuck it, what kind of a messed-up world is that? How is a person supposed to survive that?'

We turned a corner and a long narrow hill greeted us. The car began to groan.

'It's the knack of life,' Alison said.

'The knack of life?'

'First you're a child or like a child and you trust the world and everybody in it because you don't know any better.'

'And then?'

'And then a time comes in everyone's life when one way or another you discover that everybody isn't trustworthy. Try dropping into second – the hill is too steep.'

I nodded and changed down through the gears and the car stopped complaining and made slow progress up the steep road.

'That's for sure,' I said, 'and if you've any sense that's when you learn not to trust anybody.'

'That's no good either.'

'I don't know about that – look at Tim and Chrissie and . . . and other people.'

'What about them?'

'Well, take Cassandra for example – I'd say she might be sorry she trusted Tim.'

'I know,' Alison said.

'So – simple answer, trust nobody.'

Alison shook her head. 'Apart from making you miserable that's not real either. Lots and lots of people are trustworthy, so if you trust nobody I think it's just as stupid because you're living as far outside reality as if you trusted everybody.'

'Yeah, yeah, but it's safer not to trust people,' I said, swerving slightly as I took a sharp bend. The blue van bobbed up and down on the road ahead. 'For fuck's sake, be realistic. If you stand in the middle of the road all the time you deserve to be run over. It's the same thing – trust and you'll get hurt. Don't trust and then you don't get hurt.'

'Sure, but you don't get anything else either.'

'Do you remember,' I said, pausing as the van disappeared momentarily from my view and then returned. I relaxed, 'Do you remember what you told me about your ex-husband and his sister and all of that?'

'Sure.'

'How can you say what you're saying, so?'

'That's why I can say it. I had no choice but to work it out.' Alison laughed suddenly. 'I realized it was a package deal. This whole thing, I mean – if you choose not to feel the bad stuff then you don't get to feel the good stuff.'

'Total fucking bad deal. Nobody ever told me I was signing up for this shit.'

Alison laughed again. 'It's just a knack, Séamus, like driving or cycling or opening jars of jam.'

A quick flash of indicator caught my eyes and the top of the blue van disappeared to the right down a side road.

'Look!' I shouted. 'Look, they're turning off the main road. Turning right. Thank God for those low stone walls. If this was Kerry we'd never see them behind all the high hedges.'

'This is the main road?'

'Haw-haw. Phone Paul Richardson. Quickly.'

I drove to the junction where the van disappeared and turned right, scouring the flat fields at the crossroads for something distinguishing to tell our would-be saviour.

'Detective Richardson?' I heard Alison say, she held the phone towards me.

'You speak to him. I can't, the road is too twisting. I can't steer and talk on the telephone.'

'OK. Detective Richardson? Hello, my name is Alison Chang, we haven't spoken before. Yes, all right, Paul. We have bit of a situation. The van has just turned off the main road and we're following it. Sorry? No, I'm not sure. It all sort of looks the same around here.'

'It's a T-junction,' I said. Alison looked at me and held the phone close to my face. 'And there's a red-roofed barn on the left just before the turn-off. Take a right and just around the corner you'll see a statue of the Virgin Mary in a small grotto near a gateway.'

I nodded and Alison pulled the phone away. 'Did you get that, Paul? OK, great. No, we won't. OK, we will. See you soon, hopefully.'

Alison put her phone back into her pocket. 'Very observant. I'm impressed. I didn't notice half of those things.'

'I was looking for them. I knew I'd have to tell him something. Now, as there haven't been any side-roads off this road I presume they're up along here someplace. I have just one problem with this whole thing.'

'What?'

'Well, what the fuck will we do if we find them?'

'I have no idea. But I suppose we'll think of something. Look, Séamus, what's that?'

I looked to where Alison was pointing. A high green wire fence ran along the right-hand side of the road and up ahead of us two tall, black iron gates were open and swinging to and fro in the wind.

'It looks like a gateway,' I said. 'I'm not a farmer, but as far as I can tell it's a gateway.'

'Be serious, that's not what I mean. What is the whole place?'

I shrugged.

'I think I know what it is. Stop the car, I need to look at something.'

'No. If I do they'll be gone and we won't catch them.'

'It's an airfield, Séamus,' Alison said, grabbing my arm. 'I bet you anything it's an airfield. Stop the car and let me look. I think I see some kind of a sign over there on the fence. Let me look.'

'They'll get away,' I said, but I was already slowing down and stopping. Alison opened the door and sprung out of the car. By then the drizzle had stopped and it was raining heavily. I craned my neck to see her, but all I could see was that she was fumbling with something tied to the green fencing and then running back towards the car.

'It is, it is,' Alison said, sitting into the car. Large drops of rainwater ran off her face and she slicked back her hair with the palm of her hand. 'I was right. The sign says Mara Airfield, it looked like it's long since closed down but it probably still has an airstrip that they could use.'

'But I can't see or hear anything.'

'It must be a bit in off the road.'

'It must be,' I agreed. My heart pounded. What should we do? Should we wait for the police? Should we go in? If we waited would Cassandra be gone – or dead – by the time we got there? If we went in would we disrupt the whole apple cart and put her in danger? Alison was fumbling on the floor for something. She sat up in her seat and caught my arm.

'OK. Drive into that field over there – see it? It's empty. We can leave the car behind the wall. No one will see it there.'

'Who would want to steal this heap of junk anywhere let alone in the middle of nowhere?'

'No,' Alison said, laughing and coughing at the same time, 'I mean Tim and those – the bad guys, Séamus, remember them? If they come out they won't see it.'

'Oh,' I said, and I wanted to pretend that I knew all along what she meant. 'Now?'

'Now,' Alison said, so I drove across the road and through the open gateway and parked my car as close as I could to the wall. I turned off the engine and looked at Alison. She was pressing buttons on her phone.

'I hope the battery holds out on this thing,' she said as she waited. She moved the phone away from her ear and shook it and dialled again. She looked up at me. 'It won't work. Jesus, Séamus, what's wrong with it? Why do I keep getting a message that the customer has switched off his phone or –'

'Is out of coverage,' I finished for her. 'He's just hit a patch of mountainy land or something. He'll be back in a few minutes.'

'We can't wait,' Alison said, her eyes wide apart and her voice climbing on each word. 'They'll be gone if we wait.'

'No. We can't wait.'

'I'll send a text message to tell him where we are and he'll get it when he comes back into coverage won't he?'

I nodded. 'Come on, let's go. Take the phone with you. We'll start walking and we'll call him again as soon as we can.'

'OK,' Alison said, not looking at me as she tapped in the message to Paul.

'Come on, so,' I said, opening the car door and stepping out into what had become torrential rain. Alison walked around the car and stood beside me.

'It'll be all right,' I said to her.

She smiled but this time there was a wobble in her mouth that I hadn't seen before.

I took her hand and began to walk.

'Come on, hurry up, Paul,' I said, as we walked on to the road, hoping, vainly, to see a chubby detective driving towards us. But the narrow road was wet and empty. There didn't even seem to be any houses in the environs. Alison tightened her grip on my hand as we stepped through the airfield gateway.

'There are trees along the edge, there,' she said. 'We should go along by the trees so that we won't be so obvious.'

I nodded and we jogged across the wet grass until we reached the belt of conifers that somebody had obviously planted in the hope of protecting the place from the sea winds. Freezing rain-laden wind pelted into our faces. Alison shivered as we slowed our pace to a walk and made our way under the dripping trees. The wind wasn't much better in here.

'Jesus,' I muttered, trying to tighten my collar to stop the rain running down my neck, 'I hope I never meet the fucking eejit who planted these trees and thought he was making some kind of a wind-break. Because if he asks me if all his hard work was worthwhile I'm afraid I'm going to have to disappoint him.'

I looked at Alison and her face was wet and white and her black-brown eyes were wide and terrified.

'Do you know something,' I said, and paused until Alison looked at me, 'the way to look at this is that what we're trying to do is catch a plane. That's all. It's like when you're up in a plane and it's rolling or hopping around the sky, I always imagine that we're going over pot-holes and then I'm not even slightly afraid.'

Alison wiped some rain out of her eye with the hand that wasn't holding mine. 'You're barking mad, Séamus Considine.'

'Damn fucking right. I hope Tim Winter remembers that.'

Alison and I walked for a long, long time around the per-imeter of an apparently endless field. There didn't seem to be anything to see and I was starting to get a bit worried that we'd made a mistake and that the blue van with my captive cousin was careering off down some other roads in County Clare with neither us nor Detective Richardson in pursuit.

'What do you think of Pádraig Harrison?' I said, trying to find something else to occupy my head.

'What?' Alison said, coming closer. 'I can't hear you. What did you say?'

'What do you think of Pádraig Harrison?'

Alison laughed and her eyes wrinkled up at their elongated corners. 'You're joking.'

I frowned at her. 'Just making conversation. I mean if we can philosophize while part of a car chase we might as well talk about something as we creep along here in the rain. But if you don't want to say how you feel about him, that's fine with me.'

Alison and I walked pace for pace, in the inadequate shade of the tree belt, our strides shortening in unison as we grew tired.

'I don't mind telling you what I think of him,' she said, after a few seconds. 'I think he's a nice man.'

'Really?'

'Why? Don't you like him?'

I shrugged. 'He's OK,' I said, looking down at the wet patches that were creeping slowly up the legs of my jeans from the saturated grass and listening to our ever more exerted breath. 'No, actually no, that's a lie. I don't like him. I think he's a pretentious pain in the arse. Always going on and on about himself and what he has and how good he is – it'd make a cat vomit.'

'I know. But he *is* very wealthy and accomplished, isn't he? And he's very handsome as well, you have to admit that.'

'I suppose.'

'Oh, he is,' Alison said and her voice sounded amused, but when I looked at her her face was impassive. 'Even Cassandra said it, didn't she?'

'Mmm.' Bloody bastard, I thought. It was bloody bastards like Pádraig Harrison that were ruining my life. Handsome, rich, self-centred bastards. Jesus, I thought, I hated them more and more every second. Maybe I even hated them more than I hated Tim and his Afrikaner buddies. At least they were just bad, they weren't obnoxious, self-important fuckers as *well* as being evil.

'You know why he goes on like that?' she said.

'Because he's a gigantic pain in the arse?'

'No,' she said, slowly, 'because he's not sure of himself.'

'Don't make me laugh, Dr Freud.'

'Well, be like that if you like, but you don't have to be a psychiatrist to know that he's always trying to impress people.'

'But why would he want to impress me?' I asked, in disbelief. And I thought I heard Alison answer, but I couldn't be sure because just then something hard and unrelenting hit me on the head and I dropped into unconsciousness like a stone in a pond.

13

'Your Funeral and My Trial'
Sonny Boy Williamson, 1955

When I woke up I tried to sit forward to throw up, but something was restraining me so I threw up all down the front of my coat.

'Fucking brilliant,' I said, moving a hand to wipe my face, but that was restrained as well. I turned my head sideways and wiped my mouth on my shoulder. My head throbbed and my mouth tasted like I'd eaten my socks and I thought that maybe I was blind because everything was so dark.

'Séamus?' somebody said. 'Séamus? Are you awake? Are you all right?'

'Goddamn it!' I said, as I tried to turn my head in the direction of the voice. I couldn't see anything except a vague shape at the other side of the room or whatever it is I was in.

'Séamus,' the voice called again.

'Cassandra! You're alive!'

'Or else you're dead as well, and we're meeting someplace awful where we have to be tied up and pay for all the terrible sins we've committed in our lives,' Cassandra's voice said.

'No way. I know we're alive because God is not cruel enough to tie me up with you for eternity no matter what crimes I've committed.'

'It's good to see you too,' Cassandra said.

I stared into the gloom and gradually began to bring her small shape into focus. OK that was good, at least I wasn't blind.

'You too. Fuck it, what did they do to me? My head is killing me.' I instinctively lifted a hand to rub my head but it was still restrained and my head throbbed as if protesting. 'Fuck it,' I said, again, a wave of self-pity washing over me. 'What is it with these bastards? Why do they have to go around hitting me over the head all the time. I'm really getting pissed off with it.'

Then I remembered and my heart froze.

'Where is Alison? She was with me, Cass. We were together, she found you.'

'I know, she's there, beside you on the floor.'

I struggled to turn my aching head in the other direction. My eyes had adjusted to the darkness and I could see that I was sitting in the middle of the floor, propped against some sort of a wooden barrel while over against the wall a long, prone shape formed a crescent. That had to be her. I shuffled on my backside to get closer, every movement creating a cacophony of pain in my head. Alison was completely still.

As I reached her I could hardly breathe with the combination of pain and exertion and fear. I sat beside her unmoving form in the dark straining my eyes to see if I could detect some reassuring movement and straining my heart to steel itself against what might be true. I couldn't keep doing this. There's only so much any human heart can be expected to take.

'No,' I said, out loud.

'What?' Cassandra called.

'Nothing. Talking to myself.'

I kept my eyes on Alison, but I couldn't see anything and then – suddenly – like an explosion inside me, all the terror was replaced with anger. Wild, white, searing anger that ran through me like a train until the adrenaline that came with it made my headache abate and I wanted to rip Tim Winter's head off his goddamn, treacherous body with my bare hands.

She'd better not be dead, I thought as I leaned close to

her, she better not even be hurt. If that bastard had hurt Alison I was going to kill him and I didn't care if it was right or just or honourable or legal. I didn't care about any of that – I was still going to fucking murder him.

'Alison?'

'Shh!' Cassandra said. 'Keep it down. They'll hear you.'

I moved closer to Alison and my heart lifted because I thought I could see her body move as if she was breathing.

'Alison?' I whispered, leaning forward until I overbalanced and toppled on to the ground beside her. I landed so that we lay almost face-to-face on the floor. Alison didn't move, so I lay as still as I could and tried to listen. Then I heard it. Breathing. Soft breathing and I felt the tiny breeze of it on my face. Thank you, God. Thank you, God.

'Alison?' I said, softly, she still didn't move. 'Alison, Alison. Wake up. Come on, good girl, wake up. It's time for work. Come on, you'll be late. Wake up.'

Alison's head moved and she uttered a small groan.

'You are one cruel bastard. Honest to God, Séamus Considine,' Cassandra said.

'Alison,' I said, ignoring Cassandra, 'come on. Work. Wake up.'

'Séamus?' Alison said, opening her eyes.

'Alison. Are you OK?'

Alison moved her head a little and groaned again. 'Yes. I think I am. My head hurts and my arms hurt, but I think I'm OK. Are you?'

'Well, pretty much the same story.'

We lay there for a few seconds, breathing small, soft breaths that brushed the other person's face. I looked into Alison's face as we lay, prisoners on that filthy floor, and I didn't feel angry any more, but I also didn't feel afraid. In spite of everything I felt right. It was as if, suddenly, in this shittiest of places I was the person I was supposed to be.

'What happened?' Alison said, breaking the silence but not moving.

'No idea,' I said, watching the way her lashes reached almost to her eyebrows.

'They found you creeping around outside in the airfield,' Cassandra said.

'Cassandra?' Alison said, looking at me and then lifting her head to squint in the direction of Cassandra's voice.

'How's it going?' Cassandra answered.

'Oh, my God – it's so good to hear your voice,' Alison said, smiling with delight at me. 'We were right, she was here.'

'*You* were right,' I said, laughing as I rolled on to my back but my hands were tied in a bunch behind me so I had to roll back on to my side and face Alison.

'God, I hope we don't have to spend too long in here, it's freezing. I hope Paul hurries up and gets here,' Alison said.

'Paul?' Cassandra questioned.

'The cop – Paul Richardson,' I said.

'I never knew he had a first name,' Cassandra said, 'but that's good news. The cavalry are coming.'

'I wouldn't be too sure about that,' I said.

'Why?' Alison said.

'No reason,' I said, 'just might take them a while.'

'But they'll come,' Alison said.

I nodded because I couldn't bear to tell her what I thought. Alison shuddered with the cold.

'Oh, my God! It's freezing in here. You must be perished being here so long, Cass,' Alison said.

'Freezing,' Cassandra agreed.

'I can believe it. My nose feels like a block of ice,' Alison said.

'Try blowing your breath upwards. That's what I do.'

'OK, enough pleasantries,' I said, 'we have to make a

plan, we can't stay here. Cass – have you any idea who is here or what is happening?'

'Jesus, you still have no manners,' Cassandra said.

'Someone has to think practically.'

'Yeah. Practically obnoxious. Anyway, we're in a warehouse-office kind of place in some sort of a deserted airfield.'

'Obviously.'

'Do you want me to tell you what I know or not?'

'OK, OK. Go on. Sorry.'

'All right. I think I might move over closer to you guys. Hold on.'

I rolled on to my back and rocked until I pulled myself into a sitting position, meanwhile Cassandra shuffled across the room on her bottom. Once sitting up I wished I'd stayed lying down, as my head reeled and my whole body ached and I wanted to puke.

Shuffling sideways I positioned myself until I was leaning against the wall and closed my eyes to relieve the spinning and nausea. I could hear Alison moving around in front of me and when the nausea abated to the point of controllability, I opened my eyes and found that she was sitting in front of me, head drooping, breathing noisy.

'OK?' I asked her.

She lifted her head and looked straight at me and smiled. 'What did they hit us with?'

'No idea. Sit in here against the wall beside me.'

Alison moved to sit beside me and Cassandra arrived in front of us.

'Oh, God, lads,' she said, and I could hear in her voice that all the bravado had evaporated and she was going to cry. 'I'm so glad to see you.'

'Poor old Cassandra,' I said.

Cassandra sniffed loudly. 'Yeah,' she whispered. She sniffed again. 'Now, what was it you asked me?'

'Just what do you know?'

'OK,' Cassandra said, her voice steadying. 'This is an airfield – a private airstrip of some kind. And what else? – oh, yeah, OK and there's a plane coming tonight to take them away.'

'Where?'

'Don't know. But I overheard Tim – the bollocks – saying it to that big henchman. He was saying that they'd have to put lights along the runway so that the plane could land and something about ten o'clock. I couldn't hear all of it.'

'And what about us?' Alison said. 'Did they say anything about us?'

'Well,' Cassandra said and her voice wobbled again, 'I don't know what the plan for you two may be – I haven't overheard anything good since you arrived – but I think Tim was planning to kill me.'

I saw Cassandra shrug her small shoulders in the dark. She dropped her head to wipe her nose on her upper arm. 'He told me a lot of stuff – in the house, wherever it was.'

'Lahinch,' I interrupted.

'Really? I used to like Lahinch.'

'What did he tell you?'

'Oh,' Cassandra let out a loud sigh, 'he was drunk – I think. Maybe stoned as well. They had me tied up like this in a shed at the back of the house. I was hoping they'd leave me there and I think the big South African wanted to leave me – I heard him and Tim having some kind of an argument just before we left. Tim was saying – "No, she comes with us" and your man was saying, "That's stupid. We agreed we'd leave her." I think that was about me.'

Cassandra's voice drifted off with her concentration.

'When did he tell you this stuff?' I said, in an attempt to focus her.

She looked at me. 'Before we left. He brought me some food and sat on a stool in the shed while I was eating and started talking. Loads of mad stuff, I didn't understand half of it.'

'Like what?'

'Oh, really mad stuff. I couldn't even repeat it, most of it was totally bonkers. I got parts of it, though – like the fact that he and Chrissie were born in South Africa.'

'Is Chrissie here?'

'No. At least I haven't seen or heard her if she is. Why?'

'Just wondering if she's involved.'

'Well, she *is* his sister,' Alison said, suddenly.

I looked at her. 'So?'

'Blood is thicker than water and all that,' she said, looking away.

'Maybe, maybe not. She doesn't seem like the type, that's all I'm saying.'

'Well, I wouldn't imagine Tim seemed like the type either, did he, Cassandra?'

We both looked at Cassandra.

'No. The bastard.'

'There,' Alison said.

'What? What does that prove?'

Alison shrugged and looked at her bound feet. 'I think you should be careful about who you trust, that's all.'

'I know that and that's really rich out of you, Alison, after what you were saying in the car. All I'm saying is –'

'Listen,' Cassandra interrupted, 'do you think you two might listen just for one minute? You asked me to tell you what Tim said, Séamus, and you haven't shut up since I started speaking.'

'Sorry,' Alison said, lifting her head to look at Cassandra. 'I'm very sorry, Cassandra. Of course, please go on.'

Cassandra looked at me in the gloom and I shrugged.

'OK. Tim – the bollocks – said that he and Chrissie were born in South Africa and they lived there until they were six and eight.'

'That explains all the Afrikaners,' I said.

Cassandra nodded, 'Exactly what I thought myself. Then he started babbling and crying and stuff, said a load of stuff I couldn't understand. I think some of it was drunk talk and some of it was actual Afrikaans.'

'Really?' I said.

'Or else fucking Klingon – whatever it was I had no idea what he was saying.'

'So what did you do?' Alison asked.

'I didn't say a word. I just ate the cheese sandwich he'd given me and he seemed to forget I was there half the time. Anyway their mother abandoned them, I worked that much out.'

'Whose mother?' Alison said.

'Tim and Chrissie's mother. She ran away with a man. He said they were told she was dead and they didn't know she'd run away until she came back for them, which she did when he was six, I think, and Chrissie was eight. Or else it was the other way around, I'm not sure.'

'No, she's older,' I said, shrugging when both women looked at me. 'What? She told me.'

'Whatever,' Cassandra said, 'their mother left and they thought she was dead and then their father died. They were sent to stay with relatives of their father – nice people – Tim liked them as far as I could make out.'

Cassandra paused. 'Then one day their mother turned up – back from the grave – and told them she was taking them away with her.'

'Where had she been?' I asked.

'No idea. I didn't want to ask him questions and he never said. Maybe he didn't know. He was only a small child at the time.'

'But you'd think she'd have told him later on.'

'Well. That's the thing, isn't it? She couldn't tell them anything because she was dead. A couple of days after they left the farm – they lived on a farm – their mother was killed in a car crash.'

'You're joking,' I said, trying to follow.

'No, I'm deadly serious. Their mother, who they thought was dead and who came back from the dead, really actually died. It must have been pretty horrible.'

'Christ,' I said.

'William Ormston,' Alison said.

'What?' I said.

'William Ormston,' Alison repeated. 'I bet he was the man their mother ran away with. It has to be him. His first wife was killed in a car crash in South Africa.'

'Could be,' Cassandra said.

'Did Tim say anything else?' I asked.

'Oh, yes. Their mother's husband – he never named him, or if he did I couldn't understand what he was saying – anyway, he brought them back to Ireland and had some relative of his own foster them in some part of Co. Cork.'

'Ballyintra,' I said. 'Chrissie told me that. I'd never heard of it so I remembered the name. Ballyintra. She didn't seem to like it very much.'

'I'd say that's an understatement. According to Tim, they hated the place. I couldn't really follow everything he was saying but from the way he was talking – raving, really – the things he was implying were fairly awful. The least of it was that they were made to work like servants on the farm and in the house. Polish the other children's shoes, wash the floor, that sort of thing.'

'And did they have any contact with William Ormston?' I asked.

'Don't think so.'

'And how did they get out?' Alison said.

'I think when they finished school,' Cassandra said.

'It's amazing that they let them keep going to school,' I said.

'He said that. But he thinks there was some sort of a deal with the man who left them there – probably William Ormston, all right. Tim figured he paid for their upkeep and insisted they finish school. Anyway, whatever the explanation, they did both finish school. Chrissie went to Dublin and got a job and then, the following year, Tim followed her to study medicine.'

'But why did his men kill Mattie? What was that all about? What was he doing? What would make it worth shooting a stranger?'

Cassandra shook her head. 'I don't know. I think he probably told me but he was incoherent a lot of the time, slipping back and forth between Afrikaans and English, pacing up and down the shed, agitated out of his mind. What I've told you is about all I could glean from what he was babbling.'

'And this is why you think he's planning to kill you?'

Cassandra nodded. 'Well, he told me all this stuff – he probably told me more than I actually understood – and somehow I can't imagine that he wants to leave any loose ends.'

'Probably not.'

'Did he give you any idea of why they were outside Pádraig Harrison's the night of the murder?' Alison asked.

Cassandra didn't answer for a minute. 'He said loads of bits of things that I can't put together. I need to think about it. It's like searching in the bottom of your handbag. You know the stuff is there but it's all mixed up with other things. And some of it was upsetting.'

Cassandra's voice trailed off and I looked at her and she seemed to be crying again.

'Like?' I said.

'Well, he told me he loved me,' she said, in a rush, sniffing loudly. 'Can you believe that? What kind of a person does something like that? Said all this stuff like he never met anybody like me in his life before and he wished things were different.'

Alison tutted and puffed an angry sounding breath. 'Bastard,' she whispered.

I looked at her and realized that that was the first curse I'd ever heard Alison utter. Which is more than I could say about Cassandra – or myself.

'Yeah,' Cassandra said, sniffing, 'bastard. Rotten fucking bastard.'

I tuned back into Cassandra's story. 'He even tried to kiss me there when I was tied up in that shed, can you believe that? Bollocks!'

How fucking dare he? I thought as I listened, adrenaline pumping inside my tethered limbs which made them ache even more. But I didn't say anything.

Cassandra paused and took some deep breaths. 'I spat in his face,' she said, in a calmer voice.

'What?' I said.

'You heard me. I spat in his face when he tried to kiss me.'

'Jesus, Cass. For fuck's sake – he could have killed you on the spot.'

'I didn't care. I still don't care. Bastard had decided to kill me anyway. I'm glad I did it.'

'Jesus,' I said again, but I was glad she'd spat on him as well. Especially as she'd survived it.

'Leave her alone,' Alison said.

'It was dangerous though, you have to admit that.'

Alison shrugged and jostled me with her elbow.

'OK, OK,' I said to her. I looked at Cassandra. 'Still. Fair play to you, Cass.'

Cassandra smiled at me. 'Thanks.'

'Now,' I said, so that Cassandra would stop talking and I wouldn't have to keep hearing the distress in her voice. 'Now, down to business. How the hell do we get out of here?'

Both women looked at me.

'Look. We can discuss all the details later. Right now we need to get out of here.'

'Bloody men,' Cassandra said and Alison laughed. 'Always have to find something to fix when the going gets emotional.'

'It's nothing like that. Unless, of course, you two are happy to stay here and let Tim Winter kill you.'

'No,' Alison said, leaning sideways so that the whole length of our upper arms were pressed together, 'we'd prefer to escape, but what Cassandra said is true.'

'Believe what you like,' I said, moving away, slightly, and then moving back because I found it too hard to stay away from her, 'back to the job at hand. I bet he's planning to torch this building.'

'Could be,' Cassandra said.

'Yeah. I bet that's what he'll do,' I said. 'Burn it. And us. That should despatch all three of us off to heaven without him ever getting blood on his hands. Tragic accident. Nobody will even know who we are.'

'Except Paul,' Alison said. 'He's out there somewhere looking for us. It's all going to be fine.'

'Oh, right,' I said, but I didn't believe anything was going to be fine and if Paul Richardson was still out there looking for us, then where the fuck was he? I thought about my poor old car hidden in the field across the road and how easy it would be to miss it and how hard it was to find the airfield and how I would definitely have missed it if Alison hadn't made me take a look.

'What time is it?' I asked. Cassandra shuffled and swung her hands that were tied behind her back as far out to the left as they'd go and then craned her neck backwards.

'About a quarter to five. Far as I can see.'

'Oh,' I said. Fuck, I thought but I didn't say it out loud. 'Must be almost dark outside.'

'Yeah,' Cassandra said.

Dark, I thought, and we're as good as dead. If it's a quarter to five then it's hours and hours since we were captured. And if we're in this godforsaken place for hours it can only mean one thing. Paul Richardson had missed the car and the airfield.

'Anyway,' I said, 'I'm not saying the cavalry aren't coming, but while we're waiting to be rescued why don't we try and escape from here anyway?'

'OK,' Cassandra said, 'but do you mind me asking exactly how we do that?'

'I don't know yet,' I said, shuffling away on my bottom from Cassandra and Alison, 'I think we should have a look around. I'm a man, I like to keep active. Humour me.'

'OK,' Alison said, shuffling across the floor in the opposite direction.

'For God's sake,' Cassandra said, but I heard the rhythmic sound of her jeans being moved across bare floorboards. 'At least all this arsing around is making me warm, though I think my toes may have fallen off, I've no shoes on.'

My eyes had adjusted to the gloom so I stopped moving to try and see as much as I could see. It was a large room, obviously disused for years, with closed blinds on the windows, bare floorboards and strangely shaped objects pushed against the walls. One of which was right in front of Alison.

'What is that in front of you, Alison?' I called across the room.

'A desk. A big, wooden desk. The drawer side seems to be pushed against the wall, but it's definitely a desk.'

'And this looks like a filing cabinet,' Cassandra said from another wall. 'Again the drawer side pushed into the wall.'

'Obviously the airfield office,' Alison said.

'A bit big for an office.'

'Well, yeah,' Cassandra said. 'Probably stored stuff here as well.'

'The phone is hardly still connected, I suppose,' I said, giving up on the empty part of the room I was in and shuffling towards Alison. I reached the big dark object.

'OK. You were right, it's a desk.'

'Gee, thanks,' Alison said and I heard Cassandra snort a laugh. I decided to ignore both of them. I knew that I wasn't exactly great for observing the fine points of human relationships at the best of times, but in all fairness expecting me to be able to do stuff like that when I was tied up in a freezing cold office in a deserted airfield with a pain in my head and in imminent danger of death was asking a bit much.

'I don't suppose you still have your phone, Alison?' I said.

'They seem to have taken off my coat, and the phone was in the pocket.'

'And we all know there's no point in asking if you brought yours, Séamus?' Cassandra said.

'Oh, give it a rest,' I said.

Shuffling close to the wall I leaned against it and, using the muscles in my back and legs, inched my way upwards until I was standing. My legs screamed with the effort, but at least I was upright and that made me feel at less of a disadvantage, even if it didn't make much difference in reality.

'Hey, Scamie!' Cassandra called. 'Look at you! See how you've grown.'

'Maybe I'll be able to see something,' I said, walking in baby steps to a long, venetian-blind-covered window. I nudged the warped blinds with my shoulder and they swung, scattering dust and flies' legs into my face. I coughed and stepped back and then nudged the blind again, this time holding it out of the way with my shoulder. I looked out at the bleak, twilight rain-spattered landscape, hoping to see a police car or at least an anoraked policeman.

Instead I could see a large skip overflowing with miscellaneous rubbish, an expanse of grass maybe sixty feet wide and the line of the conifers Alison and I had mistakenly believed would hide us from the bad guys, bending and swaying their narrow-trunked bodies in the wind and rain.

'Well?' Cassandra asked.

'Nothing. Trees, grass, rain. No sign of a runway or even a blue van. Maybe they've left already.'

'Nah,' Cassandra said, 'we're around the back. I saw the runway when I arrived. A bit overgrown, but fairly obviously still a runway.'

Alison inched herself into an upright position and hopped over to stand beside me at the window. I couldn't help smiling at her as she approached. What was it with this woman?

'I have an idea,' she said, as she stopped in front of me.

'OK. An escape sort of idea, I hope.'

'Exactly. But don't lose your mind when you hear it, OK? Listen to the whole idea before you dismiss it, OK?'

'Sure.'

'That'll be a first,' Cassandra said, who had also made herself stand and was hopping towards us.

'Shut up.'

'All right. We need to get something to cut these ropes that are tying up our hands – yes?' Alison said.

'Yes,' Cassandra and I chorused.

'Hold back the blinds with your shoulders, Séamus,' Alison ordered. I positioned myself for maximum nudge and pushed the blinds out of Alison's way.

'OK,' she said, hopping closer to the window and looking out, 'pretty deserted looking all right.'

The blind slipped a little so I jammed my shoulder against the window frame to keep it back. Cassandra had arrived by the window and hopped closer to have a look as well.

Alison smiled at her. 'What do you think?'

'Deserted,' Cassandra confirmed.

'Great. We're all agreed.'

'So what's you idea?' I said, biting back my impatience so that I could prove Cassandra wrong.

'I'll tell you now in just one minute. Cass would you mind standing back a bit? Yes, that's great. Now if you wouldn't mind moving out a bit and facing me. That's it.'

Cassandra hopped in front of Alison who turned her back to the window and edged back until her head was resting against the windowpane.

'Your idea?' I repeated from the end of the window where my shoulder was beginning to ache from holding back the blind. 'Can I let this go?'

'In a minute,' Alison said, leaning her head forward and then suddenly slamming her head backwards until it made contact with the glass. It was like a slow-motion action replay as each tiny movement became exaggerated in front of our disbelieving eyes.

The glass shattered behind Alison's head and I jumped forward and knocked her away from the window on to the floor. Cassandra shouted and all around us glass tinkled like rain and cold rainy air poured into the already freezing room.

'For fuck's sake,' I said, panting with fear, lying across Alison's chest, 'what the fuck were you thinking? Are you cut? Are you all right?'

'I'm fine,' Alison said, smiling up at me, a look of delight on her face. 'Now we have something to use to cut the ropes.'

'Unless they heard,' Cassandra said, 'then they'll come in and God only knows –'

We stopped talking and listened. I'm not sure what I was expecting to hear. Jackboots marching along a corridor. Machine gun fire. Screams of attack. But there was no sound of anyone approaching.

'They can't have heard,' Cassandra said. 'They mustn't be right outside any more. I wonder where they've gone?'

Then we heard it. The low whirr of an aeroplane engine, growing closer and closer.

'I think we have an answer to that question. Get off me, Séamus.'

'Sorry.'

She sat up and wiggled on her bum across the floor. Swivelling around she picked up a long shard of glass.

'Alison, be careful.'

'Séamus, really. Come over here.'

I made my way towards her on my bottom hoping I wasn't going to sit on glass. Cassandra hopped towards us.

'If I watch –' Cassandra began.

'Exactly,' Alison said.

'What?' I said.

'Go behind me, Séamus, sit behind me, back to back,' Alison said.

'Why?'

'Just do it, Séamus,' Cassandra said. 'For once in your life, just do what you're asked without a huge song and dance.'

'For fuck's sake,' I said, but I did as I was asked.

'This is my plan. You promised you'd listen the whole way to the end.'

'I don't hear you doing much talking, Alison. More head-butting windows, really.'

'It's all part of the plan.'

'Now what?'

'Cassandra can you see Séamus' hands?'

'Yes.'

'Do you think you can guide me?'

'Sure.'

'That's your plan? To cut the ropes around my wrists with a piece of broken glass when you can't even see what you're doing?'

'Exactly. Don't worry, it'll be fine. Cassandra will tell me what to do.'

'I hope so.'

'Oh, shut up whinging, Séamus. By the way, Alison, do you realize your head is bleeding?'

'You see!' I said, trying to turn around. 'Are you all right?'

'Sit still, Séamus, please. We can't have too much time if the plane is here. I won't cut you.'

'I'm not afraid of that.'

'Good,' Cassandra said, 'because I'm fucking terrified of being murdered by Tim Winter.'

'The bollocks,' Alison said.

'The very one,' Cassandra agreed and both women laughed. 'Now move the glass to the right, Alison. Up a bit, very good, now down a little. Can you feel the rope?'

'Yes,' Alison said, rocking back and forth.

I could hear a sound from behind my back that was a hybrid between sawing and gnawing.

'That's good. Try not to go too far back, though. He's a bit close to the point of the glass.'

'Great,' I said, straining my neck to see behind my back. 'A kidneyectomy.'

'Oh, be quiet, Séamus,' Cassandra said, crouching down. 'And sit still. You're disturbing my concentration and you wouldn't want my concentration disturbed when you're relying on me for your safety.'

'I don't believe this,' I said, wriggling my wrists a bit as I felt the bonds loosen. 'Jesus, it's working.'

'Told you,' Alison said, between her teeth, as the sawing noise continued.

'OK, brilliant! Brilliant! Move the glass a bit to the right or you'll cut his thumb otherwise.'

I pulled my hands as far apart as they'd go to make the rope as taut as possible. Alison sawed. I pulled again and heard a snapping noise. Alison sawed harder. I pulled again.

More snapping noises and then, suddenly, my hands sprung free.

'Ohmygodohmygodohmygod!' Cassandra squealed.

I pulled my hands in front of me. Orange nylon washing line still hung from both wrists and my arm was bleeding where Alison had obviously nicked it with the glass. I never felt happier to be injured.

'Glass,' I said, spinning around on my bottom to face Alison's back, 'give me the piece of glass.'

Alison dropped the long, dusty piece of glass from her hand on to the floor and I picked it up and began to saw at the ropes on her wrists.

'Do the ropes around your own ankles first,' Alison said.

'No.'

'Yes. In case somebody comes in and catches us we need at least one of us to be fully able.'

She was completely right of course.

'OK,' I said, transferring my sawing to the orange washing line around my ankles. It gave away gratifyingly easily under the razor sharpness of the glass shard. Alison was a genius. A mad genius, head-butting the window like that, but still a genius. I looked up from sawing and noticed that the hair at the crown of her head was matted with blood. I stopped sawing and reached my hand out to touch it.

'Ouch! Séamus! Don't!'

'Sorry. Just want to see if it's still bleeding.'

'And is it?'

'No, at least I don't think it is. Is it sore?'

'No. Not really. Only when you touched it.'

'You don't have that many nerve-endings in your scalp anyway. Did you know that?' Cassandra said, from above us.

'Shut up,' I said.

'Séamus stop telling me to shut up, you're always telling me to shut up.'

'No, you're mistaken there, Cass. I don't tell you to shut

up,' I said, recommencing my sawing, 'you're the one who tells me to shut up. I tell you to fuck off.'

'Worse. So stop it.'

My ankles came apart and I stood up. 'Oh, the relief,' I said, bending back down to cut Alison free. I sawed at the ropes round her wrists and then at the ones on her ankles.

'Now me,' Cassandra said, as I finished with Alison.

'I'll think about it.'

'Bastard,' Cassandra said.

'I can't believe they didn't gag you,' I said, walking behind her to cut her ropes. 'I mean I would if I had half a chance and, to be honest, if they *had* gagged you I wouldn't take off the gag no matter what the consequences. The peace and quiet would be too good to give up.'

'Fuck off,' Cassandra said, thumping me on the arm as soon as her hands were free.

I knelt on the floor to cut the ropes around her ankles. 'Now, now. Role reversal. Leave me alone.'

'Tut, tut children – don't bicker,' a man's voice said from the other side of the room. We all looked up. Tim Winter stood, tall and swaying from side to side just inside the door. In one hand he held what looked like a petrol can. I'd guessed correctly. The barbecue was on.

'Tim,' I said, standing up and slipping the long piece of glass into the back pocket of my jeans. Tim walked back to the doorway and switched on a light that was obviously located just outside. Four long, fluorescent strip lights turned purple and flickered until, gradually, a wash of cold light flooded the filthy office. I had a quick look round and noted that we'd been right – this was definitely a deserted airfield office.

But even with the lights on it was still so gloomy that it was impossible to see anything clearly. I hoped Tim hadn't seen me pocket the glass. I was pretty sure he hadn't and, anyway, as I looked at him I figured he was probably so out of it he wouldn't have noticed whatever I did.

'You broke the window,' he said as he walked into the centre of the room, his walk that tell-tale, over-careful walk of the seriously bombed.

'We did that,' I said, in a normal voice.

Tim looked at me as he walked, and I couldn't help thinking he looked as if he was walking a tightrope. 'You smashed it all,' he said, and his words were slipping into each other like mad skaters. 'That's not a good idea. Look at that! All the rain is blowing in and now the fire will be hard to start.'

'Too bad, Tim,' I said, moving forward, slowly. I was sure he probably had a gun somewhere on him and if we could get hold of it we might stand some chance of escaping.

'Why did you come here, Séamus?' he said, suddenly letting his arm fall, limply at his sides.

'To find Cassandra. I couldn't let you take her. You might hurt her.'

Tim let out a long, loud, shuddering breath, 'I know that, really. I don't know why I'm asking you. We knew you'd come. That's why we found you, we were expecting you all the time.'

I looked over my shoulder, briefly and saw that Alison had crept as far as the wall and was edging her way behind him in the shadows of the wall. Tim didn't seem to have noticed.

'You shouldn't have taken her, Tim.'

'But you came along – as usual – and I had no choice, Séamus.'

'And not only did you take her, Tim – you lied. You promised me you wouldn't hurt her and all along you were planning to kill her.'

Tim moaned. 'I know. I know I did, I did promise you,

but she knows things now – I don't want to hurt her but I have no choice. I love her, you know –'

He turned his gaze to Cassandra who was still standing beside me. She was swaying back and forth like a reed in the wind. I put my hand out and squeezed her arm.

'I do,' Tim said, still walking, slowly towards us, 'I love you, Cassandra. I don't want to – I never loved anyone else – never felt like this –'

The wooden barrel I had been leaning against earlier came crashing down on Tim's head and he fell on to the floor. Alison stood behind Tim, looking at me as he fell in front of her.

'Good work,' I said.

She grinned and placed the barrel neatly on to the floor beside Tim's body.

Cassandra ran forward and picked up the can of petrol that had fallen on to its side as Tim collapsed. She carefully carried the can across the room and stood it upright on the desktop.

'These things are very volatile,' she said in an odd, adamantine voice.

I walked quickly to where Tim lay and began to search his pockets.

'What are you looking for?' Cassandra asked, coming to stand beside me.

'I don't know. A gun, something, anything.'

A loud woman's laugh rang out in the room. At first I thought it was Alison and I wondered why she was laughing and not only laughing, but laughing so loudly when we were surrounded by people who wanted to cook our goose – literally.

'You must think I'm a complete idiot if you think I'd arm that junkie,' the woman's voice said.

I looked up from where I was crouched over Tim's body.

'You saw what happened the last time I let him carry a gun,' she said, leaning against the doorpost, her arms folded across the chest of her immaculate cream linen jacket.

I stood up, slowly. 'Chrissie.'

'Hello, Séamus. Nice to see you.'

14

'So You Want to be a Rock'n'Roll Star?'
The Byrds, 1967

'Tim was right, you shouldn't have come,' Chrissie said, not moving from her relaxed position.

'You saw him being knocked out?' I said.

Chrissie smiled. 'Sure. It'll be good for him. He can sleep off some of that shit he injects into himself. I knew you weren't going anywhere, so why not?'

'Why not. He's obviously only a fucking junkie.'

Her smile froze and she walked across the room and slapped me in the face. I grabbed her hand, but she wrenched it free and I saw that in her other hand was a small gun, which she was pointing directly at me.

'Don't speak about my brother like that,' she said, waving the gun from side to side. '*Never* speak about him like that, Séamus.'

'Sorry. I didn't mean to imply anything. I think it's tragic, really, when somebody abuses drugs like that. I blame society, Chrissie, don't you?'

'Shut up, Séamus,' Chrissie said as she walked over to where Tim lay and bent down beside him. She lowered her head for a second to look at him and her sleek blonde hair fell over her face. I half thought of trying to take the gun from her but the only part of me that seemed capable of movement were my eyes as I watched.

Reaching out a slender hand she touched Tim's fair hair and gently smoothed it back from his forehead. 'Poor old

Timmy,' she said, lifting her head to look at me, briefly, as she spoke and stroked. 'Poor, poor Timmy.' Chrissie looked back down at Tim.

Cassandra was still standing by the desk, her hand resting on the petrol can. She looked at me and back at the can and I could see that she was wondering if we might be able to use it. I nodded and she stepped in front of the desk, concealing the can from Chrissie's view. Chrissie continued to stroke her brother's head as if we had all the time in the world.

Where were the henchmen? I wondered, as my brain began to function. How many of them were there? Were there reinforcements on the plane or were they just hired help brought in to fly Tim and Chrissie out of Ireland? What would happen if they heard gunshots? Would they rush in and kill us all or would they just fly away and save their own skins?

Chrissie stood up and bent forward to brush dust from the leg of her cream trousers. 'I know that this won't mean much to you, Séamus,' she said, straightening up and pushing her shoulder length hair behind her ears with her free hand – as soon as she had arranged her hair she readjusted her stance so that her gun was trained more accurately on the area around my heart. 'And it's a pity really because I mean it: I'm sorry Tim shot your friend. It was an unfortunate accident and a very unfortunate turn of events for all of us. Even me. None of this would have snowballed out of control if he hadn't been so stupid that night.'

She paused as if she was waiting for a response.

I laughed. 'What do you want me to say? *Oh, Chrissie, don't worry. It doesn't matter. It's fine. Everything is all right?*'

Chrissie tutted angrily. 'No. That isn't it. I'm explaining, that's all. I thought I owed you an explanation. If you don't want it, well, there isn't much I can do about that.'

'And what about all the lovey-dovey stuff?' I said, as the beginnings of a plan formed vaguely in my head.

'What do you mean?'

'You know what I mean, Chrissie. What's the explanation for that? You and Tim targeted us. You used us.'

Chrissie smiled. 'And all the while you thought it was your irresistible rugged charm. Sorry about that.'

'Well, it's a bit hard to take.'

'Oh, for God's sake, Séamus. Get over yourself.'

I took a tiny step towards Tim. 'I don't know what you mean.'

'Yes you do. I know we never managed to consummate our relationship, but whether we did or we didn't, you'd have to admit you were using me every bit as much as vice versa.' Chrissie laughed. 'Anyway! How did we start talking about this? I only wanted to explain – apologize – about your friend.'

'The problem is,' I said, lowering my voice, purposely so that Chrissie would have to concentrate harder on what I was saying, 'that it's not going to make much difference to me, is it, Chrissie – if I'm going to be dead.'

Chrissie shook her head as if she could shake off my words like a dog can shake off water. 'Fucking drugs. You don't know how bad it gets. It was ages before I knew he was using again. He had stopped. I really believe that, and for a long, long time too.'

She paused and seemed to disappear into herself for a second before coming back again. It was weird. Like a light being switched on and off. I took another tiny step.

'But I think . . . well, when the stuff happened with William Ormston, it was too much for Timmy. And once the drugs come into the picture – I didn't know it was Timmy – that night at Pádraig's, I mean. I didn't know, and I felt bad for you. You were so –'

'Devastated.'

Chrissie nodded. 'Yes, actually. In the real sense of the word. Like a building that had been knocked down.'

'I remember. And I accept your apology.'

Chrissie smiled. 'Thanks.'

'Now. Why don't you let us go? Or at least just tie us up and go on your way? Why keep making things worse? Tim shot Mattie.'

I looked down at the prone Tim and I would have sold my soul there and then for a drink of water as the words came out of my mouth like sloes, drying my mouth with bitterness. I licked my cold cracking lips with a thick, dry tongue.

'Tim shot Mattie,' I made myself repeat, 'and there is no going back on that. However, *we* are still alive. Why add to your crimes. Why kill us as well?'

Chrissie shook her head again and looked over all three of us as if checking we were in place.

'Listen,' I said, stepping forward towards Chrissie, 'I know that this isn't your fault and, I told you, I accept your apology.'

'Move back, Séamus,' she said, a smile stretching across her face. 'The strongest drug coursing through my veins is caffeine. I'm not Tim.'

I stepped backwards. 'OK, OK, I'm not going to try anything. You're the boss. You have the gun.'

'Good. Remember that.'

'Let us go.'

Chrissie sighed. 'I'd like to. Honest to God, I would like to, but I can't. It's too risky.'

'Not as risky as killing us.'

'It doesn't matter. We've already killed Mattie Ahern – that was your friend's name, wasn't it?'

'Well, you didn't kill him. Tim did.'

'Makes no difference. And then, of course, there's the business with our father –'

'Your father? But your father died when you were children, didn't he?'

'My, my. Somebody *has* done his research. No. Not Peter Winter. He was our mother's husband. William Ormston was our father.'

'What?' I said, genuinely surprised, though I could have sworn that nothing else in the world would ever surprise me again.

'Look, I don't have time for this. We have to get out of here. I need to get Daniel to carry Tim out to the plane.'

She walked to the door. 'Daniel!' she called into the darkness. There was no answer. 'Where is that man? Daniel! Come here, right now!'

I walked closer to Tim's body while Chrissie's attention was distracted. She turned around and looked at me and then walked straight at me. Had she noticed that I was closer? She didn't say anything, just stopped in front of me.

'Who is Daniel?'

Chrissie sighed. 'The idiot you heard in the village.'

'The Afrikaner?'

'The Afrikaner. Though why I'm telling you this – move back a few steps, Séamus.'

I stepped two steps backwards without taking my eyes off her. 'How could William Ormston have been your father?' I said. Maybe if I could talk to her, stall her, I could give Paul a chance to come. Why had I told him not to bring reinforcements? 'I can't believe he was your father as well. There seems to be nothing but controversy about William Ormston's children.'

Chrissie tutted loudly. 'I don't have time for this,' she said, turning towards the door. 'Daniel! Daniel!'

'Come on Chrissie – tell me – get it off your chest,' I said, winding my voice around her like a net and smiling as if I liked her. 'Anyway, who am I going to tell where I'm off to?'

Chrissie laughed softly and turned around to face me again. 'Arrogant, aren't you? What do you know?'

'Well,' I said, inching forward as if I was just shifting my weight from my left foot to my right, 'I know that he was married to your mother and that she abandoned you and Tim and ran off with him.'

'She didn't abandon us. She came back. She had no choice. She and William Ormston had been lovers all the time that she was married to my – to Peter Winter.'

'So you could have been Peter Winter's children.'

'So we thought, and I wish we were, but we're not. He thought we were, or maybe he didn't, maybe he told himself that to make himself feel better. I see that people do that a lot.'

'How do you know?'

'Know that people tell themselves stories to make themselves feel better?'

'No, the rest of it. Who your father was – the details of your mother's life.'

'I found a diary that belonged to my mother. It was in a trunk Tim and I brought from South Africa. I went there – to Cork – about ten years ago and collected the trunk. I didn't want any part of us left behind in that – that place. I'd never seen it before. They must have thrown it in after we arrived. Anyway, she describes it all in her diary. Her marriage – with separate bedrooms. Her affair with William Ormston. His children. Me and Tim.'

'So?' I said, edging even closer to Tim's body. He groaned and wriggled on the floor and Chrissie looked down at him, so I took another step closer. 'Why did she leave you?'

'Why?' she repeated as if she was tasting the word. 'Why? Because Dad – Peter Winter – loved us and wanted us and told her he wouldn't follow her or make her life difficult if she left us with him.'

'So she left without you?'

Chrissie nodded. 'But she came back. When our father died, she came to take us with her.'

Chrissie paused again and put her tongue between her

teeth and noisily sucked saliva. Her face seemed to change shape a few times before it reformed into its serene mask. She looked at me and smiled.

'We thought she was dead. Daddy told us that and he cried a lot of the time so we believed him and then – then there she was.'

'It must have been weird. Your mother dies and then comes back from the dead.'

'You could say that. When she came back after our father died, Timmy thought maybe Daddy might come back as well and everything would be all right again.' Chrissie stopped talking and looked into the distance. Her eyes were wide and looked to be full of tears.

'I bet you came from a lovely home,' she said, the line of her mouth thin and hard as she spoke. 'Mammy. Daddy. Happy families. You couldn't even imagine our lives. The cruelty. The way they treated us. The things they made us do . . .' Her voice trailed off.

'Even so? Killing us won't make that go away. And at least you had your mother. She came back for you.'

Chrissie blinked her eyes and cocked her head to one side. The tears cleared from her eyes and she laughed a tinny laugh. 'I know you're trying to stall me. And it's a nice try but it won't work. Daniel! Daniel!'

'I'm sure he's outside cranking up the engine of the plane,' I said, smiling at her.

Chrissie smiled back, and as usual I noticed the scar near her lip.

'Where did you get that scar?' I asked her, shifting my feet by tiny increments until I was standing almost by Tim's head.

She looked levelly at me as if she was trying to sell me a mortgage. 'In the crash that killed my mother. A week after she came back for us we were all in a car crash.'

'That's a bit shit,' I said.

Chrissie shrugged. 'William Ormston was driving, of

327

course, and he'd been drinking and hit a school bus and our car rolled over and that was that. He took us back to Ireland after the crash and dumped us in Cork and we never saw the bastard again until we went looking for him last year.'

'That's awful,' I said, and I meant it in spite of everything. 'Really fucking shite.'

Chrissie laughed the tinny laugh again, and the sound of it frightened me more than the sight of the gun. 'Shit happens. The thing is that it wasn't too bad when we thought he was a stranger. Discovering he was our father is what seems to have made it all too much for Timmy.'

Suddenly Alison walked towards where we were standing. 'Stop!' Chrissie shouted at her, turning slightly and pointing the gun at Alison. 'Stop right now or I'll shoot!'

Alison stopped walking and looked at Chrissie. 'Shoot. Go ahead, I'm sick of this. William Ormston was obviously a bastard. You're not the only ones he abandoned.'

'I don't care and I don't want to talk to you. Go over there and stand beside Cassandra or I promise I'll shoot you,' Chrissie said, in a voice so ordinary that it was hard to reconcile it with the words she was using.

'William Ormston was my father as well,' Alison said.

Chrissie shrugged. 'I already know that – you went to his funeral and told Stella, for Christ's sake!' Chrissie laughed. 'How stupid can you get?'

'All I'm saying is that you and Tim aren't the only ones,' Alison said, her voice as level as Chrissie's.

Chrissie focused her full attention on Alison. 'William Ormston was your father? La-de-da! Whoop-de-do! So what? Really and truly I couldn't give a shit.'

Chrissie walked over to Alison and pointed the gun upwards until it was two inches from Alison's cheek. Alison didn't flinch and I knew she thought it was a bluff, but there was something about the way Chrissie was holding herself that made me certain she was past the point of threats.

I reached behind me and felt the glass poking up from my pocket. I was still at the point of wondering if I'd make it as far as Chrissie before she blew Alison's face into smithereens, when the barrel that had knocked out Tim went rolling across the floor towards her.

'Fuck you!' Cassandra's voice screamed as the barrel hit Chrissie in the legs. Cassandra stood in the middle of the room, hands on hips, face flushed. 'Fuck both of you!'

'Cassandra!' I shouted as Chrissie staggered to the left.

Chrissie steadied herself, swivelled round and in one long, undeniably graceful movement swung her gun up and towards Cassandra.

'No way!' Chrissie shouted as she righted herself. A loud shot snapped through the air followed by a hideous slapping noise. Cassandra looked startled and I opened my mouth to speak but no sound came out. She looked down at her thigh and placed her open hand across a rapidly spreading bloodstain on the pale blue leg of her jeans. Cassandra folded on to the ground into a kneeling position.

'Stupid bitch,' Chrissie said, as she walked towards Cassandra, kicking the barrel as she passed it. 'Stupid, stupid bitch. Whatever did he see in you?'

Cassandra looked up at Chrissie as she stopped in front of her. It was like a horror tableau: one woman standing, one kneeling – a gun trained on her forehead.

'Chrissie!' Alison shouted.

'Shut up,' Chrissie said, without turning to look at Alison. Cassandra still said nothing just looked up at her assailant.

'Chrissie! Don't!' Alison shouted again.

Chrissie's hand moved tightly around the gun and I knew Cassandra was as good as dead.

Pulling the long shard of glass from my back pocket I ran to where Tim was still lying, unconscious, on the ground.

'Chrissie!' I shouted. 'Don't even think about it or I'll fucking kill him.'

Chrissie swung around and looked at me – her beautiful face pale in the gloom and framed by her luminous hair. Her eyes grew frightened as she registered the sight in front of her.

'See what I have here?' I said, leaning close to Tim and resting the glass against his throat. 'Drop the gun.'

Chrissie took a step towards us.

'I'm warning you,' I said. She stopped walking. Alison ran behind her to where Cassandra was still sitting on the ground.

'Cass? You OK?' I said.

'Fine,' Cassandra said, her voice a bit wobbly.

'Drop the gun, Chrissie,' I said, encouraged by the sound of Cassandra's voice. 'Drop it or I'll cut his throat.'

I pressed my hand heavily against Tim's chest to keep him on the ground if he woke up. His heart beat erratically against my palm and he made a whimpering noise.

'No,' she said, softly, like a prayer being muttered, 'please, Séamus. Don't hurt him.'

I watched as Alison helped Cassandra across the room and sat her up on the desk. Alison moved the petrol can out of sight and pulled off her jacket and wrapped it around Cassandra. My heart began to slow down and I took a deep breath. All right. The main thing was that Cassandra was all right.

OK, she'd been shot, but at least she was alive and didn't seem too badly injured. Still, we needed to get the fuck out of there before somebody was actually dead. I looked up at Chrissie.

'I don't want to hurt him, Chrissie,' I said, the feral terror on Chrissie's face making me think that maybe we actually had a chance after all. 'Drop the gun.'

Chrissie's hand drooped like a flower and her gun pointed towards her foot as she looked at me holding the broken glass to her unconscious brother's throat.

'You'd never do it,' she said, suddenly, the gun straightening and aiming at my head as she spoke. 'I know you, Séamus, you don't have it in you to hurt another person.'

'I wouldn't be too sure about that,' I said, as Tim stirred underneath my hand. 'There was a time when that was true, but not now, Chrissie. Now it's about survival and that changes everything.'

Chrissie smiled. 'Come on, we both know you won't hurt him. He didn't mean to shoot your friend. He was afraid. Tim has always been afraid. When our uncle did those – those things I wanted to kill him, but not Timmy. Timmy was young.'

'Timmy's only two years younger than you, Chrissie.'

Chrissie shook her head. 'But it wasn't like that. It was as if there was a ten-year age difference. He would cry when it was happening, especially if my uncle's friends were there.'

Chrissie stopped talking and looked at Tim. I noticed that her free hand was fiddling with the edge of her jacket, but her face had assumed its professional mask and was impossible to read. Suddenly she looked back at me.

'I never cried,' she said, smiling as if she was telling me some great news, but her eyes were colder and harder than any eyes I'd ever seen. 'I wouldn't give them the satisfaction. Timmy suffered so much – more than me, and when he gave those pills to William Ormston it was because he was mad at him, can't you see that? Doesn't that tell you everything? If Timmy was a bad person he'd have poisoned him.'

'What sort of pills?'

Chrissie sighed. 'He didn't tell me until afterwards. It was stupid. Timmy was angry, especially after we found out he was our father. So was I. Ormston had a serious condition of some description, something to do with blood clots – I don't know – or care.'

Chrissie paused for a second. 'We'd been in contact with him for about six months.'

'Did you know he was your father by then?'

'Sure – that's why we looked for him – but we didn't pretend that we knew. He thought we still believed he was our mother's lover.'

'And?'

'And nothing, really. Timmy offered to prescribe for him. Ormston was a stingy bastard – free doctoring – he was happy to go along with it and Timmy prescribed something that made his blood clot instead of stopping the clotting – something like that. He was taking them for a while – that's why he died so suddenly.'

'So Tim killed William Ormston?'

'I wouldn't put it like that.'

Tim groaned and opened his eyes. 'Séamus?'

'Stay still, Tim,' I said. 'Don't move.'

Tim's eyes grew huge in his face and his lips quivered. 'Chrissie?' he whispered, turning his head, 'Chrissie!' he shouted.

'I'm here, Timmy, I'm here,' she said, moving towards him.

'Back. Get back, Chrissie, or I'll hurt him. I mean it. Drop the gun.'

Chrissie stepped back to her original position, but still held on to her gun.

'Chrissie?' Tim said, again, turning his head until he found her with his eyes.

'It's OK. It'll be fine, Timmy. He won't hurt you.'

'I will,' I interrupted.

Tim shrank away from me and pulled his arms and legs and chin in close to his body. I bent forward and, grabbing a handful of hair, jerked his head until I exposed his throat.

'Chrissie!' Tim whispered hoarsely, as his wild eyes looked up into my face. I hoped I looked as desperate as I felt, and that they couldn't see how astounded I was that I felt I could slit Tim Winter's throat if the need arose. But the need hadn't quite arrived, so I adjusted the glass until it was still almost making contact with his throat.

'Chrissie,' he whimpered, 'help me. Make him stop.' Big tears flowed down Tim's cheek on to the dusty floor and my resolve began to melt. My hand shook. How could I do this? She was right. I couldn't hurt him. For God's sake, he was a total fuck-up already. What would be the point in hurting him even more? Tim stopped crying and looked at me as if he could hear my thoughts.

'I'm sorry. Don't hurt me, please, Séamus. I didn't mean it.'

'Don't hurt him,' Chrissie said. 'You can see it now, if you look at him. You can see what I told you. He's destroyed. He's not responsible for his actions.

And I *could* see it. She was telling the truth. Tim Winter lay on the floor under my weapon and though he was a man and older than me, it didn't feel like that. I felt as if I was pinioning a terrified boy. It was as though there was a tiny, defenseless child under my knee with a razor-sharp piece of glass to his throat.

My head exploded with the thoughts of all the abuse he had experienced in his life, and my heart seemed to be actually physically swelling in my chest. I couldn't do this.

What was I thinking? That I could slit this man-child's throat with my weapon of glass? That I could take his life? Spill his blood on to the floor of this shit-hole? Like he had spilled Mattie's blood on to the frosty tarmac? Like Chrissie would have done with Cassandra?

I looked at Tim again and this time he seemed different. Maybe not a man but also not a child. I saw in his eyes something like the look in the eye of an animal studying his prey. As I looked at him he exchanged a quick glance with Chrissie. I looked up at Chrissie and yanked Tim to his feet, all the time holding the glass to his throat.

Tim groaned as if I'd hurt him and maybe I had. I didn't care.

'You OK, Cass?' I called.

Cassandra didn't answer.

'Cass?'

'Fine,' she said, in a voice that was a good bit weaker than the last time she'd spoken. Her voice frightened me, but I knew I couldn't afford to be afraid. I looked at her. She seemed OK. It was probably only shock. It was bound to be a bit of a shock to be shot in the leg like that – and very sore no doubt – but probably not that serious. Just a big, bloody, flesh wound.

'Alison?' I called, just to be sure.

'She's OK,' Alison answered.

'What's the matter with Cassandra?' Tim said and I jerked reflexively. He muttered in pain as I tightened my grasp on him.

'Your sister shot her,' I said.

'Chrissie?' Tim said.

Tim tried to turn his head. 'You OK, Cass?' he shouted. 'Where are you hit? She's not dead, Séamus, is she? I couldn't bear it if anything happened to her.'

'Oh, shut up, Tim,' I said. 'For fuck's sake – you wanted to cook us.'

'But I love her –' he started.

I yanked back his head until he groaned. 'Shut the fuck up, Tim, and pay attention. Cassandra's not dead, but you will be in a minute if your sister doesn't drop the gun.'

'Chrissie,' Tim whimpered.

Chrissie moved towards us and I moved the glass so close to Tim's throat that he had to pull his head upwards and stretch his neck to try to escape contact with it.

I saw a tiny line of blood appear as I readjusted our stance. So I'd hurt him, I'd cut him, so what? Big deal. He'd shot Mattie. He wanted to kill us and still would without a second thought if he got a chance.

'Ow!' Tim said, struggling in my grasp. 'You're hurting me.'

I yanked him around so that I could make eye contact. 'Aw, really. Poor, poor Timmy. Did I hurt you?'

Tim sniffed and his face took on a self-righteous look. 'Yes, Séamus, you really hurt me.'

I looked into his thin, pale face as he spoke and saw the slipping focus of his eyes and waves of emotion thundered inside me.

'You're a ruthless bastard aren't you, Tim?' I said softly into the air right in front of his face.

He looked at me and blinked and I could almost see how he was trying to force his drug-melted brain to work. How many patients had he accidentally killed in that stupor?

'Sorry?'

'You – are – a – ruthless – bastard,' I said, opening and closing my mouth in wide arcs as I spoke. 'A bit of a lad – is that what they call it nowadays? You set out to get what you want and you won't let anything stand in your way. A go-getter.'

Tim gave me a half-smile. 'Well, I suppose so.'

'And the business with the medication you prescribed for Ormston – he never even knew, did he?'

'He had no idea,' Tim's face contorted and his eyes flicked from side to side as if he was searching his brain for something. 'How did you know about that, Séamus?'

'Chrissie told me – didn't you, Chris?'

'Shut up, Séamus,' Chrissie said.

'I have to say that that was clever, Tim – very clever,' I said. 'Everybody would think he'd just died of natural causes. What was it you said at Pádraig's? A question of *when*, not *if*, he'd have a stroke – ingenious.'

'That was the idea.'

'But when he died suddenly like that in Castleannery, weren't you worried they'd find something that would tip them off about what you were giving him?'

Tim frowned. 'I was a bit – especially at first. But when there was no suspicion around his death . . .'

'Natural causes. I was there when he died and you're right, Tim, it looked entirely natural.'

'That meant the only problem was the blood.'

'Timmy!' Chrissie shouted.

'The blood? What blood, Timmy?' I said.

'Timmy,' Chrissie repeated, in a low, menacing tone.

I smiled. 'Stop it, Chrissie, for God's sake,' I said, softly as if I was teasing her or we were sharing a joke. 'What harm is there in him telling me? Didn't you tell me about the medicine.'

'Go on, Timmy,' I said. 'What blood are you talking about?'

'The blood I'd taken to send to the lab, I took it earlier that day – the day he died.'

'Why did you take it?'

'He expected it – patients on anti-coagulants have their blood tested all the time – he was used to it. Usually I threw away the sample but that day I'd held on to it because I was going to send it to a lab in Dublin; I was curious to see exactly what effect the stuff was having on him.'

'So why didn't you just destroy it when he died?'

'I was going to – I was worried the police might ask about it. But then Chrissie said it was DNA – it was her idea to hide it in Pádraig's freezer.'

'Clever Chrissie,' I said.

Tim nodded. 'Good job we had hidden it there as it turned out.'

'The police?' I said.

Tim smiled. 'The police never even looked for blood samples – why would they? They never suspected anything. The real beauty of hiding the blood in Pádraig's was that Stella Ormston couldn't find it. You don't know what that woman is like.'

'Ruthless?' I asked.

Tim nodded. 'A total bitch. But we had her by the short and curlies with that blood. There's no denying DNA. So William dying like that turned out to be a stroke of luck for us, considering everything.'

'I can see that,' I said.

Tim's face contorted as he remembered. 'I was a bit worried about the post-mortem, though.'

I stared into Tim's pale eyes. 'Post-mortem?'

'On William Ormston – if they'd done one they'd have found out I was giving him coagulants. They didn't. They took my word. I was lucky there too.'

'You make your own luck, as they say, Timmy. I think you were clever, that's why they didn't find out. Who signed the death certificate? You?'

Tim nodded again and a small, almost embarrassed smile tugged at his lips.

'If everything was going so well, why would you take a chance like you did and go to Pádraig's house with a gun?'

Tim shrugged and looked away. 'His stupid Fort Knox.'

'What?'

'He was building that secure room for his work. Remember?'

'Timmy,' Chrissie warned.

'What difference would that make?' I said.

'Codes, Séamus. Codes and security and all that. He was converting the garage into a vault and the blood was in the deep freeze in the bloody garage. I'd never be able to get access to it without Pádraig being with me.'

'Oh, I see.'

Tim smiled. 'I should probably have waited, but I panicked. Then Mattie came along out of the blue and I lost the plot entirely. Shot him before I could even think about it.'

'But why?' I said. 'Why did you shoot him?'

'I was afraid he'd recognize me. I recognized him.'

'But I saw you and I didn't recognize you. It was dark and your face was covered.'

'It's lucky I didn't see you on the road that night, Séamus. I'd probably have shot you as well.' Tim laughed then as if he were recounting the tale of some minor misunderstanding. I wanted to smash his face.

'My luck was pretty short-lived, if you're going to kill me now,' I said, struggling to control the emotion in my voice.

'I suppose,' Tim said, 'and I'm sorry about that but when we leave for –'

'Shut up, Tim!' Chrissie shouted. Tim turned his head and we both looked at her. She had her gun trained on Alison.

'I'm sick of this. Let him go, Séamus, or I'll kill at least one of these stupid bitches. Daniel! Daniel!'

'Where *is* that bloody Daniel?' I said, ignoring her words as a sudden calm descended on me. 'Jesus, you just can't get good staff these days, can you, Tim?'

'Tell me about it,' Tim slurred beside me.

'Do you mind me asking, Tim, who exactly is he? Daniel, I mean. He keeps popping up all over the place and I just can't figure out what he's doing here.'

'He's just Daniel,' Tim said.

'I'm warning you, Séamus,' Chrissie said.

I smiled at her and looked back down at Tim. His pupils were wide enough to let in a small egg and his face was as slack and blasted as his eyes. He really was fucked. But then, so were we.

'Séamus,' Chrissie said again. I turned my head to look at her, still holding the glass to Tim's throat. I knew that at any minute, Daniel was going to come in and beat the crap out of me – that is if Chrissie hadn't shot me first. It was all too much to take in so there was no point in worrying about any of it, really. I looked back down at Tim.

'I mean I can see how you'd need Daniel around now –'

but the night Mattie was killed? I can't figure that. Why was he here?'

'He was bringing some stuff we needed for a meeting with Stella,' Tim said. 'That's where I got the photograph of Alison Chang — didn't you ever wonder where that came from, Séamus?'

Chrissie groaned.

'He's a sort of a distant relative,' Tim continued, ignoring her disapproval.

'From the home place?' I said.

Tim nodded. 'Yes. He moved to England a few years ago and looked us up. Chrissie gave him a job as a driver. She was a big-shot in TV at the time.'

Tim laughed suddenly, and the sound was raw like a scream. 'Not that driving was the only *service* he rendered for my lovely sister. If you get my drift.'

'I've had enough of this,' Chrissie said, in a hard, low voice. 'Let him go now, Séamus. I'm losing my patience and I'm in a hurry to catch my plane and I swear to God that I'll finish off your precious cousin if you don't let him go right now.'

Everybody looked at Cassandra who was huddled forward on the desk. I could see her small body shivering.

'Cassandra?' I called. Her head moved at the sound of my voice, but she didn't quite manage to lift it up. 'Are you OK, Cass. Alison? Is she OK?'

Alison didn't answer, just moved closer to Cassandra and put her arm around her. Chrissie trained her gun on Alison and Cassandra.

Tim tried to pull away from me.

'You OK, Cass?' he called. She didn't answer. He turned his head to look at me. 'Where is she hit? Why won't anybody tell me where she was hit?'

I wanted to cut his fucking stupid throat and force the whole thing to a head. I could hardly stand it another second.

But that was no good and I knew it. If I killed Tim then Chrissie'd definitely shoot Cassandra and that would be the end of it. I had to stay calm.

'She's all right,' I said, to try and control my impulses. 'She's hit in the leg. She'll be fine.'

'Unless the bullet hit the femoral artery,' Tim said, almost casually.

'What?' I said.

He smiled. 'That'd kill you in seconds though – like cutting the bottom out of a paper cup.'

'Well, she's not dead,' I said, more scared now than I wanted Tim to know.

'No,' Tim said, 'unless it just nicked it and the bleed is slow – or it could be the vibrations – you said Chrissie shot her, didn't you?'

'Christ!' Chrissie said. 'Shut up!'

'It's just that the bullet might not have damaged the artery, but the vibrations created by the bullet can cause a delayed effect. Not sure how long that takes, though, I'd have to look it up. That's more forensics than ordinary family medicine, really.'

I felt the terror rising inside me. I tightened my grip on Tim. 'Shut up, just shut the fuck up, Tim.'

Tim snorted. 'I'm only telling you what might be wrong.'

With a kind of moan, Cassandra suddenly slumped low and began to fall forwards. Alison grabbed her just before she fell. Chrissie walked straight towards them, gun held out in front of her.

'Chrissie! Drop the fucking gun!' I screamed, but Chrissie ignored me and kept walking, and somehow I knew she wasn't on her way to lend assistance.

Alison stepped in front of Cassandra. She folded her arms across her chest and smiled defiantly at Chrissie.

'Go ahead,' Alison said, 'go on, Chrissie, shoot. You're going to kill me in a few minutes anyway so why not just get it over with now? I think I'd prefer it anyway. I don't like the idea of dying in a fire.'

Chrissie walked straight up to Alison and hit her in the face with her gun. Alison's head flew back, but she turned back to face Chrissie and tried a smile. Blood flowed from her upper lip, which was split open like a burst peach. She pressed her hand against it and the flow slowed.

'Don't make the mistake of thinking I'm some sort of pathetic half-wit like my brother.'

'Only a half-wit would do something like this,' Alison said thickly.

Chrissie lifted the gun and went to strike her again, but this time Alison ducked and warded off the blow with her right arm. A loud, cracking noise accompanied the contact. Chrissie pushed the gun up against Alison's cheek and her breathing was loud and angry.

'Leave her alone, Chrissie. If you don't leave her alone I'll slit his throat from ear to ear and he'll be dead before you can cross the room.'

'Fuck you!' Chrissie shouted, her gun still shoved into Alison's face but her head turned so that she was looking over her shoulder straight at me. 'Kill him, I've fucking had it.'

'I will.'

'Chrissie!' Tim said, in a bleat. 'No, no, please.'

'Oh shut up, Tim. You can kill him, Séamus, but not before I kill this big-mouthed Chinese bitch and right now it seems worth it. She'll be dead and if you kill Timmy then you'll have no leverage and I can just shoot the fucking rest of you and get out of this shit-heap once and for all.'

'Chrissie, look –' I began.

'Shoot me,' Alison said in a steady voice. 'Go on, Chrissie, shoot me. What are you afraid of?'

'I'm not afraid,' Chrissie said, turning back to face Alison. 'You're the one who should be afraid, but you're too fucking stupid. You haven't even enough sense to be afraid.'

Alison shrugged and my breath caught in my throat as I saw the gun move up on her cheek. 'I'm going to die anyway,' she said, taking her hand away from her mouth. 'Why bother to kow-tow to you. What difference will it make?'

'Shut up you stupid half-breed,' Chrissie said, moving her face closer to Alison's bleeding, defiant face.

Alison, much taller than Chrissie, pulled her head back to get away from Chrissie's face.

'You shouldn't call your sister names,' Alison said. 'I always wanted a sister, didn't you? Maybe we could share make-up tips and talk about boys, or is it too late for that?'

Chrissie laughed suddenly, that sharp, tinny, gut-terrifying laugh.

'See you, sis,' she said, her finger flexing on the trigger. I abruptly let go of Tim and he fell on to the ground. Then I ran at Chrissie. Launching myself into the air before I reached her so that my body crashed into hers and threw her forwards. As we fell a gunshot ripped through the air.

'Stay right where you are!' Paul Richardson's voice was shouting. 'Nobody move. Police!'

I turned my head and saw the puffy orange jacket move in front of me as Paul scooped Chrissie's gun off the floor. I jumped up and ran to where Cassandra lay flat out on the desk, her left jeans leg now almost black with blood.

Her face was still and whiter than a kabuki mask against her dark hair and I could feel in the air around her that she was dying. I picked her up and ran out of the building, through a long corridor and out into the sleety darkness. A moustached policeman moved towards me as I emerged and I heard Paul Richardson shout at him.

'She shot her in the leg,' I said, to the policeman. 'Only in the leg, but she's unconscious and look –'

I looked down at Cassandra, limp in my arms. She was so small. Had she always been that small or was she just shrinking now because she was dying? A middle-aged policewoman threw open the back door of the squad car.

'Put her in here,' she said.

I didn't move. The woman looked at me but I still didn't move.

'Garda Healy!' Paul Richardson's voice called. The woman turned around. 'The ambulance?' he said.

'We don't have time,' she said. 'We can take her in the car to the Regional but he needs to put her down so I can apply pressure to slow down the bleeding.'

'Séamus,' Paul began, but I had moved already and deposited Cassandra into the squad car. Garda Healy didn't say a word, just jumped in beside Cassandra. 'Drive!' she shouted, and the car pulled off with a spray of gravel and the back door still swinging open. A blond boy-faced Guard ran after the car and slammed the door. Then the siren screeched and they were gone. Behind me voices called and car doors slammed and I noticed that Alison and Paul Richardson were standing beside me.

'She isn't dead, Séamus,' Paul said, handing me a cigarette.

I lit it and inhaled deeply. 'I know,' I said.

'She'll be OK,' Alison said and I turned to look at her. Her lip was split and swollen and her face was streaked with blood. 'I know she will, Séamus.'

I nodded and looked into the darkness because I didn't know any such thing.

15

'I'd like to thank gravity for keeping me down'
'The Wondering Geologist', Fred, 2001

Paul suggested that Alison and I sit into his car. The young
Guard who had slammed the door of the car that took
Cassandra away, handed us two plastic cups of lukewarm
coffee as soon as we sat into the back seat.

'Detective Richardson said to tell you he won't be long,'
he said.

I nodded and Alison tried to smile, but her upper lip was
so swollen it hardly moved.

'Can you manage that?' I asked as he walked away.

She shook her head. 'Doesn't matter. It's lovely and warm.'

Alison and I sat in silence for what felt like ages. I wasn't
able to talk and my guess was that neither could she. Eventually, the driver's door opened and Paul Richardson sat in and
started the engine. He twisted in his seat and looked back
at us.

'Cassandra is going to be fine.'

'What?' I said.

'Just heard on the radio – they met the ambulance in
Lahinch and they managed to stabilize her.'

'You're sure,' I said, leaning forward.

He nodded. My breath exploded in my chest as if I'd been
holding it for ages. Maybe I had. Paul Richardson turned
around in his seat and began to drive. I looked at the tall
pine trees still flapping from side to side in the wind and
rain. It had been a long, long day.

'Are you absolutely positive that she's OK?' I said.

'Definite. She lost a lot of blood but Garda Healy managed to slow it down in the car and then they met the ambulance. I don't know what the medics did, but I presume they did their stuff. The important thing is that she's going to be fine.'

Alison started to cry then. Loud, hard, shuddering sobs. I put my arm around her shoulders and she cried harder.

Paul speeded up along the dark deserted road and rubbed his hand across his face. 'Alison?'

'I'm fine,' she said between sobs.

'I would have been here earlier. But I couldn't find the car, or this place. I drove past it. It took me a while to realize that I'd passed it and then I doubled back and found Séamus' car and radioed for help but that took a while in getting here as well. I tried ringing your number.'

'They took the phone,' I said. 'Well, we presume they did – they took our coats.'

'Then when I found you, I had to disable Daniel and that other bastard before I could do anything else,' Paul continued, his voice very quiet. 'And Chrissie had that gun . . .'

Alison cried on, unable to answer what he was saying. I knew he meant well, which made me feel bad for him, but it didn't make a bit of difference to what had happened. Not one bit. I wanted to try to explain that to him, but I didn't really know how to do it. Instead I said, 'It's all right. You did come.'

He shook his head. It couldn't have been easy for him either. What a job. What a night. What a fucking world.

'Thanks for everything,' I said, to him, reaching a hand forward to pat his orange puffy shoulder.

'You're welcome. More than welcome.'

My head ached – it had started to throb again as soon as the police swooped in and gathered up all the criminals. Alison's sobs subsided and she slumped against my shoulder, quiet now except for a long, shuddering breath every few minutes.

'Can we go home?' I asked.

The tired detective nodded his head. 'I'll bring you all home, right now. We can talk tomorrow, but right now I'd say we could all do with a good night's sleep.'

'Good idea,' I said.

'Where will I bring you?' Paul asked.

'Castleannery?' I said, looking at Alison. She nodded her assent.

'Castleannery it is,' he said, as we drove along the long driveway out of the airfield and on to the narrow road.

'At least we might all get some sleep there,' I said.

Alison nodded again and then I think we both fell asleep. I didn't know for sure. All I do know is that I did.

The next day was Christmas Eve. While the rest of the Christian world was running to and fro in desperate preparation for the festivities Alison and I woke at seven and went immediately into Limerick to see Cassandra. She was awake when we arrived.

'So you were wrong and I was right, Séamus,' she said as soon as we walked into her hospital room. Alison and I both kissed her paper-white cheek and she smiled up at us. 'The cavalry did come.'

I grinned at her. Typical Cassandra – always doing the big woman. I loved that about her. I kissed her again and sat on the side of the bed holding her hand.

'How do you feel?' Alison said.

Cassandra laughed. 'Pretty good actually, but I think it might be the drugs.'

'And what did they say about your leg?' I asked.

Cassandra looked at me. 'They think it'll be fine – they have to operate some more and I'll be here for a couple of weeks, but then it should be OK.'

Cassandra's voice petered out and she closed her eyes. Alison and I sat in silence and watched as she drifted off to sleep.

'Strong medicine,' Alison said.

'Jesus, I could do with some of that myself,' I said, laying Cassandra's hand on the pale green coverlet. 'Will we go to the police station and make our statements and get that over with?'

Alison nodded and we left.

We spent a large part of that morning giving statements to the police, then back to Castleannery to collect Alison's car from my mechanic. Alison drove back to my house to collect her few belongings before setting out for Dublin.

'Well, that's it, so, I suppose,' I said, suddenly awkward, as we stood together, alone, in my kitchen. 'Are you sure you don't want to eat something before you go?'

Alison shook her head. 'I'm fine.'

'Maybe you should stay the night. You probably need to see a doctor about your head and lip.'

'It's not serious,' she said, automatically raising her hand to her swollen upper lip. I saw that a huge bruise had formed on her forearm where Chrissie had hit her with the gun.

'And what about your arm? Is it OK?'

'I'm fine, really, nothing broken – everything will be grand in a few days. I'll go see my doctor tomorrow.'

'Christmas Day?'

Alison shrugged. 'Maybe not tomorrow then. But I know it's all OK.'

I nodded and smiled. She smiled back and then grimaced slightly as the swelling on her face pulled her mouth back into a straight line.

'You could stay here. I have to go home or my mother will have an apoplectic fit, but you could stay.'

'You'd trust me not to steal the silver?'

'Sure. They're all monogrammed heirlooms anyway, you'd never sell them.'

Alison buttoned her coat. 'No, I'll go. I can always stop en route and book in somewhere if I get tired, but I'm sort of looking forward to the drive.'

'Yeah. Peace and quiet.'

'Peace and quiet,' she echoed.

We stood and looked at each other for a few more tense seconds.

'OK, then,' Alison said, suddenly, grabbing her handbag off the kitchen table. 'Take care, Séamus.'

And then she was gone. The shock of her leaving the room almost impelled me into action. I didn't think I wanted her to leave, but I didn't know why that was, didn't know what I wanted to do or say. Some kind of ridiculous hostage bond, I told myself.

She was obviously dying to get away if she was willing to drive the whole way to Dublin with a bust lip and an arm that had to ache like hell. I didn't blame her after what she'd been through. After all she'd seen.

I was exhausted and dispirited and confused, and all I could think of doing was what I knew my mother wanted. So I threw assorted clothes and underwear into a bag and drove home for Christmas.

'Can I ask you a question?' Eamon said on St Stephen's Day, as we lay draped on the couch waiting for the big match to begin.

'Sure. What is it?'

'Well,' he said, leaning on the arm of his chair and looking at me, 'well, I know I've been told this – but what was the big deal about the blood samples?'

'William Ormston's blood?'

'Yeah. I never really got it.'

'OK,' I said, glad to be asked to relate a simple catalogue of facts, 'Tim Winter was poisoning William Ormston, giving him stuff to make his blood clot.'

'I got that much,' Eamon said.

'And he took a blood test the day he died. Then hid the phial of blood in Pádraig Harrison's freezer. That night – the night he shot Mattie – he decided to go get it back because Pádraig was having this super-duper security system installed.'

'I even know all that. But what about your man's widow and all that?'

'Oh, that. After William Ormston died there were a clatter of people claiming to be his children and looking for a slice of the pie.'

'I see.'

'But unfortunately it wasn't possible to do a DNA test to prove or disprove their claims as there wasn't one verifiable scrap of William Ormston's DNA to be had.'

'How unfortunate,' Eamon said, with his trademark cocked eyebrow that I'd spent most of my childhood trying to imitate.

'Absolutely terrible,' I said, with a grin. 'And his widow – Stella – thought she was home and dry. No way to prove paternity and all the doctors said William Ormston had had a vasectomy and was infertile. Then Chrissie contacted her about the blood that Tim had in his possession.'

'Holy shit. And was he shooting blanks?'

'Seems not. He had a vasectomy all right, but it doesn't appear to have taken as they say. And it seems that he was happy enough in his old age to start acknowledging his children. Mad fucker.'

'I'd say that's an accurate enough diagnosis, doctor. Mad fucker syndrome,' Eamon said.

'Exactly. Anyway, it seems that Ormston's grieving widow didn't want to share her inheritance.'

'And didn't have to if nobody could prove paternity –' Eamon said.

'– which is where Chrissie and Tim come into the picture. And clever Chrissie decided not to bother sharing either so she offered Stella – the widow – the blood sample.'

'DNA evidence. I get it now. Jesus! Mad – but sort of clever – fuckers the whole lot of them.'

'I agree. Anyway, the deal seems to have been that unless Stella gave Tim and Chrissie a third of the estate – which alone would amount to tens of millions – Chrissie would give the blood sample to the lawyers. But if she gave them what they wanted . . .' I paused as a sense of all the insane things that had happened floated over me like a vague smell.

'But if the lawyers got hold of the blood mightn't they discover that the doc had been messing with his da's medication?'

'Most likely,' I said, 'but Chrissie was probably sure enough that Stella wouldn't take the chance of letting it go that far.'

'Why?

'Well, it made little material difference to Stella if Ormston was murdered – unless he was the love of her life – which I doubt. On the other hand it could make a big difference to her if she had to share his money with a load of offspring.'

'OK, I see. So they offered her the blood if she gave them what they wanted – what then?' Eamon said.

'Stella could do whatever she wanted. Once the deal was done and dusted, Stella could tip the phials of blood down the sink and pour bleach in after them and they'd all be happy.'

'And were they all really his children?'

'Probably.'

'Prolific mad fucker that Ormston guy.'

'Fertile fucker.'

'Fecund fucker, even,' Eamon said, grinning. 'And your friend, what's her name – Alison Chang? Is she his daughter?'

I nodded again. 'Looks like it.'

'And what will happen to the widow? Will she end up sewing mailbags? Do they still sew mailbags?'

'Paul Richardson says nothing can be proven against Stella Ormston – she hasn't done anything illegal, whatever she was planning.'

'Where is the blood sample now?'

'Who knows.'

'I wonder if all the alleged children will go ahead with their cases?' Eamon said.

'Maybe.'

'Will Alison Chang?'

'I doubt it.'

'Why?'

'I think she's probably certain enough at this point that William Ormston was her father.'

'Still she might get a few bob,' Eamon said.

'She doesn't need it – she's already loaded.'

'Is she now. Any chance of an introduction? I could do with a rich woman in my life.'

'Don't you think she has suffered enough?'

'Ha, ha,' Eamon said tonelessly. 'Tell me one other thing.'

'What?'

'Did mam say they killed Prince as well?'

'Yeah. Tim did – who else? He was spooked. Cassandra was going around asking questions and he thought it might frighten her. Put her off. So he poisoned Prince and smashed up the kitchen.'

'Jesus. What a bollocks.'

I nodded again.

'You were lucky,' Eamon said. We both continued to watch TV as the camera focused on a man in a green tweed jacket who welcomed us to the match coverage. 'Not to be killed, I mean. It was a close thing, wasn't it?'

'I suppose,' I said.

'Well done, anyway.'

'Why?'

'Just for all of that. You handled it very well – looked after Cass and all that. Jesus, I'd never have heard the end of it if you were toasted in a Clare airfield. They'd have made you a saint.'

'Thanks,' I said, knowing that was about as close as we were ever going to get to Eamon telling me he loved me and was glad I was alive. I didn't mind – it was close enough.

'Have you the remote?' he said. 'Turn the damn thing up, I can't hear a word the man is saying.'

After the match was over I went into the kitchen to make some tea and found my mother sitting at the table staring into space. I filled the kettle and switched it on and still she didn't acknowledge me or move or speak.

'All right, Ma?' I said, though it was clear that she wasn't.

She looked at me, taking a minute to focus and reminding me of Tim Winter's drugged stare.

'Alison seems to be a nice girl.'

'When did you meet her?'

'Never. Cassandra told me, and from what I understand we have Alison to thank for finding Cassandra.'

'Yeah,' I said, walking towards the fridge. 'Any food?'

'Turkey. Make a sandwich.'

I carried the remains of the Christmas turkey on its platter to the table and fetched bread and butter and began to make sandwiches for everyone.

'Why did you lie to Jessica?' I asked, not looking at my mother. 'The last weekend I was home. Why did you lie to her?'

She didn't answer for a minute. 'Because –' she said, at last, pausing again. 'Because – look, what about Alison? Cassandra says she's very fond of you.'

I laughed. 'When did she say that?'

'Last night, when I visited her.'

'Have you any idea how many different kinds of drugs your niece is taking at the moment?'

My mother shrugged. 'I thought she was perfectly lucid. So? Tell me about this girl, Alison?'

'Look, Ma, I've had a hard few weeks – no, months – no, forget that, I've had a shit year. I don't think I need to complicate my life any more than it's already complicated. I'm not even divorced, for God's sake.'

'Yes, but you will be.'

'Even so.'

'Even so, what?'

I sighed. 'Cassandra is wrong, she always thinks women are after me – or at least she always tells me that, probably to make me feel better.'

'But it doesn't, does it?'

I shook my head and concentrated on the slice of bread I was buttering. It swam in and out of focus as my eyes suddenly filled with tears. Fucking self-pity. Got me in the back of the knees every fucking time. Typical. I couldn't even just get on with it. Everything was fine – so why didn't it feel like that to me?

My mother reached across the table and put her hand on my arm and I couldn't hold on any more. Big, fat, salty tears dropped on to the slice of bread on the table. She never said a word, just kept her hand right where she'd put it. I managed to rein myself in after a few seconds and proceeded to butter the tears into the bread.

'Seamus,' my mother said. I didn't answer but I looked up at her. She moved her hand away for a second and then returned it to my arm. I liked it better when her hand was on my arm. 'Look, love. I know that I don't know this girl but maybe you should –'

'Look, Mam. You don't understand. You're talking about girls like I'm fifteen. I've been there. I've even been married, for fuck's sake, and I made a balls of it and I don't even know why and I'm not able to – I don't know – be in the world. I don't seem to know how to do it the way you're supposed to do it.'

'That's not true.'

'Yes, it is. You just don't want to believe it. You're my mother – you love me, that's why you can't see it.'

'Tell me this,' my mother said, her voice barely a whisper. 'Tell me why you don't attach any importance to the fact that people love you?'

'I do. That's not what I mean.'

'No, you don't. But forget it, I'm not even giving out to you. I wish I could fix it all for you – think of something to say that'd be the perfect thing. But I can't. The only thing I can think of is that you could be dead and you're not and so you should be grateful to be alive.'

'I am. I am grateful.'

'Show it then. Live your life.'

I looked away and then I looked back at her. My mother was staring at me. 'Live,' she repeated, as soon as we made eye contact. My mother smiled at me then and all the worried look seemed to melt off her face. 'Why don't you go see Alison tomorrow? Bring her back here for a couple of days if she'll come. I'm sure Cassandra'd love to see her.'

'I –'

'No. Don't answer. Just think about it.'

I wanted to answer. I even knew what I wanted to say, but I stopped and just nodded as if I'd consider her suggestion. I knew I wouldn't contact Alison, but it didn't matter. My mother meant well.

And she was right about one thing. It was important that I had a family who loved me. That was *very* important and I probably had taken it for granted. I'd learn to appreciate it more and then maybe that'd be enough.

'Séamus?'

'What?'

'Make some ham sandwiches as well, your father prefers ham.'

That night I went to bed full of drinking chocolate and turkey, and still I couldn't drop off to sleep. I eventually gave up and sat up in bed and turned on the bedside lamp and retrieved the book I had been reading from where it had slid on to the floor.

I lay there staring at the book jacket for a few minutes and then I leaned over to the other side of the bed and grabbed my discarded jeans off the floor and shook them until my cigarettes and lighter fell out of the pockets.

My mother would kill me if she knew I was smoking in bed. Fuck it, so what? I was a full-grown man now, she'd just have to put up with it. Anyway, how would she find out? It was three in the morning and she was fast asleep.

I propped myself up in bed with my book and cigarette and tried to read, but the thoughts that were keeping me awake danced around on the page like ants. I closed the book and tried to face up to them.

Why had my mother tried to get me to invite Alison home? She just didn't understand, that was all. I knew what I needed. I needed things to calm down. I'd go back to Castleannery, back to school, back into my life.

Maybe I'd study something next year. Something that would get me a job with more money. I could do that. That'd fill my life. I could worry about exams and lectures and essays and projects instead of faithless wives and murderous bastards. It'd be a picnic.

I might also try to be friendlier to Pádraig Harrison to make up for all the bad things I'd thought about him. Penance. And I might join a gym. I could at least be physically tough, who knew — it might sink inwards. I could get a dog as well. A dog would keep me company even if he couldn't be Prince.

I lay down, suddenly swamped with sleep. That was good. That seemed like a plan. That was really good. Everything was going to be all right. And about fucking time too.

16

'A Man Can't Lose (What He Don't Have)'
Blandamer, 1982

Then Cassandra had an exhibition. I went to all the trouble of sorting my head out in December, and in March Cassandra had an exhibition of her Spanish photographs just as she said she would.

'Jesus, Cass,' I said, as I walked around the gallery after her, looking at her photographs and feeling prouder and prouder as I looked at each giant image. She still had quite a pronounced limp when she walked. She said she didn't mind too much though, as the doctors had said it'd probably improve and had informed her she was lucky to be alive and still have both legs.

'Kind of gives you perspective,' was her stock reply whenever she was asked how she felt about it. I wasn't sure what that meant because we didn't talk that much about what had happened. It was all still a bit fresh and sore – like Cassandra's wound.

'Well, well, well,' I said, as we finished the circuit of the gallery, 'you were telling the truth. There was film in the camera.'

Cassandra stuck the tip of her tongue between her teeth and crossed her eyes, then she swivelled around towards the sound of clacking high-heels. A short, well-padded, marooned swathed woman was approaching.

'Cassandra!' the woman announced, as she reached where we stood.

'Billie,' Cassandra said, as they hugged.

'Everything looks fabulous. Just fabulous.'

'Thanks.'

Then the woman called Billie dropped her voice to the volume of a drug dealer offering heroin. 'Great response to the invitations,' she said, clapping her hands together and touching her lips with the tips of her joined fingers.

'That's good.'

The woman nodded. 'Really great, it's been really, really marvellous – almost everyone is coming.'

'That's good news,' Cassandra said, as she smiled and shook her head. 'Really, Billie, that's terrific. Thanks for all your work. By the way, this is my cousin, Séamus. Have you met?'

Billie looked at me as if I'd just dropped out of the sky. I extended my hand and she responded by allowing me to shake her soft, white, plump hand. The hundred or so silver and gold-coloured bracelets along her arm made as much noise as a five-piece orchestra as I pumped her arm.

'Nice to meet you,' I said.

The woman smiled and looked away as soon as I let go of her hand. 'Have to fly. Talk to you later.'

'Who is that woman?' I asked, as we stood watching her straighten a picture before she disappeared through a doorway with a final flap of silk.

Cassandra looked at me. 'What?'

'Who is she?'

'Oh, the gallery manager, she's the gallery manager. Fuck it, Séamus, I hate this. I should have waited until June to have the exhibition. I'm not ready for this yet. We had a very traumatic time, you know.'

'I know. But everything is all right now. So calm down, Cassandra.'

Cassandra let out an annoyed sigh. 'And look at my dress, for God's sake. Why did I wear this thing? It was a mistake, wasn't it? I should have worn the long one. I look like a slut now, as well as everything else. Can you see the dressing on my thigh?'

'No, you can't see a thing. You look fine. Just calm down.'

Cassandra stood up straight and if she had had bristles she would have bristled. 'Don't tell me to calm down,' she said, through clenched teeth. 'I'm warning you, if you tell me to calm down again, I'll slap you in the gob.'

'All right, all right! For God's sake, have it your own way, Cassandra. Don't bother calming down. I don't know what the hell is wrong with you, you look very nice.'

'Really?'

'I swear to God.'

'You're not just saying that to make me feel better?'

I laughed. 'When did I ever do that?'

Cassandra tugged at the end of her short, red, sleeveless dress and ran a hand through her fashionably tousled hair. 'I suppose. Is my make-up all right?'

I nodded.

Cassandra sighed. 'I wish you were a woman.'

'Thanks.'

'Yeah, well, it would be better, if you were a woman. You'd be more useful to me, you'd know about stuff then. It doesn't matter. I need to pee anyway. I can check my make-up in the Ladies. And Rachel is coming. She'll know. Sisters always tell you the ruthless truth.'

'Sisters and cousins.'

Cassandra nodded. 'You are telling the truth about the dress?'

'Cross my heart.'

'And you can't see the dressing on my leg?'

'You'd never guess what was under that skirt, I swear.'

'It's a dress.'

'OK, dress. What time does this thing start?'

Cassandra looked at her watch. 'Fuck it – five minutes. I have to go find the toilet. See you later.'

'Stop.'

Cassandra stopped and turned towards me.

'Good luck. They're great pictures – everything will be fine.'

Cassandra smiled and limped back to kiss me on the cheek, then she disappeared in the direction of the toilets. They really were great pictures, I thought as I helped myself to a glass of wine from the rows of filled glasses on a white, table-clothed table just inside the door. And even greater considering everything that had happened to her in recent times. Unexpectedly I heard my name spoken in a stranger's voice. I looked up.

'Pádraig!' I said as I recognized the face in front of me.

Pádraig Harrison smiled his wide, professional smile and gave me a hearty handshake.

'Great to see you, Séamus. Really, really great to see you. I haven't seen you in an age. Not since all the high drama.'

'Good to see you, Pádraig.'

He looked his usual handsome and confident self and it had its usual effect on me – I wanted to punch him, or at least mess up his hair. But I'd been wrong about him – as I had been about almost everybody I'd ever met in my life and I was resolved to make up for it. It was time I made a real effort to get to know him instead of just hating him for breathing air.

Maybe what Alison said to me when we were edging around the airfield in the rain was true, after all? It was possible, I supposed, that I found him such a monumental pain in the arse because he was trying to impress me. It was a bit hard to believe, especially when I was looking at him in the flesh. I couldn't see what it was about me, exactly, that would threaten him, but it made me feel less like throttling him to think that, so I was willing to give the idea a shot.

Then, almost as if she was conjured up by my thinking about her, I saw Alison. Tall and graceful as a sapling in a long, shiny, silver dress and black jacket. Her hair was tied up in some way and she had a nervous smile on her face that was no longer covered in bruises. I said her name without meaning to.

'Alison.'

Pádraig looked at me in surprise and then turned around and caught her by the hand.

'See who's here? It's Séamus. Well, we knew you'd be here, but it's still great to see you, isn't it, Allie?'

Alison moved forward to stand beside Pádraig and I hoped they couldn't see on my face what I was feeling inside.

'Good to see you, Séamus,' she said, in a soft voice that inexplicably made me remember lying beside her on the floor of that airfield office. Looking into her face in the gloom, so glad that she was alive that I could scarcely breathe.

'Alison,' I said, too loudly as I shook her hand for the shortest time possible. 'Great to see you. Now you two go look at the lovely pictures. That's what we're here for after all, I won't delay you.'

'Yes. They look great. Who'd have thought Cassandra was so talented?'

'Who'd have thought, eh, Pádraig? Who'd have thought? Talk to you later. Enjoy. Buy lots.'

I waved my hand and turned away, not even looking at Alison. The gallery was beginning to fill with people arriving for the opening. I saw my mother and father in the distance coming in with Cassandra's parents and younger sister, Rachel. My mother saw me and pointed me out to Rachel who waved at me.

And they were probably planning to come over to talk to me except that I waved and pointed and nodded and maniacally gestured as if I was engaged in an important mission and then I walked directly towards the toilets. But I didn't go in. Instead I waited for about two minutes outside the door and then turned and headed for the exit.

As soon as I stepped through the doors into the spring evening I lit a cigarette. It was a mild evening for March, warmish in that edgy springtime way and fresh smelling. I walked quickly around the back of the building as I smoked, I didn't want to meet anybody else.

I felt as if I was sliding down a mud-slope. It was all too much. Too fucking much. I was completely overwhelmed with seeing Alison. Submerged in confusion, especially as she was now, obviously, somehow attached to Pádraig Harrison.

That thought nearly made me laugh. Pádraig Harrison – symbol for all the fuckers who had it easier in the world and were more accomplished and more urbane and earned more money than me and had taken a bigger slice of the world than I seemed to be able to hack off for myself. I knew I was just feeling sorry for myself. None of it was true. Well, except for one thing. A fucker like Pádraig Harrison did take my wife.

I knew that Pádraig Harrison was a different person, and that he didn't break up my marriage. I knew that I only disliked him because of what he symbolized. But when I stopped to think I saw that that wasn't true any longer. Now he had actually done something to me. He'd taken Alison.

I stopped walking as I repeated that short sentence in my head. *Pádraig has taken Alison from me.* No, I answered. That's not true either. *I* never had her in the first place so while he may have taken her, he never took her from me. I was such a fuck-up it wasn't funny any more. If I was objective then I had to admit that they were suited. Both beautiful, both wealthy. Both nice, good people. A lovely couple.

Anyway, so what? It had nothing to do with me. My mother had told me to go and find Alison and bring her home and I hadn't even tried. I'd decided it was better not to risk my fragile new self and so . . . so, what did I expect?

I lit another cigarette and looked at the stars in the clear sky. It should be all right. I'd thought it all out and all the pieces and plans and bits of my life added up like a logical budget. And that should make it OK, but somehow it didn't. Somehow I still felt like shit and I was tired of it.

All I needed was to see Jessica and her architect pull into the car park. More nails Centurion. That was just paranoia, though. It'd never happen. Cassandra hated Jessica far too much to invite them to her exhibition.

I wondered if Cassandra knew about Pádraig Harrison and Alison? Probably. Why hadn't she told me? Then I remembered Cassandra trying to talk to me about Alison and how I'd headed her off at the pass thinking she was going to try to do my mother on me and make me believe Alison liked me. Maybe she was only trying to tell me about Pádraig and Alison?

I felt like a squashed fly. An insignificant little fucker who'd been run over by the world. How could I go back into the exhibition and act all night as if nothing was going on? I needed to leave. Surely it wouldn't make a difference if I left and I really, badly wanted to go home to Castleannery and lie on the couch with Fido – my new pup – and fall asleep watching the news.

But if I left Cassandra might be upset. Goddamn her.

I wasn't able for any of it. I sat on a low stone wall behind the gallery and smoked and thought and swung my legs so hard that I knew I had to be scuffing the backs of my shoes where they were hitting off the wall. I didn't care. I was certain sure Pádraig Harrison never burst into tears like I had. I bet his neuroses were as neat as his house. Labelled and catalogued and filed away to be dealt with when he was ready.

I hated him. I could feel it inside me and it was no good pretending otherwise or rationalizing or hoping to talk myself out of it. I hated him. And it didn't matter that he didn't deserve it, it was just a fact.

I'd promised myself I'd change. I'd said I'd stop fattenin'

frogs for snakes, stop wasting my time, and here I was destroyed by . . . by what? By the sight of a woman with another man?

No, it wasn't that. It was something else. What was it? I jumped down off the wall and paced up and down in the dark. Squares of yellow light patterned the ground from the high windows of the gallery. Why was I so upset?

Then I knew. When I saw Alison in the gallery something I hadn't even admitted to myself had been lost, was – suddenly – found. And it wasn't even my fault that I hadn't known about it because my life was as full of holes as a sieve.

There were just so many holes, in truth, that I hadn't been able to tell that there was another hole. A big one. Until it wasn't empty any more. And then no sooner was it filled than it emptied again. And it hurt like fuck and I wanted to choke Pádraig Harrison.

But I couldn't choke the bastard. They'd try to stop me and my mother would be embarrassed and Cassandra would lose her mind if I wrecked her exhibition. So I needed to go home. I could say I was ill. Suddenly taken ill in the car park while I was smoking a cigarette.

Food poisoning? Good idea, food poisoning. My family – even Cassandra – would whinge at me and get over it. Anyway, I'd explain to Cassandra, sometime. Not that she deserved it, she could have tried harder to warn me Alison was coming.

Lighting my third cigarette in a row I made my way back around the building and found my car in the dark. Then I drove home to Castleannery. To Fido. To bed. To TV. To nurse my grievances. To wish I had more courage. To fall asleep.

17

'Whatever Gets You True'
Paddy Casey, 1998

I did all those things when I got home. Watched TV, cuddled the downy golden puppy, dozed off on the couch with him asleep on my chest. And next morning, I got up and went to school and taught my class about division and Alexander the Great and how he tamed Bucephalas and conquered much of his world.

I never let myself think about Alison. Not even once. I never let myself dissolve into that mire. And it was hard to keep her out of my head. In fact, there were moments when it was nearly impossible, but I managed it.

Every time Alison came into my head, I beat back the idea of her with numbers and facts about phalanxes and battles and ancient codes of heroism. I wasn't having it. As far as I was concerned I'd already done my time with a fucked-up head because of Jessica and at least I'd been married to her when she'd dumped me. At least I'd had a reason to be upset. I knew for sure that I was never going to put myself through something like that again.

Especially with Alison Chang. After all, Alison was a stranger and I had no real relationship with her, so that meant I didn't have to be upset. I really just had to take hold of myself. I could see that I was out of control.

I needed a plan. Maybe I should give up teaching and become a farmer? Stay out of circulation altogether. Mattie had been a farmer and he'd been a good man and he'd been dumped as well. There was no need for any of this self-inflicted suffering.

After all the children had left and I'd tidied my classroom and fixed the hinges on the staffroom door and unblocked a toilet in the boys' cloakroom, I reluctantly went home. Fido licked my hand as soon as he saw me and I knew he loved me. Even if it was a self-interested type of love at least it was honest.

I fried some fish and ate it standing at the draining board. I couldn't seem to find a comfortable place inside myself and so I couldn't seem to find one outside myself either. The telephone rang and on the short walk to answer it I imagined it was Alison. But it was my Principal to tell me that the hurling match scheduled for that evening had been cancelled.

'OK,' I said.

'So you'll have a free evening.'

'Yes. Yes, I will.'

'Séamus?'

'Yes?'

'Are you all right? You're not coming down with anything are you? There's a lot of flu about at the minute.'

'No,' I said, trying to force life into my voice, 'no, Dick, thanks. I'm grand.'

'Well, I'd take a strong dose of Vitamin C if I were you, just in case. I find that usually does the trick.'

'I will,' I said, deciding it was better if he thought I had the flu rather than knew the truth. 'I think I have some here in the house. Thanks, Dick.'

'See you in the morning, Séamus.'

'See you,' I said, and hung up.

I picked up the golden puppy at my feet and held him close to my chest as I walked to the sitting room and turned on the TV. Maybe I *was* getting the flu, maybe that was why I felt so bad? But I knew I was fine physically, it was just every other way that I was fucked.

Life was way too sophisticated for a hick like me. Looking at everything that had happened, that much was obvious. I hadn't been able to stop or even second-guess any of it.

Mattie was dead. Cassandra was almost killed and I could be dead as well, for fuck's sake. If Chrissie and Tim had had their way we all *would* be dead. But we weren't dead. I wasn't dead.

No, I wasn't dead.

I was alive.

Mattie was dead and I was alive, and funnily enough he was the one who used to talk a lot about living life.

'It's an awful shame to act as if you're dead for years before they put you in the ground,' he'd say about someone or other who was wasting their chances. Wasting their lives.

Maybe he'd meant me as well?

Jumping up, I deposited the puppy on a cushion that he got down to chewing without delay and I ran into the kitchen. I had it somewhere. Somewhere in the pile of paper confusion I lived in, I knew I still had Alison's telephone number.

And I was right. On the kitchen windowsill underneath a telephone bill was her card with her telephone number. Before I could change my mind or lose my nerve or Cassandra or my mother could ring, I dialled the number.

The receiver felt hot against my ear and my heart was thumping like a horse's hoof as I waited. Maybe she wouldn't be there? Oh God, maybe she wouldn't and part of me wanted that, but most of me didn't because I didn't think I'd summon up the courage a second time and I couldn't keep living my life as a hollow man. The echo from the nothingness inside me was deafening.

The telephone rang. Still no answer. What if she *was* there? What would I say? I didn't know what I felt so I couldn't say that, so where did that leave me? Maybe I should hang up and wait until I'd worked out what I wanted to say? No.

That'd never happen. The telephone kept ringing. How long do phones ring before they ring out or the answering service clicks in?

'Hello?'

Alison's voice.

I took a deep breath. 'Alison?'

'Séamus?'

'Hi. How are you?'

'Fine, fine. Are you better? Cassandra said you got sick at the exhibition.'

'I'm fine. Bad chicken I think.'

'Oh, right. That's horrible.'

'Ah, well. It didn't kill me. Which brings me to why I rang you.'

I paused. Alison didn't say anything.

'Are you still there?'

'Yes. Yes, I am. Did something happen?'

'No,' I said, scrabbling inside my head for things to say, 'I just wanted to check something with you.'

'OK,' Alison said, her voice cautious, and I didn't blame her. I sounded insane even to myself. Oh dear God let me think of something to say.

'Nothing bad or anything. No murderers or kidnappings or arsonists.'

Alison laughed. 'That's good news.'

'Have you heard from Paul Richardson?'

'Not recently. Why?'

'Oh, no reason, just wondered.'

'OK.'

'And work,' I said, as a drop of inspiration trickled in, 'are you back at work?'

'Yes. I have a new job. And you?'

'Of course. I'm back since straight after Christmas.'

'That's good,' she said.

'Yes.'

Then there was a pause. I felt so weak I was hardly able to hold the telephone receiver in my hand. Maybe I'd had a stroke, or an aneurysm – were they the same thing? I didn't know. Couldn't think.

I couldn't believe I'd been stupid enough to call. Hadn't I had enough slaps in the face in the last while? Why was I doing this to myself? Then I remembered all over again. I wasn't dead. I was alive, so I had to live.

'Alison?'

'Yes?'

'I've been thinking and I was wondering if you'd like ... on Saturday ... if you're not busy. How about going to Lahinch? It's a very nice place, you know, and if you had a chance to see it in better circumstances than the last time ... But if you'd prefer to go to Spanish Point, well, that would be great. Maybe you wouldn't like Lahinch after everything that happened –'

'Oh. Well, you see, Séamus. I can't, I –'

'Look, no problem,' I interrupted, hating myself. It wasn't surprising she didn't like me – even I didn't like me. 'Anyway, great to talk with you. See you soon, I hope, Alison. Take –'

'Séamus.'

'Yes?'

'Sunday.'

'What?'

'Sunday would be better. I have to go to a christening on Saturday morning. Maybe we could go to the seaside on Sunday.'

'Oh.'

'Well? What do you think?'

'That would be – great,' I said, and I paused then to allow a small trickle of oxygen into my lungs so that I wouldn't faint. That helped so I followed it with a deep breath.

'Actually, Alison, that's not true, that would be better than great, it would be fucking brilliant.'

369

Alison laughed and I wanted to laugh as well because I felt like laughing but I was too shaken to co-ordinate the necessary bodily functions.

'Good. That's a plan. There's just one thing, Séamus.'

'Yes?'

'Maybe we could start with Spanish Point and when we feel up to it go visit Lahinch?'

'That's a good idea. How about you come down Saturday night – if you can – and we can get an early start.'

'Sounds good. See you on Saturday.'

'I'll look forward to it,' I said, and I hung up.

And that was it. As easy as that after all the fuss. Not that everything was solved or anything like that. As they say – to be alive is to have problems.

I know, for example, that sometimes, no matter what I do, I'll still feel sad and shocked and lonely without Mattie. I know I'll always be horrified by what Tim and Chrissie did and heartbroken by the thought of their lives as children. I don't think I'll ever understand any of it properly, but I now understand something I didn't know before all the shit happened. I understand now that the knack of life is to live it. No matter what happens to you.

Mattie had the knack of life. While he was alive he knew how to be alive and keep his heart open even when it was broken. If I had to say what he did I suppose I'd say that instead of shrinking and closing off to the world, Mattie made his heart bigger every time it was attacked so that, eventually, it became like an enormous expanse of water – an ocean, maybe – which couldn't be polluted by the insignificant drops of poison the world threw at it.

I think I'll try that.